THE POOL OF ST BRANOK

Angelet – known as Angel – daughter of Annora and Rolf, was born into the magnificent mansion of Cador on the coast of Cornwall, where she lived in happy security with her family until one day, at the legendary Pool of St Branok, she had an encounter with a dangerous murderer who had escaped from jail. It was an adventure she shared with Benedict Lansdon, and it was the pivot of the dramatic events which were to follow later in her life.

In London, as a debutante, she met the charming Gervaise Mandeville, and all seemed contentment until she discovered a flaw in the charm and consequently the scene changed to the goldfields of Australia.

There she met again the forceful Benedict – Ben – and memories of the horrifying incident were revived. Life was primitive among the shafts and windlasses and Angel was alarmed by the lust for gold which she saw around her. She likened these men to acolytes in the temple of the Golden Goddess and felt that they would abandon honour, integrity and all finer feelings to win her favours. Gold had become the meaning of life to them; every day they hoped to find it, and when it eluded them their desire to possess it seemed all the greater. They lived for it and some died for it.

Among them was Ben – the strong man, always one step ahead of the others, determined to go home, but not until he had found gold in such quantities as would give the riches and power he had decided to have.

He won – but not without a price.

When there was a disaster underground, Angel returned home where Disraeli and Gladstone were fighting for power; and she was caught up in the political scene.

There was Timothy Ransome, the good man who could help her to achieve a life of quiet peace; and Fanny the waif who knew what it meant to live dangerously. There were the heiresses Morwenna and Lizzie, exploited by the gold hunters. And there was Grace, who appeared at the time of Angel's frightening adventure at the Pool and who in time became a member of the family; and there was the mysterious Justin. Angel had much to learn from them and when she discovered their secrets, she began to wonder whether she herself was in acute danger.

The Pool of St Branok is the fourteenth in the '*Daughters of England*' series.

The 'Daughters of England' series

DAUGHTERS OF ENGLAND

The Pool
of
St Branok

Philippa Carr

COLLINS
8 Grafton Street, London W1
1987

William Collins Sons & Co. Ltd
London · Glasgow · Sydney · Auckland
Toronto · Johannesburg

BRITISH LIBRARY CATALOGUING IN PUBLICATION DATA

Carr, Philippa
The pool of St Branok. – (Daughters of England).
Rn: Eleanor Alice Burford Hibbert   I. Title
II. Series
823′.912[F]   PR6015.I3

ISBN 0-00-223247-2

First published 1987
© Philippa Carr 1987

Photoset in Linotron Times by
Rowland Phototypesetting Ltd
Bury St Edmunds, Suffolk
Printed and bound in Great Britain by
Robert Hartnoll (1985) Ltd., Bodmin, Cornwall

CONTENTS

Encounter
at the Pool

From the moment Benedict made his dramatic entry into the family circle I was aware of a special attraction between us – that was even before we were involved in the nightmare experience at the Pool of St Branok which was to haunt us in the years ahead, and to have such an effect on our lives thereafter.

My parents, with my young brother Jack and I, were in London to visit the Great Exhibition, for it was the year 1851 and I was nine years old. Benedict was seventeen, but when one is nine eight years is a great deal.

We had travelled up on the train from Cornwall – an adventure in itself – to the house in the Westminster square which was ruled over by Uncle Peter and Aunt Amaryllis. They were not really my aunt and uncle, but relationships in our family were very complicated and I always addressed them as such. Uncle Peter had married into the family and dominated it. Aunt Amaryllis was my grandmother's niece, although they were more or less the same age. My mother had always had a grudging admiration for Uncle Peter, which made me feel that there was some mystery about him. He was ebullient, charming, with a definite hint of wickedness about him which made him fascinating. I had often thought it would be exciting to discover what that meant. Aunt Amaryllis was quite different. She was gentle, kindly and had a rather innocent manner; and she was dearly loved by all. There was nothing secretive about her.

They were constantly entertaining important people at their house. I did not attend these occasions, of course, but even I, at my age, had heard the names of some of these guests.

Their son and daughter had exciting lives of their own. Helena was married to a successful politician, Matthew Hume. He was

9

constantly at the house, even without Helena, and spent a good deal of time in the company of Uncle Peter who took a great interest in his political career. I heard my mother say that Uncle Peter was the *éminence grise* behind Matthew Hume. Then there was the son, Peter, who had been known as Peterkin since his birth to distinguish him from his father. He and his wife, Frances, ran a Mission in the East End of London, and did much good.

My mother told me a great deal about them. She loved to talk of the past. She had been born in our old house, Cador, which had belonged to the Cadorsons for hundreds of years. My mother had inherited it, so we were not Cadorsons now. My father was Rolf Hanson, who had inherited the house through marriage with my mother; but I think he loved the place even more than the rest of us. I had heard it said that the estates had never been run so well as when Mr Hanson took charge of them. They had never been so large either, for his contribution to the family estates had been the manor property, which he had brought in when he married my mother.

He was not a Cornishman, but what they called in those parts a 'foreigner', which meant that he had been born on the other side of the Tamar in that alien land called England. He was amused by it. We were a very happy family. My father seemed so wise; he understood every little problem that arose and made no fuss about solving it, so it seemed to me. I had never seen him lose his temper. I thought he was the most wonderful person in the world. I used to ride with him round the estate. Jack, who was three years younger than I, was just beginning to do the same. There had been a time when they had thought there would not be another child to follow me and it had been assumed then that one day Cador would be mine. But Jack came.

My mother used to say: 'Cador is a wonderful house – not because of its towers and stone walls, but because of the people who lived in it and made it a home. Never, never,' she would add, 'let yourself believe that houses in themselves are important. It is the people whom you love and who love you who matter. I lost time when I could have been with your father because I thought he cared more for Cador than for me. Then

10

I was lucky. I learned my lesson in time . . . but only after we had missed a few years of life together. So some day Cador will be Jack's, and when the time comes for you to marry you will know that you are wanted for yourself and not because you are the owner of a great house.'

She spoke vehemently. My mother was a great talker – unlike my father. I liked to see him sitting there smiling at her indulgently and lovingly while she talked in her vivacious way. I think I resembled her more than I did my father – although I had his looks. I was fair-haired with large dreamy-looking greenish eyes and a wide mouth. I looked as though I should have been serious, thoughtful, but the effect was spoilt by my pert nose which was quite unlike my father's rather noble-looking long one. It gave the contradiction to my seriousness, as it were. My father would touch it sometimes when I said something outrageous as though my audacity was due to my nose.

I did not realize how lucky I was to have such parents in those days; but that, after all, is the sort of conclusion one comes to later in life.

They were the glorious days of childhood before I was suddenly aware that day at St Branok Pool that the world can be a very frightening place.

I remember those pre-Branok days when the sun seemed to shine perpetually and each day was a week long. I had a governess, Miss Prentiss, who despaired of turning me into the little lady she felt would be worthy of the House of Cador. I ran wild, and as my parents did not seem to disapprove of this, what could a governess do? I believe she bemoaned her task to Mrs Penlock, our cook, and Watson, our butler, when she deigned to go to the kitchen, which was on special occasions only, she being very well aware of the echelons of society which placed her on a higher rung of the social ladder than the domestic staff.

But Mrs Penlock, who had been at Cador in the days when my mother was a girl, in her stately black bombazine, reigned majestically below stairs and could deal adequately with Miss Prentiss. So could Watson – a very dignified gentleman, except

11

when he was making himself agreeable to one of the prettier maids, and he even did that with an air of condescension.

They were happy days. I suppose I *was* allowed to run wild, as Miss Prentiss said. My mother had had a certain amount of freedom when she was young and wanted me to have the same. There was nothing of the stern parent about her or my father. 'Little children should be seen and not heard,' said old Mrs Fenny who lived in one of the cottages near the harbour in East Poldorey, shaking her head, ominously considering the fate of those who were heard as well as seen. She was one of those old women who look for sin and seem to find it. She spent hours looking out of her tiny window on to the quay to where men sat about mending their nets or weighing up their catch, and noting everything that went on. In the summer she would be sitting at her door, so much more convenient for discovering any misdemeanour and passing on any bit of scandal that came her way.

'There will always be people like that,' said my mother. 'It is because their lives are so dull. They are unhealthily curious about others whose lives seem more eventful, and because they are envious they seize every opportunity to slander them. Let's hope none of us ever get like that.'

There were several rather like Mrs Fenny in both East and West Poldorey. The people of the east side regarded those of the west as aliens – though slightly less foreign than those who came from the other side of the Tamar. Mrs Fenny always referred to them as 'They West Poldorers' with a certain contempt. I always laughed when I heard her western counterparts speak of the inhabitants of the east side with equal scorn and superiority.

I loved the harbour with the little fishing-boats swaying on the tide, secured as they were to the great iron rings which made you watch your step as you ran along. I liked to stand by and watch the men as they worked.

'Good day to 'ee, Miss Angel,' they would call.

Angel. It was so incongruous. It was Angelet really. My mother was very interested in the family and she told me of an ancestress who had lived during the time of the Civil War.

Her name had been Angelet and I was named after her. I am afraid the diminutive form did not exactly suit me. Perhaps people used it to try to make me live up to it.

They all knew who I was, ''er from Cador, Miss Angel who might have inherited the place but for Mr Jack'. I could imagine their conversation when he was born. 'Well, it be right and proper for a lad to be the master. 'Tis no place for a maid.'

I knew them so well, these people around me. I sometimes knew what they were going to say before they said it. Old Mrs Fenny with her prying eyes, scenting out secrets; the Misses Poldrew who lived in a little house on the edge of East Poldorey which was as neat as they were. I knew they looked under their beds every night to see if a man was hiding there, so eager were they to guard their virtue which nobody so far had shown any inclination to assail. There was Tom Fish who was always about with his wheelbarrow when the catch came in; he trundled it through the two towns and up and down into the nearby villages calling 'Fish, fresh from the sea this morning. Come, women. Tom Fish be at your door. I'm here, me darlings.' There was Miss Grant who kept the wool shop and sat by her counter crocheting as she waited for customers; there were the bakers with the enticing smell of hot bread, and Pengelly's who sold everything from thimbles to farm implements; and there was the Fisherman's Rest where the men went after they had disposed of their catch, mingling with the mining community. 'Throwing away all that they snatched from the sea or grubbed from the land,' Mrs Fenny would comment, sitting at her window watching them reel out of the inn. 'Old Pennyleg ought to know better than serve 'em,' was her comment. She had resigned old Pennyleg, the innkeeper, to the flames of hell long ago.

I was very interested in Mrs Fenny. I liked to see her sitting with her Bible on her lap tracing the lines with her finger and moving her lips. I wondered why she did this, for I knew she could not read.

I loved to sit on a pile of rope with its tang of seaweed and listen to the waves while I looked out to sea and I would think of the men who had gone off into the unknown to explore the world . . . men like Drake and Raleigh. I would imagine the

13

sails fluttering in the breeze and the bare-footed sailors running hither and thither while I strode the sloping decks, shouting orders. I imagined Spanish galleons, full of treasure; sending out raiding parties, bringing them in and taking the treasure back to England. I was constantly losing myself in daydreams. I was often Raleigh or Drake. Those dreams were difficult because I had to change my sex; but there were others in which I indulged with even greater frequency. I would be Good Queen Bess knighting these men. That was better. I could see myself very well as the great Queen. Three thousand dresses and a red wig and power . . . glorious power. Sometimes I was Mary Queen of Scots going to her execution. I made touching speeches on the scaffold and there was not a dry eye near me. The executioner was so touched that he refused to cut off my head. One of my ladies, who worshipped me, insisted on taking my place. We tried to stop her but she insisted. And then . . . I pretended to be her . . . until some gallant man came and rescued me. We lived in happy security to a great age and no one ever discovered that I was the Queen because everyone thought I had been executed in Fotheringay Castle.

Such dreams were more real to me than what was happening about me. This was before that terrible time at St Branok Pool. After that I changed. I dared not indulge in daydreams then in case they led me back to the pool.

Cador was about a quarter of a mile out of the two towns of Poldorey. We were on a hill looking out to sea. The house was very splendid with its towers and turrets and its grey stone walls which had stood against the sea and the weather for hundreds of years – a fortress if ever there was one. One could lie in bed at night and listen to the wind playing about those stone walls – sometimes shrieking like a madman, sometimes whining like an animal in distress; sometimes shrill, sometimes melancholy. It had always fascinated me before that encounter; after that I hated the sound of the wind. It was like a warning.

There was a richness about life in those days. I was vitally interested in everything about me. 'Miss Angel's nose b'ain't what you'd call a big 'un,' was Mrs Penlock's verdict, 'but it be into everything.'

14

I loved the little cottages with their whitewashed cob walls all huddled together on the quay. If ever I had a chance to get inside I seized it. I would go visiting with my mother at Christmas when we took gifts to the cottage folk in accordance with the custom of years. Those homes of the poor consisted of two dark rooms divided by a partition not as high as the roof which I understood was to allow the air to circulate. Some of the cottages had a *talfat*, a sort of shelf close to the ceiling, and there the young would sleep, climbing up by means of a rope ladder. The only light was what they called the *Stonen Chill* – an earthenware lamp in the shape of a candlestick having a socket in which they would pour oil before inserting the *purvan*, the local name for the wick.

The woman of the house would dust a chair for my mother to sit on, and I would stand beside her, eyes wide, noting everything and listening to the talk about how our Jenny was getting on as maid up at the rectory or when our Jim was expected home from sea. My mother knew their business. It was part of the duties of the lady of the big house.

There was always a smell of food in the cottages. They kept the fires going with the wood they picked up from the beach. I loved the blue flames which they said were due to the salt in the wood and betrayed the fact that it had been salvaged from the sea. Most of them had cloam ovens in which they did their baking, while a kettle, black with soot, hung on a chain over the flames.

They had a different language from ours, I often thought, but I learned it. They ate different foods, such as *quillet* which was a mixture of ground peas rather like a porridge, and there was *pillas*, a kind of oatmeal which they boiled into a mixture called *gurts*. My mother told me that in the last century when these people were very poor they used to pick the grass and roll it in a pastry made of barley and bake it under the ashes.

They were more prosperous now. My mother frequently pointed out to me that my father was a good man who looked on it as his duty to see that no one in his neighbourhood should starve.

The poor fishermen depended so much on the weather and

15

the winds on our coast could be violent. A certain melancholy descended on the Poldoreys when the knowledgeable predicted fierce winds and storms which would keep the boats idle. Of course, sometimes these appeared without warning and that was what fishermen and their families dreaded most. I heard one fisherman's wife say: 'He do go out and I never knows as whether he'll be coming back.' I thought that was very sad. It was the reason why they were so superstitious. They certainly looked all the time for signs and portents – mostly evil ones.

The members of the mining community were the same. The moor began about two miles from the town and close to the moor was Poldorey's tin mine. It was affectionately known as the old 'scat bal' which meant useless, worked-out old has-been. It was far from that, for it had brought prosperity to the community. We were on visiting terms with the Pencarrons who lived in a pleasant house close by, called Pencarron Manor. They had come to the district some years ago, bought the place and started working the mine.

The superstitious miners used to leave a *didjan*, which was a piece of their lunch, in the mine for the knackers in order to placate them and stop their wreaking some mischief, which it was very easy to do in the mine. There had been some fearful accidents and there were several widows and orphans who had lost their breadwinner to the old Scat Bal. They, like the fishermen, took notice of signs. They could not afford to ignore them.

'They are naturally fearful,' said my mother. 'One understands it. And if it means giving up a little of their lunch in order to buy safety, this is a small price to pay for it.'

I was very curious to hear more of the knackers. They were said to be dwarves – spirits of those Jews who had crucified Christ. My mother did not believe in them. It was easy for her. She did not have to go down the mine. But she was very interested in superstitions.

She said: 'How they would laugh at us in London. But here in Cornwall they do seem to fit sometimes. It's the place for spirits and strange happenings. Look at the legends there are

16

. . . all the wells that give special qualities . . . all the stories of the piskies and the unexplained mysteries. And then, of course, there is Branok Pool.'

'Oh yes,' I said, round-eyed and eager, 'tell me about Branok Pool.'

'You must be careful when you go there. You must always have Miss Prentiss or someone with you. The ground's a bit marshy round the pool. It could be unpleasant.'

'Tell me about it.'

'It's an old story. I think some of the people round here actually believe it. They'd believe anything.'

'What do they believe?'

'That they hear the bells.'

'Bells? What bells?'

'The bells that are supposed to be down there.'

'Where? Under the water?'

She nodded. 'It's a ridiculous story. Some say that the pool is bottomless. In that case, where could the bells get to? They can't have it both ways.'

'Tell me the story of the bells, Mama.'

'What a child you are! You always want to know everything.'

'Well, you said that people should try and learn as much as they can.'

'Of the right things.'

'Well, this is one of them. This is history.'

'I'd hardly call it that.' She laughed and put a lock of my hair behind my ear, for it had fallen out of the grip of the ribbon which was meant to be holding it back. 'Long ago, it is said, there was an abbey there.'

'What! In the water?'

'Not in the water then. That came after. At first when they built the Abbey they were all very good men, very religious; they spent their time praying and doing good works. It was when St Augustine brought Christianity to Britain.'

'Oh yes,' I urged, fearing it was going to stray into a history lesson.

'People came from far and wide to visit the Abbey and they brought gifts with them. Gold and silver, wines and rich foods,

17

so that instead of being poor the monks all became rich. And then they took to evil practices.'

'What were those?'

'They loved their food. They drank too much; they had wild parties; they danced and did all sorts of things which they had never done before. Then one day a stranger came to the Abbey. He brought them no rich gifts. He just went into their church and preached to them; he told them that God was displeased. They had turned their beautiful Abbey, built to serve Him, into a den of iniquity, and they must repent. But the monks by this time were too much in love with their way of life to give it up, and they hated the stranger for warning them. They told him to leave without delay and if he did not go they would drive him away. He would not go and they brought out whips and sticks which in the past they had used to chastise themselves, which was supposed to make them holier – though I could never see why. They turned on him and beat him, but the blows just glanced off his body and did not harm him at all. Then suddenly a great light surrounded him. He lifted his hands and cursed St Branok's. He said: "Once this place was considered holy, but now it is accursed. Soon it shall be as though it never existed. Floods shall carry it away from human sight. Your bells will be silenced . . . save when they shall proclaim some mighty disaster." And with that he disappeared.'

'Did he go to Heaven?'

'Perhaps.'

'I bet it was St Paul. It was just the sort of thing he would do.'

'Well, whoever it was, according to the legend, he spoke the truth. When they tried to ring the bells no sound came. Then the monks began to be afraid. They started to pray but it was no good. The bells were silent. Then one night it started to rain . . . and it rained and rained for forty days and forty nights and the rivers were overflowing and the water rose and rose until it covered the Abbey and in place of it was St Branok's Pool.'

'How far down is the Abbey?'

She looked at me and smiled. 'It's just a story that has been made up. When there was a disaster at one of the mines people

18

said they heard the bells. But to my mind, when something dreadful happens, people fancy that they heard them, because you never hear about the bells until after the event. It is just one of the old Cornish legends.'

'But the pool is there.'

'It's just an inland lake, that's all.'

'And is it bottomless?'

'I doubt it.'

'Has anyone ever tried to find out?'

'Why should they?'

'To see if the Abbey is down there.'

'It's just one of those old Cornish superstitions. No one investigates them. No one examined the water in Nun's Well at Altarnun to see what it contains to prevent insanity, or St Uny's Well at Redruth to see if it could prevent those who drink it from being hanged. There are just people who like to believe these things . . . and the rest are sceptical. It is the same with Branok.'

'I should like to hear the bells.'

'They don't exist. I doubt there was ever an abbey there. You know how these legends grow up. People fancy they see or hear something which they can't explain. Then the legends start to grow. Don't go too near the place, though. It's unhealthy. Stagnant water always is . . . and as I say, the ground is marshy.'

I must say I did not think very much about the pool then. There were all sorts of stories about weird happenings, such as certain people ill-wishing others and how some had the power to do harm by making waxen images of them and sticking pins in vital parts. There was a man who died suddenly and whose mother accused his wife of killing him by sprinkling salt round his chair – a method which would not be considered evidence of murder in a court of law. There was Maddy Craig who was a Pellar, which meant that an ancestor of hers had helped a mermaid, who had been stranded on the shore, to get back to the sea. Pellar families were those which had been endowed with special powers because they had assisted mermaids. So I did not attach much significance to the bells of St Branok.

My mother was very interested in our family and knew a great deal about it because so many of them had kept an account of their lives. Most of these were all bound and kept at Eversleigh which had been the original home of the family; but marriages throughout the years tended to send people off to different places; and Eversleigh was now the home of what was almost another branch of the family. We visited rarely because it was such a long way to the other side of England – the south-east, whereas Cador was in the south-west.

My mother had seen some of the volumes and she would tell me about them. I was very interested in my ancestor Angelet. She had had a twin sister called Bersaba and both had married the same man – Angelet first and her sister Bersaba afterwards: that was when my namesake had died.

At Cador there was a picture gallery, and the portrait which was of greatest interest to me was that of my grandfather. As he looked down on me his eyes seemed to follow me wherever I was in the gallery and I could fancy his face changed as he watched. It was a clever portrait, I suppose, because one had the impression that at any moment he was going to step out of the frame. He was dark; there was a great strength in his face; his mouth seemed to turn up at the corners as one watched and there was a twinkle in his eyes. He looked as though he thought life a great joke.

My mother discovered my interest in the picture.

'You are always gazing at it,' she said.

'It seems as though he is really there. The others are just paintings. He looks alive.'

She turned away; I knew she did not want me to see how moved she was.

Then she said: 'He was a wonderful man. I loved him . . . dearly. When I was young he was the most important person in my life. Oh, Angel, how I wished you could have known him! I sometimes think that our lives are planned for us. He had to die young. He could never grow old. He had lived adventurously, violently even . . . and then he came to peace with the family he loved dearly . . . my mother, Jessica, Jacco and me.'

She stopped, too emotional to go on.

I slipped my arm through hers.

20

'Let us not look at him, Mama,' I said, 'if it hurts you.'

She shook her head. 'If he were here he would laugh at me. He would tell me not to grieve. She went with him . . . my mother . . . and Jacco too. They all went. They left me alone. Even now . . . I remember it so vividly. I can never forget . . . even now I think of that day when they went away and never came back.'

She told me the story of Grandfather Jake Cadorson. 'This was his home. He had an elder brother who was the heir to the Cador estate. They didn't get on well together. Jake left home and lived with the gypsies.'

'He looks a little like a gypsy.'

'It was in his nature. He was never afraid of life. He challenged life and life met the challenge . . . and won in the end. When he was living as a gypsy he killed a man. The man was some aristocrat who had attacked one of the gypsy girls. Jake sought to save the girl. There was a fight and during it he killed the man. He was transported to Australia for seven years. He would have been hanged for murder if your grandmother Jessica had not prevailed upon her father to do all he could to save him. Her father was a very influential man. And so . . . the punishment was transportation to a new land for seven years, which was considered a slight punishment for killing a man.

'While he was away his brother died and he inherited Cador. He returned to England and married your grandmother. My brother Jacco was born and then I was. We were a very happy family. Then we went to Australia. Jake had prospered there when his seven years term was up and he had some land there. It was while they were in Australia that he went sailing on that terrible day . . . he, my mother and Jacco. They never came back.'

'Don't talk of it.'

'It affects me . . . even now. It seems so clear.'

I put my arm round her. 'Never mind. You have Papa and us now . . . Jack and me.'

She held me tightly. 'Yes. I have been lucky. But I can never forget it. We were all together . . . and then . . . no more. That is how life goes sometimes. One must be prepared.' She kissed

21

me and said: 'I should not be sad. There were so many happy times with them. I must remember those instead and be grateful for those times. And now I have your father and you and Jack.'

When I had heard the story of my grandfather, I came more often to the gallery to look at him. In those daydreams of mine I projected myself into the years long ago before I was born. I was a gypsy riding in the caravan with him. I was on the ship which carried us overseas. I was with him on the fateful day when they went sailing. I rescued them all and there was a different end to the story. My grandfather had a prominent place in my repertoire of dreams.

Then came the day in early April. It was spring and Jack was in the garden with Amy, our nursery maid, and I was with them when my parents came out.

Jack ran to my mother and clutched at her skirts. She lifted him up. Then she smiled at me. 'We've heard from your Aunt Amaryllis.'

Aunt Amaryllis wrote frequently. She liked the family to keep in touch, and she had always felt she must look after my mother since the death of my grandmother in that fatal incident in Australia; for Amaryllis and my grandmother Jessica – although they were of an age – had been brought up together.

'She's excited about the Exhibition,' said my mother. 'The Queen is going to open it on the first of May. She suggests we ought to go up to see it. It is some time since we visited.'

I gave a little jump of joy. I loved visiting London.

'There seems to be no reason why we should not go,' said my father.

'I'm going too,' announced Jack.

'Of course you are, darling,' said my mother. 'We shouldn't dream of leaving you behind, should we?'

'No,' replied Jack complacently.

'It will be exciting,' went on my mother. 'They've been months planning it. And the Queen is particularly enthusiastic because it is Prince Albert's idea. He's been behind it all along.'

'When shall we go?' I asked.

'In a few weeks,' said my mother.

'We'll have to,' added my father. 'We want to be there for the opening.'

'By the Queen,' I put in. 'Oh, I can't wait to see it.'

'I shall write at once to Aunt Amaryllis,' said my mother.

And from then on there was little talk of anything but the Great Exhibition.

When we arrived in London Aunt Amaryllis greeted us warmly. There was something very thrilling about the London residence. It was situated in a dignified square in the middle of which were enclosed gardens – for the use of the residents, all of whom had a key. They were beautifully kept and there were trees, shrubs and little paths with seats here and there. I thought of it as an enchanted though miniature wood. From the top windows of the house there was a glimpse of the River Thames. I loved to look down on it and imagine the glories of the past when the river was the great highway of the capital. I was Anne Boleyn going to her coronation and later going to her doleful prison in the Tower of London. I was in the royal pageant listening to Handel's *Water Music*. I was at the centre of many brilliant events and always playing some heroic part in them.

Aunt Amaryllis must have been nearly sixty by now but she had one of those smooth, unruffled, almost childlike faces which made her seem much younger. Uncle Peter was older still but he gave the impression of being indestructible.

Amaryllis embraced my mother with rather special affection. Her eyes filled with tears and I knew she was thinking of my grandmother, which she always did when seeing my mother after an absence.

'It is lovely to have you here,' she said. 'It seems so long. And, Angelet, how you have grown! And little Jack! No longer little, eh?'

'I am rather big,' Jack admitted modestly.

And Aunt Amaryllis kissed him tenderly.

'And Rolf . . . So lovely to see you. And now your rooms. Your usual, of course. By the way, Helena and Matthew will

23

be here tomorrow for luncheon. Matthew has some business to discuss with Peter in the morning.'

And there I was in my little room at the top of the house. Aunt Amaryllis knew that I loved to watch the river. She thought of things like that and seemed to have spent her life trying to please everybody.

There was a great deal of talk about the family during the rest of that day.

'You must take the children over to Helena's,' said Aunt Amaryllis. 'Jonnie and Geoffrey will look forward to seeing Angelet.'

'Jonnie must be getting on now.'

'He's soon to be thirteen.'

I looked forward to seeing Jonnie.

The next morning my mother took Jack and me to see the Humes. Matthew was of course with Uncle Peter, but Aunt Helena welcomed us warmly. Aunt Helena was very like her mother but she lacked that innocent belief in the goodness of life which was her mother's outstanding quality; she adored her family and was very proud of her husband's achievements. She talked to my mother about Matthew's progress in the House of Commons and how she hoped the Party would soon regain power and if they did there would certainly be a post in the cabinet for Matthew. Her father was sure of it and, of course, he had his ear to the ground.

I went off to see Jonnie's collection of books on archæology which he showed me with great enthusiasm. I did not care very much about old weapons and coins and pieces of urns and things which had been dug up and proved when the Stone Age merged into the Bronze; but I did like to be with Jonnie. He was very interested in the Exhibition and told me that he was often in Hyde Park watching the progress of the work. It was going to be wonderful when it was opened and we could see the wonders of that glorious glass palace.

Geoffrey, two years my senior, was inclined to view me with a certain aloofness as being too young to engage his attention. Jonnie, who was four years older, was quite different. There was something special about Jonnie.

24

When we returned to the house in the square Matthew was still with Uncle Peter.

Uncle Peter was very affable to me and I fancied he gave me a rather special affection. Once he said: 'You may not look like your grandmother but you are another such as she was.' And I felt that was a compliment. He must have been fond of Jessica.

He dominated everything, although he was quite an old man. His hair was almost white now, but he was very handsome; but what was different about him was that rather secretive smile as though life was great fun to him because he had found the perfect way to live it. I could well believe he had.

The *Eminence Grise* . . . well, there was no doubt of that. Matthew, famous politician though he might be, regarded his father-in-law as a master. Matthew had done a great deal since he had returned from Australia and written that book about transportation and prisoners which was becoming a classic, *the* book on the subject. Transportation was still in existence and so were the infamous hulks in which prisoners were kept; and the conditions in prisons were still appalling; but Matthew had called attention to these matters and the subject of transportation was constantly being given an airing; there were many who supported Matthew's views that it should be abolished and it seemed only a matter of a short time before it would be. Matthew had also written a book about child chimney-sweeps and labour in the mines. Matthew was a natural reformer. It meant that he was a highly respected member of Parliament, beloved by his constituents, highly thought of by the leaders of his party, and certain of a ministerial post when it was returned to power.

I was allowed to sit with the family for luncheon.

'I shall have Angelet beside me,' declared Uncle Peter. He had great charm and an endearing way with him. It was small wonder that innocents like myself admired him.

He did most of the talking. He seemed to have, as was once said of him, 'a finger in many pies'. I was not sure at that time what his business was, but I knew that it was highly profitable and made him very rich. Later I learned that he owned several clubs of somewhat dubious reputation, but in his view these were a necessity for the community. It kept certain persons from committing misdemeanours which could be a menace to society, so he was doing a great service to the country. Amaryllis believed this absolutely, though there had been a great scandal about his activities at one time and through it he had lost his place in Parliament. Even he had to compromise in some way, for he had to content himself with being outside the main action and give himself up to guiding Matthew in the way he wanted him to go. I thought of Matthew as the puppet and Uncle Peter as the puppet-master.

It was not only Matthew whom he manipulated. I was sure Uncle Peter made a number of people do what he wanted.

It was gratifying and made me feel important to be selected to sit beside him.

The talk was of the folly of John Russell who was the Prime Minister and a Whig; and as Uncle Peter was a Tory, he had nothing but contempt for Little John, as he called him.

The Exhibition was discussed at great length.

'You are looking forward to seeing the opening, are you not, Angelet?' he asked, turning to me.

I assured him that indeed I was.

'It will be something to remember all your life. It is an historic occasion.'

'I understand the Queen is opening it,' said my mother.

'But of course. Her diminutive Majesty dotes on the idea. And why? Because it was Albert's brainchild. Therefore in her eyes it must be perfect.'

'Is it not wonderful to see how happy they are?' said Aunt Amaryllis. 'They set such a good example to the nation.'

'There are the occasional storms, I believe, my dear,' said Uncle Peter. 'But I fancy Albert usually comes out best in these encounters, which says something for his wisdom . . . or is it his pretty appearance?'

'Oh Peter!' said Aunt Amaryllis, half scolding, half admiring.

'At least,' put in Matthew, 'the whole project is nearing completion and all should be well.'

'Little John will do his best to make difficulties,' said Uncle Peter. 'What's his latest, Matthew?'

'He wants the salute of guns fired in St James's Park. He says if they are let off in Hyde Park they may shatter the glass of the dome.'

'And will they?' asked my mother.

'Of course not,' retorted Uncle Peter. 'It is just that he wants to put in his spoke and cause a little trouble.'

'I believe Albert is going to stand out against him,' said Matthew.

'What if it does shatter the dome?' I asked.

'My dear Angelet,' said Uncle Peter, beaming at me, 'then Albert will be proved wrong and Little Johnny right.'

'Isn't it a risk?'

He shrugged his shoulders. 'I don't think Albert will give way on this matter. Don't look so glum, I doubt it will happen, and I feel sure the crystal dome will remain intact, and if it does not . . . well, then I say . . . what a to-do!'

'It seems rather silly to risk it,' I said. 'It would be awful if it were spoilt after all this fuss.'

'Life, dear child, is full of risks. Sometimes it pays to take them. If the Prince gave way on this we should have Little Johnny raising other objections. Albert can't admit he's wrong . . . so he takes this little risk.'

I was thoughtful, considering this, and I saw Uncle Peter's amused glance on me.

He went on to talk of the beautiful Exhibition and how the Prince had thought of it as a festival of Work and Peace. How much better for nations to mingle in friendship, to show their achievements in technology than facing each other on a battlefield. Art and Commerce should stand side by side.

The great day dawned. How fortunate we were to be of a party which could attend the opening. For the first time I saw the Queen. She looked magnificent in pink and silver; across her breast was the Garter ribbon and on her head a small crown in which the Koh-i-Noor diamond glistened. I caught my breath in wonder. I had never seen such a beautiful vision. I was so proud as I joined in the cheers as she arrived in her carriage, two feathers waving gently on her head attached in some way to the crown. She looked proud, happy and completely regal, everything that a queen ought to look.

27

It was a wonderful day. It had lived completely up to my expectations. The music was splendid. I loved the Hallelujah Chorus. The Queen and her husband were on the royal dais and sat under a blue and gold canopy. I could not take my eyes from her. In my mind I was there. I was Victoria – the proud wife, the wise mother, the great Queen – an example to the nation. I was very contented.

It was an exhausting day. There was so much to see; I found the displays of workmanship, the efforts of all the countries to send of their best, and the famous people like the Duke of Wellington, very interesting. But nothing could compare with the sight of our little Queen, so radiantly happy, so human, yet very much the Queen. I loved her from that moment and it was the memory of her which would remain in my mind as the most thrilling spectacle of that day.

There was talk of nothing else but the Exhibition. We discussed it endlessly.

Aunt Amaryllis said: 'Of course you will go again before you return to Cornwall.'

My mother said we must.

'Will the Queen be there?' I asked.

'It would not surprise me,' replied Uncle Peter. 'This is Albert's conception and therefore in her eyes must be perfect.'

'They fired the guns in Hyde Park,' I said, 'and they did not shatter the glass dome.'

'You remembered that, did you?' said Uncle Peter, smiling.

'Well, it was important.'

'And a bit of a risk. But didn't I tell you that risks have to be taken . . . and if you are bold they will work out in your favour.'

We retired that night; and as soon as I lay down I was into a beautiful sleep of happy jumbled dreams . . . myself in pink and silver walking majestically up to the royal dais, everyone cheering me. It was a beautiful dream.

It happened the following day.

We were at luncheon, Matthew was there again – he was a

very constant visitor – being coached in the way he must act in Parliament, I supposed.

We were still talking about the Exhibition and were on the last course when there was a quiet knock on the door and Janson, the butler, appeared.

He gave a discreet little cough and said: 'There is a young gentleman to see you, sir.'

'A gentleman? Can't he wait until after luncheon, Janson?'

'He said it was important, sir.'

'Who is it?'

'He calls himself a Mr Benedict Lansdon, sir.'

Uncle Peter sat very still for a few seconds. It was hardly noticeable but I was watching him closely and I thought he was a little disturbed.

He half rose in his chair and then sat down again.

'Oh,' he said. 'Oh, very well, Janson, I'll see him. Ask him to wait.'

Janson went out and Uncle Peter looked at Aunt Amaryllis. She said; 'Who is it, Peter? The name . . .'

'It could be some long-lost relative. I'll sort it out . . . if you'll excuse me.'

When he went out the chatter began.

'I wonder who it is,' said Matthew. 'It must be someone in the family. That name . . .'

'How exciting,' I said.

My mother smiled at me but said nothing.

We had finished luncheon so we rose. Uncle Peter, I gathered, was still closeted in his study with the visitor.

It is so frustrating to be young and have things kept from you. That there was an enormous mystery about Benedict Lansdon, I had no doubt. My father and mother talked of him in hushed whispers. Aunt Amaryllis looked a little dazed. I heard Matthew say to my father that he hoped it wouldn't 'get about'.

I wondered what that meant.

I listened; I watched; and gradually I began to learn the truth.

Benedict was Uncle Peter's grandson. He had been born in Australia seventeen years ago. His father was Uncle Peter's son. Uncle Peter had been married only once and that was to

29

Aunt Amaryllis, but that did not prevent his having a son of whom Amaryllis, until this moment, had never heard.

I listened to my mother talking of it to my father. She said: 'He passed it off as you would expect him to. A youthful misdemeanour . . . before he met Amaryllis, of course.'

So Benedict was the result of a youthful misdemeanour.

It was from Benedict that I heard more of the story than I could get from anyone else. He and I were immediately attracted to each other. I to him because he was different from anyone I had previously known and he to me perhaps because I so blatantly admired him.

He was tall for his age; he had very blue eyes which were startling in his bronzed face; his hair was very fair, bleached by the fierce sun of the Antipodes. He had an air of insouciance, as Uncle Peter had, but it was almost a swagger in Benedict; I thought Uncle Peter would have been very like him when he was his age. There was a look of amusement as though he saw the world as something made for his advancement and benefit. It was a look I had noticed in Uncle Peter. There could be no doubt of the relationship between them.

The house in the square had only a small garden. It had paving stones and rather stunted bushes and a pear tree which produced very hard pears. Aunt Amaryllis had had pots put in with flowering shrubs and there was a rustic seat.

It was in this garden that I had my first meeting with Benedict.

'Hello,' he said. 'You're a cute little girl. Who are you?'

'I'm Angelet. Some people call me Angel which is misleading.'

'I hope it is,' he replied. 'I'd be rather scared of an angel.'

'I don't think you would ever be scared of anything.'

That was how I felt about him; and he liked to hear it. His blue eyes shone with pleasure. 'I'm not scared of much,' he admitted. 'But angels do have a habit of recording people's sins.'

'Have you committed many?'

He nodded conspiratorially and I laughed.

I said: 'Who are you?'

'Benedict Lansdon. Call me Ben.'

30

'Ben suits you better. Benedict sounds a little holy . . . like a monk or a saint or something.'

'I fear I should never be one of those.'

'Ben's much more suitable.'

'They call me Ben way back.'

'Why are you here?'

'To see my grandfather.'

'Uncle Peter?'

'Oh, he's your uncle, is he?'

'No, not really. They call people uncle when they don't know what else to call them. He's just married to my Aunt Amaryllis, but she's not my real aunt either. It really is one of those relationships which are too complicated to explain to people.'

'Well, mine is not a bit complicated. He really is my grandfather.'

'But there's something odd about it. He didn't seem to know he had you for a grandson until you came here to tell him.'

'Not odd really. All very natural. People sometimes have children they don't intend to. It takes them by surprise, so to speak, and then what are they going to do with them? That's what happened to my grandmother and your Uncle Peter.'

'I see.'

'And she then went to Australia. He paid for her and sent her money for as long as she lived. My father was born. He was called Peter Lansdon after his father . . . Peter Lansdon Carter in fact but the Carter was dropped. My grandmother never married but my father did, and they had me. That's how I come to be your Uncle Peter's grandson. My grandmother was always talking about England and what a fine fellow my grandfather was. Once there was something in the papers about him. It was not very good, but she laughed over it, and said there was no one like him. When she died we lost touch with him, but he was often spoken of. My mother died and there was just my father and me. We had a small property but it was hard going. The land wasn't good . . . too dry and there always seemed to be droughts . . . and then there were pests . . . locusts and that sort of thing. When my father knew he was dying he used to talk to me about the future. He knew someone who'd buy

31

the property. He wanted me to go to England and find my grandfather. "You'll find him easily," he said. "He's a well-known gentleman." And when he went I thought I'd like to see England, so I sold up and came.'

'That was a very brave thing to do.'

'I don't look at it like that. I just wanted to come.'

'What will you do now?'

He shrugged his shoulders. 'Have to see which way the wind blows.'

'I hope it blows in the right direction.'

He gave me a confident smile. 'I'll see it does,' he said.

'I am sure you will.'

We smiled at each other and I had an idea that he liked me as much as I liked him.

I said: 'My grandfather went to Australia.'

'Is that so?'

'Yes. First he went as a convict.'

'Never!'

'Oh yes. Seven years' transportation for killing a man.'

'I can't believe it.'

'It was very extraordinary. He joined the gypsies and became one of them although he had been brought up at Cador. You'll come to see Cador, won't you? It's a wonderful place. It was in the Cadorson family for generations.'

'One of those old places, eh?'

'It's my home.'

'Tell me about your grandfather.'

'Well, he went off with the gypsies and a man who called himself a gentleman attacked a gypsy girl. My grandfather stopped him and in doing so, killed him. It was said to be murder and he was sent to Australia for seven years.'

'A light sentence for murder.'

'It wasn't really murder. It was a righteous killing. And my grandmother, who was a little girl then, saved him, or she made her father do so. My grandfather served his term, prospered out there and when he came back to England, he and my grandmother were married.'

'A happy ending, then.'

32

'At first. They had my Uncle Jacco and my mother and were very happy, but they all went out to Australia and they were drowned there . . . all but my mother. She was the only one left because by chance she hadn't gone sailing with them that day.'

'So Australia kept him in the end.'

I nodded.

'I've heard some tales of people who have come out.'

'Yes, I dare say. It seems to be a place where things happen.'

'Everywhere is a place where things happen.'

'Well, I'm glad you decided to come here, Ben.'

'So am I.'

Amaryllis came out with my mother. Amaryllis looked a little nervous of Benedict but he smiled at her without embarrassment. He was quite at home.

He talked for a while about Australia and how he was finding London as exciting as he had thought it would be. He asked if he could ride here. Aunt Amaryllis said that people rode in the Row and she was sure that could be arranged.

'I bet you're a regular horsewoman,' he said to me.

'Well,' I replied, 'I love riding and I do quite a lot of it at Cador.'

'Perhaps we could take a ride together.'

'I'd love it.'

My mother and Aunt Amaryllis looked a little apprehensive and Aunt Amaryllis said that luncheon would be served in half an hour.

I did go riding in Rotten Row with him and Jonnie and Geoffrey. I found it very different from riding in Cornwall. Many of the fashionable people were there and there were continual nods of recognition. I could ride every bit as well as the London boys, but I could see that Benedict was a very fine horseman indeed; and I rather wished that we were somewhere where he could show off his skills.

He talked – most of the time to me. 'You ought to see the outback,' he said. He described the land. 'Scrub and hills,' he said, 'with the gumtrees everywhere.'

'And kangaroos?' I asked.

33

'Surely. Kangaroos.'

'They have little babies in their pouches. I've seen pictures of them.'

'Little things about half an inch long when they're born.'

He told us about Sydney with its wonderful harbour . . . all the little bays and inlets, the beautiful foliage and the brightly coloured birds.

'And convicts,' I said.

'Yes . . . still them. But less than we used to have and there are many settlers there now who have come out to make something of the place and they're doing it.'

Jonnie came up on the other side of me. Geoffrey was a little way ahead.

'Would you like to go, Jonnie?' I asked.

'Well . . . for a visit. I'd rather live here.'

'How do you know?' I demanded. 'You've never been there. Ben will be able to tell us which is best because he'll have been there and here. What do you think, Ben?'

'I haven't made up my mind yet.'

We were able to canter for a while. It was very exhilarating.

I was liking Ben more and more.

Ben was accepted into the household, and as no one seemed to find his presence an embarrassment, it wasn't. This was largely due to Uncle Peter, who behaved as though it was the most natural thing in the world for the result of an early peccadillo to come home to roost. He carried everything before him, as I learned later he had once before when a scandal had threatened to wreck his career – and did so to a certain extent except that he would not allow it to go further, and as he behaved as though it did exist, in time everyone began to do the same.

Uncle Peter seemed quite proud of Ben. I dare say he recognized in him another such as himself and I think he was rather pleased to discover he had a hitherto unheard-of grandson.

He discussed with my father what should be done with the boy. I heard my father talking about this afterwards with my mother.

34

'I must say,' said my father, 'one thing about Peter, he does not shirk his responsibilities. He wants to do everything he can for the boy. He wants to send him to university for a year or so, as he said to put a polish on him. He thinks he has talents.'

'I am sure he has,' replied my mother. 'He certainly gives me the impression of being a chip off the old block.'

They became aware of my attention and changed the subject. Maddening! For myself I was enormously interested in Ben and wanted to hear more of him.

We all went to the Exhibition once more and this time Ben was one of the company. He managed to be near me often which gave me great pleasure; and he was quite knowledgeable about some of the exhibits.

I said to him: 'Are you glad you came to England?'

He pressed my hand. 'You bet,' he said.

'I'm glad too,' I answered.

'Oh, it was a good thing all right. My grandfather's a great man, don't you think?'

I said I did.

'I want to be like him.'

'You are,' I told him.

'In every way. I want to go into business. He's talked to me a lot. First he wants me to go to learn to be more like an English gentleman. Do you think that's a good idea?'

'I think you're all right as you are.'

'He doesn't think so. And he's a very wise man.'

He grinned at me. There was satisfaction shining in his eyes. He was glad he had come.

I was sorry when it was time to go home. I hated saying goodbye to Ben.

'You'll come here again soon,' he said. 'Or I might come and see this wonderful Cador.'

'That would be lovely,' I replied.

He came to the station to see us on to the train and stood on the platform waving.

35

'You two did seem to take to each other,' commented my mother.

'He has a colourful personality,' added my father.

'What did you expect . . . Peter's grandson and that unconventional life.'

'I wonder if he *will* come to see us.'

'He will,' I said. 'He said he would.'

'People don't always keep their word, dear.'

'But he meant it.'

'But people do mean things when they say them . . . and then they forget.'

I was sure he would not.

I thought about him for a long time afterwards, and then the memory began to fade.

A year passed. We had heard from Aunt Amaryllis at intervals. Peterkin and Frances had added another wing to their house of refuge; Jonnie and Geoffrey were away at school most of the time. Peter's hopes for Matthew had been realized with the end of Little Johnny's government and the beginning of Lord Derby's ministry and their son-in-law had his post in the Cabinet. Peter's grandson had changed quite a lot. 'He is becoming more and more like one of us. He is really quite an English gentleman now . . . or almost. Peter is concerned about him. He thought he might like to go in for estate management, and he is going to ask you if you will have him at Cador for a time . . . say a month or two . . . just to see how he likes that kind of life. Peter thinks he might be rather suited to it.'

'Of course he may come and stay a while,' said my father. 'I dare say it might be just the thing for him. He was brought up on what they call a property in Australia. No doubt he was born to the life.'

My mother said she would write to Amaryllis at once; and I felt excited at the prospect of seeing him.

A few days later I saw Grace Gilmore for the first time. I had taken my horse, Glory, down to the beach for I loved to gallop her over the sands at the edge of the water. It was very rarely that anyone came down there at that spot. The stretch of shore was only about half a mile from the harbour and it was part of Cador land, but there was no restriction about people's using it.

I was surprised when I saw a young woman there. She was seated on an upturned boat close to the old boathouse which was never used nowadays, and she was staring out to sea.

She looked startled when she heard me galloping towards her. I pulled up.

'Good afternoon,' I said.

She returned my greeting. She was quite young – just under twenty, I decided. There was something about her which interested me. She looked serious, anxious, and when she saw me a little alarmed.

I wondered who she was, and that natural curiosity, deplored by Mrs Penlock, always got the better of me. She was a stranger and we rarely saw strangers here. Visitors were usually relations of the inhabitants and their presence was always a matter of gossip. I had heard nothing of this one.

'It's a lovely day,' I went on. 'Are you staying here?'

She replied: 'I'm staying a few days at the Fisherman's Rest.'

'Oh? Are you comfortable there?'

'Well . . . yes.'

I knew Pennyleg had little to offer paying guests; there were so few of them. I believed there were only two rooms available and they were small and cramped. Most of the trade was provided by the local miners and fishermen.

'Are you staying long?'

'I'm unsure.'

She was not very communicative.

She said suddenly: 'Do you live here?'

I nodded and pointed upwards to where Cador stood, on the top of the cliff.

'It's magnificent,' she said.

I warmed to her, as I always did to anyone who praised Cador.

'Is this your boathouse?' she asked.

37

'I suppose so. It is never used.'

She interested me, but then people always did . . . particularly strangers. I fancied I detected a certain tension in her. Then I told myself it was my imagination again.

I said goodbye and rode up the incline through the gorse and valerian and sea pinks to Cador.

I forgot all about her until next day when I saw her again.

I was with my mother in the garden. She had come through the courtyard and was standing there looking at us. She seemed very sad and pathetic.

My mother said: 'Good afternoon. Do you want to see someone?'

'Are you the lady of the house?' she asked.

'Yes.'

'I met your daughter.'

'That's right,' I said. 'On the sands by the old boathouse. Are you staying at the Fisherman's Rest still?'

She nodded. 'I was wondering if there was any work . . .'

'Work?' echoed my mother.

'I'd do anything,' she said with an air of desperation, which I could see touched my mother as it did me.

'Watson, the butler, engages staff,' said my mother. 'You could see him.'

I imagined Watson. He would be condescending. What work could he give her? As far as I knew we did not need another servant and she did not look like a house or parlour maid, or anything like that. She was good-looking in a severe sort of way. Not the kind who would attract Watson.

'I . . . I can sew,' she said.

My mother looked at me. I could see that the girl had aroused her sympathy as she had mine and we both wanted to do all we could to help her.

I read my mother's thoughts. This might be a possibility. Clothes were bought on trips to London or even in Plymouth. There was one stylish dressmaker there. But I had often heard my mother say: 'How I wish we had dear old Miss Semple here.' Miss Semple had had her room in the attics somewhere and up there was a big airy and light room which had been used as a

38

sewing-room. Miss Semple had worked there until she died three years ago.

At that moment the girl swayed a little; she would have fallen to the ground if my mother had not caught her.

'Poor soul, she has fainted,' said my mother. 'Help me, Angelet. Get her head down. That will revive her.'

In a few seconds she had opened her eyes.

'Oh, forgive me,' she said.

'My dear child,' began my mother, 'we're going to take you into the house. You need to rest awhile.'

We took her into a room leading off the hall where people waited if they wanted to see my parents about anything.

'Ring and tell someone to bring me some brandy,' said my mother.

I did so.

The girl was sitting in a chair. She said: 'I'm all right now. I'm sorry. It was foolish of me.'

'You're not all right,' said my mother firmly. 'You're going to rest awhile.'

A servant brought the brandy which the girl took half reluctantly. She seemed to recover a little.

She half rose to her feet but my mother gently pushed her back into the chair.

'Tell me,' she said. 'Where have you come from? And why is a girl like you looking for work?'

She smiled ruefully. 'It's no use pretending, is it? I have to find work . . . quickly. I'm desperate. I have nowhere to go.'

'I thought you were staying at the Fisherman's Rest,' I said.

'I have to leave tomorrow. I have no . . .'

'Why did you come here?' asked my mother.

'I knew there were one or two big houses in the neighbourhood. I thought I might find work in one of them. So . . .'

'I see,' said my mother. 'And where have you come from?'

'My home was in Barnton . . . in Devon. My father was the rector. He was much older than my mother and my parents were not young, either of them, when they married. I was the only child. I looked after my father and when my mother died

39

. . . well, it was not easy. He was ill for some time and he had to retire. All his savings were used up. There were some debts and when everything was sold I had very little. I knew it wouldn't last. I had to find something I could do. You see, I have never been trained for anything but I used to do a lot of sewing for people in the neighbourhood and acquaintances. I'm really good at it . . .' she ended almost pleadingly.

My mother had made a decision. 'You could see how you liked it here,' she said. 'We had Miss Semple who worked for us for years. She died three years ago. We were all very fond of her and she has never been replaced. Her room has never been used and there is the sewing-room next to it.'

Her face was illumined with joy. She said: 'Do you really mean it . . . ?'

'Of course,' replied my mother. 'Now let us be practical. I'll take you up to see the room right away.'

She had taken my mother's hand; her eyes were closed. I thought she was going to burst into tears, but she did not.

My mother was faintly embarrassed by this show of gratitude. She said quickly: 'I suppose you have some things which you will want to bring.'

'I have a few clothes at the Fisherman's Rest. That's all.'

'I'll show you your room and then you can go to the inn and collect your things. You can settle in right away.'

'You are so kind . . . This seems too wonderful to be true.'

We took her up and showed her the rooms. In the sewing-room was a big table at which Miss Semple had sat; and there were the dummies she used, and in the drawers of the table her cottons and tape-measure just as she had left them.

She told us then that her name was Grace Gilmore, and that she hoped one day to repay us for all the kindness we had shown her.

That was how Grace Gilmore came to Cador.

There was a certain resentment below stairs where what was called 'Interference from the Top' was not approved of; but my mother told them that Miss Gilmore was a genteel young lady who had fallen on hard times and she wanted them all to be as helpful towards her as possible.

Watson and Mrs Penlock both agreed that they would do all they could to help 'the young body' settle in and they implied that although it was Watson's prerogative to engage staff, they did see that sewing was something outside his domain; so perhaps on this occasion it was not such a breach of household protocol as it had at first seemed.

Later that day, Grace Gilmore arrived with her personal belongings and was settled into the rooms at the top of the house.

She was very eager to begin work and we soon discovered that she was an excellent seamstress.

'We've been lucky,' said my mother. 'And she is a lady, which is a help too. We must be very kind to her, poor girl. She has had such a bad time and she is really quite young. I have no doubt that she could help Miss Prentiss in some ways.'

I was pleased that we had been able to help her. Grace Gilmore interested me. There was something mysterious about her.

Benedict arrived at Cador. He was even more handsome than I remembered.

'Why,' he cried, 'you've grown. You're almost a young lady now.'

He laughed. I noticed that he had beautiful white teeth and his eyes were bluer than I remembered.

'I'm settling in now,' he said. 'I'll soon be as English as you.'

My parents greeted him with pleasure and in a few days he seemed to become part of Cador. He spent a good deal of time with my father. Jack was very taken with him and he was soon popular with the servants.

Whenever I could be with him, I would. He seemed to enjoy my company. But of course he had come with a purpose and he was kept busy. He was full of enthusiasm for the estate; and when he was not with my father he seemed to be with John Polstark, our manager. He was very popular with all. I knew that in the kitchen they discussed him constantly, especially the younger and more frivolous maids.

41

'He's what you might call one of them charmers,' was Mrs Penlock's verdict. 'You girls want to watch out with them sort. They can be all nice words and smiles till they get what they want from you girls . . . and then it's "Goodbye, I'm off now to the next."' But she herself was not immune. She would simper a little when he was near. He was full of good will and if he did cast a sparkling eye on the younger and prettier of the girls, he did not forget the older ones either. He would give the same sort of attention to Mrs Penlock herself – who admitted to being in her sixties, but I was sure she had forgotten to add a few years, for she had been at Cador when my mother was a girl and had not been exactly young then. He made everyone feel that there was something special about them which he found lovable. I supposed that was called charm.

I tried to discover what it was about him which had that effect on people. It was more than just his attitude towards them; he was the sort of man who wanted power and I came to the conclusion that that was the very essence of masculine attraction.

My mother talked to me about him.

'He seems to have a way of making himself known,' she said. 'He has only been here a short time and he is making an impression.'

'There is something different about him,' I answered. 'He's unlike anyone else I know.'

My mother smiled. 'He's getting along with John Polstark and your father. They seem to think he will make a good estate manager.'

'What do you think Uncle Peter intends to do? Buy him an estate somewhere?'

'Probably . . . but for himself, I should imagine. He'll keep a firm hand on it and perhaps let Benedict manage it.'

'I shouldn't think Ben would want that.'

'No. He's like his grandfather, I dare say. He would want to have complete charge. It will be interesting to see what happens. They're a strong-willed pair. By the way, Miss Gilmore is settling in well, I think. Don't you?'

'She's so grateful, it's almost embarrassing.'

42

'Poor girl! I don't know what she would have done if we hadn't taken her in. She seemed pretty desperate. She has asked me for a day off.'

'A day off! So soon!'

'She's got an old aunt who lives somewhere near Bodmin. She wants to go and see her and tell her that she's settled and where she is and all that, I suppose.'

'I thought she hadn't got any relations.'

'I don't think she said that. Well, this is her father's sister . . . and I dare say she is very old . . . as the father was. In any case I have said she may go.'

'Near Bodmin, you say?'

'She mentioned Lanivet.'

'That's some little way.'

'She said she would be away one night and she was so grateful when I said that would be all right. I think she is going to be very useful. She's made a very good job of that alpaca. You know I was very fond of that costume. I didn't want to discard it, but the bottoms of the sleeves were so marked. She's done something so that it doesn't show. And she's tightened up the skirt which was too loose. It almost looks like new. Dear old Semple was getting a little past it, though she would never admit it. I don't think she could see very well towards the end.'

'I think you are rather pleased with Miss Gilmore, Mama.'

'It is nice to be able to do a good turn to someone and find you've done yourself one too.'

'Is she getting on all right with the servants now?'

'I think they consider her something of an outsider.'

'Well, anyone who comes from the other side of the river is that.'

My mother laughed. 'She is quiet and causes no fuss. I don't know what goes on in the kitchen. It's like the case of Miss Prentiss. They are so strict about levels of society that they are a little complicated to follow. She seems to have become quite friendly with Miss Prentiss.'

'Perhaps they both feel they can be friendly without upsetting the rules of protocol.'

'That must be so. However, she is going off in the morning.'

43

I often wondered about Grace Gilmore. There was an air of mystery about her which intrigued me. I did not mention it to anyone. They would say – or even if they didn't say it they would think it – that I was daydreaming again. I imagined her life with the poor old rector – so feeble and demanding. I was sure she had waited on him, caring for him, living for him and letting her own life slip away.

My mother would say: 'You are building up what isn't there, Angel. That imagination of yours . . . It's all very fine but don't let it run away with you.'

I saw Grace Gilmore going to the station to get the train. There was something purposeful about her. I smiled and wished her a good journey.

I began to wonder whether she would come back. There was a certain unreality about her. It occurred to me that she might suddenly disappear and we would never hear of her again. I was so obsessed by this thought that when I returned to the house I went to her room. Everything was neat and tidy. I looked in the wardrobe. Her clothes were hanging there. Her nightdress lay neatly folded under her pillow. Yes, I was inquisitive enough to look there.

It was the room of someone who intended to return.

In the afternoon I went riding with Ben and all thought of Grace Gilmore departed during such a pleasant time.

He talked about running an estate of his own.

'Like Cador?' I asked.

'Just like Cador only bigger.'

I laughed. 'Everything about you has to be bigger than everyone else's.'

'I admit it.'

'Do you realize that this estate has been built up over hundreds of years?'

'I do.'

'And you are going to come and start and immediately have something bigger?'

'It is what I should like.'

'We don't all get what we like.'

'I intend to.'

'Pride goeth before a fall.'

'Oh, moral, are we?'

'It's supposed to be true.'

'I shall be prouder than ever and not fall . . . just to prove it's wrong.'

'I should be rather disappointed if it were, when I think of the number of times I have had to write it out for Miss Prentiss.'

'It is a great game to prove the moralists wrong. And for every one of these adages there is a contradiction.'

'"Too many cooks spoil the broth" and "Many hands make light work"?'

'Exactly. So I shall make my own laws. They will be the laws of Reason.'

'Oh, Ben, it is nice to have you here.'

'Shall I tell you what is the nicest thing about being here?'

'Yes, do.'

'Angel is here.'

'You always say such wonderful things. Do you mean them?'

'Not always. But on this occasion, yes.'

'If you don't mean them, why do you say them?'

He paused for a moment and laughed at me. 'Well, it makes people feel good. They like you for it, and it is wise to have people liking you. Never make enemies if you can help it . . . even in the smallest way. You never know when the most trivial thing can be turned against you. It is what you call keeping the wheels well oiled.'

'Even though it is false?'

He shrugged his shoulders. 'It's harmless. It makes people feel happy. What's wrong with that?'

'Nothing, I suppose, only I like things to be true.'

'You are asking too much.'

We had come to open country and I started to gallop. He was beside me.

'We're almost on the moor,' I shouted.

I pulled up. There it was – miles of moorland with its boulders and little rippling streams and here and there the flowering gorse.

45

'There's something strange about it,' I said. 'Do you feel it? I mean strange in a certain way. Uncanny.'

'Out of this world.'

'Yes.'

'You might have strayed on to another planet.'

'That's it. Strange things happen here. When I am here I can believe the stories one hears of the piskies and the knackers and the rest.'

We walked our horses for a while.

He said: 'We could tie our horses to that bush and sit here for a while. I'd like to, would you?'

'Yes,' I said.

So we tethered the horses and sat with our backs against a boulder inhaling the fresh air. There was a faint wind which whistled through the grass, making a soft moaning noise which was like a human voice.

I was glad he was aware of the spirit of the moors.

'The mine is not far from here.'

'Oh yes. It belongs to the Pencarrons, I believe.'

'Yes. We'll ride over there one day. They'd like to meet you.'

'Profitable concern, the mine, I take it.'

'Yes, I think so. It's a great boon to the Poldoreys. Quite a number of the men work there. The population seems to be made up of fishermen and miners . . . apart from the farmers and people who work on the land. They are safe.'

'Safe?' he asked.

'They are not in danger. Fishermen and miners always look out for disasters. With the miners it's black dogs and white hares which appear now and then to announce some disaster . . . and disaster in the mine or at sea can be terrible. Then there are those knackers who have to be placated all the time. The miners have to leave them bits of their lunch when, poor things, they are hungry and could do with it all themselves. Then the fishermen . . . they never know when some mermaid is going to appear to give some dreadful warning or they are going to meet a ghost ship. Apart from all that, there is the weather. So you see, those who work on the land have rather a peaceful time.'

46

'Why do they not all want to work on the land?'

'If they get a good catch they earn a lot of money. And the miners? Well, I suppose they earn more than the farm labourers, because their jobs are so dangerous.'

'Logical reasoning,' he said. 'Yes, up here one could believe in some of those stories.'

'These stones, for instance, could come suddenly to life. Look at that one. It is rather like a woman's shape. It's the one they call the Stone Novice. She was turned out of her convent because she disobeyed the laws of the Church.'

'I wonder what law?'

'She had a lover. They say that at certain times, if you come up here alone, you can hear her weeping.'

'I expect it is only the wind.'

'It could easily be mistaken for weeping.'

'Tell me more.'

'There is the story about the mine.'

'Polcarron's.'

'No. No. There are lots of mines in Cornwall. This was somewhere else. It is supposed to have happened years ago. It's an old Scat Bal now.'

'I thought Pencarron was that.'

'Oh no. That is not a Scat Bal. It's used just as a term of affection for that. I do hope the knackers understand that. They might be annoyed if they didn't. This one I am telling you about is a very different matter.'

'I'm longing to hear more.'

'It was a tin mine. There was a terrible accident there. Several men were killed. After the accident a lot of people remembered seeing black dogs and white hares hanging around. It was a complete disaster. They said that was the end of Cradley Mine. Those who escaped lost their jobs; there was a great deal of hardship in the neighbourhood. People used to say the mine was haunted. They heard strange knockings there at night. There were two men . . . brothers . . . miners who had lost their work and lived in great poverty. One night they decided to go into the old mine and see what the knocking meant. This was dangerous, for the mine had collapsed once and could do so again. However, one dark night they went in. They crawled along in the direction from which came the knocking, expecting at any moment that the earth would collapse on top of them. They saw a light. They went towards it and there were twenty little men all digging away with tiny shovels. They had tiny pails and these were full of gold. They were knackers.'

'And gold . . . in a tin mine?'

'That's the story. The two were terrified, and then they lost their fear for the knackers were so small . . . just the size of a sixpenny doll, they said. The knackers were not angry with the men, because they had been brave to come there in the dead of night. The men just marvelled at the sight of the gold they could see in the earth. They said that if they brought proper implements in one night they could mine twenty times as much gold as the knackers were doing in that time. They came to an arrangement with the little men. They would mine the gold and sell it and for every ounce they sold ten per cent should go back to the knackers. This was agreed and every night those two men went to work. In a short time they were very rich. They bought a beautiful house and they lived like gentry and everyone was in awe of them because of their sudden fortune, which they said had been left to them by a relation from overseas.'

'I hope they remembered to surrender the ten per cent.'

'Oh yes, they did. They never forgot. As soon as a transaction was made the knackers received their due. Well, the men married. They each had a son, and when the boys were old enough they told them the secret of their wealth, and they brought them into the mine so that when they were dead their sons could go on mining gold. So they did and in time the two men died and there were only the sons.'

'I can guess what's coming.'

'What?'

'They didn't pay their dues.'

'That's right. They said: "Why should we? We do the work." They never saw the knackers. They just had to take the commission and leave it there. But it was always gone on their next visit. They made up their minds that it was a fantastic story and their fathers must have been mad to throw away so large a proportion of the profits. They did not work hard as their fathers had; they gambled and drank too much and they went only to the mine when they needed to replenish their coffers. And then one night they went to the mine and all the gold was gone. There was nothing there. It had returned to being an old Scat Bal.'

'Well, it served them right, didn't it? They should have kept to the bargain . . . particularly when dealing with people who can produce gold out of a tin mine and cut off supplies when they are being cheated!'

'You are very sceptical, I think.'

'Never mind, I liked the story. There are two morals in this one. Don't be afraid, for if you are bold you will prosper. That is shown by the two men investigating the knocking; and then: Don't cheat . . . especially if your victim is more powerful than you are.'

I laughed at him.

I said: 'If Uncle Peter buys an estate and you manage it, I wonder where it will be.'

'I have to make up my mind,' he said. 'There are so many possibilities. What I shall do, I think, is look for some obliging knackers and ask them to find me a gold mine.'

'You are never really serious, are you?'

'Yes, sometimes, very serious.'

We were silent for a while. I inhaled the strong moorland air and was happy.

When I look back at that day, I think it was the end of my happiness.

In spite of my imaginings about Grace Gilmore she returned to Cador as she had arranged. I saw her in the sewing-room on the morning after she came back. I had a dress which I rather liked and I thought it was too short. I wondered if it were possible to let it down without spoiling it.

I felt then that there was a restrained excitement about her, and I wondered what had happened when she visited her aunt.

I asked her if she had had a pleasant visit. For a moment she looked startled. Surely she could not have forgotten?

She said: 'Oh yes . . . thank you, Miss Angelet. Very pleasant.'

'I suppose your aunt was very interested to hear you had come to Cador.'

'She seemed pleased that I had found a place.'

'Mama was very pleased with the alpaca.'

'I am very happy about that.'

'Is your aunt a dressmaker, too?'

'Oh no, no.'

'I thought perhaps it ran in the family. Miss Semple, who used to do dressmaking here, had a mother who was a dressmaker . . . and so was her grandmother, I believe.'

She said: 'I am sure I can make a good job of this hem, Miss Angelet.'

I had the impression that she thought I was prying and my mother had told me as well as the servants that that was forbidden. She knew how interested I was in people and how I could not rest until I had discovered what I wanted to know about them.

I said: 'Thanks, Miss Gilmore. I'll leave the dress with you.'

I left then but I continued to think about her.

The very next day we heard about the escaped convict.

I had been riding with Ben and we had gone out as far as the Pencarron Mine. He seemed to have become interested in mines since I had told him the story of the knackers' gold.

When we came back we rode down to the harbour. He wanted to look at the sea.

As we came through the town we saw a little knot of people gathered together staring at something fixed to the wall. We went close. It was a poster.

I saw Jim Mullens, one of the fishermen whom I knew well, and I called to him: 'What's all the fuss about, Jim?'

'Oh, Miss Angel, there be a terrible to-do. It's this here convict who has got out of Bodmin Jail. Real dangerous they say he be.'

50

I dismounted and led my horse forward. Ben did the same.

We saw the rather crude drawing of a man. He had strongly marked brows under a pair of wild-looking dark eyes and thick dark curly hair.

'THIS MAN IS DANGEROUS' said the big black words on the poster.

I read on. He was one Mervyn Duncarry and he had been about to go on trial for murder when he had escaped from Bodmin Jail.

Mrs Fenny was there, having left her cottage to be closer to the excitement.

'This be a shocking thing,' she said. 'We could all be murdered in our beds.'

The Misses Poldrew stood by. I heard the whispered words. 'He assaulted the poor young thing before he strangled her. He deserves to hang twice over . . . and here he is . . . He could be in Poldorey this minute . . .'

The Misses Poldrew would have to make a double check under their beds this evening, I thought.

There was a little about this dangerous man. He had broken out of jail during the night and could be anywhere in the Duchy. Ports were being watched. The public should keep a lookout. If they thought they saw him they should not attempt to approach him, but report it at once.

We mounted our horses and rode through the town.

'He'll soon be found,' said Ben. 'He can't get far with everyone on the alert for him.'

At luncheon we talked about him.

'He'll hang for this,' said my father. 'It is sad, for he is apparently quite a well-educated young man. He was a tutor.'

'Looking after children!' cried my mother. 'How terrible!'

'He suddenly seemed to go mad. It was some girl in the village. A child of about ten . . .'

My mother avoided looking at me. She was about my age . . . this poor girl who had been assaulted and murdered.

My mother said fiercely: 'I hope they catch him . . . soon. He deserves everything he gets . . . and more. Why do people do such things?'

51

'It's a madness,' said my father. 'He must have become suddenly insane.'

'Perhaps he could be cured,' I suggested.

'Perhaps and perhaps not,' said Ben. 'And who would ever know that he was cured? It might break out again and someone else be murdered.'

'Yes,' agreed my mother. 'It seems that eliminating such people is the only way. He won't get far,' she added. 'No fear of that.'

When luncheon was over Ben said to me: 'What about a ride this afternoon?'

'I'd like that,' I replied eagerly.

'You said you were going to show me that pool.'

'Oh yes. Branok.'

'The bottomless pool where the bells are heard when some disaster is about to occur.'

'Yes,' I giggled. 'It's one of those places . . . like the moor. You can laugh, but you can feel it when you are there.'

'Right. In half an hour?'

When I went down to the stables Ben was already there, mounted.

He said: 'I've just had a command from John Polstark. He wants me to go out with him and look at one of the cottages.'

I was disappointed. 'So you can't come.'

'It won't take very long. Are you ready to go? I believe the cottage is somewhere near the pool. You go on. Wait for me there.'

I brightened. 'I'll do that.'

And so, innocently happy, I rode out to the pool, not realizing that life was never going to be the same again.

It was a warm day with just a light, coolish breeze. I reached the pool. How silent it was! There was no one about. There rarely was here. I listened intently. I almost felt I could hear the tinkle of bells. It was easy to fancy such things in such a place.

I felt a desire to touch the water. It shimmered in the sunshine. It was still, though; there was not a ripple on the surface. I halted my horse and, slipping off her back, looked round for

52

somewhere to tether her. She was docile enough, but I did not want her to wander.

I patted her and said: 'Just for a while. Ben will be here soon.'

I went down to the pool and trailed my hand in the water. I half wished that I could hear the bells; and yet I should have been terrified if they had begun to peal. How would they sound under water? Muffled, I supposed. I should be rather frightened but only because I was alone.

My horse whinnied.

I stood still without turning round. 'It's all right, Glory,' I said. 'He'll soon be here . . . then you'll be free . . . though he might want to walk for a while.'

I heard a footstep.

'Ben,' I called. I looked round, but it was not Ben.

'Good afternoon,' he said. He was a youngish man in his early twenties, I imagined. He smiled pleasantly. 'I've lost my way. Perhaps you could direct me.'

'I expect so. I live round here.'

'Not at that magnificent house I passed?'

'Was it on a cliff?'

'Yes. Like a castle.'

He had come closer and was looking at me intently. He had thick eyebrows and dark curly hair.

'That's Cador,' I told him. 'It's my home.'

'Congratulations. It must be wonderful to live in such a place. It is certainly very fine.'

'It's very old, of course.'

'I guessed so.'

'Where do you want to go?'

'Is there a good inn?'

'There is the Fisherman's Rest. It's very small. There was the King's Arms. That was an old coaching inn . . . but there was no business after the railway came, and it closed down. There is only really the Fisherman's Rest.'

'You're a nice little girl,' he said, and he came closer to me.

It was then that I felt the first twinge of fear. He seemed to change suddenly. I had thought that he was a student . . . exploring the countryside. Now I was not so sure.

53

'Thank you,' I said as coolly as I could and started to walk past him, but he caught my arm.

'You're frightened,' he said. 'Why?'

'No . . . no,' I stammered. 'I . . . I just have to go.'

'Why?' he cried, shaking me.

A terrible thought came into my mind. I remembered the poster. I looked at his face. His eyes now looked wild; they seemed to bore right into me. I thought: It's the escaped prisoner . . . and I'm here . . . alone with him. I wanted to cry out but my mouth was dry and no sound came. My heart was beating so fast that I thought I should suffocate.

I heard myself say shrilly: 'Who are you?'

He did not answer. I moved backwards. I was very close to the water.

He advanced too. He had changed. He was no longer the pleasant student. There was a dreadful light in his eyes. His pupils seemed to be distended.

He said: 'I like little girls.' And he laughed horribly. 'I like them when they are nice to me.'

'Yes . . . yes,' I said, trying to sound normal and wondering if I could slip past him and run . . . and run.

He gripped my arm. I tried to wrench it free, but he laughed again in that frightening way. Then he put a hand out and touched my throat.

'No, no,' I screamed. 'Go away. Let me alone.'

It was the wrong thing to have done. As I tried to dodge past him he caught me by the shoulder.

'Let me go,' I sobbed. 'Let me go.'

Panic had seized me. I could not think. I was only aware of his closeness . . . his motives, which I only half understood but which I knew ended in death.

I was young; I was agile; but he was a grown man and stronger than I. I knew that if he caught me I was doomed.

I heard myself screaming at him. He put up a hand and covered my mouth. I kicked and he freed me. I ran. I was trying to reach Glory, but how could I get away in time? He would catch me before I had a chance to untie her.

I started to run on but he caught me and I fell. I was sobbing

54

with fear and screaming at the top of my voice. Who would hear me? Few people came to the pool.

He was loathsome. He was horrible. He nauseated me. He was pulling at my clothes. I kicked and struggled and I think I hurt him, for he called out in sudden pain, cursing me. He gave me a blow at the side of my head which set up a singing in my ears. I felt blood in my mouth.

'No . . . no . . . no,' I sobbed.

I had never fought like this before. I knew that my life depended on my ability to defend myself. I was sobbing like a baby, calling for my mother and my father. Oh, if only they knew what was happening to their beloved daughter! What *would* happen to me? I should be found . . . dead . . . another victim.

There was a lot of fight in me. I saw blood on his face and the more I fought the more angry he became.

I could not go on much longer. I felt my strength failing me. I had no idea how long this struggle had gone on, but I knew that for me it was a losing battle.

I prayed, I think. One always does, if only subconsciously on such occasions. It is at times like this one that one believes in God . . . because one has to.

And . . . as if by a miracle my prayers were answered.

I heard my name. 'Angel!' It seemed to come from a long way off. 'For God's sake, Angel!'

And there was Ben.

My assailant was on his feet. I saw Ben running towards us. He was still calling my name. 'Angel, Angel. Oh *no* . . .'

The murderer was lunging towards him, but Ben was ready. I watched, too stunned to move for a moment. I just lay there. I saw the man strike out at Ben . . . but Ben parried the blow and came at him. He hit him hard between the eyes. The man staggered and fell. I got to my feet and rushed to Ben.

He held me tightly in his arms. 'Angel . . . dearest Angel . . . Are you all right? Oh . . . my God!'

'I'm all right now, Ben. I'm all right now you are here.'

He stared at me . . . the blood on my face . . . I knew there was blood on my clothes. I could not imagine what I looked like.

We turned to gaze down at the man.

'It's the one,' said Ben. 'It's the wanted man.'

'I thought he was you,' I said. 'He asked me the way . . . and he seemed quite normal. Then suddenly he changed. He got hold of me and I couldn't get away. Ben . . . oh Ben.'

'It's all over now. He looks as if he is really out. We'll just go and let them know we've found him.'

'He might get away and escape.'

Ben knelt down. The man had not moved since he had fallen. He looked strangely still. Ben lifted his head. It fell back with a jerk but not before we had seen the blood staining his thick dark curly hair. The back of his head was covered in blood. So was the stone on to which he had fallen.

Ben looked at me in horror. His next words sent a tremor of fear through me. 'He's dead,' he said.

He let him fall and then he added: 'I've killed him.'

'Oh Ben . . . it can't be . . . What'll happen?'

'I don't know,' said Ben.

'You just saved me . . . that was all. He can't be really dead . . . not just like that.'

'I hit him pretty hard . . . but it wasn't that only. He fell on that stone. There's a sharp edge. It looks as if it has penetrated his head.'

I just stared at him in sudden terror. My thoughts went back to the picture in the gallery. I saw clearly my grandfather's laughing eyes. Jake Cadorson, who had killed a man who was attempting to assault a young gypsy girl. It was murder, and in spite of the fact that he had saved the girl from her attacker he had been sentenced to transportation for seven years.

Ben had killed a man . . . a murderer wanted by the law. But it would be called murder or at least manslaughter . . . and my grandfather's punishment for the same offence had been seven years' exile.

It must not happen to Ben.

Ben had lost his bravado. I could see that he was thinking what I was.

He said slowly: 'I . . . I killed him.'

'You didn't mean to. You had to stop him. If you hadn't killed him he would have killed you.'

'It was murder,' he said. 'They'd say it was murder.'

I began to tremble. 'My grandfather,' I began. 'It was the same . . . almost exactly the same . . . But this man was a murderer . . .'

'What do you say they did to your grandfather?'

I replied through chattering teeth: 'They were going to hang him but my grandmother saved him . . . and then they sent him away for seven years. It was considered a light sentence.'

Ben was silent. He could not take his eyes from the man.

I said slowly: 'Ben . . . no one must know.'

'They'd find out,' he said.

'How?'

'They do. There are clues and things like that. You don't know you've left them but they find something you didn't think was important. And what about this blood?'

He stood for a while in silence, staring at the water. 'That's it,' he said.

'What, Ben?'

'We're going to throw him into the pool. Nobody will find him there. We'll put some stones in his pockets to weigh him down.' He seemed to regain his old fire. 'Come on. Help me, Angel. We'll get him to the pool.'

I thought wildly: It's the answer. He'll disappear. No one will think of looking for him there.

He was heavy. We pulled him across the grass, leaving a trail of blood. We had him right to the edge of the pool. I noticed that his eyes were open; he seemed to be staring at me. I thought: I shall never be able to forget him.

I turned away and as I did so I caught sight of something glittering near the water's edge. It was a ring. I picked it up and slipped it into the pocket of my skirt. I don't know why I bothered to do that at such a time. I supposed because I had to stop looking at that man and thinking of him, even for a split second.

'What are you doing?' asked Ben, who had been gathering

57

large stones which he thrust into the man's pockets. 'Here. Help me get him into the water.'

We pushed the body into the pool, but it was shallow and we had to wade in so that we were sure of getting him to the deeper part.

The water was cold. I was shivering. He slipped out of our grasp. For a moment I saw his head with the dark wet hair, the odd pallor of the skin, the open accusing eyes.

As I turned away I fell. I was completely immersed. Ben picked me up and said: 'It's over. We've done it.'

We stood on the edge of the pool, Ben's arm about me.

'Stop shaking, Angel,' he said. 'He's gone. No one will ever find him. There are no tides in the pool to wash his body ashore. He's gone forever. Let's get away from here.'

He held me close to him as we walked to the horses. His, fortunately, had remained waiting. I could not stop looking at the trail of blood on the grass.

Ben looked up at the sky. 'There'll be rain tonight. That will wash it all away.'

'Suppose someone sees it before?'

'No one will. Few come here. Besides, you'd have to look for it to find it . . . and nobody could be sure that it was blood.'

'It's a terrible thing to kill a man,' I said.

'We didn't kill him. It was an accident. And, remember, he would have done to you what he did to that other girl. It was justice. If we are sensible we shall feel no regret about him. He deserved to die. He would have been hanged after he was tried and found guilty, which he obviously was. We've got to be sensible about this. Oh God, Angel, you are so young.'

'I . . . I don't feel young,' I told him.

He took my face in his hands and kissed it.

'It's our secret, Angel.'

'But he's dead, Ben, and it was because of us that he died.'

'No, it was because of himself. It was justice. I feel no remorse.'

'But when they know . . .'

'They are not going to know. Why should they ever know?

58

If they found out there would be a fuss. They would say we killed a man. We disposed of his body.'

'We shouldn't have done that, Ben. We should have gone and found them and told them . . .'

'There would have been such a fuss. They would have accused us. They might even call it murder. They did with your grandfather, didn't they? It's a similar case.'

'But the man he killed was not a murderer.'

'It makes no difference. Listen to me. We are in this together. It is our secret. We can't bring all the scandal there would be on our families. There would be endless gossip. You know how people exaggerate. Imagine the press getting hold of it. No, as far as we are concerned it is over.'

'How can it ever be over?'

'It will be . . . if we don't let anyone know. They will hunt for him and they won't find him. They'll think he has escaped. There'll be questions and more questions. They'll never let us rest. They'll say I killed him and you were an accessory after the fact . . . that's how they talk. We don't want a great fuss. It would be exaggerated and remembered for the rest of our lives. It is always so in these cases. Consider all your legends. How they have grown up through distortion and exaggeration. We should be branded forever and they would punish us in some way . . . even though they would have hanged him . . . which would have been far worse for him than the way he died. So we've got to think of a way out of this. We have to think of our families. It's the only way. I know what we must do.'

'What?' I asked.

'We must get away from here at once and not let anyone know we came here. We must say nothing about what happened. Can you do that, Angel? Not to anyone . . . not a word.'

'Yes . . . yes, I think so.' But I looked down at my sodden clothes. There was blood on my jacket.

'We'll have to give some sort of explanation,' went on Ben. 'We'll say you had a fall. That's the answer. It will account for the state you are in. But there must not be a word about what actually happened . . . about him.'

'There'll be some way they'll find out.'

59

'Not if we play it carefully. Stop shaking, Angel.'

'I can't help it. I just feel so cold.' I started to sneeze and for a few moments could not stop.

He looked at me anxiously and said: 'Listen, Angel. This is terrible, but we're in it now and we have to get out of it.'

'When they don't catch him . . . ?'

'They'll think he's got away. It will be as easy as that.' Ben was beginning to regain his confidence. There was even a look of excitement in his eyes. 'We'll do it. But we've got to plan very carefully. He's gone. He won't be able to murder any more young girls . . . never again. We've done a good thing. No one will ever know that he is at the bottom of the pool. His clothes will be waterlogged. He's right down at the bottom. He'll never be found. We've saved him from the hangman's rope, and that was what he deserved and what would have come to him. We've done him a good turn. We've done all those little girls whom he might have murdered a good turn . . .'

Cold and shivering as I was, I felt better. Ben was so convincing. I began to believe that if he decided what we must do was the best thing for us, it would be for everyone else too.

There was nothing I wanted more than to get away and forget.

He was talking coaxingly. 'You see, Angel, how awful it would be for us and our families if it were known. I don't know what they would do to us. They wouldn't let us go off scot free. When people are killed there is always trouble. But we mustn't stay here. What are we going to do? You're wet through . . . and so am I. We can't say we've been in the pool. We'll have to say we were wet through by the sea. Look. It happened this way: you were galloping along the beach. You know how you like to do that. Glory stumbled over a boulder and threw you. You were close to the sea and the waves washed over you. You hurt yourself on a rock. That will account for the blood. You just went over Glory's head. You lost consciousness for a few seconds. Thank goodness I was with you. That's how it will have to be. Can you do it?'

'Yes, Ben, I think I can.'

'Then let's get away from here. The sooner the better.'

He took my hand. I was still trembling.

'You'd better not ride,' he said. 'We'll get you up on Glory and I'll walk you home.'

He was right. I realized I could not have ridden. There were times when it seemed as though the earth were coming up to meet me and I was shaking all over.

Ben murmured soothingly to me as we rode along. 'The thing is not to talk too much about it. Make yourself believe it happened the way we said it did. You can come to believe it . . .'

'I'll never forget it . . . the way he looked at me. Oh, Ben, it was so horrible.'

'You've got to forget it. It doesn't do any good to go on remembering that sort of thing. We did the best possible thing . . . the only possible thing . . . and now we've got to forget it and make our story the real one. When the truth is too distressing to contemplate it's not a bad idea to substitute it with fancy.'

'You'll be there to help, Ben?'

'I'll be there.'

'I think I can do it, then.'

'Angel,' he said, 'you know I love you.'

'Oh really, Ben? I love you, too.'

'When I think of that man . . . and you . . . dear innocent Angel . . . I'm *glad* I did it.'

'I wish someone else had. I wish he had never escaped out here.'

'It's no use wishing it away. It won't go that way. It's our secret, and dear Angel, you will be all right. It will be better as time passes.'

'I feel very strange, Ben. Everything seems far off.'

'It will be all right.'

He held me firmly. I was hardly aware of the road as we travelled along.

I vaguely remember my mother as she rushed out crying, 'What is it? What's happened?' And Ben replying, 'Angelet's had an accident. Glory threw her.'

'My darling child!'

I was so relieved because my mother was there.

61

My father came running out, fearful and horrified to see the state I was in.

'We'll get her to bed quickly,' said my mother. 'She's had an accident . . . riding.'

'Riding? Riding Glory?'

'I don't think she's in a fit state to talk,' said Ben.

My mother took me up to my room. She took off my coat and for a second or two studied it in consternation, and putting my hand in the pocket of my skirt, I felt the ring I had picked up.

'What's that?' asked my mother.

'Oh . . . nothing . . . something I picked up.'

'Never mind that now,' said my mother, and I opened a drawer and put the ring into it, vaguely wondering why I had bothered to pick it up except that I had always been interested in things I found and did it automatically.

'We'll soon have you comfortable,' said my mother. 'You're soaked to the skin. We'll get you out of just everything.'

She wrapped me in a blanket and put me into bed. I still could not stop trembling.

'Your father has sent one of the men to get Dr Barrow,' said my mother.

'I'll be all right.'

'The doctor is going to have a look at you. You never know when you have a fall like that. I don't think anything can be broken.'

I lay in my bed. My mother sat beside me and in due course the doctor came.

He examined my head. There was now a vivid bruise on my cheek.

'Did you fall on your face?' he asked.

'I . . . I can't remember. It is all so confusing.'

'Hm,' he said. 'Open your mouth. You've bitten yourself, I think. You must have done that as you fell. You've got some good bruises.'

I was terrified that what he discovered would not fit in with our story.

'On the beach . . .' he murmured, looking puzzled.

'I can't remember much about it. Suddenly I was down . . .'

He nodded and turned to my mother. 'Might be a little concussion. It's a good thing she fell on soft sand. It's the shock more than anything else. Keep her warm and I'll give her a sedative that will ensure a good night's sleep. Then tomorrow we'll see.'

A good night's sleep! I thought: I shall never sleep peacefully again. I shall dream of that awful moment when he had his hands on me . . . and when he fell down . . . the trail of blood as we dragged him to the pool . . . and that moment before he went down when he seemed to stare at me with his dead eyes and the water was pink with his blood.

I knew I could never forget and nothing would ever be the same again.

I did sleep deeply, due to what Dr Barrow had given me, and when I awoke next morning my head was heavy. I felt dizzy and very hot. Memory came back to me and hung over me like a stifling cloak. I just wanted to get back to blissful forgetfulness.

My mother was alarmed when she saw me and Dr Barrow was immediately summoned.

It was a blessing in a way. It saved me from too many questions and I believe that if I had had to face them while the incident was fresh in everyone's mind, I might not have been able to support our story.

I had a cold which, during the next few days, developed into bronchitis and then pneumonia. I was very ill and there was a possibility that I might not recover. I lived through the days in hazy dreams. For a lot of the time I was floating in a strange world. I was not sure where I was. I would see my mother's face watching me so tenderly that I felt I must get well. Then I would be back at the pool. I would see that face floating on the water and I would cry out 'No, no.' Then I would hear my mother's voice: 'It's all right, darling. I'm here. Everything is all right.'

There was a great deal of activity in the room. Through the haze of unreality I saw Grace Gilmore. She seemed to be there

63

often. Ben came to see me. I was aware of him as he was standing by my bed; and I thought we were at the pool together. I started up.

I heard my mother say: 'I don't think she should have visitors . . . yet.'

Then they were talking about the crisis. There were many people in the room . . . faces which swam vaguely before me . . . voices which came from a long way off. My mother was trying to smile, but I knew she was crying and I thought: I am dying.

And then the fever had gone and everyone was smiling and my mother was bending over the bed and saying: 'How are you feeling, darling? You are better. You will soon be well.'

I was like a new person – not a child any more. I had grown up. The world in which I had complacently lived before that day at the pool had evaporated. It was a different place now – a world in which terrible things could happen. The fears of the past had been shadowy . . . something one only half believed; they were for other people; not for me. I had my parents, my secure home, and nothing could harm me. Ghosts and witches, cruelty and horror, pain and murder, that might happen to other people, but not to me and those around me. They were something to talk about, to frighten oneself about . . . but with the delicious fear of childhood . . . when you terrified yourself knowing that Mother was close behind and you could run to hide yourself in her skirts and the bogey would go away.

But I had left all that behind now. I had come face to face with horror. I knew a little of what that man would have done to me before he killed me. The awful realization had come to me. It could have happened to me!

My mother would not let me look in the glass for some time, and when I did it was a stranger who looked back at me. Pale and thin, my eyes seeming bigger, but my hair . . . it was short like a boy's.

My mother touched it gently. 'It will soon grow. And look, it is wavy. We had to cut it off because of your fever.'

64

I could not stop looking at that face in the mirror. There were secrets there. Those were not the innocent eyes of childhood. They had looked on the fearful realities of life.

I felt older. My illness had changed me. While I had lain there in limbo, I had grown up. I knew now that what we did was the only thing we could have done. Ben had been right. He had killed a man, but it was something which had had to be done; the man was a murderer; he would have committed more murders. It was not like killing an ordinary person.

But I had to stop going over it. I had to accept what was done. Ben had said I had to believe what we had said had happened, and he was right.

I was feeling better. I was sitting up now.

My mother said: 'Watson was down at the quay this morning and found this John Dory. He thought it would be just the thing to tempt you. Mrs Penlock has done it in a special way. You'd better eat every scrap of it. You know what they are.'

I smiled. I cherished every aspect of normality, of the return to the old days.

I heard my mother whisper to my father: 'Better not say anything about the accident. It seems to upset her.'

I was glad of that. I didn't want to have to talk of it. I did not want to have to lie more than was necessary. That was a great help.

I learned that I had been very ill for three weeks.

'Jack has been so upset,' my mother told me. 'He's been wanting to bring you his train and you know that is his dearest possession. You should have seen the glum faces in the kitchen. Mrs Penlock is full of ideas as to what she is going to give you to eat. She says she is going to "build you up" as though you are some sort of edifice. You would be the size of a house if she could have her way. We've all been so worried . . . every one of us, and we are so happy now that you are getting well. But don't think you are going to rush it. You're going to spend another week in bed; and then we are going to take it very slowly.'

'I must have been very ill.'

She nodded, her lips trembling.

'You thought I was going to die.'

'Pneumonia is very serious . . . and there was a fever. You seemed to be so disturbed. But it is all over now.'

All over? I thought. It will never be all over. He will always be there . . . lying at the bottom of the pool.

I said: 'How is Ben?'

'Oh, he has gone. He waited to see if you . . . he waited until we knew you were going to recover. He couldn't go till then. Well, you know, he was only coming here for a month or so.'

'He didn't come to say goodbye.'

'No. I didn't want you to have visitors . . . and you seemed a little upset when he came.'

'Didn't I speak to him?'

'No . . . not really. You muttered something we couldn't understand . . . and I said that I thought too many people in the room was not good for you. He went back to London about a week ago. There is a lot to tell you when you are stronger.'

I was feeling a little better every day. Nothing had been discovered, then.

How right Ben had been! It had happened. It was over, and we had to forget.

I was very weak and was surprised how tottery I felt when I got out of bed.

'It will take time,' said my mother.

She would sit with me during the afternoons. Sometimes she read to me; at others she sat at her sewing . . . and we talked.

It was some little time before I could bring myself to say: 'Mama, I haven't heard anything about . . . that man . . . that convict who escaped.'

'Oh, him. That all died down. They never caught him.'

'What . . . what do they think happened to him?'

'They think he must have got out of the country.'

'Would he be able to do that?'

'Oh yes, it's possible. I expect he had friends to help him.

66

There was quite a little bit of news about his background. It was most extraordinary. He was apparently quite a well-educated young man. He had been tutor to a family not far from Bodmin, Launceston way. Crompton . . . I think was the place. How dreadful to think he had been in charge of children! I think his late employers must be feeling very grateful just now.'

'A tutor,' I murmured.

'Yes . . . to a young boy about your age. There was a little girl in the family, but I think she had a governess. There was quite a story about them. His employers were astounded. They had always thought so highly of him.'

'You don't think he might have been . . . innocent?'

'Oh no . . . no. No question about that. He was caught red-handed, as it were. It was some local village girl.'

I shivered.

'Apparently something suspicious had happened to him before . . . but it hadn't been proved. That was a pity. If it had been, that poor girl's life might have been saved.'

'And he escaped?'

'Yes. He had a knife. They don't know how he managed to have that. They think it must have been cleverly smuggled in to him. He attacked a warder with it. The poor man was badly hurt and is now slowly recovering. He got keys from him and just calmly walked out of the jail. They traced him to Carradon . . . not very far from here. Then they lost the trail and he disappeared into the blue.'

Oh no, Mama, I wanted to say. Into the pool.

'It was a nine days' wonder. I think it is something the authorities would rather forget. But the press won't let them . . . not until people get tired of the case. They do of course get tired of reading about chases that go on and on and never get anywhere. It's rarely mentioned now. They accept the fact that this was one who got away. I think it is almost certain that he left the country.'

There was no need to worry, I thought. He will never be found. Ben is right. We have to forget. We did nothing wrong. He was a man who was going to die in any case and we had made it easier for him.

My mother went on: 'Grace has been wonderful. She is more than a seamstress. She is an educated girl. I always think it is hard for those who have been brought up in a genteel family suddenly to be confronted with the need to earn a living. She dressed my hair the other night. She has quite a flair for it. Not that I need a lady's maid. But when we go to London I always feel I could do with one. And she was wonderful . . . so wonderful when you were ill.'

'She seems such a pleasant woman.'

'I am so glad we were able to help her. She is so very grateful and can't do enough for me.'

'It has been a case of casting your bread upon the waters.'

'I am glad to see you remember your Bible,' said my mother, lightly planting a kiss on my forehead.

When Grace came to see me she told me how pleased she was by my recovery.

'Praise be to God, you are on the mend now.'

'Thank you for what you did. My mother said you were very helpful.'

'It was the least I could do after all your kindness to me. I can't tell you what a relief it is that you have been getting a little better every day.'

'I know I have been very ill.'

'You were indeed . . . apart from the fever. You seemed so distressed. You kept muttering to yourself. You mentioned the pool once or twice.'

I felt a sharp shock run through me. What had I said when I was delirious?

'Pool . . . ?' I repeated foolishly.

'I suppose it was St Branok. Well, there was talk about it. The usual. People hearing the bells down there. Who ever heard of bells under water?'

'Have they been saying they heard them . . . lately?'

'I did hear it mentioned once. Someone was going past at dusk and thought he heard the bells. It's in their minds, if you ask me.'

'Yes, I expect so. There have always been people fancying they hear the bells.'

I changed the subject. I did not want to talk about the pool; but I was disconcerted that she had noticed my preoccupation with the place.

A few weeks had passed. I was out of my room now. I took walks round the garden. My hair was beginning to grow. It clustered round my head, giving me the appearance of a boy; but my mother said she was sure it was growing very fast indeed. Everyone was so pleased when I came downstairs. I rode out with my father who would not let me go alone. Nor did I want to. I did not ride Glory now. She was in disgrace, poor creature, having been accused of throwing me. I muttered an apology to her and would have preferred to ride her, but they insisted that I did not. My father was anxious that I should not be overtired; so the rides were short.

There was news from London.

'They have all been so upset by your illness,' my mother told me. 'Your Aunt Amaryllis has not let a week go by without writing. She is so delighted that you are getting better and always sends love and good wishes from them all.'

'Dear Aunt Amaryllis,' I said. 'She is so good to everyone.'

'My mother always used to say that she sailed through life quite unaware of evil and therefore evil passed over her; and she never saw it even when it was very close to her.'

'It is a good way to live. But then, if you don't see evil how can you avoid it?'

'It is true. But Amaryllis is so good herself that she thinks everyone else is the same. So she sees no evil, hears no evil and speaks no evil. Therefore for her it does not exist.'

'It is wonderful for her but everyone cannot be like that.'

I wondered what she would have thought if she had been confronted by a murderer, as I was at St Branok Pool.

Everything came back to that. I must stop myself brooding on it. I had to remember Ben's instructions. 'Tell yourself you fell from your horse when you were riding along the shore. Make yourself believe it.' But I could not make myself believe something which did not happen. Even Aunt Amaryllis would not have been able to do that.

My mother came to my bedroom. I had to rest in the afternoon

69

– doctor's orders – although it was not necessary to sleep unless I wanted to. My mother used to sit with me.

It was on one of those occasions when she brought Aunt Amaryllis's letter to read to me.

Dear Annora [she had written],

We are all so absolutely delighted that Angelet is recovering so well. Poor darling, what an ordeal for her. But she is young and healthy and I am sure will soon be quite well. We are longing to see her . . . and you all, of course. I was thinking that when she is a little stronger, Angelet might like to come up to London and stay for a while. It is not the country, of course, but a change is always good. Do think about it. We'd love to have her . . . and you, of course. Peter joins in my good wishes and says he hopes Angelet will come to see us. He always had a soft spot for her, you know. He says she reminds him of Jessica, of whom he was really very fond.

Benedict has left us, so we are missing him rather. Such a lively young man!

My mother smiled, thinking, I was sure, how like Amaryllis it was to take the result of her husband's youthful indiscretion to her heart.

He did enjoy his stay with you, but he was so upset about Angelet's accident and illness. I gathered he was the one who was with her when it happened and that he brought her home. He seemed really unhappy about it, and he hated talking of it. It seemed to upset him.

Although he enjoyed being with you, I don't think he wants to go into estate management. Peter thinks it would be too quiet a life for him. What do you think? He's gone back to Australia! He has a project. You may not have heard of all the excitement there has been about the discovery of gold in Australia. Well, Benedict has gone back to find gold. He expects to come back a rich man.

Peter didn't really want him to go. After all, he has only just found him, but he did not want to stand in his way. He

70

said it was just the sort of thing he would have wanted to do himself when he was young. Peter thinks the chance of making a fortune from the Australian goldfields is a remote possibility – as all the good stuff must have been found long ago, but he thinks it will be good for the boy to have a try. He said he would regret it all his life if he didn't go. He would imagine he had lost opportunities. So he has gone out there and we now await the return of the golden millionaire.

I suppose he is almost there by now. Benedict does not let the grass grow under his feet. Peter says he reminds him of himself when he was young – which is rather nice.

Well, don't forget. We should be delighted to see Angelet and you in London to stay for a while. I am sure it would do her good.

With much love,
Amaryllis.

So Ben had gone away to a new country. I supposed that was the best way of forgetting. I felt a tinge of resentment, as though the burden of our secret had been left to me to bear. That was foolish. He had to make his fortune. He would come back.

And then I shall see him again, I thought. In the meantime I must keep our secret.

We did not go to London that year. I know my mother was very worried about me. I had changed so completely. The impulsive, rather garrulous girl had become a quiet, secretive one. It must have seemed strange that my illness should have changed my character. Sometimes I was on the verge of confessing, for if they only knew what had happened to me they would understand.

But I was resilient and ebullient by nature and I gradually found myself forgetting my secret for long periods at a time. Then I would have a dream or something would remind me, and memories would come back to me and I would revert to the quiet, withdrawn girl once more.

I knew they were puzzled and was deeply touched by their concern for me.

Mrs Penlock tut-tutted at the sight of me. 'A beanpole, that's what you are, Miss Angel. You want to get a bit of flesh on them bones of yours. I could make you a beautiful taddage pie. That 'ud put some life into you, that would.'

I used to enjoy her taddage pies, made with young sucking pigs; but I had no desire for them now. She was always trying, as she would say, 'to tempt me', as though food was the cure for all ailments.

They were all very kind to me and when they saw my spirits lifted were so obviously pleased that I felt I must cast off my melancholy to please them.

In any case I was coming to terms with it.

We were getting very friendly with the Pencarrons who owned the tin mine close to the moor. They were a very old Cornish family and had orginally come from somewhere near Land's End. They had owned a mine there which had been worked out and that was why they had come to our neighbourhood. They had acquired the mine which was now known as Pencarron Mine, and their house was Pencarron Manor. Since they had arrived some ten years before, they had become part of the community.

Morwenna was a quiet girl, rather serious; she suited my mood at that time; she did not ask questions and although she was a year older than I she would follow me. She was very good-natured and hardly ever ruffled her governess. Miss Derry was friendly with Miss Prentiss and they took pleasure in comparing their pupils. I was sure I suffered in the comparison.

Morwenna was a great help to me at that time. She was so undemanding. We used to ride together round the paddock. My mother did not want me to go out without her or my father, or at least a groom; that made me restive, but I was too listless to protest at that time.

One day my mother and I rode over to the Pencarrons to have lunch with the family – a fairly frequent occurrence. We were passing through the town, as my mother wished to call on one of the old ladies in East Poldorey to take her some wools for her tapestry which my mother would have to buy when it was finished. We had quite a stack of this kind of work in one of the storerooms. My mother felt in duty bound to buy the wools and silks and then the finished product.

As we rode through the town young John Gort came running up to us. His grandfather, Jack Gort, had been one of the leading fishermen of his day and he was still to be seen on the quay supervising the family as to the best way of conducting the business they had inherited from him.

Young John looked rather anxious.

'What is it?' asked my mother.

'I've just been wondering, me lady,' he stammered, 'about that there boat by the old boathouse.'

'Oh?' said my mother. 'Why?'

'Well, 'tas been there for years and as no one wanted it, like . . . I thought as how . . . if no one wanted it, like . . . I thought as how . . .'

'You want it?' said my mother.

'Well, seeing as 'ow it ain't used, like.'

'You take it, John.'

'Oh thank 'ee, me lady.'

He darted off.

'Do you know that old boat he was talking about?' asked my mother.

'I think I've seen an old one there at some time.'

'Well, he might as well make use of it, then.'

And we rode on to Pencarron.

Grace Gilmore was often in my company. She was always pleased to do something for me. She would kneel at my feet, pins between her lips, turning up a hem, or make me stand on a chair to assure herself that she had got the length absolutely right; and I always had the impression that she was particularly interested in me – as indeed I was in her.

I was beginning to feel better. I was quite enjoying Mrs Penlock's muggety and lamby pies. My hair was growing. It was down to my shoulders, long enough to tie back with a ribbon.

I no longer looked like a wraith. I was laughing more frequently and indulging in those daydreams in which I had played the central and heroic part. I was returning to normal.

I had not been to the pool since it happened and it was beginning to seem like a bad dream. Benedict had gone right out of my life. I was hurt about his going. I remembered vividly how he had said to me so vehemently, 'I love you, Angel,' and I had replied that I loved him, too. And now he was on the other side of the world and perhaps I should never see him again. I should have thought he was running away from our terrible secret, but I could not believe that Benedict would ever run away from anything. No, he had gone to find gold . . . like the men in the story of the old scat bal. But I was left where it had all happened.

They were less careful of me now. I used to go off on my own. I even rode Glory again. She seemed glad to have me back. Horses are very intelligent and I wondered whether she knew she had been disgraced and wrongly accused.

'It had to be, Glory,' I whispered to her. 'It was all part of the secret.' She seemed as though she understood. After all, she had seen it happen.

I must not think of it.

It was gone. It was past. It wasn't the same as killing an ordinary man. I kept telling myself that he had been going to die in any case . . . far more horribly. It had just happened more quickly and easily than it would in the hands of the law. How often had I gone over and over that point!

One day, when my thoughts were running on these lines, I felt I had to exorcize the ghost which was haunting me. I had to go back to the pool. I had to see it again. I had to convince myself that I was cured of my guilt. I kept telling myself that I was not to blame. I should have been the victim. I had just helped to keep his death a secret and that had been the right thing to do. But I had to go to the pool. I had to convince myself that I was not afraid of it any more.

I rode over there. It was less than a mile from the house. I wanted to turn back but I would not allow myself to do so. I rode through the trees and there it was . . . glittering in the

74

sunshine . . . still mysterious . . . just as it had been on that dreadful day.

I dismounted and tethered Glory to the same bush as I had on that other occasion.

I patted her head, wondering if she remembered. 'Don't fret,' I said, 'I've just got to do this. It won't be anything like that other time. And then we'll think nothing of coming here.'

I walked down to the edge of the pool and stared into the still water. There were weeping willows hanging over it and some bedraggled-looking plant-life floated on the surface of the water. I wondered how many secrets besides mine it was hiding.

I continued to look into the water, fearing to see his face again. The water was greenish brown, and now there was no trace of the pink which had once coloured it.

I strained my ears. I half fancied I could hear the tinkle of bells – but it was the faint breeze ruffling the trees. How easy it was to fancy one heard music.

I closed my eyes, trying to wipe out memories. I had been foolish to come. Oh no. This was the way to be reasonable. To say to oneself: There was nothing wrong about it. Ben had to do what he did. We both had to.

I opened my eyes. Silence and then . . . what it was, I was not sure, but I guessed I was not alone. I just felt a presence. I stood very still looking at the water. The movement came from behind. Someone was standing close to me.

I half expected to see him there . . . his ghost risen from the waters of the pool.

I turned sharply.

'Grace!' I cried in immense relief. 'What are you doing here?'

'What are you, Miss Angelet? I saw you standing by the water, so quiet and still. I wondered if you could hear the bells.'

Relief swept over me. It was only Grace . . . not some grisly ghost . . . the murderer resurrected from the dead.

'I . . . I was just looking at the pool,' I said.

'You are very interested in the pool,' she replied.

'I suppose it is because of the bells. I've always been interested in things like that.'

She came close and looked at me intently.

75

'You talked of it . . . when you were ill. But come away. It's damp and cold . . . an unhealthy place.'

'Yes,' I agreed.

I noticed that there was a baffled look on her face and I wondered what she was thinking. There was something eerie about the situation . . . the two of us standing there, as though we were both hiding something.

I said: 'Did you walk here?'

'Yes. Then I saw you at the pool and I wondered what you were doing. I thought it might be damp and you'd catch a cold.'

I walked back to Glory, Grace beside me.

'You'll go straight home, I suppose,' she said.

I nodded. 'You too?'

'Yes. I must finish that petticoat for your mother.'

I mounted Glory and rode away.

I was glad I had been to the pool. I felt better after it. It was no longer a place to avoid. I was growing away from my memories. I no longer had to tell myself we were not to blame. I *knew* we were not. All we did was what had to be done and it was what was best in the circumstances. I should come to the pool again and again and next time I should not try to recall. I should simply forget.

When I look back I think it was rather strange how Grace Gilmore had become almost a member of the family. I liked to be with her. She intrigued me. I felt there was a part of her which I did not know. Subconsciously I wanted to find out about her; I think that was why she was rather exciting to me.

I talked to Morwenna Pencarron about her. 'What do you think of Grace?' I asked.

'Oh, she's very nice.' Most people were 'very nice' in Morwenna's opinion. She reminded me a little of Aunt Amaryllis.

'But do you think there is something different about her?' I persisted. 'She doesn't talk much about her past. Do you know where she comes from?'

'She comes from somewhere near Devon.'

76

'I know. But she never really *talks*.'

It was no use trying to explain to Morwenna.

My mother encouraged our friendship because she liked someone to be in charge of me when I went out; she knew my spirit and did not want to restrict it, but since what she thought of as my fall, she did like me to be in the company of an adult. In London I should never have been allowed to go out alone; but here, where everyone knew everyone else, it seemed safe. I had discovered that this was not always so.

So if Miss Prentiss or Miss Derry did not accompany us, it was usually Grace.

One day we went to the fair with her, Morwenna, Jack and I. I had always loved the fair. There were several of them – they were annual occasions, and the best of all was St Matthew's Fair which was held on the first of Ocotober.

It was so full of life. People from the surrounding villages converged on to the place. There was noise and bustle everywhere. The horse- and cattle-dealers were there; one heard the continual lowing of cows and the grunting of pigs. There they would be in their pens while the farmers leaned over the rail and poked the pigs with sticks to see how fat they were and cast shrewd eyes over the lambs, the cows, the bullocks. But what I liked best were the stalls with their goods for sale; comfits, fairings, china jugs, cups and saucers, teapots, farm implements, clothing, saddles, ribbons, dresses, boots and shoes, pots and pans, and even cloam ovens; and all the traders shouting their wares. Then there was the food: the constant smell of roasting meat, bread, potatoes in their jackets, sugar animals, hearts in pink sugary sweets with 'I love You' on them. There were the peepshows and the puppets, the marionettes, the dwarves, the fat woman, the bearded lady and the strong man; and of course the gypsies who would tell your fortune.

On this occasion Miss Prentiss had a headache and my mother asked Grace Gilmore if she would take us so that we should not be disappointed. She accepted with alacrity, and we set off.

We had a wonderful time roaming among the stalls. We visited two of the shows and marvelled at the rippling muscles of the strong man and tried our hand at the hoopla; we bought slabs of hot gingerbread, eating it as we went along, which Grace was not sure we should have been allowed to do.

Jack assured her that people could do things at a fair which they could not do elsewhere. He was more excited than Morwenna and I were. I suppose we were a little blasé.

Fiddlers were playing and several people were dancing.

'The most exciting part is when it gets dark,' I said, 'and then they light the flares.'

'Your mother will want you home long before that,' Grace told us.

'I should like to have my fortune told,' said Morwenna. 'Ginny, our parlourmaid, had hers told at Summercourt Fair. She is going to marry a rich man and travel overseas. It was a wonderful fortune.'

'How can they tell?' asked Jack.

'They can see into the future . . . and into the past,' Morwenna replied. 'They can see all you've done. It's all clear to them. It's all in your hand, particularly if you've done something wicked. That's easiest to see.'

Jack looked uneasy, but Morwenna clasped her hands and said: 'Oh, I wish we could.'

I thought: It's all very well for you. You have never done anything except cheat at lessons a bit . . . copying out something from a book which you're supposed to know . . . taking a jam tart from the kitchen when the cook's back is turned and saying you didn't. Little sins . . . nothing like killing a man and hiding his body.

The pleasure of the fair had gone. That was how it was. Memory came up suddenly . . . as that man had come to the pool . . . and the pleasure in the day was spoilt.

I was glad when Grace said there was no time to have our fortunes told. She said: 'We must start for home now.'

And we left the fair. As we walked away the sound of the fiddlers grew fainter but we could hear them singing:

'Come, lasses and lads,
Get leave of your dads
And away to the maypole hie,

78

For every he has got him a she
And a fiddler standing by . . .'

Jack was disappointed at leaving the fair. He had expressed
his displeasure and demanded to know why we could not stay.
Grace explained that we must get back before dark. Jack never
sulked for long and in a few minutes he was himself again. He
had a very lovable nature.

The gypsy was sitting by the side of the road. She had a basket
full of clothes-pegs beside her and I was not sure whether she
was coming from or going to the fair.

'Good day to 'ee, ladies and little gent,' she said.

'Good day,' we replied.

'How would you like the gypsy to give you a nice fortune?'

I heard Morwenna murmur, 'Oh *yes*. Oh, Miss Gilmore, may
I?'

Grace hesitated, but Morwenna turned such a happy face to
her that she was unable to resist.

'All right then, dear. But we mustn't stay long.'

'Cross the gypsy's hand in silver,' said the woman.

Morwenna drew back. 'Oh . . . I don't think I have enough.'
She produced some coins.

'Well, seeing as you be such a nice little lady, I'll take what
you've got. Wouldn't want to disappoint a little love like you.'

Morwenna dimpled prettily and held out her hand.

'Oh, I see a long and happy life. You're going to have great
good fortune, you are. You're going up to London to see the
Queen . . . when you're a little older, that is . . . and there you
are going to find a rich husband and live happy ever after.'

It seemed very little for all the money Morwenna had left;
and I knew she had wanted to buy a pink sugar mouse and had
hesitated because she had thought it too costly. It was very
likely that Morwenna might go up to London for a season when
she grew older and the object would be to find a suitable
husband for her.

She turned to me. 'And you, me 'andsome. There's a nice
fortune for 'ee, I can see.'

She had taken my hand. I was terribly afraid. Was it written

79

there? Was she seeing the pool and that inert body . . . those eyes staring at us as the head disappeared?

'Nought to be frightened at, lovey. 'Tis all fair and smiling for a little lass like you. You're going to London, too. Perhaps you'll go with your little . . .' She was trying to decide on our relationship and added: '. . . little companion.' Then I felt that if she didn't know who Morwenna was she would not know about the pool.

Now she turned her attention to Grace.

'Life writes as it goes along,' she said. 'There'll be more to be seen, little lady, when you be a few years older. And now, my lady, it be your turn.' She had taken Grace's hand.

'No,' said Grace, 'I don't think . . .'

The gypsy was looking at her intently. 'Oh, there be trouble 'ere . . . deep sorrow . . .' Grace had turned pale. The woman went on: 'I can see water . . . water between you and what you desire . . .'

I felt myself go limp with apprehension. It was clear to me that she had thought the fortunes of young girls – as she regarded Morwenna and me – were not worth telling. Little did she know! I had a vague idea how this fortune-telling was done. There was a good deal of chance in it, I had no doubt, but I did believe that flashes of truth occasionally emerged; and if something really violent had happened . . . it might be possible to detect it. I felt that she might have seen something in my hand which she could not explain. Who would have thought that a girl of my age could be involved in such an experience? She was transferring it to Grace.

'You will be strong,' she was saying. 'You will overcome.'

The gypsy seemed a little shaken. Her eyes were fixed on Grace's face.

Grace withdrew her hand. 'Well . . . thank you . . .'

'It's trouble . . . trouble . . . but nature made you strong. You will overcome. All will be well. You'll find happiness in the end.'

Grace opened her purse and gave the woman money.

'Come on,' she said. 'We shall be late back and that will not do.'

The gypsy was silent. She slipped the money into her pocket and sat down.

We walked away.

'We should never have stopped,' said Grace. 'It was a lot of nonsense.'

'It cost a lot of money,' commented Jack. 'You could have bought six slices of gingerbread and a pink pig with what you gave her.'

'It was rather silly of us,' admitted Grace. Her voice was cold and her face looked different somehow.

She might say it was a lot of nonsense but I believed the gypsy had frightened her.

I looked over my shoulder. The woman was still seated by the side of the road staring after us.

I told my mother of the encounter.

'She promised Morwenna and me that we should go to London and find rich husbands.'

'You'll have to go up for a season, but that's some time away. And as to the rich husband . . . we'll have to wait and see.'

'I think she rather upset Miss Gilmore. She talked about some trouble.'

'One doesn't take any notice of them.'

'Not unless they tell you something nice.'

'That's the idea,' said my mother, smiling. 'By the way, soon we shall be going to London. I've been talking to Grace about new clothes. She says she could make them. I wonder if she could. One doesn't want to look countrified. What passes here might look a little dowdy in London. But I thought we might give her a try with the blue linen. It's just the colour for you.'

Grace was very anxious to try with the linen. She came to my room with some patterns which she wanted to discuss with me, and she had the blue linen with her.

She said: 'I thought we'd have a little piping round the sleeves . . . as it is in this pattern. Don't you think that would look nice? I think a lightish brown . . . very light . . . would look effective.'

81

'Yes, perhaps,' I said. 'I have a scarf which I think would be just the right colour to match up with the blue. It will be in that drawer behind you.'

'May I?' she said, opening the drawer.

There was a short silence. She was staring at something in the drawer. She picked up the ring I had found at the pool. I had put it there when I came home and forgotten all about it.

'This gold ring . . .' she said. 'Is it yours?'

I felt uneasiness gripping me as it always did when there was any reference to that day.

'Oh . . .' I stammered. I held out my hand for the ring. 'I . . . I found it.'

'Found it? Where?'

'It . . . was when I had my accident. I remember it now. I picked it up without thinking.'

'On the beach?'

I did not answer. I ruffled my brows as though trying to remember . . . although I recalled perfectly well every detail of that fearful time.

'What? When you fell?'

'Y . . . yes . . . it must have been. I fell . . . and there was the ring.'

'On the beach,' she repeated. 'And you picked it up then. Why?'

'I don't know. I always pick up things. I suppose I do it without thinking . . . It's difficult to remember . . . I must have seen the ring and picked it up and put it in my pocket.'

'It's rather a nice one,' she said. 'It is gold, I think. What are you going to do with it?'

'Oh . . . nothing.'

'You didn't think of returning it to its owner?'

'I don't know whose it is. I shouldn't think any of the fishermen have a ring and it wouldn't be theirs because they don't come to that part of the beach. It might have been there a long time. Some visitor lost it, I expect, and it's so long ago they've forgotten about it.'

'If you don't want it . . . may I have it?'

'Of course.'

82

She slipped it on to the first finger of her right hand.

'This is the only one it fits,' she said.

I found the scarf and we set it side by side with the blue linen. But I was not really attending. It was incidents like that which shook me terribly and brought it all back to my memory.

Miss Gilmore seemed a little absent-minded too.

Grace Gilmore was quite a good horsewoman. My mother was constantly urging her to accompany me when I went riding.

'Angelet is so independent,' I heard her say. 'She does love to ride off on her own. But I'd rather someone was with her.'

Grace Gilmore was nothing loath. There was little she seemed to like better than regarding herself as a member of the family.

We were riding along the beach one day when we came close to the boathouse. She pulled up suddenly.

'It must have been somewhere near here where you found the ring,' she said.

I nodded. I hated telling a lie, but it was necessary.

She was looking along the shore, past the boathouse to where the harbour was just visible. She took off the ring.

'Look at these initials inside it,' she said. 'Did you notice?'

'No. I didn't look at it . . . much. I just picked it up.'

'You weren't in a fit state to examine it closely, I suppose.'

'No. I don't know why I picked it up and put it in my pocket. Just force of habit, I expect. I wasn't really thinking of it.'

'No, you wouldn't at such a time. Do you see what the initials are?'

She handed me the ring. Engraved inside were the initials M. D. and W. B.

'I wonder who they are,' I said.

She took the ring from me. What a fool I had been to pick it up. If I tried to return it the people would want to know where I found it. It might well be that the owner of the ring had never been near the sea. Ben had talked of clues. This could be one of those. I wished that Grace had never found it. I would have thrown it away if I had remembered. I should have remembered. When one practised deceit one had to be careful.

83

Her next words made me shiver.

'Those initials M. D. What was the name of that man who escaped from Bodmin Jail?'

'I . . . er . . . I don't remember.'

'It was Mervyn Duncarry, I'm sure. M. D. You see?'

'There could be lots of people with those initials.'

'He must have been here . . . on this beach. I feel certain it is his ring.'

'And who is W. B.?'

'Some woman I suppose who was fool enough to love him.'

She held the ring in the palm of her hand and then suddenly she flung it into the sea.

'I couldn't wear the ring of a murderer, could I?'

'No,' I said vehemently, 'of course you could not.'

She could not guess how relieved I was to see the end of that ring. It was what I had begun to see as a piece of incriminating evidence.

A Marriage
in a Far-Off Land

We were going to London to pay that long-delayed visit to Uncle Peter and Aunt Amaryllis.

It was the year 1854 and I had now passed my twelfth birthday. There was a great deal of preparation, as there always was for these trips. Grace Gilmore had made a success of the blue linen and had made other dresses for me and for my mother.

Grace was really part of the household now. She had taken charge of my mother's wardrobe, and was able to dress her hair for special occasions. She was no ordinary lady's maid, of course. My mother had a real affection for her and was eager to help her in every way and Grace showed her gratitude by making herself almost indispensable to my mother.

'I don't know how I managed before she came,' she used to say.

Grace was treated more and more like a member of the family. She was clever. There might have been revolution in the kitchen at such elevation of one who was in their eyes a mere servant, though an upper one. But Grace Gilmore was possessed of great tact. She always treated Mrs Penlock and Watson as equals; and although they felt they should be given the respect due to the heads of the servant oligarchy, they did accept that Grace was outside the usual laws of protocol. She now had her meals with us. At first Watson was inclined to sniff at that, and we wondered whether the parlourmaids would be allowed to serve her or whether she would be expected to help herself. My mother soon put an end to this nonsense and as Grace herself was the essence of tact, the situation was eased and finally accepted.

So Grace had become almost like a daughter of the household – and a very useful one.

She would travel with us – as one of us – but she insisted on lady's-maiding my mother; keeping an eye on our wardrobes; and she was helpful with Jack.

This hovering between upper and lower parts of the household might have presented a problem to a lesser person, but Grace dealt with it calmly and efficiently, as she did all things.

We were greeted with great delight by Aunt Amaryllis, who scolded my mother for delaying so long. She embraced me and looked at me anxiously.

'My poor darling Angelet,' she said. 'What a terrible accident that was! Well, you look quite healthy now, doesn't she, Peter?'

Uncle Peter looked a little older, but the years only added to his distinction. He kissed me on both cheeks and said how pleased he was to see me.

'Matthew and Helena will be over with Jonnie and Geoffrey,' said Aunt Amaryllis. 'When Jonnie knew you were coming he was so pleased. He is really very cross with you for staying away so long – so are we all.'

'It couldn't be helped,' replied my mother. 'Don't think we did not miss our visits. But why didn't you come to Cador?'

Aunt Amaryllis lifted her shoulders. 'Peter has been so busy and we are all here . . . the whole family. It is so much better for you to come to London.'

'And this is Grace,' said my mother. 'Grace Gilmore.'

'How do you do, Miss Gilmore. We are so pleased you came. We have heard so much about you.'

'You are all so kind,' murmured Grace.

'Now then . . . to your rooms. Luggage will be sent up . . . and dinner is at eight. Do come down when you are ready. Matthew and the family will be here at any minute.'

Grace helped my mother unpack and then came to me.

'What a lovely house!' she said.

'I've always been fascinated by it,' I told her. 'And Aunt Amaryllis always gives me a room overlooking the river.'

She went to the window and looked out.

I stood beside her. 'You can just see the Houses of Parliament. They really are magnificent. Did you know the Queen opened the Victoria Tower and the Royal Gallery only two years ago;

and she knighted the architect? It really is a wonderful sight when you look across the river.'

'It is a great pleasure for me to be in London. It was a very fortunate day when I walked into your garden.'

'I know we all share that view,' I told her.

It was wonderful to see the family, particularly Jonnie. There had always been a special friendship between us. He was four years older than I, which had seemed a great deal when we were younger, but as we grew older the gap seemed to lessen. I had hero-worshipped Jonnie in those days but when Ben had come I had been rather fickle and transferred my adoration to him.

He took my hands and gave me that rather gentle smile which had always made me feel cherished.

'Why, how you've grown, Angelet. And you've been so ill. We were all so anxious about you.'

'I'm all right now, Jonnie. How are you getting on? Still concerned about all those old relics . . . still digging up the past?'

He nodded. 'I'm getting completely immersed. There is a party going out to Greece next year. I'm hoping to go.'

'What are you hoping to find . . . a lost city?'

'That's hoping for a lot. Generally it's just dig . . . dig . . . and you're lucky if you find a drinking vessel.'

'Oh, this is Miss Grace Gilmore,' I said as Grace appeared.

'How do you do?' said Jonnie. 'I've heard so much of you. Aunt Annora has told us how good you have been to her.'

Grace laughed: 'It is more she who has been good to me.'

She looked not so much pretty as interesting. She was elegant. Her sense of dress was perfect. Her clothes were simple and yet noticeable for that very reason. She wore a gown of a light biscuit colour which toned with her hazel eyes; her smooth brown hair fell rather loosely over her ears and was caught in a knot at the nape of her neck. She was wearing a garnet brooch which my mother had given her – her only jewellery. Everything was plain but decidedly elegant.

Jonnie smiled at her. If he thought she was some sort of higher servant he would be especially gracious to her. Jonnie was that kind of person.

Ben had been so flamboyantly attractive that he had made me forget what a very delightful person Jonnie was.

Grace said: 'I heard you are interested in archæology. I've always been fascinated by things that belong to the past. What an exciting time you must have!'

'I have just been saying to Angelet that people imagine we are coming upon old treasures all the time. That, if one is lucky, is the experience of a lifetime.'

'I'd love to hear more about that.'

'Well, you'll stay for a while and we shall meet again. There's plenty of time for us.'

Matthew and Helena came in to welcome us and in turn were introduced to Grace. Geoffrey was growing up. He must be nearly fifteen by now.

'Peterkin and Frances will be coming,' announced Aunt Amaryllis. 'I was determined to muster as many of the family as possible. It is such a long time since we have seen you all. I know it was due to Angelet's accident and subsequent illness . . . Well, all that is over now. It is wonderful to see her so blooming.'

In due course everyone was assembled and we were seated at the dinner table, Uncle Peter at one end, Aunt Amaryllis at the other.

There had been occasions in the past when I had sat at this table and I remembered the conversation. It always seemed to be dominated by Uncle Peter as far as I remembered and everyone deferred to him. There was a good deal of politics, which I believed interested him more than anything else. Of course I had been very young then and my opportunities to listen had not been very frequent.

Now, of course, I was older but perhaps not yet of an age to take a great part in the discourse.

The talk at this time was about the situation between Russia and Turkey and the part England should play in it.

'Palmerston has the people with him,' said Uncle Peter.

'But is he right?' asked Matthew.

'I think war is wrong in any circumstances,' said Frances.

Frances was a very forthright woman, one of the few who

would directly contradict Uncle Peter. For many years she had been running what was called a Mission in the East End of London; she had married Peterkin and they worked together. She was rather a plain woman, but attractive because of her vitality and enthusiasm; she was highly respected in many quarters because of the work she had done, and was doing, for the poor.

'My dear Frances,' said Uncle Peter, with a kindly but faintly condescending smile, 'we all think war is wrong, but sometimes it is inevitable, and a prompt action in which a few suffer may prevent the deaths of thousands.'

'In my opinion,' went on Frances, 'we should keep out of this.'

'I am inclined to agree,' said Matthew. Matthew was a reformer by nature. He had come into prominence with his book on Prison Reform and from that had stemmed his career in politics. Uncle Peter had been of inestimable help to his son-in-law; and Matthew never forgot that; he must have felt very strongly on this matter of war to express an adverse opinion.

Uncle Peter came in firmly. Lightly he might brush Frances aside, but he was really concerned about Matthew.

'My dear Matthew,' he said, 'often it is necessary to take the long-term view. You will never have the support of the people by a weak pacifist policy.'

'But if it is *right* . . . ?'

Uncle Peter raised his eyebrows. 'In politics we have to think what is best for the country. What is going to keep power in our hands? We cannot allow sentiment to play a part in our judgement. The people are even now turning against the Queen . . . and Albert is the villain-in-chief.'

'They are always against Albert,' said Frances.

'Yes, but they now think he and the Queen are considering their Russian relations rather than the country. The people want Palmerston and his gun-boat policy. You have to admit that it is not without its merits.'

I could see Matthew wavering. He would conform with Uncle Peter's wishes. He always had. That was how he had got on. He had been made by Uncle Peter.

'The point is,' said my father, 'is there going to be war?'

'I think it is almost certain. We shall have to go to Turkey's aid. We shall have the French with us and we shall settle this matter very quickly and show the world that we are masters of it.'

'Aberdeen is against it,' said Matthew.

'Aberdeen is too weak. The people are clamouring for Palmerston. Mark my words, Palmerston will be back. We shall go to war. It is what the people want. Palmerston is the hero of the day.' He looked at Matthew sternly. 'It is necessary to be on the winning side.'

So the conversation went on. Then we talked of Cornwall and my father and Uncle Peter were in deep conversation about the estate. Aunt Amaryllis told us of the London scene, that she had recently been to the opera and that she hoped we would all go very soon.

But the talk did keep coming back to the possibility of war and that was really what was in everybody's mind.

I lay in bed that night and thought about the evening. London always made an impact on me. It was not only the streets, which always seemed so alive in contrast to our country lanes. Perhaps it was the feeling that life here could never be dull. Something important was just about to happen, I always felt. That was probably the impression I had in this house and it was largely due to the impact of Uncle Peter's personality.

Already I was aware of the impending disaster of war and I had seen opposite reactions to it; and what had impressed me was Uncle Peter's control of Matthew, and as Matthew was one of those people who make our laws, I thought of Uncle Peter as a puppet-master jerking his protégé in the way he must go. Matthew's instincts were against war; but he was going to support it because Uncle Peter was jerking him.

It was so interesting that St Branok's Pool seemed a long way away.

The days began to fly past. There was the visit to the opera which Aunt Amaryllis had promised us; we went riding in the Row; Jonnie was a constant companion. He had not yet

90

completed his education but as he had decided to take up archæology as a profession he would interrupt it to go to Greece for a period of practical study; and was at the moment preparing for it.

He usually spent his mornings in private study but in the afternoons he would be free and that was the time that he was in our company. I say 'our' because Grace Gilmore seemed always to be with us.

In the mornings we often went shopping with my mother, Grace with us. Being in London, said my mother, gave us an opportunity to replenish our wardrobes. She and Grace liked to study the fashions in the shops and consult together. Grace was very knowledgeable about materials and styles.

Sometimes in the afternoon we rode in Rotten Row. It was not, of course, like riding at home. It was more like a parade; Jonnie, and occasionally Aunt Amaryllis, were with us and when they were they were constantly being greeted by people. Riding there was more like a social event.

I enjoyed very much walking in the Park, which we did frequently. Jonnie or Geoffrey would accompany us. Sometimes we took Jack, who was wide-eyed with wonder at everything he saw and asked interminable questions.

The best times of all were with Jonnie and Grace. She and Jonnie had taken quite a liking to each other. She was so interested in everything and she asked all sorts of intelligent questions about archæology; he had lent her books on the subject.

I used to love to sit by the Serpentine in blissful forgetfulness of that terrible day which during the visit to London seemed so far from what I thought of as the scene of the crime. It had faded into the past and was of far less significance than it had been in Cornwall.

There was one day, I remember, when we talked of Ben, that brought it back a little, for I had not seen Ben since it happened. I had been aware of him at my bedside, I supposed, but that was all.

'You remember Benedict, Angelet,' said Jonnie one day.

'Oh yes, I remember him.'

'Of course you do. Do you know, Miss Gilmore, I was quite jealous of Benedict at one time. Angelet used to be my particular friend and when he came along she completely forgot me.'

'Who is he exactly?' asked Grace. 'I know he was at Cador for a while but I was never quite sure.'

'He took a bit of explaining,' said Jonnie. 'He's my grand-father's grandson. I suppose that makes him a cousin. What complicated relationships we have in our family.'

'Perhaps that's why you are rather complicated people,' said Grace.

'That must be the answer. Do you know, I never thought of that.'

'I wonder if he has found gold and become rich,' I said.

Jonnie said to Grace: 'That was what he went to Australia to find. Gold! Do you remember some time ago there was a great deal of comment about the goldfields of Australia. A place called Ballarat, I believe. Well, Benedict just thought he would like a share of it and he went in search of his fortune.'

'I expect if he had found gold he would have been delighted to let us know,' I said.

'Yes, I'm sure of that, too,' agreed Jonnie. 'Benedict was not one to hide his light under a bushel.'

I wished they wouldn't talk of him. They were bringing it all back to me again.

'Perhaps he is having a hard time,' I suggested.

'Well, I should think it is not a very easy life . . . until one strikes gold.'

'He sounds a very interesting young man,' said Grace 'I remember him only slightly.'

'He is rather overpowering, wouldn't you say, Angelet?' said Jonnie. 'In fact he is very much like my grandfather.'

'I see what you mean,' said Grace. 'Tell me, when are you planning to go to Greece?'

'Next spring, I think.'

'How very exciting! I think it must be one of the most thrilling things one can do . . . to discover the past, for that is what it is.'

'Exactly,' agreed Jonnie. 'Then I hope to get to Pompeii. I

feel there is a good deal to discover there. People have explored a little. I have been there once . . . two years ago.They have worked on it . . . spasmodically. There is no system, though. I believe work on it would be very rewarding.'

'How fascinating,' cried Grace rapturously. 'It was the volcano which erupted, wasn't it?'

'Yes, but there were a series of earthquakes before that. It was the shocks which set Vesuvius erupting and sending out those ashes and hot stones pelting down on the cities and utterly destroying them.'

Grace shivered. 'It makes you realize how uncertain life is.'

'It does indeed. Well, I intend to get out there and work. I shall do everything I can to make that possible. There is so much to do, I am sure we can uncover a whole city.'

'How did they know there was a city there?' I asked.

'The walls of the amphitheatre marked the spot, but it was just a lot of hardened mud with sparse grass on it . . . enough, though, to show that there had been a city there. As far back as the sixteenth century they came upon ancient buildings. There have been excavations but they have never been carried out in a scientific way. It's time they were. Then heaven knows what treasures we shall uncover.'

'I think it must be a wonderful profession,' said Grace enthusiastically. 'I'd love to be concerned in it.'

'It's hard work . . . digging and all that.'

'I'm strong.'

'I tell you what: I'll lend you some more books.'

'Oh, will you?'

'Of course.'

He did, and soon they were involved in intelligent discussions and I felt rather left out. It was the first time I had been made aware that I was still a child and Jonnie and Grace were adults. She must have been two or possibly three years older than he was. I liked Grace very much but I did wish that she was not always present when we went on our rides and walks. I also wished that she were not quite so clever; she seemed to have acquired quite an understanding of archæology which she had certainly not had when she came to London.

93

I remember one day when we were walking back to the house we encountered a band of men walking along carrying banners. We stood watching them. They were singing something. It was hard to decipher but Jonnie translated for me. It was:

> 'You jolly old Turk, now go to work
> And show the Bear your power.
> It is rumoured over Britain's Isle
> That A is in the Tower.'

'What does it mean?' I asked.

'Well,' said Jonnie, 'the people are all for war. People always are if the war is taking place elsewhere. They like to hear of the glory but they would certainly not want to suffer the discomforts. This war is far away. Therefore they are all for it. Palmerston is all for making England the greatest power in the world. If anyone utters the mildest word against us he sends out the gun-boats to parade along their coasts, to show them our power. The people like it. They love Old Pam, as they call him. He's colourful. Of course he's very old now, but in his youth he was a rake. I believe he may still be. Funnily enough, the people like that. They don't want a good man; they want a colourful one. Poor old Aberdeen, with his pacific policies, is dull. The fact is the people are blaming the Queen and Prince Albert for our reluctance to go to war. It is quite unfair. They say the Russians are the Queen's relations and she cares more for them than for England. But they prefer to blame Albert, so they are calling him Traitor.'

'And he is the A who is rumoured to be in the tower?' said Grace.

'That's so. But it is all nonsense. Albert is by no means a prisoner. But I daresay war will be declared on Russia sooner or later.'

The next day an article appeared in *The Morning Post* written by Mr Gladstone setting out the Prince's virtues and commenting on the folly of blaming him. John Russell and Benjamin Disraeli made speeches about him in the Houses of Parliament – the latter's was brilliant; and this with Mr Gladstone's article made a deep impression on the people.

94

And still the threat of war hung in the air.

An ultimatum was sent to Russia to the effect that if she did not return the Danube principalities which she had annexed we should declare war.

When no answer was received, there was only one action the government could take.

We were at war with Russia.

It was amazing how quickly people's views could change. Matthew was now in full agreement with the declaration. This was probably due to Uncle Peter's influence. But Jonnie, too, had changed his mind. He was now for teaching the Russians a lesson, and saving little Turkey from the bully.

War fever swept over the country. It would all be over in a few weeks, they said. The Russians would soon see what happened to those who thought they could bully their neighbours.

They would find they had to face the wrath of powerful Britain.

That was April and in May we returned to Cornwall. Life settled down to normality. There was little talk down there about the tension between Turkey and Russia. It was all a matter of whether there would be a good harvest this year and whether the rain would keep off until Midsummer's Eve.

The rain did keep off for that important occasion and as if to make up for it, it then began to pour; and as often in Cornwall, as Mrs Penlock said, once it started it did not know how to stop.

There was speculation whether the Tamar would overflow its banks; and the possibility of high tides was considered with some apprehension. Some of the fields were flooded and there was consternation among the farmers.

Then one day I heard disquieting news.

The Pencarrons were coming to dinner and my mother had asked me to go down to remind Mrs Penlock that Mr Pencarron could not take any dish with pilchards in it. Mrs Penlock was very fond of starting a meal with a special dish of which she was very proud, and even when my mother had not suggested it, she had a habit of slipping it in. The fish was served with oil

95

and lemon and some ingredient which Mrs Penlock would not divulge. 'Fair Maids' was what she called it which, I had discovered, was her version of *Fumadoe* – which meant 'Fit for a Spanish Don', and reminded us that there was a certain Spanish element in the Duchy after the defeat of the Spanish Armada when the galleons had been wrecked along our coast and many Spaniards found refuge here.

When I arrived in the kitchen a great deal of excited talk was going on.

Mrs Penlock was saying, 'Stands to reason. People don't invent such things. They'm handed down . . . generation to generation. I reckon 'tis true then and some 'as heard them bells.'

I felt that twinge of fear which I always had when people referred to the pool.

'Truth in what?' I demanded.

''Tis all this rain we'm 'aving. That there pool . . . St Branok's, you know. 'Tas overflowed. Well, stands to reason . . . all this rain. 'Tas washed away the soil and they do say 'tis true. There be the remains of an old monastery . . . bits of rock and things sticking out of the ground. They'm saying you can see it . . . clear as daylight . . . and it's a wall . . . an old stone wall.'

'You mean . . . right there by the pool?'

'That's where I do mean. It be all this rain . . . loosens the soil, it do. And there be this bit of a wall, they do say. 'Tis unmistakable.'

I told her about the pilchards.

'There's some as don't know what's good for 'em,' she grumbled. 'I do reckon them Fair Maids be a real and proper way to start a meal. Gives you appetite, they do say, and they'm right. No bones about it.'

'Well, not for Mr Pencarron.'

I wanted to ask her more about the pool but I was afraid to; and as soon as I could I rode out there.

The ground was very wet and soggy. I saw two people standing close to the water and recognized one as John Gurney, the other was his son. They farmed on the Cador estate.

96

I rode up to them.

'I have heard that a wall has been exposed,' I said.

' 'Tis all this flooding, Miss Angelet. No good to the crops . . .'

'They are saying there really is a monastery here.'

'It seems they'm right. This here's a wall.'

'Is it really?'

'Could well be, Miss Angelet. Not much of it to see . . . just enough to show it might have been. Look, 'tis over there.'

I shivered. I wondered if there was any sign of blood on the stone. It was there that he had fallen and struck his head. Foolish thought! The rain would have washed it away even before the last deluge.

I walked Glory over and looked at it. I couldn't help but see him in my mind's eye. I glanced across to the pool. It was swollen and the water was dribbling beyond that spot where we had stood by the willows and let him slip down to his watery grave.

I turned back to the men.

'I suppose all sorts of things could be brought up on the water?'

They looked puzzled. 'Things that may have fallen in,' I said.

'Oh no, Miss Angelet. Reckon anything that went in would go right down to the bottom.'

'They say it's bottomless.'

'Must have a bottom somewhere, Miss Angelet.'

'But they did say . . .'

'Well, them bells 'as got to rest somewhere, 'asn't 'em?'

They laughed.

'I reckon there'll be some as 'ull be hearing 'em after this,' said John Gurney.

'You can bet your life on that,' said his son.

I rode back. It was foolish to worry but anything connected with the pool made me uneasy, and I supposed it would as long as I lived.

I was amazed when a letter came from Jonnie to my mother. When I went down to breakfast she was reading it.

'Good morning, Angelet,' she said. 'This is from Jonnie. He wants to come down.'

'That will be nice,' I said.

'He wants to bring a friend.' She glanced at the letter. 'Gervaise Mandeville. They've been studying together. So I suppose he's an archæologist as well. Shall I read to you what he says?'

'Please do,' I replied.

'"We're so excited about this find at the pool. It sounds quite fascinating. We should love to come down. I am referring to a friend. He's very enthusiastic and if I could bring him with me, it would be wonderful. Ever since Miss Gilmore wrote about the exposed wall, I was eager to come and see it. Could you put up with us both? We could of course stay at the inn if it wasn't convenient . . ."'

My mother looked at me. 'What nonsense! As if we would let them stay at the inn. Of course they will come here.'

'He's quickly learned about the discovery at the pool,' I said.

'He and Grace have been writing to each other. Naturally she would tell him such a piece of news.'

I felt a certain resentment. It was foolish. Why should they not write to each other?

'I suppose she thought he'd be particularly interested in that sort of thing,' said my mother. 'And she was right. He's hoping to unearth a monastery.' She added lightly: 'He'll be wanting to get down to the bottom of the pool to see if there are any bells there.'

I could not share her lightness, though I tried to pretend to.

And this friendship with Grace? He had not written to me. Of course she had shown a marked interest in his archæology. It must be due to that.

A few weeks later they arrived.

Jonnie embraced me warmly. He was full of enthusiasm. 'And this is Gervaise . . . Gervaise Mandeville,' he said.

Gervaise was very good-looking, tall with blond hair and blue eyes. He seemed to be laughing all the time – even when one would expect him to be serious. It was as though he found everything a joke and such was his personality that when one was with him, one felt the same. I liked him from the moment

98

I saw him. He was not so intense as Jonnie, although he was excited at the prospect of discovering a monastery – but even that seemed like a joke to him – as everything else was.

Having visitors from London was always refreshing. We were rather cut off from affairs in the country and the first night at supper we seemed to be catching up with what was happening in the outside world.

The war was by no means over. The Russians had not, contrary to the expectations of the people in the streets, given up as soon as they knew the British were on the way.

'It looks,' said Jonnie, 'as though it might go on for a long time.'

He was very sad about it.

'Some people think we should never have gone into it.'

'Peterkin and Frances and Matthew do, I know,' I said.

'Peterkin and Frances certainly. Matthew has swung right round. He has made some stirring speeches in the House.'

I smiled, thinking of Uncle Peter jerking his puppet.

Gervaise said lightly: 'I'd give it another three months. Then we must win . . . if only to oblige me. I have a bet on with Douglas.'

'Gervaise likes a gamble,' Jonnie explained to us. 'And Tom Douglas is as bad as he is. When the two of them get together they'll wager on how many cabs they'll see on the way to the club. I've seen them watching rain drops falling down a window . . . urging the particular one they have put their money on to move faster . . . as though it were a horse in a race.'

Gervaise grinned. 'It brings an added zest to life,' he explained.

Grace was full of information about the discovery at the pool and she could talk knowledgeably on the subject. I wondered how interested she really was and whether she was doing this to please Jonnie.

They talked enthusiastically of what they were going to do.

'I suppose,' said Jonnie, 'if we're going to dig we have to get permission from the owner.'

My father smiled. 'The Cador estate extends to the pool. It's all Cador land.'

99

Jonnie beamed. 'So all we have to do is ask you and Aunt Annora.'

'Exactly,' replied my father.

'And have we your permission?'

'I can only say,' said my father, 'that I should be most interested to know if it is really the site of an old monastery.'

'Hurrah!' cried Gervaise. 'We can go ahead.'

Grace said: 'Shall I be allowed on the site?'

Jonnie turned to her, beaming with pleasure. 'I should be put out if you were not there.'

'I dare say you would like to be there, Angelet,' said my mother.

Jonnie smiled at me. 'Of course,' he said. 'You must come and help, Angelet.'

I felt very pleased that he obviously wanted me to go.

'We shall make the place famous,' said Gervaise. 'Imagine the Press. "Great Find by Students. Jon Hume and Gervaise Mandeville have outclassed the experts. Hitherto unsuspected monastery has been excavated from remote part of Cornwall . . ."'

'It was not unsuspected,' I reminded them. 'People have been saying they heard the monastery bells for ages.'

'Ah, the Bells of St Branok! That will fascinate people . . . We ought to have some bells rung . . . just to create the right atmosphere.'

'The bells,' said my mother, 'are supposed to herald a disaster.'

'That makes it all the more exciting.'

'Heralded disasters often come to pass,' I said, 'because people expect them to.'

'She is a wise woman, this daughter of yours,' said Gervaise, smiling warmly at me. 'I'm all eagerness to get to work. Jon, I wager you twenty pounds that we've got that wall uncovered within a week.'

'I'm not the betting man you are,' said Jonnie. 'I'll wait and see.'

The next day they inspected the site. I went with them – so did Grace.

100

The place seemed to have lost its eeriness. It was only when I was there alone that the atmosphere seemed to envelope me. They inspected the jutting stone on which that man had cut his head.

'Yes,' said Jonnie, 'it's part of a wall. We'll have to start digging here.'

He walked down to the pool, examining the water.

'I reckon,' he said, 'that this was once a fishpond. They always had fishponds in their monasteries. They provided food for the monks.'

'We'll try to fish,' said Gervaise. 'Ten pounds for the first one who makes a catch.'

'Be serious,' said Jonnie. 'Any fish in that pool would have been poisoned long ago. Heaven alone knows what has gone down into that water over the years.'

'Well, it will be fun to try. Let's say a tenner for the first one who brings up anything at all. It might not be a fish. Angelet is looking disapproving. I'm sorry, Angelet. I'm really a very serious character under my skin.'

He smiled at me so charmingly that I wished I could tell him what I was thinking. I was sure he would have made some light-hearted comment and made me feel that I was worrying unduly.

That very afternoon they started to dig. They had brought the necessary equipment with them and they wore what they called working gear. My parents were very amused by them.

There was a great deal of comment throughout the neighbourhood and it was largely critical. Mrs Penlock expressed the general feeling.

''Tain't natural,' she said. 'If it was meant to have been seen, it would have been. If the good Lord sees fit to cover it up, that's how He wants it.' I knew it was serious when the good Lord was brought in. His name implied that it was a question of right and wrong, and on such occasions Mrs Penlock and the Lord were always together on the right side.

So I gathered that the exploration was unpopular.

'If it were meant to be discovered,' said Mrs Penlock to me, 'it would never have been covered up.'

'But it has been covered up, over the years. People have to discover these things. It teaches us about the past. People want to know, and the Lord helps those who help themselves, remember.'

''Tain't natural,' was all she would say.

Protests came vociferously from one quarter. This was from old Stubbs. He lived in the cottage near the pool. He and his daughter Jenny were a strange pair. They had lived alone since Stubbs's wife had died. She had been a kind of white witch who grew herbs and was said to be able to cure all sorts of ailments. Jenny Stubbs was, as Mrs Penlock said, 'Not all there.' She was in fact a little simple. She would go about crooning to herself, but she would be on the quay when the catch came in, picking up any fish that was thrown aside because it was not up to standard. I had seen her once or twice gathering limpets and snails. She made a broth of them, I believe.

They lived a hermit-like existence. Old Stubbs was said to be a footling, which meant that he had been born feet first and therefore had special powers. He did occasional work, like clipping hedges; and my father had allowed the family to go on living in the cottage.

We were there, with Jonnie and Gervaise digging and Grace and I fetching and carrying, when the old man suddenly appeared. His eyes were wild, his hair unkempt.

He said: 'Lay down them shovels. What be doing on our land?'

Gervaise smiled charmingly. 'We are exploring and we have permission to do so.'

'Get off our land or 'twill be the worse for 'ee.'

'Really,' began Jonnie. 'I don't see what right . . .'

'This land ain't meant to be disturbed. There's people that don't want it and won't have it.'

'Why, there's no one here.'

The old man looked crafty. 'They be 'ere . . . but you can't see 'em.'

Jonnie was exasperated. Gervaise of course thought it was a joke; but nothing concerned with this place could be a joke to me.

'This land belongs to the dead,' said old Stubbs. 'Woe to them as worries the dead.'

'I should have thought,' said Gervaise, 'that they would have liked us to find their buried monastery.'

'You'm worrying the dead. 'Tain't right. 'Tain't proper. You go away from 'ere. Go back to your big city. That's where you belong to be. No good will come of this, I promise 'ee.'

With that he shook his fist and hobbled away.

'What an interesting character!' said Gervaise.

I told him about their cottage nearby and how he and his daughter scratched a living from the soil.

Gervaise was quite interested but Jonnie wanted to get on with the dig.

For three days they worked, but knowing the people well, we in the family were aware that there was general disapproval of the excavations.

'It's so silly,' said my father. 'Why shouldn't we know if there was really a monastery there? Why all this objection?'

'You know how the people hate change,' my mother reminded him.

'But this is not going to change anything in their lives. I'd like to know how the story got about that there was a monastery there.'

'You don't propose to drag the pool, do you?' said my mother.

'I hardly think that would be possible. But it would be nice to know that at least the monastery was there.'

What followed was inevitable.

A groom, exercising one of the horses, passed the site. It was dark, and he distinctly heard the sound of bells. They were coming, he thought, from the bottom of the pool.

Then there was talk of nothing but the bells.

They rang, didn't they, when disaster was threatened. Someone had displeased God and you didn't have to look far to see who that was. Dead folks didn't want to be disturbed and it was reckoned that 'all they monks at the bottom of the pool don't take kind, like, to people coming up from London and starting to dig all round their resting-place.'

People were saying they heard the bells and it was always at dusk.

Two weeks had passed and I think that even Jonnie was beginning to realize that it was no use going on. They had uncovered what could be part of a stone wall. It might have been an old cottage. There was nothing to show that it was part of a monastery.

'We should need to have special equipment,' said Jonnie. 'We'd have to go down a long way . . .'

'And possibly find nothing,' added my father.

'What a pity!' said Grace. 'I am so sorry. It was my fault. I shouldn't have mentioned it.'

'Oh, no,' cried Jonnie. 'It was the greatest fun, wasn't it, Gervaise?'

Gervaise said that he was satisfied. He had found new friends which was far better than an old monastery.

'Charmingly said,' replied my mother. 'But I know you are disappointed. Never mind. Perhaps Pompeii will be more rewarding.'

'Well, we shall certainly find something there,' said Jonnie.

There had been some talk of our going back with him and staying in London for a while, but my father said he could not go, for there were all sorts of problems to be dealt with on the estate.

I was disappointed, but relieved that they had stopped digging, and the recent activity at the pool had made me feel that I wanted to escape for a while.

'Angelet does so love London,' said my mother. 'I don't see why *you* shouldn't go, darling. Grace could go with you.'

Grace said: 'Oh, that would be wonderful.'

So it was arranged.

It was the day before we were to leave when Gervaise said to me: 'I want to take one last look at the site. Will you come with me, Angelet?'

'Why do you want to look at it?' I asked.

'I just have the fancy to. I tell you what. We'll go at dusk. There won't be anyone there. That is the witching hour.'

I shivered.

'Come,' he said. 'I know the place fascinates you. It does me too.' He added: 'You'll be safe with me.'

We rode out together and he had arranged it so that we reached the pool just as the light was beginning to fade.

'We haven't improved the countryside, have we?' he said, looking ruefully at the piece of wall with the heaped soil about it.

'Never mind,' I said. 'I believe it is the fate of many archæologists.'

'Well, if you didn't look you would never find, and it has been a lot of fun being here.'

'Even though you failed?'

'I don't look on it as failure because I have found some new friends. And now you are hoping to come back to London with us.'

'I'm pleased about that.'

'Listen,' he said. 'Listen to the silence.'

How eerie it was! But perhaps it was memories which made it so. The water was just visible in the darkness. There was the faintest breeze, which ruffled the grass and now and then broke the silence with a gentle moan.

'I can understand people's building up legends about this place,' said Gervaise. 'Did you come here often?'

'No . . . not now.'

'Listen . . .'

There it was . . . faint in the stillness of the air but unmistakable. It was like the tolling of a bell.

I turned to look at Gervaise. Had he heard it too? His expression told me that he had. Blank amazement showed on his face. He was staring at the pool. There it was again. The distinct tolling of a bell.

He said: 'You've gone quite pale. Do you feel all right? There must be a church somewhere near.'

'You couldn't possibly hear church bells here.'

'How then . . . ?'

I shook my head.

'It can't be . . .' he began.

105

There was silence between us. We stood very still straining our ears, but there was only silence.

'Don't be scared,' he said. 'There must be an explanation.'

'It seemed to come from the pool.'

'Impossible.'

'Then where?'

'Let's look at it like this. We came here to hear bells.'

'Did we?'

'Yes, I think that was in our minds. We were expecting to hear them . . . so we imagined we did.'

'Both of us . . . at the same time?'

'It must be so.'

He started towards the pool. I hesitated. 'Come on,' he said, taking my arm. 'We'll go right up to it and listen . . . hard.'

I followed him. We were so close now that another step would have taken us into the dark water.

He shouted: 'Who's there? Play the bells again.'

His voice echoed back. It was uncanny.

But there was no sound at all except the faint noise made by the wind in the grass.

'It's chilly here,' he said. 'Let's get back.'

After we had left the pool he did not speak for some time. Then he said: 'We imagined it.'

But he knew, and I knew, that that was not so.

When we arrived in London I noticed at once that the mood of euphoria about the war had changed considerably.

There had been no speedy conclusion; news had arrived of a cholera epidemic which had been responsible for the death of many of our men. Everyone was talking about William Howard Russell who was sending home disturbing articles which appeared in *The Times*. Men were dying of disease and there was a lack of medical supplies to deal with the epidemic. There was chaos, little organization; and this was an enemy more formidable than the Russians. The war was ugly and frustrating – not the glorious road to victory which so many had been led to expect.

British and French armies had won the battle of Alma and hopes revived for a speedy conclusion to the war, but those articles in *The Times* were more disturbing than ever.

There was talk of little else but the war. It seemed to me that everyone knew what should be done. Palmerston should have been brought in earlier; his advice should have been taken. If it had been, the war could have been averted. Palmerston was the hero of the day and war fever was rampant.

I noticed how thoughtful Jonnie had become. He was deeply concerned about news and studied the papers avidly.

Once when we were out we saw soldiers marching on their way to the wharf where they would embark for the Crimea. The people cheered them; bands were playing and they looked magnificent.

Then we went into the Park and sat on a seat watching the ducks on the Serpentine.

'It's a righteous war,' said Jonnie. 'We cannot allow one nation to subdue another just because it is strong and the other weak.'

Grace said that those men were heroes to go into an unknown country and fight for the right.

We walked home in a somewhat sombre mood. I thought Jonnie had something on his mind. I wished that he would confide in me and wondered whether he had in Grace.

I had to conquer a smouldering resentment because he really did take more notice of Grace than of me; and not so long ago we had been such friends. He had once implied that he was a little piqued because I seemed to transfer my affection from him to Benedict Lansdon. He had spoken jestingly, of course, but I wondered if he had meant it . . . just a little. Now I felt the same about him and Grace. Of course she was older than I . . . older than us both . . . and she had read so much of archæology since she had known Jonnie that she could talk to him almost as a fellow student would have done.

I did not see Jonnie all the next day and on the following one he told us what had been on his mind.

He made the announcement just before we went into dinner. Helena looked very solemn and so did Matthew.

'I have joined the army,' said Jonnie. 'We don't have to do much training. There isn't time. I expect I shall be leaving soon for the Crimea.'

Jonnie's action aroused a great storm in the family. Helena was very worried and tried to persuade him to change his mind; Geoffrey was resentful because he was not old enough to do the same. I think his father, in his heart, agreed with Helena, but Uncle Peter saw how the situation could be turned to advantage. There had been hints, in pacific circles, that those who were eagerly clamouring for war were not those who would have to go and fight it. But here was a prominent politician whose son had volunteered. He was a student studying archæology but as soon as he understood his country's need he had rallied to the flag.

'This will do infinite good,' said Uncle Peter soothingly. 'The war will soon be over. Perhaps before Jonnie gets out there.'

Even so the Russell reports did not echo that view. There was an outcry in Parliament and throughout the country. Something would have to be done.

Then we began to hear a great deal about a lady called Florence Nightingale. Uncle Peter and Aunt Amaryllis knew her family fairly well. They had always thought that Florence was a difficult girl who had caused her parents some concern because she would not do what every girl was expected to do – make a good marriage and settle cosily into society. Florence had all the necessary accomplishments; she was handsome and intelligent, charming and attractive to the opposite sex. But she had a passion for nursing. How ridiculous! they said. Nursing was not for ladies. It was the sort of work people did when they could find no other employment. It was rather like the drifters and ne'er-do-wells who went into the Army. Only this comparison was not stressed now for the drifters and ne'er-do-wells had been miraculously turned into heroes.

But now those who had ignored Miss Nightingale began to notice her.

'I heard,' said Uncle Peter, 'that Miss Nightingale is being

108

taken very seriously at last. Sidney Herbert is most impressed. They realize the need for good nurses out there. She is suggesting taking a group of women out there . . . women whom she will train. It is an important step forward.'

Jonnie looked splendid in uniform. We were all very proud of him, but of course with each passing day his departure grew nearer.

Then a strange thing happened.

Lord John Milward, of whom I had never heard before, died. There was a column in the paper about him. He had suffered an attack of the dreaded typhoid fever which had in a very short time proved fatal.

I had not thought that this could affect us at all. That was because at that time I was ignorant of the family history. Lord John Milward had left quite a large sum of money to Jonnie.

Jonnie was astonished and then suddenly he seemed to accept it.

It was some time later when I learned the truth.

Lord John Milward was, in fact, Jonnie's father and not Matthew Hume, as I had always been led to suppose – and so had Jonnie himself.

Apparently when she was very young, Helena had been engaged to John Milward; there had been a scandal involving Uncle Peter and his night clubs and the Milward family had insisted that the engagement be broken off.

My grandmother and grandfather Jake Cadorson, who had been visiting Australia to look after some property which Jake had acquired after his sentence had expired, took Helena with them. My mother was there too. Helena was at this time pregnant and my grandparents helped her over a difficult time. Jonnie was born in Australia. Matthew Hume had been on the ship taking them out; he was going to get material for his book on prisons – transportation being an important part of it – and there he met Helena and married her; and Jonnie had always thought that he was Matthew's son.

109

John Milward, however, did not forget his son and thus it was that Jonnie was on the point of becoming a rich man.

He said his new affluence would be of great use in his work and everyone was very pleased for him. I did love Jonnie; he had been a hero of my childhood. I was sorry that I had for a time allowed Ben Lansdon to usurp his place in my heart. Jonnie was gentle and reliable; Ben was powerful and exciting. Ben had gone away and left me with our secret. I wondered how Jonnie would have behaved. Jonnie would never have been in such a situation. He would never have thought of hiding the body in the pool.

But Shakespeare said that comparisons were odorous; and how right he was.

Then came another bombshell.

Grace came to me one day and said she must talk to me.

She said: 'I wish your mother were here. I am sure she would understand. But I want you to explain to her.'

I was mystified.

'I've made a decision,' she said. 'If they will have me I am going to Scutari.'

'To Scutari!' I cried. 'But how?'

'With Miss Nightingale's nurses. I have been along to see about it today. They will let me know if I am accepted. I feel sure I shall be. They told me it was almost a certainty. They do not get many educated young women and these are the sort that are wanted.'

'But you are not a nurse.'

'Nor are most of the others. In fact there are no real nurses anywhere. The hospitals are full of incompetent people who take to nursing because they cannot get work elsewhere. I've been talking to people. I want to go, Angelet. Please explain to your mother. It seems so ungrateful to leave like this, but I always felt she took me in out of charity and created work for me so that I should not feel I was imposing.'

'Oh nonsense, Grace. My mother is fond of you.'

'I feel that and it makes me unhappy. I am very fond of her . . . and you and everyone at Cador.'

'I wish I could come.'

'Your mother will be glad you are too young. I imagine it will not be the most comfortable way of living . . . but I want to do it. Seeing Jonnie in his uniform . . . Angelet, please do not say anything to anyone until I am sure of being accepted.'

I promised I would not; but in a few days she heard that her application was successful.

Everyone was astounded, but they applauded her enterprise and bravery. Jonnie was overcome with admiration for her and again I felt that twinge of jealousy.

'I would have gone if I had been old enough,' I said.

Jonnie gave me that loving smile of his and said: 'I know you would.'

Grace received her uniform – not the most glamorous of costumes. There was a grey tweed dress and jacket of worsted of the same colour, with a white cap and a woollen cape.

'You just have to take the nearest that fits,' explained Grace. 'They are certainly unbecoming.'

'They are to impress on you that you are meant to be useful rather than ornamental. But they would look better if they fitted.'

Grace was easily able to alter hers to make it a better fit; but it still remained a most unattractive outfit.

Jonnie had gone. That was a sad day. Aunt Amaryllis insisted that Helena and Matthew come to the house in the square for dinner.

We drank to the success of the war, the conclusion of hostilities and Jonnie's speedy return.

In October Grace set out for London Bridge where she was to join the band of nurses.

I felt deflated after she had gone. I wondered when I should see her and Jonnie again.

My parents came to London when they heard that Grace had gone.

'She's a good brave girl,' said my mother. 'She always wanted to make herself useful. I was so glad that we were able to help her. Poor girl, she was quite desperate when she walked into the garden that day. She was always so grateful, and we had to

111

be grateful to her, too. We shall miss her. I hope this wretched war will soon be over and she will be back with us.'

Soon after that we returned to Cornwall.

And the war dragged on.

Life seemed more than usually uneventful in Cornwall after that visit to London.

We were deeply concerned about the war. There was no good news. The winter was setting in and that could be a greater foe than the Russian armies. We had news of the disastrous Charge of the six hundred Light Cavalry at Balaclava; few men returned from that. There was the battle of Inkerman in which we lost more than two thousand men, and even though they told us that the Russians lost twelve thousand, that was little consolation to sorrowing relatives.

Aunt Amaryllis wrote constantly. She said that Helena was taking Jonnie's departure sadly. She was like a wraith; she thought of little but the danger Jonnie was in.

'I wish,' wrote Aunt Amaryllis, 'that that man Russell would stop writing such terrible things and sending them home. It makes us fret so. Poor Helena is beside herself with grief, and I think all the time of our dear Jonnie out there in that terrible place . . . and that nice Grace, too. Although, of course, she is not in the battle. I do wish it would all be over. It is so far away. What has it to do with us? But that's wrong of me. Peter says the war is right and we have to preserve our influence all over the world. It is so necessary for everyone . . .'

'Poor Aunt Amaryllis,' said my mother. 'Usually she can let ill fortune sail over her . . . but this is a little too close . . . with Jonnie at the front.'

The siege of Sebastopol continued. Once that fell into allied hands, it was said that the war would be all but over, but the Russians were a stubborn people; they would not give in; and our men on the outskirts of Sebastopol suffered more through the terrible winter than those who were within the city . . . many dying of the cold, so said Russell. Miss Nightingale and her nurses were doing a wonderful job but what could the most

112

efficient nursing do without supplies? And conditions were still terrible.

It seemed to go on and on. The winter was over; spring came. Each day we waited for news, but all through that year there was nothing that was good.

Then came the sad letter from Aunt Amaryllis.

I don't know how to tell you. We are all devastated. Jonnie has been killed. He was so brave, they say. He was a wonderful soldier. But I am afraid that is no consolation to poor Helena. She is prostrate with grief; and we are all very, very sorrowful. Peter is most affected. He saw that there was a fine piece in the papers about Jonnie's bravery and how he gave his life for his country. He says that, sad as this event is, it will increase public appreciation of Matthew. That does not console poor Matthew. He loved him. We know Jonnie was not his son but he had always been brought up as such and the fact that John Milward was his real father makes no difference to Matthew's affection for him. It is such a sad time for us all. I wonder if you could come up. It would be such a help if you could. Helena is so fond of you. She talks quite a lot now of how wonderful you were to her in her trouble . . .

My mother stopped reading. She stared ahead of her and I knew she was too emotional to go on.

She said: 'It is terrible, Angel. You know the story now. We were on the ship together going to Australia when I heard she was going to have Jonnie. She was so distressed. She was going to throw herself overboard, but Matthew saved her. He is a very good man. But he has allowed his father-in-law to lead him in every way. Only what can he do? Peter made him. He would never have got far without him. He cared about people. Those books of his show that. But no one would have taken any notice of them if Peter hadn't thrust them forward. Matthew knows that and he's ashamed in a way . . . and yet he is bound to Peter. He couldn't do a thing without him . . .'

She was talking as though to herself. Then suddenly she

remembered my youth, as people often did. I had developed a way of lapsing into silence when people talked like that so they forgot how young I was and said more than they would if they remembered it. I had learned a good deal that way.

She stopped abruptly.

'I think,' she said, 'that we ought to go up. We might be able to help. I'm afraid it won't be a very happy visit. Poor Helena. She is like Amaryllis. She needs to be cared for. And all that business of John Milward's being brought up again must have been very upsetting for her.'

'I think Jonnie must have been a little pleased. His real father remembered him and he had such plans for his diggings. The money would have been a great help in that and now . . .'

The knowledge that I should never see him again enveloped me and I felt the tears in my eyes.

My mother put her arms round me and we wept together.

'Yes,' she said at length. 'We must go up. We must be able to comfort them a little.'

My father said that, although he would be unable to accompany us to London, my mother and I must go.

There were high hopes now that Sebastopol would fall. Surely they could not hold out much longer? People were full of hope and then these hopes would be dashed and we would seem no nearer to the end.

When the Emperor of Russia died there had seemed to be a chance of peace, but like all hopes this evaporated. That had been early in the year.

We had had the news of Jonnie's death late in August and just as we were ready to leave the Russians evacuated Sebastopol.

There was great rejoicing in the Poldoreys, for this could only mean that the war was virtually over.

It was too late for us, my mother said. Jonnie had already died.

That was an unhappy visit. My mother went to stay with Helena at their house in Westminster. I remained with Aunt Amaryllis and Uncle Peter. When Frances and Peterkin came

114

they talked to me of their houses of refuge in the East End of London. They now had several of these.

'We have always been greatly helped by my father-in-law,' Frances said. 'He always likes it to be announced when he gives a donation and we all know it is for the glorification of Peter Lansdon. He would have had a title by now, I am sure, if his business was not so disreputable; but I think he hopes to override this difficulty in time.'

Peterkin said: 'My father is a man who always overrides *all* difficulties.'

'Of course we received the money most gratefully,' went on Frances. 'To me it seems unimportant where it comes from as long as it is put to good use. I have had three more soup kitchens this year through his bounty. So who am I to complain?'

'The money comes from the pockets of the rich who squander it at my father's clubs,' said Peterkin. 'It is fitting that it should be used for the benefit of the poor – some of it, anyway.'

'It is good of Uncle Peter to give it,' I said.

'It is very good for us . . . and Uncle Peter,' added Frances.

'It seems to me,' I replied reflectively, 'that it is not always easy to tell what is good or bad.'

'I can see young Angelet is going to be a wise woman,' said Frances.

When I visited the Mission she put me to work. I ladled soup out of the great tureens for the people who lined up for it in the kitchens. I was deeply touched by the experience and very sorry for the people who came to be fed . . . particularly the children.

During that time I met poor women who had been ill-treated by husbands or male acquaintances; I saw women about to give birth and having no place to go. I watched Frances deal with them; she was brisk and without sentimentality; she rarely expressed pity; but she always solved their problems.

Peterkin was with her in everything she did, but she was the leading spirit. He adored her; but he was more easily affected than she was; and somehow this made him less effective.

I thought how strange it was that Uncle Peter should have a son like Peterkin. I think he must have had a great respect for Frances, although he always spoke of her with a hint of cynicism.

115

She saw right through him and Uncle Peter was the sort of man who would respect her for that.

That was necessarily a melancholy visit and I was relieved when we returned home. There was nothing we could do to disperse the gloom.

Time, I hoped, would help to do that.

People were right about the fall of Sebastopol. It did virtually put an end to the war although it dragged on in a desultory way until the end of the year, when peace negotiations were started. These seemed to go on and on. The winter passed. March was with us before the Peace of Paris was signed and the forces started to leave the Crimea.

Aunt Amaryllis wrote again:

Helena seems to have recovered a little. Matthew is so good and kind to her. He has been a wonderful husband. Of course he has no post in Palmerston's government, but Peter says Palmerston won't stay. He was popular during the war but people do get tired of war and he expects Derby to be back in the not too distant future and then Matthew's chances will be high . . .

There was a great deal of celebration and rejoicing when the treaty was signed. Now we are awaiting the return of the soldiers . . . only Jonnie won't be among them. Some of them are already home. Poor souls, how they have suffered. I don't think people will be shouting in the streets for war for a long time. They are saying that we lost twenty-four thousand and the Russians five hundred thousand and the French sixty-three . . . So we came off best. And poor Jonnie was one of the twenty-four thousand. How dreadfully sad it all is! I wish they would settle their differences in some way other than killing people who have really nothing to do with it and perhaps do not even know what it is all about.

They say that some of the nurses are remaining in Scutari till the last of the soldiers have left. Then they will come home. Some of them have come back. There are some terrible

116

cases and the nurses came with them . . . to nurse them on the way. I wonder what happened to that nice girl, Grace. What a wonderful job she has done!

We are all hoping that we shall see you soon. You know how we love to have you. There are special times when families should be together. Now that I am getting older I find these times very frequent.

So do come soon.

'We must go again,' said my mother. 'I always used to enjoy those visits to London so much. Last time, of course, it was very sad . . . but Helena must grow away from her grief.'

So once again we found ourselves in London.

This was the year of peace and I was fourteen years of age and rather grown up for my years. I think events of the last few years had brought me right out of my childhood – although perhaps I had emerged from that after my terrifying encounter at the pool.

Strangely enough, because of all that had been happening that event now seemed remote; there were occasions when I did not think of it for weeks. So there was some good in everything.

It was September, a lovely time of the year, unexpectedly warm during the days with a tang of autumn in the early evenings and the leaves in the square and the parks turning golden brown.

Opposite the house in the square was a garden which was for the use of residents. There was a key which hung in the hall; I could at any time take this key and go over there and sit among the flowering shrubs and trees. Although there would have been an outcry if I had gone into the Park alone I was permitted to go into this garden.

I loved to be independent of everyone and it was a favourite spot for me during my stay in the house in the square. In fact they had begun to call it Angelet's garden.

I used to sit there and listen to the clop-clop of horses' hoofs as the carriages passed through the square and occasionally scraps of conversation floated to me as people passed by, which

117

I found intriguing. I would imagine how those conversations went on after they had passed out of earshot and what the lives of the people who were making them were like.

It was what my mother would call exercising that over-worked imagination of mine.

One day when I was seated near the bed of asters and chrysanthemums, I saw someone standing outside the railings which enclosed the square.

It was a woman. I could not see her face, for she was in shadow. I did not look intently – people often gazed in at the gardens as they passed – and when I looked again she was gone. I wondered why I had noticed her. Perhaps it was because she seemed to linger. It was as though there was something purposeful about her.

The next day I saw her again. She came to the railings and looked in. I was sure at that moment that she had some special interest in the place.

'Hello,' I cried and went to the railings.

I stared in amazement. It was Grace.

'Grace!' I cried.

'Oh Angelet, I've seen you once or twice in these gardens.'

'Why didn't you speak? Why didn't you come to the house?'

'I . . . I didn't know . . . till I saw you . . . that you would be in London.'

'What are you doing here? When did you come home? Oh, Grace, you must have had some strange adventures.'

'Yes, I have. I want to talk to you.'

'Come to the house. Wait a minute. I'll come out.'

'No . . .' she said. 'Can I come into this garden? I'd like to talk to you alone . . . first.'

'Of course. Wait a moment.'

I unlocked the door and she came into the garden.

'Oh, Grace,' I cried, 'it's good to see you. We've talked about you so much. You've heard . . . about Jonnie?'

'Yes,' she said faintly. 'I know.'

'It was terrible. We are getting over it a little now . . . but we don't forget. How could we forget Jonnie?'

'No . . . we could never forget him.'

118

'It is so awful to think we shall never see him again.'

'Yes . . . I feel that too. There is a lot I have to tell you, Angelet. I wanted to talk to you . . . or your mother . . . first . . . before I did to anyone else. I am not sure what I should do. I want you to let me know what you think.'

'I? What can I tell you?'

'You're there.' She waved her hands towards the house. 'You'd know how things are. You'd know how they feel about . . .'

'About what?'

'I think I had better tell you from the beginning. You know we left London Bridge on that day . . .'

'Yes, yes.'

'We went to Boulogne and then to Paris. They made much of us in Paris. It was their war as well as ours. Then we went down to Marseilles where we stayed a while to collect stores. After that we set sail on the *Vectis* for Scutari. It was a fearful journey. I thought we were all going to be drowned.'

She paused. I watched her face. I was wondering why she had to tell me all this before she told the rest of the family.

'What was Scutari like?' I prompted.

'Unbelievable. It was dusk when we arrived and it looked so romantic . . . the hospital was like a Moorish palace. That was at dusk. In the light of day we saw it for what it was. The wards were very, very dirty. We had to clean up the place before we did anything else. Miss Nightingale insisted on that. The state of the patients . . . the lack of materials . . .'

I fancied she was holding something back which embarrassed her, and for that reason she found it difficult to talk of the matter which was uppermost in her mind.

'The hospital was very big; it had once been very grand. The mosaic tiles must have been beautiful at one time but they were cracked and many of them broken. The place was damp. Everything was dirty. Dirt . . . dirt everywhere . . . and there were so many sick men . . . row after row of beds. I felt desperately inadequate.'

'That was why you went . . . because they needed you so

119

badly. Mr Russell told us all about it. They must have been pleased to see you.'

'The authorities were sceptical of us at first. They just thought of us as a pack of useless women . . . but Miss Nightingale soon made them change their minds.'

'Grace, what is it you want to tell me?'

She was silent for a while, staring ahead of her at the bronze-coloured flowers, her mouth tight, her eyes almost appealing.

She said: 'Jonnie . . . was brought in. It was an amazing coincidence.'

'You mean . . . wounded? Was it such a coincidence? You were there and he was there and the wounded would be brought in for you to nurse.'

'He wasn't in my section. I happened to walk through the ward and see him. He looked so ill. I just went and knelt by his bed. I shall never forget his face when he saw me. I believe he thought he was dreaming. He was wounded in the leg. It was rather bad and they were afraid of gangrene.'

'It must have been wonderful for you to have found each other.'

'Oh, it was, it was. I asked if I could be moved to that part of the hospital where he was. One of the women changed places with me. It had happened before when someone was brought in who knew one of the nurses. So I looked after him. I had always . . . been fond of Jonnie.'

'And he was fond of you,' I told her.

'Yes, we had a great deal in common. I was with him every day. He used to look for me. I was so moved to see his face light up when I came. I nursed him. They had to take a bullet out of his leg and I was there when they did it. They had very little to kill the pain. That sort of thing is heart-rending. He held my hand while they did it. Then . . . afterwards . . . I nursed him and he began to recover. If his recovery had been longer he might not have died.' She bit her lips and seemed unable to continue.

Then she turned to me and pressed my hand. 'I had him walking again soon. They needed men. He had a few days' leave and then was to join the men outside Sebastopol. When you are in that position . . . when you feel you are facing death and the chances are that you can't be lucky twice . . . a kind of desperation gets hold of you. It might have been like that with Jonnie. Perhaps I ought to have realized it, but I was fond of him, Angelet, very fond. I loved him, Angelet. We had this little time together. I got leave and we went out together. There was little on our side of the Bosphorus and they took us back and forth to Constantinople on the other side in little boats they called *caïques* . . . and we dined in the city. We were reckless . . . like two people who know they have not long to be together. Constantinople is different from any place I have ever seen. There are two cities really – Christian Constantinople and Stamboul. Bridges connect them and if ever the nurses went out – which they did occasionally in parties – they were warned not to cross the bridges into Stamboul. I was not afraid of anything with Jonnie. It was a wonderful evening. We sat in an alcove in this restaurant which he knew of and we ate exotic foods – caviar and meat stuffed with peppers. It was all very strange and foreign. But I did not notice the food. We talked and talked . . . not of the war, not of the hospital, but of the future and what we should do when we were home again. He wanted to go to Italy. He was fascinated by the site at Pompeii and he talked as though I should be with him. Then suddenly he took my hand and said, "Will you marry me?"'

I drew breath sharply. Somewhere in my dreams I had thought of marrying Jonnie. Then I had thought of marrying Ben, it was true. But I went back to Jonnie after Ben had gone to Australia.

'I said I would,' she went on. 'It's easy there, Angelet. There is no formality. You have to pay them well and you can get a priest to marry you. It is probably some unfrocked priest from England . . . I don't know. But he married us . . . and that was what we both wanted. We spent three days together . . . and then I went back to the hospital and he went to Sebastopol. That is my story, Angelet. You know the rest. He never came back.'

'So you . . . you are Jonnie's wife?'

She nodded. 'What do you think they will say, Angelet?' she asked anxiously. 'They might not . . . accept me.'

121

'What do you mean? You are Jonnie's wife. Therefore they must.'

'I am afraid they will say it is no true marriage.'

'How can they? Don't they have certificates? Do you?'

'I have one, but, as I say, it was different from the way it is done here. We knew of this priest. He had married one or two other people. It might be that they won't accept it. They could raise all sorts of objections . . . if they wanted to.'

'They wouldn't do that. Why should they?'

'Angelet, you must see. Jonnie belongs to a different family from mine. I worked for your mother.'

'What has that to do with it?'

'They might say . . . everything.'

'I don't see how they can if you are married with a certificate to prove it.'

'If they wanted to disprove it . . .'

'They are good, kind people. Jonnie loved you and married you. We all knew that he liked you very much. That was obvious. So they wouldn't be very surprised. You were both out there. It seems natural to me.'

'I wouldn't want to embarrass them. I wouldn't want to be there . . . if they didn't want me.'

'But you are Jonnie's *wife*!'

'Yes,' she agreed.

'I am going to tell them right away . . . and you are coming with me.'

She drew back. 'No . . . no. Let me wait here. You go and tell them. But if they think it is no true marriage I will say goodbye to you . . . to you all . . .'

'My mother would never allow that. She is always saying how she misses you.'

'She made me so happy . . . you all have.'

'I shall go right away. Promise me you won't leave this garden, Grace.'

'I promise. If you don't come back in, say, half an hour, I shall know they do not believe me . . . they do not accept me. I shall understand.'

'You are being foolish, Grace, and I always thought you were so clever.'

I came out of the gardens and ran across the road.

Aunt Amaryllis was in the little room where she did the flowers, a vase of water before her and the flowers lying at the side of the sink.

'Aunt Amaryllis,' I cried. 'Grace is in the gardens. She has married Jonnie.'

Aunt Amaryllis turned pale and then pink. She dropped the scissors and wiped her hands.

'Come,' I said. 'I will take you to her.'

I was glad that they welcomed her so warmly. Jonnie's widow would have a very special place in the household.

Aunt Amaryllis was almost happy. Helena came and listened sadly to Grace's story.

'My dear,' she said, 'you made him happy before he died.'

'Yes, we were very happy,' Grace told them.

'I'm glad,' said Helena.

I wondered what Uncle Peter thought. He seemed to like Grace but he was suspicious by nature. He asked a lot of questions and I fancied that in his mind he was making notes of details which he would later verify. But even he had been deeply affected by Jonnie's death and was pleased to see that Grace's coming and her announcement had lifted the spirits of Helena and Amaryllis. He may even have felt a twinge of conscience because he had been rather pleased with what Jonnie's going to war had done for Matthew.

The rest of that visit was dominated by Grace's return to the household.

Of course Jonnie had been rather a rich young man. He had left no will but his widow would not be penniless. She said that she would be happy to leave everything in Uncle Peter's capable hands.

I don't know what arrangements were made or how much money Lord John had left to Jonnie. There was no doubt that Uncle Peter had made enquiries as to the validity of the marriage and he must have been satisfied, for Grace now became an independent woman with her own income.

Helena wanted her to live with them until she made plans. She said: 'I always wanted a daughter and that is what you will be to me now. I have lost my son but I have a daughter.'

Everyone seemed satisfied at the outcome; and there was a certain contentment about Grace. She was happy to be in Jonnie's home.

The London Season

I had reached my seventeenth birthday. Life had slipped back into its more or less uneventful groove now that the war was over and the loss of Jonnie was a sad memory rather than a bitter pain to the family.

Without those harrowing despatches from the Crimea the Press seemed full of trivialities for a while, and then came the Indian Mutiny which was even more shocking than the war. There were terrible accounts of how our people had been treated, mutilated and brutally murdered . . . those who had been friendly servants suddenly turning against men and women and children. The fate of the women was stressed; they had been raped and submitted to horrible indignities. My imagination went beyond that moment when I had heard Ben's voice calling my name. I kept thinking: Suppose he had not come in time.

I believed then that never, as long as I lived, should I be able to forget that nightmare.

Nobody was quite sure why there had been a mutiny. Some said it was because the sepoys had believed that their cartridges were greased with the fat of beef and pork which rendered them unclean in their eyes; others said they were in revolt against the East India Company. The general belief was that the Indians feared that we were imposing our civilization upon them. We were in possession of the Punjab and Oude, and they may have thought that we intended to take over the whole of India. The sepoys had learned the art of battle from us . . . and now they turned it against us.

The whole country was shocked. People argued fiercely about what should be done . . . blaming this side and that as they always do from the safe haven far from the scene of strife.

There was great excitement when Lucknow was relieved and the garrison there saved.

Uncle Peter said that good had come out of it, for now the administration of India was to pass from the East India Company to the Crown.

We had paid several visits to London. Grace was now installed in a house of her own. It was quite small, not very far from the house in the square. It was tall and narrow with four storeys and two rooms on each floor. It had been bought from the money Lord John had left Jonnie; and Grace was allotted an income. It had all been amicably arranged by Uncle Peter.

We saw Grace frequently when we were in London. I sensed that she was not happy and I supposed that that was inevitable. She had lost Jonnie just as they were about to embark on a new life together.

She confided in me a little. She said that Helena was very kind to her and so were Matthew and Geoffrey, but she felt that her presence reminded them of their loss and she hesitated to visit them as often as she would have liked.

I told her that was nonsense. They would love to see her often. She was a consolation for their loss.

She replied that she felt even less inclined to go to the house in the square. Aunt Amaryllis was very kind to her but she felt that Uncle Peter entertained some suspicions still, although she knew that he had made enquiries about the validity of her marriage. She was very relieved that he must have satisfied himself that she was truly married to Jonnie, because he had made all the necessary monetary arrangements.

'Of course I understand all that,' said Grace. 'I came to you and you helped me but I never forget that I was a kind of upper servant. Then I was received here . . . through the kindness of your mother. But I sometimes feel that Peter Lansdon does not entirely accept me. He has arranged the money, of course, but I am not allowed to touch the capital. I get my income. I have this house . . . Sometimes I feel he is keeping everything in his hands . . . until he proves something.'

'You mustn't think like that. He is a very wily businessman. He suspects everyone and everything. It's second nature to him.

You mustn't mind his being cautious, Grace. He can't help it.'

'No, I suppose not. I wish I could entertain people. If Jonnie had lived I would have helped him in his work. I would have had all the influential people here.'

'I don't think archæology is like politics. It's not a matter of meeting people but of finding out things.'

'I suppose you are right. I think perhaps I feel a little idle. Do you know, now and then I almost wish I were back in Scutari . . . that hospital . . . among all the horror. There was always plenty to do there . . . and Jonnie was alive.'

'I understand, Grace,' I said. 'You must come down and stay with us for a while. My mother would be pleased.'

She did visit us; and when she was at Cador she insisted on making a dress for my mother and doing little bits of sewing for me.

Morwenna Pencarron came often to Cador and we visited her family in the house near the mine. It was rather a grand house. It had been an old manor and the Pencarrons had spent a lot of money on restoring it. The gardens were wonderful. The Pencarrons were quite homely people. Josiah Pencarron had been extremely successful with the mine he had owned before he came to this one. He was the complete businessman. He thought business and talked it constantly; he was the sort of man who would be certain to succeed.

At the same time he was a loving father and husband; and great care was lavished on Morwenna, an only child. He used to say: 'I want the best for my girl.'

And so I had come to my seventeenth birthday. I knew, of course, what that entailed.

'You'll have to have a season,' said my mother. 'Both your father and I are agreed on that. You can't stay down here. You're growing up. We're lucky to have family in London. That will help a lot. Aunt Amaryllis knows the ropes. She brought Helena out. And Helena will of course help.'

'That was a long time ago. I expect it has all changed now.'

'Oh, not so much as all that. Anyway we shall find out.'

'I hope you won't expect me to walk off with the catch of the season.'

'My dear child, your father and I want you to be happy, that's all.'

127

'I heard Helena say she hated every minute of it.'

'Well, Helena's a very retiring sort of girl. You are not like that.'

'You didn't have a season, Mama?'

'No. Because I went to Australia with my parents . . . and you know what happened there. Afterwards it seemed unnecessary.'

I smiled apologetically. I knew she was reminded of the death of her parents. It was the last thing I wanted to do.

I said: 'Well, I suppose I shall find it amusing.'

'You will. You will enjoy it. And if nothing comes of it . . .'

'You mean if I don't find a rich and handsome husband?'

'Angel!'

'Well, that is what it is all about, isn't it?'

'My dear child, it gives you an opportunity to meet people. I know some girls suffer torments. They fear they will prove unattractive and nothing is more likely to make them so than that. I want you to go into all this in a carefree way. I've talked about it with your father. We certainly don't want you to feel you are up for auction. Just enjoy the parties and if by chance you meet someone whom you think you can love, we shall be delighted. But don't let it worry you. It will just give you a chance to go to places and meet all sorts of people. Whatever happens we have each other, haven't we? You've always been happy at home.'

I put my arms round her and kissed her.

'I am sure Aunt Amaryllis meant that with Helena, but I suppose she didn't tell her. And I think Uncle Peter might have expected a good deal. I am lucky to have you and Papa.'

'I think we are lucky too. Your father thinks Jack will do a good job at Cador when the time comes.'

'Oh heavens . . . that's years and years away.'

'Yes, please God. But what I want you to know is that we are here . . . as long as you want us . . . no matter what.'

I had an impulse to tell her then of that incident which now seemed so long ago. I wondered what her reaction would be. It was almost irresistible . . . but not quite. She would be disturbed, worried. It would make me different in her eyes – not her innocent daughter any more. I could not do it. I did not

128

want to disturb her. She was so happy in her cosy family cocoon. I could not spoil it with the grisly tale. So I said nothing.

Grace was very interested to hear of my proposed season.

'I hope I shall be able to take part in it,' she said.

'My dear Grace,' replied my mother, 'everything will be taken care of.'

Grace's face fell and my mother went on quickly. 'Oh, I am sure you will be most useful. You have a style . . . an elegance . . . You could advise about clothes. Of course there are court dressmakers and people like that.'

'I understand,' said Grace. 'But I should like to help if there is anything I can do. I get rather lonely and it would be so exciting.'

'There will be a great deal of preparation,' said my mother.

'I am sure you are going to enjoy it,' said Grace.

I was not so sure, but I promised myself that I would not attempt to look for a rich husband. I would make a turn-about of the whole procedure; and instead of being up for auction, I should inspect the gentlemen and if I did not like them, be they marquesses or dukes, I would refuse them. I laughed at myself. As Mrs Penlock would say, 'Opportunity would be a fine thing.'

But one could not enter into such an undertaking without thinking rather seriously about marriage. I remembered the two passions of my younger life: Jonnie and Ben. This was different. Those had been childish fancies. I had seen them both as heroes. I did not think that Ben was quite that. Jonnie might have proved to be one, and he would always remain one in my eyes because he had died before his claim to the title could be disproved. And in any case, I dramatically told myself, he had become another woman's husband.

Grace and I rode over to the Pencarrons.

'What a lovely old house this is,' she said.

'Oh yes,' I replied. 'The Pencarrons have done wonders with it. My father said it was almost a ruin when they took over. They call it Pencarron Manor now and the mine is Pencarron Mine.'

'They must be very rich.'

129

'I suppose so. I believe the mine is very profitable and my father said Josiah Pencarron has other interests in the Duchy.'

Morwenna came running out to meet us.

She had grown a little plump and she had the rosy complexion of a country girl and little confidence in herself. I could never imagine why. She had a kindly nature and her parents were devoted to her – especially her father. I should have thought his almost besotted devotion might have made her quite conceited.

Mrs Pencarron once told me that it had been a great disappointment to him that they had no son . . . until the day when Morwenna was born.

'She came rather late,' she said. 'I'd thought I was too old to get a child. But she is all the more precious for that. Father said he wouldn't change her for twenty boys.'

Morwenna was delighted to see Grace. She liked her. But then Morwenna liked everybody.

We went into the hall. It was essentially Tudor with enormous oak beams supporting the vaulted ceiling. The linenfold panelling on the walls had been painstakingly restored at great cost.

The staircase at one end of the hall had carved banisters decorated with the Tudor rose. There were arms on the wall . . . but of course not the Pencarrons'.

Josiah had imitated one or two features of Cador, and we were amused by this – and flattered.

He was ostentatiously gratified by his rise in life, and although he would have greatly liked to have been born into the gentry he was proud that, by his wits and good sense, he had been able to live like one of them.

My father said it was most commendable for a man to have come so far; he had the greatest respect for him.

In fact, there was something very likeable about all the Pencarrons.

Luncheon was served in the dining-room which they used for a few guests; if there was a large company they would eat in the great hall – according to the old custom. But for this occasion it was, of course, the dining-room – a beautifully proportioned

130

room with high ceiling and wall tapestries which Josiah had bought with the house.

Conversation turned to my coming out.

'I shall go up to London,' I told them, 'and be put through my paces. I believe one has to learn how to curtsy and walk backwards. There is a great deal to learn and I don't know how long one is with Her Majesty. A matter of seconds, I suppose. You curtsy . . . and that is it. You pass on and it is "Next, please". And for all that you have to have a special court dress and feathers and learn how to keep them steady and how to smile in the most genteel manner. You must not lose your balance when you curtsy. In fact, you must not make one mistake. Well . . . there wouldn't be much time to, I suppose.'

'So you are to be presented to the Queen!' said Mrs Pencarron in an awed voice. 'My word, that's something to be proud of.'

'I'm not sure how I feel about it.'

'Oh, go on with you,' said Mrs Pencarron. 'I reckon it's a great honour, wouldn't you, Jos?'

'I would that,' replied Josiah. 'And that's what's going to happen to you. Well, I never.'

They were interested to hear more about it. I told them all I knew, which was not much, but they kept plying me with questions.

Josiah was looking at his daughter with loving pride.

'What do you say, Mother? I reckon our Morwenna would look a real treat in a court dress and feathers.'

Grace said: 'I believe it is quite a sight to see all the carriages lined up in the street on their way to the Palace. Who will present you, Angelet?'

'I think it will probably be Helena. She has already been presented so she knows how to go on, and then of course she is the wife of a prominent member of Parliament . . . and the mother of a hero . . .' My voice faltered a little as it always did when I mentioned Jonnie.

'I reckon it has to be someone like that,' said Mrs Pencarron regretfully.

'It doesn't have to be a relation,' said Grace. 'Of course it's a costly matter . . . but they seem to think it is what every girl needs to launch her into society.'

'I'd like to see our Morwenna there.'

'Oh no, Pa,' said Morwenna quickly. 'It wouldn't do for me.'

'And why not indeed?' Josiah was the important businessman suddenly, bristling at the notion that there was something his little girl was not good enough to take part in.

'Do you really mean . . .' began Grace. 'Do you really mean that you would like Morwenna to be presented at court?'

'Would that be allowed?' asked Mrs Pencarron.

Grace smiled. 'I shouldn't think there would be any difficulty. You are doing good work down here . . . employing large numbers of men. You don't have to be related to the presenter. I can see no reason why, if you wanted it, Morwenna and Angelet should not be presented together.'

Grace was looking at me and I was thinking what fun it would be to have Morwenna share in this ordeal with me. She was a very pleasant girl and I was fond of her. She might be a little dull; she always agreed with everything I said; but she was straightforward and reliable; and when people were as nice as Morwenna was, one should be prepared to put up with a little boredom.

'It would be lovely,' I said. 'We'd go into it together. Helena could take us both under her wing.'

Morwenna was looking alarmed.

'Well, I never did!' said Josiah.

'Would you like us to make enquiries?' I asked.

'I'd be that grateful. Think of it, Mother. Our little girl going to see the Queen.'

They talked of nothing else for the rest of the meal: what dresses would be needed; what we should have to learn to do.

'It will be fun,' I said, to cheer a worried Morwenna. 'We will do it together.'

'Then, of course, there is the season,' Grace reminded us.

'Balls and parties and things,' I added.

The Pencarron parents exchanged excited glances. I could see that they felt this was hardly within their scope.

'It will all be in London,' I said. 'I shall probably be staying

132

with Uncle Peter and Aunt Amaryllis. My mother will surely be there. I might stay at Helena's. Morwenna could be with me.'

Josiah could think of nothing to say to this glittering prospect and fell back on: 'Well, I never did.'

When we rode home, Grace said: 'The seed is sown. It wouldn't surprise me at all if Morwenna went with you to London.'

'I hope she does.'

'I can hardly think she will be the debutante of the season. The poor girl is a little gauche.'

'Well, she has lived her life in the country. I don't think she is as happy at the prospect as her parents are.'

'She has to do the hard work while they bask in the glory.'

'I'm not sure that it is such a good idea. I am not eager and Morwenna is far more retiring than I am.'

'Perhaps we shall hear no more of it.'

'I rather think we shall. Has it struck you that Josiah Pencarron is the sort of man who, once he has made up his mind he wants something, will make sure that he gets it? Well, I think that he has made up his mind that Morwenna is going to court.'

'We'll wait and see,' said Grace.

It was as I thought. The seed had been sown in the minds of the Pencarron parents. Their girl was going to become a real lady; she was going to have all the advantages which had been denied them; and Morwenna and I went to London to begin the gruelling process of moulding us into young ladies of the court.

We had lessons in dancing and deportment from Madame Duprey. We walked round the room carrying a small pile of books on our heads. 'Shoulders back. Draw yourself in below the waist. One foot in front of the other. No, not like that, Morwenna. Just slightly.' And then there was the dancing. Sometimes I took the male part, sometimes Morwenna. 'It is *nécessaire* to know where your partner should be at every second. That is better, Angelet. No no, Morwenna, to the right. To the right! *Ma foi*, you will disrupt the entire cotillion.'

133

Poor Morwenna! She did not take to it as easily as I did. She was in despair. 'I shall never be able to do it,' she said.

'Oh yes you will,' I assured her. 'It's easy. You just worry too much.'

I would go through the steps with her in our bedroom, for we shared one in Helena's house which was not as big as the one in the square.

Helena was very kind and sympathetic. I believed it brought back her own days when she had been put through her paces and had been, I fancied, rather like Morwenna.

'What I don't want to do is disappoint Pa and Mother,' said Morwenna. 'I am sure they are expecting me to marry a duke at least.'

'Dukes are sparse on the ground,' I told her. 'We'd be lucky to get an Hon. or a mere knight.'

I could joke about it because I did not have to worry. If nothing came of my entry into high society I would just go back to Cador and everything would be as it was before. My parents would not harry me into making a brilliant marriage. As for Morwenna: it was just that they wanted so much for her; but I told her again and again that what they wanted most was for her to be happy; and if her father knew how worried she was, he would stop the whole thing.

'I know,' she said. 'They are such darlings and so good to me always. It is just that I should like to make them proud.'

And so we went on. It was amazing how much practice had to go into the perfect curtsy. We would do it correctly one day and the next day it did not work. We were the despair of poor Madame Duprey, who, I suspected, was really plain Miss Dappry or something like that and had never been nearer to France than Folkestone. But the French had a reputation for elegance and so from necessity and the success of her career she must become one of them, if in name only.

Then we had our singing master, Signor Caldori, for girls must be able to sing and play the pianoforte. One did not need to be a Jenny Lind or Henriette Sontag, but one should be able to trill pleasantly.

We must have elocution lessons. These were particularly

difficult for Morwenna, who had a slight Cornish accent which had to be completely eliminated; we had to be able to talk freely without embarrassment on any subject which might be raised, and yet not to be over-bold or force our opinons on the company. One must never try to ape the men; one must preserve one's femininity in all eventualities.

Then, of course, there were the dressmakers and what seemed like endless consultations. Grace was very good and helpful; she often accompanied us to the dressmakers and even dared make a few suggestions there. Our court dresses were made by the most fashionable dressmaker. 'I don't want any expense to be spared,' was Josiah Pencarron's comment. 'Everything's to be of the best. I don't want my girl to go to the Queen looking any less well dressed than any of the others.'

So eventually we were on our way to the Queen's drawing-room in our court dresses, each with its train three or four yards long which seemed to take a mischievous delight in getting into awkward and even dangerous positions and tripping us up if we were not careful. Our hair had been specially dressed by the court hairdresser, with three white plumes arranged in it, and we fervently hoped these would stay in place until the ordeal was over; we had been stuffed into our corsets and so tightly laced that we became breathless. It was not so bad for me because I was fairly thin but it must have been agony for Morwenna. She endured it stoically as she did everything else.

And there we were in the carriage with Helena, among all the other carriages on their way to the Palace. People looked in on us – some laughing at us, some envious. There were children without shoes or stockings. I could not take my eyes from their red chilblained feet and I felt ashamed.

Helena pulled down the blinds of the carriage but that did not shut them out of my mind. I thought then of the wonderful work Frances and Peterkin were doing and that I might like to join them.

But then we had arrived.

Into the palace we went, and there was the Queen, a tiny figure, most elaborately dressed, diamonds glittering on her

135

person and jewelled tiara on her head. There could be no mistaking her. Small she might be, but I had never before seen a more regal air. Beside her was the Prince, formidable, severity in every line of his once-handsome face. He looked strained and tired; and I remembered how the press had attacked him during the recent war. They did not like him because he was a German and they were not fond of foreigners. No people ever were. The French had hated Marie Antoinette because she was an Austrian, I remembered.

I was there before Her Majesty. I was thankful that my curtsy would have won the approval of Madame Duprey herself. I kissed the plump little hand, glittering with jewels; I received the benign smile and I walked backwards with ease . . . and it was all over.

I felt I had been weighed in the balance and found not wanting.

I was now fit to mix in English society!

Our first ball! It was given by Lady Bellington, one of the leading London hostesses, for her daughter Jennifer. The Bellington residence was a mansion which had a small garden, beyond which was the Park.

Helena, with my mother, Aunt Amaryllis and Uncle Peter, accompanied us. My mother told me not to worry if I did not dance all the evening. If we were sitting out we should indulge in animated converation and give the impression that we were not in the least concerned about not being asked to dance. It was hard to imagine Morwenna engaged in animated conversation and this only added to her worries.

'No one will surely want to dance with me,' she declared. 'And if they did I should forget half the steps. I don't know which will be worse . . . having to dance or sit out.'

'All things come to an end,' I told her philosophically. 'Tomorrow it will be something in the past.'

I was quite looking forward to it. I loved dancing for one thing; and I did find it amusing to be among these people, to watch the ambitious mammas' eyes on the most eligible of the young men, calculating, trying hard to push forward their daughters without seeming to.

I exchanged glances with my mother; she knew what I was thinking, and I had said to myself: It doesn't matter. If I sit out the whole evening they love me just the same. I gave up a little prayer of thanksgiving for my parents.

At the top of the wide staircase Lord and Lady Bellington received us graciously, Jennifer beside them.

We passed on.

The music was playing. Two middle-aged gentlemen came up to us and asked us to dance. From Helena's description of her coming out days I guessed they were needy scions of good family who were given an evening's entertainment in exchange for services rendered to the unpreferred.

They whirled us round. I wondered how Morwenna was getting on. I thought she might find this a good baptism, for the middle-aged gentlemen would do their duty which would surely include being affable and helpful to a shy young woman.

In due course we returned to our party. We had broken the ice. We had danced.

A young man appeared. He bowed before us, his eyes on me.

'May I have the pleasure . . . ?'

I rose and put my hand in his; in a short time we were in the dance.

'Quite a crowd,' he said languidly.

'Yes.'

'It is always thus at Bellington affairs.'

'You attend them frequently?'

'Oh . . . now and then.'

We talked of the weather, the floor, the band and such matters, which I could not find of absorbing interest; but we danced and, thanks to Madame Duprey, I was able to give a good account of myself.

And then I saw a face which was vaguely familiar to me. For a second I could not think where I had seen it before. He was looking at me with a kind of awestruck recognition. Then I knew. He was the young man who had come down to Cador

137

with Jonnie to dig at the pool. I remembered his name: Gervaise Mandeville.

The dance led us away from each other but my thoughts had now turned from the band, the floor and the weather, and I was back in Cornwall. I was there at the pool, and it was all coming back to me, as it still did on such occasions, even now.

I was glad when I was returned to my party. Morwenna was still sitting out.

'Was that enjoyable?' asked Helena.

'He danced well,' I replied.

'I could see that,' said my mother. 'Madame Duprey was a very good teacher.'

He was there almost immediately.

'Mrs Lansdon . . . Mrs Hanson, you remember me? Gervaise Mandeville?'

'Oh!' cried my mother. 'Oh yes . . . you came down with . . .'

He understood. He did not want to raise painful subjects. 'Yes,' he said. 'For the dig. It was not very successful, I'm afraid. I came to ask Miss Hanson if she would care to dance.'

'This is Miss Pencarron,' I said. 'She is being brought out with me.'

He bowed, smiling pleasantly at Morwenna.

'She comes from Cornwall, too. We're neighbours,' said my mother.

Helena looked very sad. She, of course, remembered Gervaise as a friend of Jonnie's. Gervaise knew this. I was to discover that he was very sensitive to the feelings of others.

He held out his hand to me. 'Shall we dance?' And we were away.

'I couldn't believe my eyes,' he said. 'At first I wasn't sure. It's a long time ago. You've grown up since then.'

'You too are older.'

'An inevitable process, I'm afraid.'

'But you haven't changed much.'

'Nor have you . . . now that I am seeing you at close quarters.'

He smiled at me, very friendly and with a hint of admiration in his face. I felt my spirits rising and the faint depression, which memory had brought, was fading.

138

'You have grown taller,' I said.

'And so have you.'

'Well, you would expect that, wouldn't you? I was about thirteen years old, I think.'

'Time passes. I liked that little girl very much. I am sure I am going to like the grown version as well . . . perhaps even better.'

'Don't make rash judgements.'

'Somehow I think this is going to be one of my more sober ones. It will be rather fun to find out if I am right.'

'Tell me about yourself. Are you still digging?'

'No. I don't think I have the aptitude for that kind of work.'

'You seemed enthusiastic.'

'Oh, that was special . . . that eerie pool and all the talk about those bells. By the way, have the bells been heard again?'

'Not recently. I used to think that people fancied they heard, but when I thought I did myself . . .'

'It's a good story. I was awfully sorry about . . .'

'Jonnie?'

He nodded. 'I'm afraid seeing me must have brought it back.'

'Well, I suppose it has to be brought back every now and then . . . but it isn't as bad as it was in the beginning.'

'Poor old Jonnie. He was made for martyrdom.'

'You did not go to the war, I suppose?'

'Not much in my line. I'm not the heroic type.'

'I often wonder what good it did in the end.'

'Ah, that's the question. But at the time it seemed the right thing to do.'

'Do you remember Miss Gilmore . . . Grace Gilmore?'

'Oh yes, I do. She was a rather striking lady, as far as I remember.'

'She married Jonnie.'

'Did she really?'

'Yes, she went out as one of Miss Nightingale's nurses. They found each other out there and were married. She is here in London now. We see a great deal of her now she is a member of the family.'

'I thought she was a most unusual person.'

139

'Yes, I suppose she is.'

'Tell me about yourself.'

'There's little to tell. You know what it is like at Cador. Well, that is my life, with occasional visits to London.'

'Where are you staying now?'

'With Aunt Helena . . . Jonnie's mother. She's bringing me out.'

'I see.'

'Are you often invited to occasions like this?'

'Frequently. They have to keep up the quota of young men to provide partners and escorts for the debutantes, and if one is not too old, maimed, or in any way afflicted, and one's family is up to a certain level in the social scale . . . one is invited. The sexes must be evenly balanced – so here I am.'

'And do you enjoy the role?'

'I am enjoying it immensely at this moment.'

'It is pleasant to renew old acquaintances.'

'Well, not always. Sometimes it can be alarming. Just imagine being confronted by one of the skeletons which have crept out of the cupboard.'

'Are there many in your cupboard?'

'It is inevitable that such a worthless character as I should collect a few. You, now . . . you have a life of virtue behind you. You are an innocent maiden just setting off on life's devious paths. That is different.'

I shivered faintly. It was inevitable that meeting him should revive old memories and his references to skeletons in the cupboard made me uneasy.

He did not notice and we had just passed our group. Morwenna was still sitting out and as she could not manage animated conversation was looking bored and uneasy.

I said: 'Will you do me a favour?'

'Even unto one half of my kingdom.'

'I shall not be as demanding as that. I want you to return me to my family and dance with Miss Pencarron.'

'Is that the young lady sitting there?'

'Yes. She is rather nervous. She is terrified that she is going to be a failure.'

140

'Which of course is the easiest way of becoming one.'

'I know. That's why I don't care.'

'You are asking a great deal.'

'Why? She is a charming girl, and she has been taught to dance. She won't tread on your toes . . . too much.'

'I would endure a stampede to please you. But you are still asking a great deal because I have to abandon the pleasure of your company, and I have a better idea. Leave this to me.'

As we went on dancing he was scanning the groups of people as we sped by. Suddenly he halted.

'Philip,' he called. 'Philip, this is Miss Hanson. What are you doing here standing partnerless? Is that the way to do your duty? Miss Hanson, this is Philip Martin.'

He bowed. 'Pleased to make your acquaintance.'

'Let's make a foursome for supper,' said Gervaise Mandeville. 'You go and dance with Miss Hanson's friend. She's very much in demand, so be quick. Let's hope she's free now. Come along, we'll take you over and introduce you.'

We went back to the group. 'Excellent,' said Gervaise. 'She's free.'

Philip Martin was introduced. He was a rather colourless young man, but he had a pleasant manner and all the usual clichés were exchanged.

He asked Morwenna to dance. There was a look of relief on Helena's face as they started off. Gervaise and I followed them into the dance.

I liked him for that. In fact I was liking him more and more with every minute. He had an ebullient personality, and a way of turning the most faintly amusing subject into a hilarious joke. He laughed a great deal; and when he was not laughing his eyes were alight with amusement.

I spent almost the whole evening with him.

We met Morwenna and Philip Martin in the supper room; we sat at a table for four, eating delicious cold salmon washed down with champagne. I could see that Morwenna was enjoying the ball and I was grateful to Gervaise for that; and there was a great deal of laughter at the table.

We arranged that we should all take a ride in the Row the

next day; and I was delighted that I was going to see Gervaise again so soon.

Riding home in the carriage we were rather subdued. I could see that they were all very pleased at the way in which the evening had gone.

I thought it was all thanks to Gervaise, who had certainly made it enjoyable for me . . . and for Morwenna. But for his timely introduction of Philip Martin Morwenna might have sat for the whole evening, uninvited except by the middle-aged gentlemen whose duty it was to ask the neglected for the occasional dance.

'He is a very charming young man,' said Helena of Gervaise.

'It was nice that we knew him,' commented my mother. 'It is always pleasant at such affairs to come upon people one knows. He's an archæologist, I believe.'

'He isn't now,' I said. 'He gave it up.'

'The parties and balls get more interesting as the season goes along,' said Helena. 'That is when you all get to know each other. At first quite a number are strangers to each other.'

'Gervaise Mandeville and Philip Martin are calling for us tomorrow,' I said. 'We are going riding in Rotten Row.'

I was well aware of the significant glances between our elders. This was how these affairs were supposed to go. I dare say there would be a great deal of discussion among our elders about Gervaise Mandeville and Philip Martin.

Morwenna and I were too excited to sleep. We lay in our beds and talked about the evening.

'I think Gervaise is very interested in you,' said Morwenna.

'Oh, it is just because he stayed at Cador once.'

'I think it is more than that.'

'He came down with Jonnie. They were digging together.'

'Yes. I know. By Branok Pool.'

Still the mention of the place made me feel as though I had been doused in cold water.

'That's why he picked me out,' I explained. 'He recognized me.'

'Well, he needn't have attached himself to you for the whole evening. He liked you. He liked you a lot. I could see that.'

'And Philip liked you.'

'I don't think so. He was just doing what he felt he had to. He told me Gervaise had given him a tip.'

'A tip?'

'Yes . . . advised him about some horse race and he won two hundred pounds. He said he was very grateful to Gervaise. I think that was why he was dancing with me, because Gervaise wanted him to. Did you ask him to?'

'What nonsense!' I lied. 'Really, Morwenna, you have to stop thinking like this. You get the notion that nobody wants you for yourself . . . and you make it so obvious that if you are not careful people will begin to think you are right.'

'You certainly don't think like that.'

'No, my dear Morwenna, I never think about it. If people like me, that's fine; if they don't . . . well, I won't like them either. We always like people who like us. I think it will be fun riding tomorrow. Gervaise is amusing, isn't he?'

'Yes,' said Morwenna.

'Are you sleepy? Good night.'

'Good night,' said Morwenna.

I could not sleep. It had been an exciting evening. I had loved the glitter, the ballroom, the splendid dresses, the flowers and meeting Gervaise. But over it all had been the shadow of the past. I could not think of Gervaise without seeing him digging at the pool and remembering the fears that had aroused in me.

I supposed it would always be like that.

My friendship with Gervaise grew apace. He visited the house frequently. We met at parties and he always arranged that we should be together there. Philip Martin had dropped out. I supposed he felt he had repaid his obligations to Gervaise for the 'tip'. So we were no longer a quartet. Poor Morwenna, she accepted her fate stoically. It was all working out just as she had expected it would.

I had made a pact with Gervaise that when we were at parties and dances, he would be sure that there was a partner for

Morwenna. He always did and I was grateful to him. He was very kind and gentle to her and provided the partners in the most tactful way, so that Morwenna did not guess she was being asked because he insisted that they should do so.

There was a ball given by Aunt Helena and Uncle Matthew, but it was held at the house in the square as there was an adequate ballroom there. Uncle Peter was present and several celebrated politicians, so it was quite an auspicious occasion.

It went off very well and by that time it seemed clear that the friendship between myself and Gervaise was progressing to something deeper.

Uncle Peter had, as he said, made discreet enquiries and discovered that Gervaise was the younger son of a rather illustrious family which claimed to have come over with the Conqueror, but could at least be traced to the fourteenth century. They had fallen on hard times, as had so many of the great families with mansions to keep up and a style of living from which it would be sacrilege to depart because it had been going on for centuries. Gervaise was by no means wealthy; there were two elder brothers and a sister. The estate was in Derbyshire. His father had married a rich heiress which had bolstered up the family fortunes for a few decades. Gervaise had charm, breeding, but a rather inadequate income.

My mother was not in the least perturbed about that. She said they were not fortune-hunting for their daughter. She thought Gervaise charming and she could see that I was becoming very fond of him.

On the rare days when I did not see him time seemed long. I missed the laughter and the light-hearted way of looking at life.

'You're lucky,' said Morwenna with ungrudging admiration. 'He is so amusing . . . but what I like best about him is that he is so kind. Are you going to marry him?'

'I'll have to wait to be asked.'

'I'm sure he will ask you.'

'Sometimes I am not sure. Has it struck you that, charming as he is, he is not really very serious?'

She was thoughtful. 'He makes everything seem amusing,

144

yes, but I think he could probably be serious about some things, and I think he is about you. He is always there. You see each other so frequently.'

'Yes,' I said slowly. And I knew I should be very unhappy if he regarded our relationship as something with which to amuse himself for a short time.

We suited each other. It amazed me how, when I was in his company, I responded to him. I was light-hearted, as he was . . . and everything seemed to be such fun. I had never felt quite so carefree since that incident at the pool. In the first place he had reminded me of it because of the fact that he had dug there with Jonnie. He reminded me of Jonnie, being interested in the same things – and yet with him I felt light-hearted. It was miraculous.

He was a great favourite with the family. My mother had written to my father; she wanted him to come up to London and stay awhile. I knew why. It was because she thought that my relationship with Gervaise was growing serious and she wanted him to inspect a possible son-in-law. They tried to be discreet but it was not difficult to see through their discretion.

The season progressed; more parties, more dinners, all of which I shared with Gervaise. We visited the opera; we shared a love of this; we heard the works of Donizetti and Bellini and a young composer, Giuseppe Verdi, whose music I enjoyed more than any. On one occasion the Queen was present. That was a gala event. I watched her, obviously enraptured by the music, now and then turning to the Prince beside her to make some comment.

This season, which I had anticipated with a certain amount of apprehension, was proving to be one of the most exciting and wonderful periods of my life. It was all due to Gervaise, of course.

He had been very interested to meet Grace again. He talked to her about Jonnie and how friendly they had been. Grace said it had been wonderful to be able to talk about Jonnie; she feared that to do so upset his mother a great deal and so his name was hardly ever mentioned. She found some relief in talking of him.

She wanted to hear the little anecdotes he had to tell of their friendship. He made them amusing and it was pleasant to hear them laughing together.

Grace told me that she thought he was one of the most charming men she had ever met and she was happy for me.

'How I wish,' she said, 'that Morwenna could find the same happiness.'

'Morwenna will be glad when the season is over,' I replied. 'But I don't think it has been as bad as she expected.'

'The good Gervaise has tried to provide her with escorts. He is a very thoughtful young man.'

I was pleased as I always was when people praised him.

I was certain now that he was going to ask me to marry him and I was equally certain that I was going to say yes.

It happened one day when we were in Kensington Gardens. It was rarely that we were completely alone together. Grace often accompanied us on our walks but on this day Morwenna had had to pay an unexpected visit to her dressmaker and Grace went with her. Gervaise was now accepted as a friend of the family; and so, since Grace was with Morwenna, there was no objection to my going for a walk with him.

We walked to the Round Pond and watched the children playing with their boats, and we strolled down the avenue of trees and sat for a while under them.

He said: 'I expect you know what I am going to say, Angelet. I think everyone knows I am going to say it some time. I was just trying to let a reasonable time elapse . . . though I don't see why I should. Why does one feel one must be conventional? If I ask you here I shan't have to go down on my knees . . . but I ask you with heartfelt humility, being fully aware of the honour you do me.'

I laughed and said; 'Oh, come to the point, Gervaise.'

'I hoped you'd say that. Will you?'

'I think you should be a little more explicit.'

'Marry me,' he said.

'But of course,' I replied.

He took my hand and kissed it.

'You are unlike anyone else I have ever known. You are

frank and honest. Almost any other girl would have hummed and hahed and said it was so sudden.'

'I could hardly say that. You have been a constant visitor to the house ever since the ball. We didn't think you came to study the architecture.'

'Did you not? Oh dear, I have betrayed myself. Was it so obvious?'

'I think it was. I hoped it was.'

'Oh, Angelet, how wise they were when they named you. You are indeed an angel.'

'Please don't endow me with saintly qualities. You will certainly be disappointed if you do.'

'Well, I never greatly cared for saints, but angels are another matter. This is wonderful. We shall make plans. An early wedding, don't you think? You'll have to meet the family. I've met yours, so that's something. We'll go down soon. They'll want to arrange things, I suppose. Let them. We'll just think of ourselves. Contemplate it, my darling. We shall be together for ever and ever.'

'For as long as we both shall live. I love that phrase. There's something so comforting about it.'

'It was rather miraculous, wasn't it . . . coming across you at the ball. Though our parths would have crossed some time or other, considering we were both in the same season.'

'And before I thought there was something rather unpleasant about these seasons. You know what I mean. Girls being paraded like that.'

He nodded. 'But people have to be brought together, I suppose, and I shall never quarrel with any system that brought me my Angelet.'

'Nor I with one which gave me you.'

'I love you, Angelet.'

'I was waiting to hear you say that.'

'Did you really want me to state the obvious?'

'I couldn't believe it until I heard it.'

'Now will *you* state what I *hope* is obvious?'

'I love you, Gervaise.'

'Then that is settled.'

147

'How strange that you should have come to Cador.'

'It was clearly Fate.'

'But then we did not see each other for all those years.'

'That was because you hadn't the sense to be older when we met. You had to grow up, and when the time was ripe Fate said, "Bring in the lovers . . ." and there we were at the Bellington ball.'

'So you believe in Fate.'

'I think we make our own.'

'Have you ever been in love before?'

He was silent.

'Confess,' I demanded.

'Must I?'

'Indeed you must. I must know the worst.'

'Well, when I was six years old I was in love with a little girl of eight. We used to go to dancing classes and she bullied me shamefully. My devotion was true and I was faithful to her for six weeks in spite of the brutal manner in which she treated me. She used to pinch my ears.'

'I mean seriously in love.'

'Never. Until now. And you?'

I hesitated.

'At one time I was very fond of Jonnie. And there was someone else.'

'Oh?'

'He was some sort of relation. He came down to Cador for a while to see if estate management would suit him as a career. His name was Benedict.'

'He sounds like a saint or a pope or at least a monk. Weren't they the ones who made that delicious liqueur? Tell me more of your Benedict.'

'He seemed very handsome and magnificent. I was about ten. I suppose one's judgement is not to be relied on at that age.'

'You sound as though this hero had feet of clay.'

'Oh no . . . no. I was ill and he went away and I never saw him again.'

'Then I can curb my jealousy regarding him. Were there others?'

148

I shook my head emphatically. He smiled at me and I thought: I am happy . . . happier than I ever thought I should be since . . .

We sat for a while on the seat watching the little boats on the water, discreetly holding hands.

'Shall we go back and tell them?' he asked.

'Yes,' I replied. 'I feel I want to tell everybody.'

'So do I.'

As we came out of the gardens a woman approached us. She was carrying a tray of violets.

'A bunch of vi'lets for the lady,' she said wheedlingly. 'Come on, young gentleman . . . I've got children at home and I've got to get rid of these 'ere before I go 'ome to them. Can't go back to little 'uns with nothing in me pocket, can I?'

Gervaise selected the biggest bunch. They were wilting slightly and I was very sorry for the woman who had this basket full of violets, past their first freshness, to sell before she went home to her family.

Gervaise gave the violets to me. He noticed my pity for the woman and I was sure he shared it. He put his hands in his pocket and pulled out a handful of coins. He put them on the woman's tray. She stared at them.

'Well, sir . . . well, me lord . . .' she began. ''ere you are. You bought the blooming lot.'

'Keep them. Sell them.'

'Gawd bless yer.'

'This is our lucky day,' he said.

'Well, bless you, sir, if it ain't mine, too.'

He put his arm through mine. I smelt the violets. They seemed very beautiful to me.

'That was a lot of money you gave her.'

'I had to. I was sorry for her.'

'Because of all those children?'

'Because she's not us. I am sorry for every man in London who is not engaged to marry Angelet.'

'You say the most delightful things.'

'They will become more delightful as the years pass.'

'I do hope so. Do you believe her story about going home to all those children?'

149

'No.'

'You didn't?'

'I expect it is what they call sales patter.'

'But you must have believed her . . . just for a moment. You gave her all that money.'

'I dare say she needs it more than I do.'

'Gervaise, I believed in those children.'

'You would, my dearest. You are good and pure and unsullied by the wicked ways of the world. To be honest, I don't care whether it was the truth or not. She'll be glad of the money. And I want everyone to be happy. Haven't you ever felt like that?'

'Yes.'

'When?'

'Now,' I said.

And we laughed as we walked back to the house.

They were all delighted with the news.

'I guessed it would happen sooner or later,' said my mother.

'Are you sure you love him?' asked my father.

'Rolf!' cried my mother. 'It is clear that she does.'

'He wants us to go to Derbyshire to meet his family,' I told them.

'I think that's an excellent idea,' said my mother.

'I do hope you are all going to like each other.'

'If the rest of the family are anything like him, we most certainly shall.'

It was arranged that he should take us to his home at the end of the following week. He was writing to his parents to tell them the news.

'I do hope they will be pleased,' I said to Gervaise.

'They'll be delighted,' he replied. 'For the last three years they've been saying I should marry and settle down. They think that will steady me.'

'Are you unsteady then?'

'Very much so. I hope you are prepared to take on the steadying process.'

Thinking of the visit, I was a little apprehensive. Everything had gone so smoothly so far. Could it continue to do so?

150

At the end of the week I went to the park for a walk with Morwenna and Grace. Grace was talking about my trousseau and she thought it would be a good idea if we looked round while we were in London.

'I could make some of your less important clothes,' she said. 'I'd love to. I'd come and stay at Cador for a time . . . if you'd have me.'

'You know we are always glad to have you.'

'I was not sure. The servants view me with some bewilderment because they don't know where to place me. Below stairs or above stairs. Married into the family . . . but not quite worthy of it.'

'Oh, no one takes any notice of that sort of nonsense,' I said.

'They do.'

'Well, if they do, just ignore it.'

'I know. It doesn't bother me really. Amuses me rather.'

We were seated on a bench. A man had passed by as we were talking. I fancied he paused for a while and looked at us rather intently. He went on for a few steps, then stopped and, turning, he came purposefully towards us.

He was looking straight at Grace. 'Good morning, Miss Burns. How nice to see you again,' he said.

Grace sat very still and then said slowly and very distinctly: 'I think you have made a mistake.'

'Oh? It *is* Miss Burns, isn't it? Miss Wilhelmina Burns?'

'N – no. There is no one of that name here.'

'I could have sworn . . .'

He kept his eyes on her face. He looked very puzzled.

'No,' said Grace firmly.

I said: 'This lady is Mrs Grace Hume.'

He took a few paces back, smiled and bowed. He said: 'Madam, you have a double. I do beg your pardon. If you could see Miss Burns you would understand the mistake.'

'It is all right,' said Grace. 'We understand.'

He stared at her for a few seconds as though marvelling. Then he turned and slowly walked away.

'I suppose we all have our doubles,' said Morwenna. 'After

151

all, when you consider we all have two eyes, a nose and a mouth
. . . you'd think a lot of us would look alike.'

'He seemed very insistent,' I commented. 'It was almost as
though he didn't believe we were telling the truth and you really
were that Miss Wilhelmina . . . what was it?'

'Burns,' said Morwenna. 'Yes, he really did seem as though
nothing would convince him that you weren't.'

Grace said quickly: 'Well, as you say, Morwenna, we must
all have a double somewhere.'

My mother received a letter from Lady Mandeville saying that
she and Sir Horace would be delighted if she, my father and
Miss Angelet Hanson would pay them a visit. She thought that
if they could possibly stay for two weeks that would give them
all a chance to know each other which, in the circumstances,
would be desirable.

My mother replied that we were all delighted to accept Lady
Mandeville's kind invitation to Mandeville Court.

I confessed to Gervaise that I suffered a few nervous qualms
at the prospect. They were bound to be hypercritical of
their prospective daughter-in-law. It was customary in these
cases.

'Oh, but they could not fail to be enchanted,' he assured me.
'They will say, "How on Earth did our son manage to secure
such a prize?"'

'I do not think that is the usual way in which parents regard
newcomers to the family.'

'Ordinary rules do not apply to us, surely?'

'Why not?'

'Because no other parent has ever been presented with such
a vision of delight.'

'You are absurd.'

'Generally, maybe. But on this occasion I am completely
sound and one hundred per cent logical.'

'It is comforting to know that you see me in such a light. I
fancy your parents will have a clearer and more penetrating
vision.'

152

'Seriously, Angelet, there is nothing to worry about. They haven't all that much of a high opinion of me. I am not the apple of the parental eyes, nor the hope of the family. They don't expect me to marry royalty. All they want is for me to "settle down".'

'You're a great comfort to me, Gervaise.'

'It's what I intend to be . . . in one of your favourite phrases, until death do us part.'

We were to leave for Derbyshire at the end of the week, and the days were spent in preparation for the visit. My mother, Grace and I, had discussions as to what clothes we would need. 'Something for the country,' said Grace, which I had not brought with me. We went to Jay's in Regent Street; and for the rest I had my evening clothes and riding habit.

'You fuss too much,' said Gervaise. 'We shall not be entertaining royalty while you are there.'

It was the day before we were to leave. I was doing some last-minute packing when Morwenna came into the room we shared.

She said: 'Grace has just come. We're going for a walk in the park. I thought you had finished your packing.'

'I have really.'

'Why don't you come with us?'

'I'd like to.'

'Come on. Get your cloak. I shall miss you very much, Angelet, when you go.'

'It's only for two weeks.'

'It is wonderful . . . you and Gervaise. You are so happy together and he is delightful. What I like about him so much is that although he is so amusing and sometimes cynical, he is so kind.'

'Yes,' I said. 'That is what I like about him.'

'You are so lucky,' she said wistfully.

'I know. I wish . . .' I did not finish but she knew I was about to say that I wished she could find someone like Gervaise. It was what she needed. Poor Morwenna. She had so convinced herself that no one could care for her that she became awkward and self-effacing in company. She would have loved to make a

153

grand marriage . . . not so much for herself but to please her parents.

'Come on,' she said. 'We're keeping Grace waiting.'

We went down together.

'Angelet has decided to come with us,' said Morwenna.

'Oh, I thought you would have too much to do,' said Grace.

'It's practically done. I'm all ready for the fray, and I thought I'd like a walk in the park.'

We were talking about the trip to Derbyshire and the coming parties which Morwenna would be attending without me – a prospect she did not relish – when a small boy, barefooted, ragged and unkempt, dashed up and almost knocked Morwenna over. She gave a little cry and put a hand to her side.

'My purse!' she cried. 'He's taken it from the pocket of my cloak.'

We were too stunned to do anything. For a few seconds we stood staring after the boy, who was running away with Morwenna's purse in his hands.

And then . . . a man appeared. He emerged suddenly from a clump of bushes near the path. He was about two yards ahead of the boy. The boy swerved, but he was too late and not sufficiently agile. The man had him in his grip.

He shook him and took the purse from him. Then he suddenly released the boy and gave him a push. The boy scampered off and the man, holding Morwenna's purse, came walking towards us.

He took off his hat and bowed. 'I saw what happened. I'm afraid I let him go. Poor creature, he looked half starved.'

He handed the purse to Morwenna. 'Yours, I believe.'

'Oh, thank you,' she said.

There was something familiar about the man. I had seen him before but for the moment could not think where. Then suddenly it came to me. He was the man who had approached us some little time ago because he thought Grace was someone else.

'Why, I do believe . . .' he said, smiling at Grace. 'Yes, of course, you are the lady who bears such a strong resemblance to a lady of my acquaintance.'

Grace smiled. 'I remember you,' she said. 'We saw you almost at this spot. It is a favourite walk of ours.'

'It is becoming one of mine.' He turned to Morwenna. 'I'm afraid that was rather a shock for you.'

'Oh yes,' she said. 'It was silly of me really . . . carrying a purse in that pocket.'

'These people are sharp. They are trained to it, you know. They can almost sniff out a stealable object. Why do we not sit down for a moment?' He indicated a seat.

He was smartly dressed in morning coat and top hat; he was young, the type of man we met in the London social circle.

'I hope you don't think this is indecorous,' he said. 'But perhaps in view of our little adventure . . .'

'I am so grateful to you,' said Morwenna. 'I am glad to have a chance to thank you. I hadn't much in the purse but it was worked by my mother, and I do value it for that reason.'

'These sentimental gifts cannot be replaced. This makes me doubly happy to have been of assistance.'

'It was so fortunate that you happened to be so near.'

He introduced himself. 'I am Justin Cartwright,' he said.

'Do you live near here?' I asked.

'I have been abroad,' he said. 'I have only recently returned home. I am staying in London . . . in a hotel at the moment. I am making plans.'

'That sounds very interesting,' said Morwenna.

He smiled at her. He seemed to be quite interested in her, for which I was glad; and she responded. She did not seem to be trying to shrink away. After all, it was her purse which had been stolen; and she could be said to be the centre of this adventure.

We chatted a little; and after a while he said he must not detain us further.

Morwenna thanked him again for his help and he left us.

'An interesting man,' said Grace.

'And very kind,' added Morwenna.

'I wonder what his business is and what he has been doing abroad,' I said.

'He was so quick after that boy,' went on Morwenna. 'And I

155

am glad he let him go. He said he looked so frightened and he was obviously very, very poor. It was kind of him. Most people would have made a fuss and there would have been a lot of trouble. Goodness knows what would have happened if that boy had been handed over to the law. I've been reading Matthew's book on prison reform. Some of the things which happened to those people are quite terrible.'

'They are criminals,' said Grace. 'And that boy would have made off with your purse. He will go on doing that sort of thing and will probably steal the purse of someone who depends on what is in it for his next meal.'

'Well, I didn't,' said Morwenna. 'And I am glad he let him go. He was touched by him and I think that shows a good nature.'

'Well,' said Grace, 'it is time we went back. It will teach you to be more careful in the future, Morwenna.'

Morwenna said it would; but I could see that she had quite enjoyed the encounter. The theft had been shocking, but the rescuer had been both courteous and attentive to her. That was rare for Morwenna and she seemed to blossom under it.

I wished again that she would lose that sense of inferiority – then I was sure she would be quite attractive.

Discovery
on a Honeymoon

Gervaise had left London a few days before we set out for
Derbyshire and he was at the station to meet us. He had come
in a carriage with the Mandeville arms emblazoned on it and
drawn by two rather sprightly grey horses.

When he greeted us he told us how delighted he was to
see us and that the family was agog with excitement at the
prospect.

Our luggage was put into the carriage by a respectful porter
whose manner indicated to us the importance of the Mandevilles
in this part of the world; and soon we were riding through the
country lanes.

And there was the house.

There had been a Mandeville Court in Tudor times, but the
old building had burned down in the early 1600s and a few years
later had been rebuilt. It was of a rectangular shape composed
of bricks and Portland stone. There was a portico and steps
leading to the front door; and the tall windows gave a touch of
elegance.

It was a very attractive house, though it lacked the antiquity
of Cador. In fact it seemed quite modern in comparison; but it
was stately and dignified – a house to be proud of.

We were taken immediately into the house where Gervaise
introduced us to his parents.

Sir Horace was benign and told us how pleased he was that
we were able to come. Lady Mandeville was pleasant, but I
could see that she was a forceful woman and her gimlet eyes
were naturally focused on me.

Then there were the rest of the family: the eldest son, William,
who would inherit the title and the estates; Henry, the second

son, who was studying law; and Marian, the daughter, the youngest member of the family, slightly younger than I was, I guessed.

We were shown to our rooms which were lofty and elegant, and mine, next to that of my parents, looked out on the gardens.

A maid came in to help us unpack, although we could easily have done it ourselves and would have preferred to. One did not need a great deal of baggage for two weeks.

My evening dresses, my riding habit and my 'country costumes' were soon all hanging up in the wardrobe and I was washing my hands in the basin provided, when my mother came.

She sat on the bed and smiled at me.

'Well,' she said. 'I don't think it is going to be all that much of an ordeal, do you?'

'I am not sure of Lady Mandeville. She looked at me so piercingly that I thought she was seeing right through me.'

'Well, naturally she would want to get to know her prospective daughter-in-law.'

'I rather like Sir Horace.'

'Yes, he resembles Gervaise.'

'I saw that and it endeared him to me.'

'It's going to be amusing. The daughter looks as if she could be fun. The brothers are rather serious. I imagine they take after their mother. I shall invite them to Cador, of course.'

'When?' I asked.

'It all depends when the wedding will be. I suppose that is something we shall decide while we are here.'

'I thought I was here on approval.'

'Then don't. I have an idea that Gervaise is the sort of young man who will make up his own mind without seeking advice; and he has already done that.'

'What does Father think of him?'

'Much the same as I do. He's interested in the second son . . . rather naturally because he is in the law . . . as your father was when he started out.'

'Well, we shall see how it goes.'

'Not nervous now?'

158

'No. Though I should like to make a good impression. I am sure Gervaise would be happy if I did.'

'All you have to do is be yourself . . . and you will.'

In the dining-room the whole family were assembled. I was seated beside Sir Horace. Lady Mandeville was at the other end of the table with my father next to her. Conversation was mostly about the house, and when we described Cador to them, they were very interested.

They had arranged one or two dinner parties so that we could meet the family's friends who lived in the neighbourhood; and they were pleased to hear that I enjoyed riding.

Once or twice I caught Marian's eyes across the table. I could almost imagine that she winked at me. My father talked about some of the old customs of Cornwall and they were very interested in these.

'We are not so imaginative here in Derbyshire,' said Sir Horace. 'I do not think we would accept the story of those little people finding gold in a tin mine.'

'I would say we were more realistic,' put in Lady Mandeville.

My mother told them the story of the Bells of St Branok to which they listened with the utmost scepticism, but which sent shivers through me; and I wished that subject had not been brought up.

'Cornwall must be quite different from the rest of England,' said Lady Mandeville.

'Oh, it is,' declared my mother. 'I am only half Cornish . . . through my father, and Rolf . . . well, he is what is called a foreigner there. You are right when you say it is different. I hope you will visit it and see for yourselves.'

They all declared they would be delighted to do so.

'Tomorrow,' said Lady Mandeville, 'I shall show you the house . . . if you wish to see it; and I will tell you some of the tales which have been handed down to us. We have had our adventures. The Wars of the Roses . . . the Great Rebellion . . . but all perfectly natural. As I say, we are a down-to-earth people here.'

'It will be most fascinating,' said my mother.

Then we chatted about the past and the elder son William

talked of the estate, and the young one in an aside to my father about the changes in law over the last few years; and the evening passed pleasantly.

I felt the worst of the ordeal was over.

I was right. After the first two days when I thought I was on trial, I began to enjoy the visit. I was falling more and more in love with Gervaise every day. I began to form a friendship with Marian; the fact that she was about a year younger than I was made me feel like an elder sister. And as I had always wanted to be a sister – preferably an elder one – I felt very contented.

I found the house very attractive but was secretly glad that Gervaise and I would not be living in it. Gervaise said he would like to live in London. He had never been exactly a country boy – unlike his brothers.

Henry would have a practice in law and might well go to London, possibly Derby or some big city; William would run the estate with his father; and Marian would have a season next year and then presumably marry.

We rode together; we attended the dinner parties which had been arranged, and the neighbours came and inspected me as Gervaise's future wife. It was all according to convention. I had done just what was expected of a young girl, and had done it rather successfully. I had had my season and before it was over I was engaged to be married, to the approval of both our families. All that had to follow now was the wedding.

My father and Sir Horace talked of settlements, of which I did not want to hear for they seemed mercenary to me. Lady Mandeville and my mother talked about the wedding, which would, of course, take place at Cador.

The Mandevilles would travel to Cornwall then; they would not come before as it was such a long journey; but the two families had this excellent opportunity of exchanging views on the subject now.

Both sides agreed that there should be no undue delay. This meant that the Mandevilles had put their seal upon the matter.

Marian and I were a good deal together. We had quite a lot

in common besides our age. I had just been presented; she soon would be; she wanted to hear all about it.

I told her of the dancing classes, the curtsies which had to be practised endlessly, the brief moment with the Queen . . . and then the season.

'And the whole thing is arranged to get us married,' she said. 'Well, it worked with you.'

'I had a good start. I knew Gervaise before, when he came down to Cornwall to dig. He was a friend of my cousin who was killed in the Crimea.'

'Yes, I know. I heard. The family thought Gervaise might take up archæology then. He seemed really keen . . . but he dropped it, of course.'

'Why do you say "of course" like that?'

'Well, he never wants to do anything for long . . . except racing. I reckon he'll get his own stables one day. It's the thing he's really keen on.'

'Yes,' I said. 'I know.'

'The family don't like it . . . not after what happened to great-great and probably a lot more greats grandfather Sir Elmore. He gambled the family estate away. You'll see him in the gallery. I'll show him to you. Ever since that happened the family have been terrified of the horses.'

'Ah,' I said, 'skeletons in the cupboard?'

'We have a few. I expect most people have. You too . . . ?'

'I'm sure of it.'

'It's rather fun getting them out and having a look at them. We ought to do that more often. It can be a lesson to us all.'

'You must show me the reckless Sir Elmore one day.'

'I will. I expect you like the horses too.'

'I like riding them.'

'I didn't mean horses. I meant *the* horses . . . which means gambling on them.'

'I've never gambled. I don't have the urge to.'

'Then you will keep Gervaise on an even keel, as they say. Don't give him any rein . . . that's apt . . . or he'll be galloping off, which he can do rather recklessly. Papa has had to bail him out once or twice. Oh, I am sorry. I'm upsetting your

161

rose-coloured picture of him. Don't take any notice. My brother Gervaise is the nicest person in the whole world. I love him dearly. If I wasn't his sister and he weren't engaged to you I'd want to marry him. He has the sweetest nature. I'm sure I shall never find anyone half as nice.'

'I know.'

'He's much nicer than my other brothers. They are steady as rocks . . . But Gervaise is the one for me.'

'I feel that too,' I told her.

'I'm glad you are going to marry him. We all think it is most suitable.'

'Oh, thank you.'

'And what is nice is your people like Gervaise, too.'

'They think he is charming.'

'So it is the ideal match. I wonder what will happen to me when I come out.'

'For that,' I said, 'we must wait and see.'

Marian showed me the picture of the reckless Sir Elmore.

'He gambled and gambled and in the end he wagered the house in the hope of recuperating all his losses.'

'And he won?'

'No, he did not. He lost.'

'But the house remained in the family's possession?'

'Only because the eldest son married a rich woman . . . just in the nick of time. It was a great self-sacrifice. He did it for Mandeville Court. But then later he weakened and went back to his first love and he set her up in part of the house. He refused to give her up. One day she disappeared. They say the wife murdered her . . . pushed her out of a window and buried her late at night. She is supposed to haunt the place.'

'And that's one of the skeletons. And a ghost! I thought your mother said that only *natural* things happened here.'

'Oh, she refuses to accept the story of the ghost. I do, though. I think all old houses ought to have a ghost. Don't you think Sir Elmore is handsome?'

'Yes, he is.'

'I always think he has a twinkle in his eyes . . . just like Gervaise has. You can imagine how, ever since, there has been a horror of anyone in the family ever falling into the clutches of "the horses".'

'And Gervaise has?'

'I don't know that it is necessarily horses, though I suppose they come into it. He just likes doing unusual things. My father wishes that he had taken up something like the law . . . something which would have a steadying influence. They weren't very keen on archæology, but it was better than nothing.'

'I thought he was very keen on that when he came to Cador.'

'He is keen . . . while it lasts. Someday he will find something he really wants to do and then he will do it better than anyone else ever has before.'

And after that I often went to the gallery to look at Sir Elmore.

One day Lady Mandeville came upon me there. I did not hear her arrive. I was standing before the portrait of the man who interested me so much and she was beside me before I realized it.

'A good portrait, is it not?' she said. 'There is something quite lifelike about it.'

'Yes, one could imagine he is laughing at us.'

She nodded. 'Do you know the story of him?'

'Marian told me.'

She was silent for a moment. Then she turned to me and said: 'It's a weakness in the family. They have no respect for money. I think you have been very sensibly brought up. That is why I feel I can talk to you.'

I felt flattered. I knew that she had accepted me, but I did not know she had any great opinion of my wisdom.

She looked over her shoulder and lowered her voice. 'You will have to look after Gervaise,' she said. 'I believe you can. That is why I am delighted by this marriage. William and Henry take after me. I have no qualms about them. Gervaise is a Mandeville through and through.'

'Oh yes . . .'

'Indeed yes. They are very charming. His father is just the same . . . but they have no respect for money. One has to keep a watch on them. I have with Sir Horace. I am telling you this, and then we will say no more about it. When I married into the family Sir Horace's finances were in disorder. I brought a large fortune with me and ever since then I have managed the affairs of this household. That is the way I have brought the family back to prosperity. You may think I should not be talking thus, but I am doing it because you are a sensible girl. I am pleased that you are to marry Gervaise. He is a delightful young man in almost every way, but he is reckless where money is concerned. He is a member of a family which simply does not understand how to handle it. When he has it, it slips through his fingers. You must keep him away from the gaming tables. You'll manage it, my dear, as I have with his father. There! I have said my say. And I think it is right that you should know this. You will be very happy with my son. He is a very good and kindly young man. He would be perfect but for this one weakness, and I think it is only right that you should be aware of it.'

She patted my cheek lightly and went on: 'You are amazed that your future mother-in-law should talk to you thus. But I do so because I like you. I like your family; I trust you; and I know you are going to be to Gervaise what I have been to his father.'

After that encounter with Lady Mandeville there seemed to be a special friendship between us. She talked to me about the house and I understood that it meant a great deal to her. I realized that she loved it with a deeper passion than the rest of the family did, although she had only come to it through marriage. She was like a convert to a new faith who seems more deeply devoted than those who have been born to it.

Somehow the knowledge that Gervaise had some weaknesses only endeared him to me. After all, paragons of virtue are often rather dull and difficult to live up to.

No one saw any reason why the marriage should be delayed. Two months would give us ample time, said my mother.

164

As soon as we returned to London we would begin our preparations. The Mandevilles would come to Cornwall for the wedding.

My parents came to my room and I could see from their expressions that there was going to be a serious discussion.

'It's the settlement,' said my father.

'Oh, I don't want to hear about that.'

'You must be sensible, darling,' said my mother. 'It's the usual arrangement, that's all.'

'But why does this have to be done? It's like paying Gervaise to take me.'

'It's just a guarantee that you are not going to your husband penniless.'

'I am sure Gervaise never thought of money.'

'I am sure he didn't. But your mother and I want you to know that you are taking this money with you . . . and . . .'

My father bit his lip and my mother went on: 'It's in your name. It is something that's there, you know . . . and it can't be touched without a lot of negotiations with lawyers.'

'I don't understand what this is all about.'

My father said: 'On the advice of Sir Horace and Lady Mandeville I did it this way. They didn't want you to have money which could be easily accessible . . .'

'They seem to think that Gervaise can be a little reckless with money and it was wise to . . . tie it up a bit,' put in my mother.

'I wish you hadn't done it,' I said.

'It's all right, Angelet,' insisted my mother. 'It's always done.'

I did not like this, particularly the suggestion that Gervaise could not be trusted, and the talk of settlements cast a little cloud over my happiness. I had been made to understand that Gervaise was a little extravagant; he was not always thinking about wealth; he was over-generous. I remembered how he had given the flower-woman that money when he had bought me a bunch of violets.

I liked it. He wanted to give pleasure to people and if he were a little extravagant in doing so, I liked him for that too.

165

I would forget all about this sordid business of settlements and money and think about my wedding day.

All the way up to London we were talking excitedly about the coming wedding.

'Two months,' my mother was saying. 'It really doesn't give us a great deal of time. While we are in London we must do some more shopping. It would be nice to have the dresses made here in London . . . but I don't quite see how. Perhaps we could buy the materials here and have them made up in Plymouth. However, we'll see. I think, Rolf, we should have another week at least. We'll need that.'

My father thought he ought to return to Cador. 'But you and Angelet could stay a little longer,' he added.

'All right,' replied my mother. 'You go ahead. Grace will be very helpful. She seems to have a natural flair for clothes. I always think she looks so elegant. I fancy she is a little lonely. What a sad life . . . to lose one's husband almost immediately after marriage.'

I was to return to Helena's and Matthew's and my parents were staying at the house in the square, so the cab would drop me first; and while my bags were being taken into the house, Helena came out.

I could tell immediately that she was extremely distraught.

I cried: 'What has happened?'

She stared at me for a few seconds, then she burst out: 'Morwenna has disappeared.'

The cabby was quickly paid off and instead of going straight to the house in the square, my parents stayed.

As soon as we were inside, Helena said: 'She has just . . . disappeared. It was two days ago.'

'Disappeared?' cried my father. 'But . . . how?'

'Grace was coming and they were going out together, and when Grace came the maid went to Morwenna's room to call her and the room was empty. The time went on . . . and Grace was waiting there. She said she would go over to my mother's house to see if Morwenna was there. It was unlikely, but we

166

did not know. We thought she had to be somewhere. She wasn't there, of course. And then we began to get worried.

'Grace was a great help. She went back to her own place to see if Morwenna had gone there and they had just missed each other. She wondered whether there had been some misunderstanding about arrangements. Of course, Morwenna rarely went out on her own. We never thought it was right that she should . . . but on isolated occasions she might have done so. Well, the plain fact is that she has gone. We can't find her anywhere.'

'Has she taken anything with her?'

'No, only what she was wearing. Everything seems to be here. It is just as though she has walked out.'

'Surely she would never do that,' said my mother.

'She was always nervous about going to places,' I said. 'She always wanted someone with her.'

'It's been driving us mad.'

'And she has been gone two days?'

'We haven't known what to do.'

'The police should be told,' said my father.

'We have told them . . . and we have sent word to her parents. I just can't think what has happened.'

'If there had been an accident we should have heard.'

My father was thoughtful. 'You . . . don't think she has been kidnapped?'

'Kidnapped?' cried Helena. 'Who would kidnap her?'

'I was thinking of a ransom,' said my father. 'There was some mention in the paper a few weeks back about mining in Cornwall and how successful the Pencarron Mine was. I saw something about Josiah Pencarron's daughter, Morwenna, being in London for the season. I just wondered . . .'

'Good heavens,' murmured my mother. 'It seems feasible.'

'What would they do to her?' I asked in terror.

My mother turned away. 'They would have to treat her well. She would be their bargaining counter.'

'It's terrible,' I cried. 'Morwenna . . . of all people. I wish she had come with us.'

We did not know how to act. The police were making enquiries. No one had any information except the maid, who thought she had seen Morwenna leaving the house late on the night before her disappearance.

We could not understand that. Why should Morwenna have left the house late at night? There was no letter or anything in her room to give an indication that she had been called away. But who could have called her at that time of night?

None of us could understand what it could mean.

The maid thought her bed might not have been slept in, although it had been turned back and made to seem as though it could have been.

We sat there in terrible dismay. We all felt we should be taking some action. But what? Morwenna just walking out of the house. It didn't make sense. There must have been a reason. There must have been a message if she went of her own accord.

And her departure might not have been discovered until about twelve hours after she left. What could have happened during those fateful twelve hours?

Uncle Peter came to the house with Aunt Amaryllis.

'This is an extraordinary affair,' he said. He felt certain that Morwenna had been kidnapped and that sooner or later a ransom would be demanded. Then we should have to go very carefully from there.

'But what is so strange,' said my mother, 'is that she appears to have gone willingly.'

'She must have left some message,' said Aunt Amaryllis.

'The servants have been questioned,' Helena reminded her. 'Nothing has been found.'

Uncle Peter said: 'She was probably lured out of the house to where her kidnappers were waiting.'

'She would never have done such a thing,' I cried. 'She would have been scared. If I had been here she would have told me. This wouldn't have happened if I had been here.'

'It is all very mysterious,' said Uncle Peter, 'and unfortunate that she should be staying at this house.'

I felt impatient with him. He was afraid, even at a time like this, that there would be some scandal which would harm Matthew's parliamentary image; yet he would also be wondering if there might not be some good publicity in it. I could imagine his weighing this up. It was how he looked on everything.

'What we have to think about is Morwenna,' I said. 'Where it happened is not important. All that matters is that it has happened.'

'We have to consider all the details carefully,' put in my father. 'Where it happened . . . might be very important.'

'Her parents will know by now,' said Helena. 'I can't bear to think what their feelings are at this moment.'

'But what are we going to *do*?' I asked.

'We shall hear something in due course,' said Uncle Peter. 'There will be a demand for a ransom, I expect. It has probably been sent to her parents. They are the ones they will have their eyes on.'

'It will be terrible for them,' said my mother.

I imagined Mr and Mrs Pencarron's receiving a demand for money in exchange for the return of their daughter and threatening . . . what? . . . . if they did not comply.

I felt frantic with anxiety. I could not bear to think of Morwenna in the hands of desperate men.

Later that day Mr and Mrs Pencarron arrived in London. They had aged considerably.

It was immediately clear that they had no news of Morwenna.

'I can't understand all this,' said Mr Pencarron. 'Our girl . . . what has she done? Why should they do this to her?'

'We should never have let her come to London,' mourned Mrs Pencarron. 'I always knew it was a wicked place.'

'We'll find her,' said my father firmly.

'You will, won't you?' pleaded Mrs Pencarron. 'What do you think they are doing to her?'

'They won't harm her, that's for sure,' replied my father. 'They can only bargain for her if she is alive and well.'

'Alive . . . you don't think . . .'

'Oh no . . . no . . . What I am telling you is that if she is well they can bargain for her. I expect sooner or later they will be asking for some money.'

'I'll do anything to get my girl back,' cried Mr Pencarron. 'They can have all I've got.'

'We'd do anything . . . anything,' sobbed Mrs Pencarron.

I went to her and put my arms round her. 'She's all right, Mrs Pencarron. I know she'll be all right.'

'Did she say anything to you ?' she asked piteously. 'Did she seem frightened that someone was going to take her away?'

'I was in Derbyshire with my parents,' I explained. 'I wasn't here. But I just feel she is all right. She must be.'

'And you weren't here,' said Mrs Pencarron almost accusingly.

I shook my head.

They were absolutely broken-hearted. Mrs Pencarron kept telling everyone that she had given up hope of having a child . . . and then they had their little Morwenna. They would give anything . . . anything they had . . .

'If the Press come round don't tell them that,' said Uncle Peter. 'The demand will go up. We will have to play this carefully.'

We were all relying on Uncle Peter. The existence of his dubious clubs from which he had made his great fortune was what my father called an open secret in the family, which meant that everyone knew of it and kept up the pretence that Uncle Peter's business was perfectly respectable. But he would have knowledge of the underworld; all kinds of people came to his clubs; the matter would be better in his hands than anyone else's.

He said there should not be too much said about the case until there was some notion as to what it was all about.

There must come a demand soon. The best thing for us to do was to wait for it.

It was hard. It was four days since Morwenna had disappeared and there was no news.

The Pencarrons, who had been taken off by my mother to Uncle Peter's house where there was room for them, did not help matters. They were in a state of utter despair. If I had a chance I would tell Morwenna that she must never again think of herself as unloved. She meant everything to her parents.

Uncle Peter was making enquiries. The police were asking questions and we were all getting desperate. And then, one morning, when I was thinking, here is another day without news, a cab drew up at the door and from it alighted Morwenna. She was not alone. A man was with her. I recognized him at once. He was Justin Cartwright, the man who had retrieved her purse when it had been stolen from her.

'Morwenna!' I cried. 'Where have you been?'

I was so delighted to see her that I had to stop myself from bursting into tears of relief. I hugged her to make sure she was real. I gazed at her. She looked very happy.

'Where have you been?' I demanded. 'We have all been frantic.'

She turned to the man and said: 'This is my husband, Angelet. I eloped with him. We were married at Gretna Green.'

The first thing I had to do was to get her to her parents and we set off immediately. As soon as the door was opened I shouted into the house: 'She's here. Morwenna's back.'

There were exclamations of joy as, it seemed, the entire household came running into the hall. When the Pencarrons saw their daughter they flew at her and the three of them were there in a sort of huddle . . . just clinging to each other. There were tears in Mrs Pencarron's eyes. I could see her lips moving and I knew she was thanking God for giving her her daughter back. They did not ask for explanations. All they cared about was that she was back with them; she was safe and unharmed; and they were ready to forget their sufferings in the sheer joy of having her returned to them.

'Oh Ma and Pa,' she said at last. 'I didn't think you'd be so worried.'

Then came the explanations.

'It was thoughtless of us,' said Justin Cartwright. 'I take the blame. I persuaded her. She didn't want to do it this way. But I feared objections. I could not bear the thought of losing her.'

Morwenna was smiling happily. I could not believe this. She was like a different person. She had cast off that hangdog look; she was desired, wanted; she was loved; she had had a romantic wedding and it was quite easy to see that she adored her husband.

171

I could have been angry with her if I was not so delighted. This was what I had always wanted for Morwenna. It was a pity she had had to put us all through such an ordeal to achieve it.

'You see,' explained Morwenna, 'it all happened so suddenly.'

Justin went on humbly, looking at Mr Pencarron, 'The moment I saw your daughter I knew she was the only one for me. I fell in love at first sight. I did not believe in such things . . . until now. I am afraid I acted thoughtlessly. But I was overwhelmed. I had to persuade her . . . You see, I feared there might be obstacles. I know I'm not good enough . . . and I was afraid. I can only hope that you will forgive me for all the terrible suffering I have caused you.'

'Well, I never,' said Mrs Pencarron. 'It's like something out of a book.'

Uncle Peter was standing by, faintly cynical; not so Mr Pencarron. It seemed to him the most natural thing in the world that a young man seeing his daughter should fall in love with her so madly that he persuaded her to elope with him.

'Morwenna wanted to leave a note,' went on Justin Cartwright, smiling wryly at Mr Pencarron, 'but I was afraid you would have us followed and prevent the marriage. I am entirely to blame. I hope . . . that Morwenna will give you a good account of me.'

Mr Pencarron said gruffly: 'Are you happy, my girl?'

'Oh, Pa . . . I am, I am.'

'Then that's all we want, don't we, Mother?'

'That's all we want,' said his wife.

Uncle Peter sent to the cellars for champagne that we might drink the health of the newly-weds.

'Then,' he added, 'I dare say Mr and Mrs Pencarron will want to have a little talk with their son-in-law.'

There was a great deal of consternation in the family. Who was this Justin Cartwright? It seemed that he had no definite employment. He had been abroad for some years and had just returned home and was wondering what he would do. He had a little money and was what was called a gentleman of

172

independent means. He and Morwenna would not be rich but he could provide for his wife – albeit modestly.

The police were called off the hunt. It was just another case of elopement. They turned up now and then and they wished people would give a little more thought to the trouble they were causing.

Uncle Peter thought that the incident could be of a little use to Matthew, for the happy bride had been staying at his house. 'People love a little romance,' he said. 'Nothing like it for fixing one in the mind of the electorate. They'll forget what happened, but they will remember it was a romantic affair and that it happened in your house. Romance only happens to nice people. It will be of some little use, I dare say.' The Pencarrons wanted their daughter and her husband to return with them to Cornwall for a proper wedding. This Gretna Green method was all very well, but what they had fancied for their Morwenna was a wedding with veil and orange blossom in St Ervan's Church with guests in Pencarron Manor to follow.

So this was to take place; and I was sure Justin would be offered some executive post in the mine – although it was difficult to imagine him in that capacity. He seemed to me entirely the man about town.

Although it was a great relief to have Morwenna back with us safe and well, there were certain misgivings. Uncle Peter thought that it was very likely that the man was an adventurer; being one himself, he very probably recognized another.

Grace was delighted for Morwenna. She said that even if she had been married because she was an heiress, was that not the reason why so many debutantes were married? It was absurd to hold up one's hands in horror because someone had used a rather different method with the same object in view.

She said Morwenna was a girl who needed romance to pull her out of that mood of self-deprecation into which she had fallen, and what could be a better antidote to that than an elopement? Justin Cartwright at worst could be the same as many men who, during the season, were looking for an advantageous marriage; at best it could be genuine love which had prompted him to elope with Morwenna.

'Let us hope it is the latter,' she added.

And that was what we all did.

The Pencarrons returned to Cornwall, taking Morwenna and her husband with them. There was to be that ceremony at St Ervan's and they would start making plans.

As for myself, I remained a little longer in London; Grace was with us most of the time; we bought materials and talked of wedding plans. Gervaise came to London and we had a few wonderful days together; we went again to the opera and we had luncheon alone together – permitted now that we were officially engaged. And then I said goodbye to Gervaise.

I should not see him again until we married.

Back at Cador there was no talk of anything but the coming wedding. Morwenna had had her ceremony. They had thought it best to have the whole thing completed so that they would feel that Morwenna was really married and they could not feel that until the ceremony in St Ervan's took place. So there were hasty preparations. Morwenna had her white gown and orange blossoms; she was married in the church and many returned to Pencarron to take part in the reception.

I wished I had been there in time to participate.

'Never mind,' said Morwenna, 'I shall certainly come to yours.'

She was like a different person. There was no doubt that she was happy and, as she had never expected to be, she enjoyed it all the more. In those days she went about in a state of dazed bliss. Justin was very tender to her. I liked him for that, although I could not rid myself of the idea which Uncle Peter had sown in my mind that he might be an adventurer. The Pencarrons were certainly very wealthy and Morwenna was their only child. Marriage with her must seem a good proposition to any needy young man seeking an heiress.

But when his father-in-law offered to take him into the business he politely declined. He was grateful. It was a great honour, Morwenna told me he said, but he could not do it.

'He is so noble,' she went on. 'He says he wants to support

174

his wife without the help of her father. He can do it, and although she may not be as rich in her new life as she was with her parents, she would be well looked after. Wasn't that wonderful of him? You see, he is so used to living in town. He wouldn't fit into a rural society.'

'I can see that,' I said.

'He's like Gervaise. You couldn't see him in the country either, could you?'

I admitted she was right.

'Pa has offered to give us a house in London for a wedding present but he is having difficulty in getting Justin to agree to take it. You see, he doesn't want to take anything.'

'Where was he living, then?' I asked.

'In a hotel.'

'He could hardly expect you to live in a hotel.'

'No. So I think that for my sake he will accept Pa's offer. They don't really want me to go to London. They would like us to settle here.'

'What do you feel about it, Morwenna?'

'Oh, I want to be where Justin is. Mother and Pa can come up and stay with us . . . often. And we can come down here.'

'It sounds like a good arrangement. And you are very happy, aren't you, Morwenna?'

She nodded. 'Life is wonderful,' she said. 'So unexpected. Those awful balls . . . those dinner parties. I never knew what to say to anybody and I would sit there feeling that everyone was trying to think up excuses to get away from me.'

'And Justin changed all that.'

'He was quite different from anyone else. He really wanted to be with me. He listened to what I had to say. He made me feel that I was interesting. It has changed everything.'

'I hope you will always be as happy as you are now, Morwenna.'

'I shall always be happy as long as I have Justin.'

I thought: The man is a miracle-worker. He has changed her completely. Or is it simply Love?

The weeks flew by. My wedding dress was ready. We had it made in Plymouth. It lacked the grandeur of my court dress but

175

it was very beautiful. There was my veil and orange blossom. I should be the typical bride.

As Morwenna had been, I was married in St Ervan's. My father gave me away and Morwenna was my Matron of Honour. Gervaise was a very handsome bridegroom and I was proud of him. The reception followed, toasts were drunk and, with the help of Gervaise, I cut the cake. We left the guests while I went up to change into my going-away costume.

Grace and my mother were with me. My mother was emotional, as most mothers are when their daughters get married. I suppose they think the relationship will never be the same again, and they have lost some part of a daughter to a stranger.

I threw my arms about her, remembering all we had been to one another.

I said: 'We are going to see each other often. I shall come to Cador and you must come to London.'

She nodded, too tearful to speak.

We were to live in London. My parents, as the Pencarrons had with Morwenna, were presenting us with a house as a wedding present. It seemed the most sensible of gifts to a married pair who had to find a home for themselves. Morwenna and I promised each other that we would have an exciting time helping each other to choose our new homes; and one thing which delighted was that we should be neighbours.

The prospect ahead seemed full of pleasure; and in the meantime Gervaise and I were about to leave on our honeymoon which was to be spent in the South of France.

Grace patted the sleeve of my jacket and smoothed the skirt. We had bought it in London and she had helped to choose it. I felt it was very elegant and there was a little hat with a curling blue-tinted ostrich feather with it.

'You look lovely,' said my mother. 'Doesn't she, Grace?'

Grace agreed.

And then I went down to Gervaise who was waiting for me and whose looks told me that he agreed with them.

*

When we arrived at the station the train was already in. We had a first class carriage to ourselves.

'How fortunate!' I cried.

'Arranged,' said Gervaise, 'with Machiavellian cunning.'

And we were laughing together.

We were to stay the first night in a London hotel before we continued our journey the next day.

'It will be the first time I have ever been out of England,' I said.

'Is that why you are so excited?'

'The sole reason,' I told him.

'Angelet,' he said severely, 'you must not tell your husband lies.'

'What will you do if I decide I shall?'

'I shall be forced to take drastic action.'

'Such as?'

'You'll find out.'

And so we bantered.

The journey, which had previously always seemed so long, now seemed quite short; and there we were coming into Paddington Station.

I was full of admiration for the manner in which Gervaise guided me through, having summoned a porter to take the baggage. Soon we were in a cab.

What a man of the world! I thought proudly.

Our room overlooked the park. It was quite a splendid room with heavy brocade curtains, gilded furniture and a bed which I imagined could have been used by Louis XIV.

'The bridal suite,' announced Gervaise. 'All arranged efficiently by your father, I must tell you.'

'He didn't tell me.'

'No, it was to be a surprise.'

'It's very grand.'

'Well, it is our wedding night.'

I changed into a dinner dress and we went down to dine. Eager-to-please waiters hovered; the discreet music was delightful; and Gervaise was sitting opposite me telling me how much he loved me.

It was a beautiful night. There was a moon which seemed suitable for the occasion. From the balcony we could look over the park which seemed to have become mysterious and unreal. He put an arm about me, his fingers caressing my neck. Then he took the pins from my hair and let it fall about my shoulders.

He drew me back into the room. He took my face in his hands and said: 'For so long I have waited for you, Angelet. I have wanted you so much. You wouldn't understand . . .'

Then he kissed me as he had never kissed me before. I felt startled. I was innocent but not ignorant. I knew of the relationships between the sexes in theory. It should be something precious; it made a bond between people, such as that between my parents, Helena and Matthew, Uncle Peter and Aunt Amaryllis. It was easy to see there was this special bond between them. But there was another side to it. There was something I had glimpsed on that never-to-be-forgotten day there at the pool.

And suddenly without warning it came upon me . . . the terrible fear. I was back there. It was as vivid as it had been on that day.

I seemed to see those other features . . . the feel of his hands . . . his breath on my face.

I heard myself scream: 'No, no.'

I tried to withdraw my hands but he held them tightly.

'Let me go,' I cried. 'Let me go.'

He released me, staring at me in amazement.

'Angelet, what's wrong? What is it?'

The sound of his voice, so tender, so loving, reassured me. I was being foolish.

'I . . . I don't . . . know,' I stammered.

'There's nothing to be afraid of. I'm not going to hurt you. I wouldn't hurt you for the world.'

'No . . . I know. It is just that . . .'

He would have taken me in his arms but I shrank away from him.

'Angelet, what on earth has happened? You're looking at me as though I'm a stranger . . . a monster.'

And I thought: I shall never forget. It will always be there.

178

I turned away from him and flung myself on to the bed. Involuntary sobs shook my body.

He was lying beside me, his arms about me. 'Tell me, Angelet. Tell me all about it.'

I knew then that he had not changed. I had nothing to fear from him. But I knew, too, that I could no longer bear the burden of my secret.

I just lay there silently; now and then shaken by a sob. He held me tightly.

'It's all right, Angelet,' he said. 'What are you afraid of? There is nothing to fear. I promise you that. Tell me what it is that worried you.'

I buried my face against him and I heard myself say: 'It was what happened at the pool.'

'At the pool?'

'It's so long ago . . . but it still seems clear to me. It always has been like that. It goes away and then it comes back. It comes back so suddenly. It will always be like that.'

'What? Tell me.'

I took a deep breath. Then it came out: 'There was a man who escaped from Bodmin Prison. There was a great deal of talk about him . . . pictures of him. I was alone by the pool. I had tied up my horse Glory . . . I went down to look at the pool . . . and he was there. He talked for a while. I thought he was a visitor who wanted to know the way . . . and then suddenly he changed.' I was shivering now. It was all coming back so clearly. 'He looked at me . . . he put out his hands and seized me.'

'Oh my God,' said Gervaise.

'I knew what he would do to me . . . what he had done to that girl he murdered. I fought him. But I was only a child and he . . .'

I could feel the horror rising in Gervaise. It was like a physical thing.

'Someone came . . . and saved me. He fought with the murderer . . . who fell and caught his head on a stone. I remember the stone. It was part of that wall you found when you came down to dig.'

179

'I know . . . I remember.'

'It killed him. We threw his body in the pool. They all thought he had escaped. But he didn't. He is lying at the bottom of the pool . . . where we put him.'

He did not speak. I knew he was too shocked. He just held me tightly, then he murmured my name and called me his little love, his darling.

'You see, Gervaise, I never told anyone . . . You are the first . . .'

'I'm glad you told me,' he said.

'I had to. I had to make you understand.'

'I understand,' he said.

There was a silence and then I said: 'What are you thinking of, Gervaise?'

'I am thinking of it. I can't stop thinking of it.'

'It was terrible. It had all happened so quickly. Everything before had been easy . . . simple . . . and after that . . .'

'Of course, of course.'

'We shouldn't have done it, should we? But you see he was fighting with Ben.'

'Ben?'

'Benedict. We called him Ben. He said that the man would have been hanged for murder in any case and that it was an easy way out for him. I don't think Ben felt it as much as I did.'

'Well, he wouldn't. He wasn't nearly assaulted and murdered.'

'No.'

'You mustn't shiver like this. I am going to send for some brandy. It'll steady you. It'll soothe you. My poor, poor Angelet, and you have had this on your mind ever since!'

He went to the bell-rope and pulled it. Then he came back to me and put his arms about me.

'I'm glad you told me,' he said. 'And all that time you kept it to yourself.'

I nodded. 'I'm glad you know. I nearly told my mother once or twice . . . but I didn't. There are only two of us who knew . . . Ben and myself . . . and now you, of course.'

He kissed me tenderly.

180

There was a knock on the door. It was a waiter. Gervaise ordered the brandy and came back to me.

He said: 'Where is Ben now?'

'He's in Australia. He went there to find gold.'

'And you have not heard from him all these years?'

'I expect Uncle Peter hears from him now and then.'

'My dear, dear Angelet, how old were you when this happened?'

'Ten . . . I think.'

'My poor child.'

'Gervaise, were we wrong? What should we have done? You see, we didn't know what to do. He was lying there dead.'

'Perhaps you could have told people what had happened.'

'But Ben said they would say we killed him. You didn't know about my grandfather. He was sent to Australia for seven years for killing a man. It was in more or less the same circumstances. He was with some gypsies and a man tried to assault one of the girls. My grandfather fought with him and killed him. He would have been hanged for murder if my grandmother had not had an influential father.'

'Surely this was different.'

There was a knock on the door. The brandy had arrived.

'Drink this,' said Gervaise. 'It will soothe you. It'll make you feel better.'

'I feel better now I have told you.'

'I'm glad of that.'

'I had to, hadn't I? Otherwise you would have thought I didn't love you. I do love you, Gervaise. I want everything to be right between us. It was just then . . . that it all came back to me.'

He put an arm round me as I sipped the brandy.

'You mustn't worry,' he said. 'It's all long ago. You've got to put it out of your mind.'

I shivered. 'Can you ever put such a thing out of your mind?'

'I think you will in time. You've taken a step towards it tonight. I'm here with you . . . for the rest of our lives . . . here to help you . . . to care for you.'

'That's a wonderful thought.'

He took the glass from me and kissed me.

'You did nothing wrong,' he said. 'You helped to hide him, it's true. It was the best way perhaps. His death was accidental. He brought it on himself. You have to forget it.'

'I have tried to forget. I do for long periods . . . and then it comes back as it did tonight.'

'It's left a scar,' said Gervaise. 'I understand. But we are going to heal that scar. I'm going to help you forget. I shall do everything I can to make you happy. What you saw on that day was ugly, but ugliness exists in the world. You have confused it with love. Believe me, the two are miles apart. You will understand. I will make you understand, and then you will know the difference and you will not be afraid any more.'

How tender he was. He soothed me. I felt as though a burden had been lifted from me. It was no longer the secret locked within me. I had shared it and it had become lighter.

I shall never forget that night – my wedding night. He understood so well. His greatest quality was that he respected the feelings of other people and he could put himself in their place. He had sympathy for everyone, I was to discover. If he wanted to make life easy for himself, he did for others at the same time. His sympathy and understanding were balm to me.

I lay in his arms all night – just that. He knew my feelings; I had shown them clearly enough. He knew that I had to banish the horror of that encounter from my mind; I had to understand the difference between lust and love before we could be lovers.

I realized later how fortunate I was in him, how much I owed to him.

I slept at last, comforted, because he shared my secret.

We travelled through France to the *auberge* on the edge of the mountains. We were staying in a village about a mile from the big and fashionable resort on the coast. Gervaise had stayed there in his student days and it was clear from the start that Madame Bougerie was rather taken with him.

Madame Bougerie was the power behind the Auberge Bougerie. Alphonse, the husband, was a small man who must

182

have learned over the years that his wife demanded absolute obedience. There was a daughter and son-in-law. The whole family worked in the *auberge*.

Madame usually sat at the reception desk with papers before her – a stern woman dressed entirely in black; she wore jet earrings and a jet necklace; her greying hair was taken straight back from her face and was worn in a knot, nestling in the nape of her neck.

We were all in awe of her, from the humblest pot boy to the most exalted guest.

I was enchanted by the place from the moment I saw it. It seemed to be hanging on the hillside. There were stables with a few horses, for in such a place horses were necessary and patrons were allowed to hire them. The *auberge* was of grey stone. There were wicker seats on the terrace which allowed one to sit while contemplating the superb scenery. There were urns containing colourful shrubs. The flowers were plentiful and wherever one looked one could see the beautiful bougainvilleas and oleanders blooming in abundance.

Below us were small houses gleaming white in the sunshine with pink roofs and green blinds to shut out the intruding sun.

It was an enchanting place.

Over the years Madame had had many English visitors to her *auberge* and she prided herself on her command of our language. If we spoke to her in French she would always reply in English. Gervaise was amused and tried to force her into her own language. I think she did the same with him. It was amusing to listen to them – he with his French just about adequate, and she with her English which was scarcely that; and neither giving way.

We were given a room with a balcony which overlooked the bay. It was the perfect setting for a honeymoon. We rode and we walked and I felt more at peace than I had since that encounter, which now seemed to have diminished in importance because Gervaise knew of it.

Sometimes Madame Bougerie would give us a packed lunch of crusty bread and cheese, fruit and wine; and we would go off on the hired horses right into the mountains. We laughed a great deal . . . and we talked. When Gervaise mentioned my experience at the pool, it no longer set me shivering. I found that through him I was beginning to see it differently. I had had a lucky escape – a very narrow one. Perhaps it would have been wiser for us to have confessed what had happened and not hidden the body. But no one would blame us. Gervaise had made me see that. There had been a fight and the murderer had fallen and in falling killed himself. No one could blame us for that. But it was over. Nothing could change what we had done. The wise thing to do was to forget it . . . or see it as it really was. A lucky escape for me and a man meeting his deserts, a happy release for him when it was considered what the law would have done to him.

And during those happy days, the inevitable happened. I was sure Gervaise knew it would but I would never forget his restraint and patience in waiting until I was ready.

We were lovers in truth and I was happy through this new relationship with this wonderful husband of mine. I felt I had laid my ghost. That incident had receded far into the past. It was no longer a shadow over my life.

So I was happy.

There came a day when we went into the town. The atmosphere down there was quite different. There were several big hotels, a promenade along which the fashionable strolled; outside the cafés were tables under brightly coloured awnings; people sat there sipping their *apéritifs*.

The sun shone on the water, making it look as though it were sprinkled with diamonds. Gervaise told me that it was one of the most fashionable resorts, and visitors were predominantly English.

We took our place outside the Café Pomme d'Or. I sipped my *apéritif*, trying to look as though I were quite accustomed to such sophistication and that this was not all new and wonderful to me.

'The Golden Apple,' I said. 'I wonder why they call it that.'

'There are golden apples all over the world,' said Gervaise, 'ever since someone gave one to somebody.'

'It was Paris. I think he had to choose the most beautiful

184

woman and he gave it to Aphrodite. There were two other contestants.'

'He couldn't have been very popular with those two.'

'Poor man. What could he do? He had to make a choice.'

'It was rather foolish of him to get himself into such a situation.'

'Apples seem to be a popular fruit in those classical legends. I believe they grew them in the Garden of the Hesperides, too.'

'You would need rather a big nugget to make it into an apple. I wonder if your friend Ben has found any of that size.'

'I don't think he can have done so. We should have heard if he had.'

It was wonderful. I could speak of Ben easily and naturally without feeling that shiver of apprehension . . . that dreaded memory coming back to me.

'I suppose the owners of these places like to remind people of these things. Perhaps the Golden Apple suggests that all the ladies who come here are as beautiful as Aphrodite and the men as handsome as Paris. After all, where you come from legends are just everyday gossip.'

I thought of the knackers who had mined gold in the tin mine; and I remembered how long ago Ben and I had lain on the moor and I had told him the story.

It was comforting to be able to look back on that without fear of remembering beyond it. Gervaise had done that for me.

Afterwards we strolled along the promenade. We came to a round building with gardens in front in which bloomed the exotic flowers to which I was accustomed.

'What is this place?' I asked.

'It is a casino.'

'Oh?' I replied. 'That is where they gamble.'

'Shall we take a look inside?'

'May we?'

'Of course.'

It was quite fun at the time. I should have remembered the warnings.

There were a great number of people there. We walked round. They were playing games I did not understand.

185

I stood for a moment with Gervaise watching the wheel spinning round on the big table. I noticed the strained eager faces and how those people kept their eyes on the numbers all the time.

Then the wheel stopped and the croupier's stick pulled in the chips.

It was all a mystery to me but I was aware of Gervaise's growing excitement.

'Shall we go?' I said.

'Just a moment. I'd like to try my luck. Sit down. I won't be long.'

He left me there. I waited. What a long time it seemed! I watched the people. They talked excitedly. Some were elated. Some melancholy. There was an atmosphere here which I had never been aware of anywhere else. It was a sort of feverish excitement.

I hoped Gervaise would not be long.

It seemed to me that I waited a very long time; when he came to me he was flushed; his eyes were brilliant; he was elated.

'I've won,' he cried. 'My luck was in.'

He showed me a handful of money.

'At first it went wrong,' he said. 'I lost three times running. I was almost cleaned out . . . then it started to change. I'd have gone on and on making us millionaires if I hadn't thought of you sitting here . . . waiting. So I came away.'

'I'm glad you did. It seemed so long.'

'I was afraid it would. You don't notice the time when you are at the tables, you know.'

'No, I suppose not. Shall we go now?'

It seemed to me that he left reluctantly; but as soon as we were out in the fresh air his spirits revived.

'I'll tell you what I am going to do,' he said. 'I am going to buy a present for someone.'

'For whom?'

'For Mrs Gervaise Mandeville, of course.'

'Oh no. Let's keep the money.'

'Money is not for keeping.'

'Isn't it? I had always thought it was.'

186

'That is where you have to learn. It's for giving presents . . . making people happy.'

'I'm just as happy without a present.'

'You're going to get one all the same and I know what.'

'What?'

'I noticed your eyes on that dress in the window of a shop we passed this morning. That glorious blue velvet creation.'

'Oh . . . that. Yes, it's lovely. It must be very costly.'

'Well, you have a rich husband now.'

'Gervaise, buy something for yourself if you must spend it.'

'Certainly not. I'm going to buy something for you. Come on.'

He led me back to the shop. It was true I had admired the dress. I had rarely seen one so elegant and beautiful.

'There is something about it,' he said. 'Is there not?'

'It's certainly very fine, but I dare say it will cost a great deal.'

'We'll go and see.'

Reluctantly I was led into the shop. A tall thin woman in black came out to us. She reminded me of something between a spider and Madame Bougerie.

The dress? Oh yes. It was indeed a special dress. She gesticulated wildly. And for Madame. Yes, yes. It was Madame's size. One could say that it had been made for Madame.

I was scurried into a cubicle and there I was divested of my own dress and stood before the mirror in the glorious creation. I had to admit it was beautiful and it suited me.

It fitted *comme les gants*. It was Madame's dress. No one else must have it. It must be Madame's.

The price appalled me, but Gervaise took it light-heartedly. I know that it swallowed up all his winnings.

This was what he wanted.

The dress was packed up and Gervaise carried it proudly from the shop.

I said: 'It is a great extravagance and you shouldn't have spent all that money.'

'But it had to be Madame's. It was made for Madame. It fits like a glove. There was no question about it. And you look quite superb in it. I am sure had you been present, Aphrodite would never have got her golden apple.'

187

'I still think of it as an extravagance.'

'Nonsense. I wanted to buy it. What is the good of having a wife if I can't spend my winnings on her?'

So we walked home and that night I wore the dress. I loved it. It was beautiful – and very precious because Gervaise had given it to me.

Later I wished we had never seen the casino. But of course Gervaise knew it was there. He had been there before. It may well have been why he had chosen this place for our honeymoon.

I enjoyed the days when we walked or rode in the mountains; but I did sense in him a yearning to be in the town; when we visited it he would lead me to the casino and he would go in, leaving me sitting there waiting for him. I could have gone with him, I suppose. I could have had my own little flutter; but I had no wish to. I always had the feeling that I should lose – and that would be two of us.

There were one or two occasions when he won but never as much as when he had bought the dress.

I remembered the family warning and what his mother had said. I was to be the steadying influence.

It was like a blight on our honeymoon. If only it could have gone on as it had begun. I had been so superbly happy in the beginning after my confession . . . happy as I had never thought to be again after that encounter at the pool. And Gervaise had made it possible. I would never forget that.

And then the visit to the casino! Every time I looked at the dress, I remembered – that feverish excitement, that desire to gamble. I, who did not have the slightest inclination to do so, found it difficult to understand the urge which seemed to come over Gervaise. He was like a different person when it was on him. Usually he was so relaxed, so carefree. This was an obsession.

We had spent two weeks at the *auberge* and were going home in three days' time. We were some little distance from the railway station and there was an old carriage drawn by two

188

rather aged horses which made short journeys when it was necessary and would take guests' luggage to and from the station.

Two days before we were to leave the carriage had to go to the station and Madame Bougerie said it would be convenient if our bags could be taken to the station then to save a journey.

I was rather sad, packing.

'Put everything you can in,' said Gervaise, 'so that there is nothing we have to carry. Then we can walk down to the station when the time comes.'

I wondered afterwards what would have happened if the luggage had not been sent on in advance. He would not then have been able to do what he did.

That evening Gervaise went down to the town alone. I was rather tired. We had walked several miles during the afternoon and the casino did not attract me. I did not wish to partake in the gambling; nor did I wish to wait while Gervaise did. I found the place rather depressing in spite of the bright lights and the splendidly clad women. I detected in the faces of so many that frenzied look which I had seen in Gervaise.

He was very late back that night. I was relieved to see him. I had visions of his coming out from the casino with his winnings and being waylaid and set upon and robbed.

When I told him this he laughed.

'No one would have wanted to set upon me after the luck I have had tonight.'

'It seems to me that you hardly ever have any luck.'

'What? Think of that beautiful dress.'

'That was the only time – and you spent all that.'

'One day you will be surprised.'

I thought that he was a little less ready to laugh than usual. I did not know how bad it was until later.

The next morning we went down to the town. I was afraid he was going once more to the casino, but he did not.

'I think,' he said, 'we should go and see if the luggage is all right.'

I was relieved. It seemed a good idea.

Even now I am not sure how it happened or why I allowed it

189

to. He had brought the luggage out. The train was in the station. It was the train we should take to Paris.

A porter had seized our bags.

I cried: 'He thinks we are going on the train.'

Gervaise did not answer. He allowed the porter to go and followed him taking me with him.

'Explain to him,' I shouted.

'It's all right,' said Gervaise. The porter put the bags on the train. Gervaise gave him some money.

I said: 'What are you doing, Gervaise? How . . . ?'

He turned to me and smiled and pushed me down into a seat.

'If you are not careful . . .' I began, 'the train will go . . . What game is this?'

'Wait and see,' he said.

The train had started to move and I cried out in alarm.

'It had to be,' said Gervaise. 'It's the only way. I was absolutely cleaned out.'

'What of Madame Bougerie's bill?'

'I'll send her the money.'

'But you didn't explain.'

'How could I? She'd never understand. I'll write.'

'What will she think?'

He shrugged his shoulders.

'Listen to me,' he said. 'It was the only way. I paid last week. It is only one week owing. It was lucky about the luggage. That's what gave me the idea last night. It is better to do it this way. There would have been a terrible fuss. Goodness knows what would have happened. I could never have got it over to her. You know she thinks she understands English.'

I sat back in my seat staring at him in horror.

'Thank goodness we had our return tickets,' he said. 'You see, it all worked out.'

'Gervaise,' I said, 'how could you? It is cheating, it is stealing . . .'

'No,' he said. 'She'll get the money. I'll see that she gets it.'

I sank forward helplessly. I felt covered in shame.

*

190

No one is perfect. I must never forget his loving tenderness. I would always remember the first night of our marriage when he had miraculously lifted me out of my terror, when he had freed me from that haunting spectre. Never, never must I forget that. And this . . . it was something they had warned me of. It was why my father had made some complicated arrangement about the settlement. I must do something. I could not allow us to cheat. I thought of the horror there would be in Madame Bougerie's face when she realized her guests had left . . . without paying. How could he have done it . . . and in such a light-hearted way!

He might send the money in time. He would probably send more than he owed to make up for what he had done. But that was not the point. The money must be sent without delay.

I must do something.

The thought preoccupied me all the way home. Gone was The magic of the outward journey. Gervaise realized this and was contrite.

'If I had known how much it was going to upset you,' he said, 'I would have thought of something else.'

'There wasn't anything else. You had gambled with the money which was really Madame Bougerie's. It's dishonest, Gervaise.'

'Not if I pay it back. I'll send her extra for the trouble.'

We were staying at the Mandeville town house until we had a home of our own. There was no one to greet us because we had come earlier than had been expected. I was glad of this. I did not want to have to give explanations.

I would not rest until I had sent the money to Madame Bougerie.

I did know that the money my father had settled on me was to be kept in my name and that the capital could not be touched without the agreement of my parents. I was to get an income which would be paid to me. This had been agreed between my family and the Mandevilles. The income would not be large and I had not yet received the first instalment. I needed money quickly and I knew approximately how much and it must be a little more because of the trouble we had caused. I wrote and asked my father for it.

191

It came almost at once. He guessed that I had had expenses on my honeymoon. I was relieved. I went to the bank and discovered I could change English money into French; and it was mailed off immediately to the *auberge*. I wrote a note apologizing for the trouble we had caused, explaining rather vaguely that we had had to return to England without delay, and if we had not caught the train we should have lost a day, so we had had to take it. I humbly begged Madame's pardon for what must have seemed inexcusable behaviour.

When the money had gone off I told Gervaise what I had done.

He looked at me sadly: 'I'm sorry, Angelet,' he said. 'You see the sort of a man you have married. Do you despise me?'

'Of course not. But it seemed . . . so awful, I couldn't bear it.'

'I know. You are so good . . . so honest.'

'I'm not. I'm not. But going off like that . . . Please, please, Gervaise, don't let us do anything like that again.'

'We won't,' he said fervently. 'I promise we won't.'

He had been so wonderful to me. I had expected too much. People were not models of perfection. In a way I loved him more for his weakness. It seemed to strengthen me. I was no longer the innocent young girl to be led and guided. I had my responsibilities; and I was going to look after him.

I would make him see the risks and follies of gambling.

I was very innocent still.

I had a letter from Madame Bougerie thanking me for the money. She had known, of course, that it must have been something pressing which had made us leave so unexpectedly and never for one moment had she put a wrong construction on this. She understood perfectly and she hoped we would visit the *auberge* again when we should be very welcome.

I did not suppose for one moment that she had not suspected the worst of us, but that was the diplomatic way of dealing with the matter and Madame Bougerie would always know how to do that. However, the incident had been brought to a satisfactory close as far as the *auberge* was concerned; and I was sure, in my new role as my husband's guide and helpmeet, that where money was concerned such a thing would never happen again.

I gave myself up to the pleasure of househunting. This was particularly agreeable because Morwenna shared it with me. It seemed the most delightful coincidence that we were in London, both recent brides, looking for houses which were being given to us by indulgent fathers.

We laughed over this and when one of us went to look at a house, the other was always there.

We inspected numerous residences. Some would be too small, some too large; some were too far from the centre of town and neither Justin nor Gervaise would like that. There was, we discovered, a similarity between our husbands. They were both what were called men about town. Justin appeared to have a private income from his family; Gervaise had an allowance from his. So it seemed inevitable that we should, on so many occasions, become a party of four.

After much preoccupation with Adam doorways and spider web fanlights, Regency and Queen Anne, we found our houses. They were not far apart. Morwenna's was Regency with a charming wrought-iron balcony on the first floor; ours was of a slightly earlier period – small but a model of Georgian elegance.

Our parents came to London and we had a pleasant time shopping for the furniture, the Pencarrons and my parents vying with each other in what they wanted to do for their darling daughters.

It was a very happy and merry time; and both Morwenna and I were examples of newly-wedded and decidedly contented wives.

Within a few months we were installed in our respective houses. Grace was naturally a great help and helped us choose colours for carpets and curtains, throwing herself into the project with the utmost enthusiasm; and the days sped by.

During this time the Prince Consort died. A feeling of gloom swept over the nation. Those who had been highly critical of him during his lifetime now saw him as a model of virtue. As for the poor Queen, she was prostrate with grief and shut herself away, refusing to appear in public.

We dined often with Morwenna and Justin and they with us. Morwenna sang rather pleasantly and I played the pianoforte – not well, but adequately. Justin had quite a good tenor voice, and Gervaise sang out of tune which caused a certain amount of merriment. We enjoyed what we called our musical evenings, but we soon realized that the men were restive. They preferred to play cards, which neither Morwenna nor I had any gift for.

We liked amusing games which did not require too much concentration and very often we would leave the men together. The first time I was amazed and a little disturbed to realize that they played for money.

Gervaise, I remember, was in good spirits when they first did this. He had taken quite a bit from Justin.

I did not like it. 'Why?' I said. 'He was a guest in our house.'

Gervaise looked at me in astonishment and burst out laughing.

'Of course, darling. We gave him a wonderful evening. He enjoyed it thoroughly.'

'Enjoyed losing money!'

'It was all part of the fun. I have discovered he likes a good gamble.'

'I don't suppose he likes losing money.'

'Well, naturally we all prefer to win.' He seized me and danced round the bedroom with me. 'You are a funny little thing, Angelet.'

'Why?'

He took my chin in his hands and kissed me tenderly. 'Such quaint ideas! Most men like a game of chance, you know.'

'Yes,' I said. 'I suppose they do.'

But it did occur to me that both Gervaise and Justin liked it better than most.

After that there were often cards. When they came to dinner or we went to them I had the idea that they could not wait to get to the card table.

They played a lot of poker. I watched them sometimes with that light in their eyes and that feverish colour in their cheeks.

194

It was more than excitement. It was obsession. It worried me a little. I used to hope that neither of them would win and they would both end just as they started.

I did gather that Justin won very often. Gervaise would shrug his shoulders.

'All have their ups and downs,' he said.

'You seem to have more downs than ups with Justin,' I commented.

'It's the way of things. It will change. It always does. The exciting thing about luck is that it is unpredictable. That's why they call it Lady Luck. It's like a woman.'

'Do you find me unpredictable?'

He put his arms round me. 'Of course not. Didn't I tell you, you were unique. That's why I love you.'

I could often forget my misgivings when I was with Gervaise; he had a convincing way of making light of difficulties.

I had thought at first that Justin and Gervaise were very much alike. They were in some ways, of course; their style of life; their affability towards everyone; their love of a gamble. Neither of them worked. I realized I had been used to people's working around me. There had always been problems on the Cador estates and my father had frequently been busy; Mr Pencarron was deeply concerned with the mine; our friends in the two Pendoreys were lawyers or doctors; Uncle Peter was immersed in his business; Matthew was at the House; Peterkin and Frances with their Mission. But Gervaise and Justin were different in this.

Justin was considering, he said. He was going to do something. He had arrived in this country from America not long ago. He had been involved with the production of cotton over there. He was, as he said, feeling his way. He wanted to do something but he was not yet sure what. Gervaise had no such pretensions. He was quite content with life as it was. He had the belief that one day he would make such a killing at the card tables that his fortune would be made.

I did try to reason with him sometimes. I said: 'If you made a fortune at the card table you would immediately risk it again.'

'Yes. And win an even greater fortune.'

195

I said: 'Do you forget what happened to your ancestor?'

'I was never allowed to. It was preached as Holy Writ in our household.'

'Well then, perhaps it is as well to keep it in mind.'

He always laughed at me when I was serious. Sometimes I found it faintly irritating; but he could always charm me out of that mood.

We were frequent visitors at the house in the square. Both Aunt Amaryllis and Helena took a motherly interest in us – Amaryllis, I suppose, because that was her way with all the young members of the family and Helena because she had 'brought us out'.

I enjoyed these dinner parties. Conversation was always lively, particularly when Uncle Peter was present. He and his daughter-in-law Frances often sparred, but I think he admired her, as he did all people who lived energetically.

Politics were often the subject of the discourse and I wished that Matthew and Uncle Peter would differ now and then; but Matthew always agreed with Uncle Peter's views.

At this time he was deploring the continued premiership of Palmerston.

'Surely it's time he retired,' said Uncle Peter. 'If he did, I think we should see a return of the party and office for you.'

Matthew said he would never retire. 'He'll die in harness. That is the old man's way. Sometimes he looks as if he is half asleep or wholly so. He sits there on the bench with his eyes half closed . . . a real dandy in his frock coat and light grey trousers, wearing his gloves. He always wears his gloves. You're certain he hasn't heard a word of the debate. Then he'll get to his feet . . . You know that way of his, poking fun at things . . . getting them laughing . . . and then he'll somehow get the vote going the way he wants it.'

'A remarkable man,' said Uncle Peter. 'He should have been with us.'

'That's true,' agreed Matthew. 'Who else could overcome all that tittle-tattle about his love-affairs? Who would believe that a Prime Minister could be nicknamed Cupid?'

I loved to hear those little anecdotes of people whose names

I knew so well. So those dinner parties were always a delight. Gervaise enjoyed them too. Sometimes I felt that Uncle Peter saw too much. I believe he knew about Gervaise's gambling, for one day he said to me: 'You want to keep a tight hand on that husband of yours. He's too fond of the tables.'

Uncle Peter should know. He had made his fortune out of those clubs where gambling – among other diversions – was in full swing.

He was very watchful of Justin and, I was sure that Justin puzzled him more than Gervaise did.

There came one evening at the house in the square which was to change our lives, although I did not know it then.

They had been discussing Palmerston's increasing age again and expressing some anxiety for the health of Lord Derby who must surely defeat him at the next election; then they went on to the antics of Benjamin Disraeli whose sights were set on the highest post of all.

Then Uncle Peter said suddenly: 'By the way, I have heard from Benedict.'

I saw Gervaise glance at me. I started, but not with that apprehension which I had known before my confession to Gervaise. He had convinced me that I was in no way to blame and that it would be sensible for me to put the incident right out of my mind.

Uncle Peter went on: 'He writes rarely. I don't think it has been as easy as he at first thought it would. But now it seems there has been a breakthrough.'

He explained to Gervaise and Justin. 'Benedict, my grandson . . . an earlier family . . . is a very go-ahead young man and had this notion of going out to Australia when he heard gold had been found there.'

'That was a long time ago,' said Aunt Amaryllis.

'Yes, it must be now. Benedict is not a letter-writing man and he certainly wouldn't communicate when times were hard. But I must say that he is a sticker. He went to Australia convinced that he would come back with a fortune and he is the sort who wouldn't want to return without one. That's why he is still out there.'

197

'Well,' said Matthew, 'there hasn't been a fortune yet.'

'He writes and says that there have been difficulties, but he thinks he's on a good strike now. There's a lot of hard work to be done, it seems, but his luck is changing. He says he has been scratching a living from the goldfields so far but he was always hopeful . . . and now it looks as though those hopes are about to be realized.'

'In what part of Australia is all this happening?' asked Justin.

'It's somewhere north of Melbourne.'

'I remember what a lot of talk there was about finds there,' said Justin. 'It was very exciting. It must be more than ten years ago. There was a similar sort of thing in America. But that was somewhat earlier, I think. A man comes across it . . . there's a lot of talk . . . and the Rush is on. Someone did very well at a place called Golden Point, I believe. That was in Australia. He made a vast fortune. People left everything to go out there. They thought they were coming back millionaires.'

'And did they?' I asked.

'Some of them did.'

'Well, let's hope Benedict is successful,' said Uncle Peter. 'Somehow I don't think he will come home until he is. He's got that bulldog tenacity. Once he gets hold of an idea he won't let it go. He'll succeed or stay out there for the rest of his life . . . trying to.'

'It is very interesting,' said Gervaise. 'I can understand how people get caught up in it.'

'It's a gamble,' said Uncle Peter. 'So much would depend on luck. You would get some working day and night and finding nothing . . . and then someone comes along and in a week or so he's stumbled on a fortune.'

Aunt Amaryllis shivered. 'I should hate that,' she said.

Uncle Peter smiled at her tenderly.

'Don't worry, my dear. I have no intention of throwing up everything to go to the goldfields of Australia.'

Everyone laughed and they began to talk of other things.

When we returned home Gervaise was thoughtful.

'Interesting about Benedict,' he said. 'He was the one you told me of.'

I nodded.

'He seems rather a forceful character.'

'Oh yes. I am sure he will find his gold.'

'It seems to have taken him rather a long time.'

'Yes, but he is bound to win in the end.'

'And come back a millionaire.'

I was wondering if he ever thought of me and of that adventure which we had shared together. It was significant that I could think of it now without that little shiver of fear. Gervaise had done that for me.

I did not notice how thoughtful Gervaise had become.

It was some days later when he broke the news to me. When we had last been at the house in the square he had left me with Aunt Amaryllis and had disappeared with Uncle Peter. When they rejoined us, Gervaise looked a little flushed – excited, I thought. Uncle Peter was his usual calm self.

I fancied Gervaise was impatient to leave.

When we finally did he was rather silent on the way home and at last in our bedroom I asked him if anything was wrong.

'Wrong?' he said. 'No. About to be right. How would you like to go to Australia?'

'What?' I cried.

'We're going,' he told me. 'That is, if you like the idea . . . I shall have to go. I hope you will come too.'

'Gervaise, what ever are you talking about?'

'I suppose,' he said, 'I had better begin at the beginning.'

'It is usually advisable to.'

'I'm in debt . . . up to my ears.'

Horror seized me. I felt limp with dismay and fear.

'But how? I've tried so hard . . .'

'I know you have. I've lost a lot to Justin. That's not so important. It's the clubs . . . I have to pay my debts. I'd never be received in any of them again if I didn't.'

'Perhaps that would be just as well.'

'You don't understand, Angelet. They are debts of honour.

199

One can make one's tailor wait . . . or the butcher, the baker and the candlestick-maker . . . but one must pay one's gambling debts at the clubs.'

'How much?'

'Too much to tell you.'

'I had better know.'

'I'm not sure . . . except that it is too much for me to handle. That's the bad news. Now here is the good. My debts are going to be settled. I have had a word with your Uncle Peter.'

'Why is he brought into this?'

'He does own several of the clubs where I play.'

'Oh, Gervaise, I thought you were getting better.'

'Sorry,' he said ruefully. 'But listen. We're going to Australia. We are going to find gold. We're going to be millionaires. Then I shall shrug aside my debts because with a lordly gesture I shall pay on the nail.'

'Do be sensible, Gervaise. This is a serious matter.'

'Sorry again, darling. Of course it is a serious matter. But it is going to be exciting.'

'What has Uncle Peter said to you?'

'He will settle my debts and pay our passage out . . . with a little to spare for the time before we get started. He's writing to Benedict asking if he will meet us and help us to get started, to be our sponsor and guardian angel. And we shall be leaving shortly for our adventures overseas.'

'Why should Uncle Peter settle your debts?'

'It's not quite so altruistic as you might be thinking. Your uncle is an astute businessman. He wants what they call collateral for his money.'

'What do you mean?'

'Some sort of security which we are in a position to offer.'

'What?'

'This house, of course.'

'It was my parents' wedding present!'

'That does not in any way detract from its value.'

'Gervaise, what have you done!'

'Nothing as yet. It's all in the air. But it is a wonderful solution. In fact it is the only solution . . . or I fear that ere long

I shall find myself languishing in prison for debt: and what chance has a poor debtor then of repaying what he owes?'

'Gervaise, you're frightening me.'

'I'm frightening myself. I am seeing more and more that I have to find a way out of this trouble . . . and this is it. I have to do something, Angelet.'

'Some work, you mean. Yes, I have thought of that.'

'This will be admirable. It will suit my temperament. Every day will be a gamble. Just imagine it . . . the excitement of going into those goldfields . . . never knowing whether it is going to be The Day.'

'We know nothing about it. Where shall we live?'

'Oh, there are places. The experienced and knowledgeable Benedict will show us the way. From him we will learn all we need to know. You don't seem enthusiastic, Angelet.'

'It's hard to. I know nothing about it. It all seems a trifle mad to me. And you have given Uncle Peter this house in order to settle your debts. You can't do that.'

'It's only on paper . . . a safeguard . . . for him. When we come back with all these millions of pounds' worth of nuggets . . . I think that's what they call them . . . we shall hand him back what we owe him and we shall have our dear little house waiting for us. But Angelet Mandeville might wish for a grander place in which to live now that she is a golden millionaire. A country mansion and a town house. I wonder if there are any castles for sale?'

'Be practical, Gervaise.'

'I'll try, but I'm so excited about this project. I know in my bones that it is going to be right for us.'

We lay awake for a long time talking about Australia. It seemed to me a wild dream . . . something that Gervaise liked to contemplate and had no roots in reality. But I was perturbed about all the debts and that he could mortgage our house in order to settle them.

I thought it might be one of those dreams with which Gervaise liked to soothe himself and that he only half believed it. But this was not so. He really had spoken to Uncle Peter. Uncle Peter himself took me on one side and said: 'I think it is not

201

such a bad idea. Gervaise is one of those people who are always going to gamble. Nothing would cure him. I'll take care of things here while you are away. If he could get himself a fortune I fancy he would not be so reckless. Young men with small incomes often try to augment them. It might be that if he were rich the urge might diminish a little.'

'Do you really think we should go to Australia?'

'I think it is not a bad idea, as I said. People are beginning to talk of Gervaise's tendency . . . not for play but not to pay. A man needs a good income to live the way he does. Let him go to Australia. It might be good for him . . . and it could be the making of him. I have written to Benedict. I am sure he will do all he can to help.'

My parents came to London. I could see that they did not like the idea – particularly my mother. That was understandable. She would be thinking of her own visit to Australia which had ended in such a disastrous climax.

I was sure that my father would have settled Gervaise's debts rather than that we should go, but I was beginning to see that that would be no real solution. Gervaise must do something for himself. If his debts were paid there would be more. I knew him now. This gambling was not merely a pastime with him; it was an obsession. It was almost like an illness; it would recur. If he did find a fortune in Australia it was just possible that that urge would diminish . . . possibly be cured. I had come to the conclusion that it was something we had to try.

Grace was horrified. She said: 'Think of all the hardships out there.'

'Yes, my mother has talked of them. But she was there a long time ago. Things may have changed.'

I was very apprehensive, but Gervaise was so eager. I think he had had a real fright when he realized the amount of his debts and what the consequences would be if he could not meet them. He was desperate and this seemed an honourable way out.

Morwenna was very sad at the thought of my going. Justin was particularly thoughtful; and then one day, Morwenna came to me in a state of great excitement.

Before I could ask what had happened, she burst out: 'We're coming with you. Justin thinks it would be wonderful to seek our fortunes in the goldfields. For so long he has been thinking of what work would suit him. This is just it.'

I looked at her and laughed; and then we were hugging each other.

I think everyone felt a little easier because the four of us were going. Grace seemed particularly relieved.

'It will make such a difference,' she said. 'I am so pleased.'

'Really, Grace,' I replied, 'the way everyone is talking you would think we were never coming back.'

'Morwenna will be a good companion for you . . . and Justin and Gervaise get on so well together.'

'I am afraid they are both too fond of gambling.'

'Well, let us hope that this gamble brings the desired results.'

After that I could view the prospect with more enthusiasm. It was to be a great adventure and, I told my mother, we could be lucky very soon. In that case we should come home at once. Who knew, we might be with her this time next year.

There had been a reply from Benedict. He would do all he could to help. There was a letter for me in which he said he had often thought of me and he was delighted at the prospect of seeing me again. 'You must be quite grown up now. A married woman! I wonder if we shall recognize each other.'

I was sure I should recognize him. He had been vivid in my mind for so long.

Much as I hated leaving my family, I was growing excited at the prospect of a completely different life.

And in due course we travelled to Tilbury and set sail on the *Royal Albert*, our destination – Melbourne.

Gold

Once the excitement of getting on board and settling into shipboard life was over, the voyage was, I suppose, an uneventful one. The ports of call were of great interest to us and Gervaise was a wonderful guide and companion. He seemed to have cast off all memory of those hideous debts which he had left behind; he was so sure that all would be well, and such was his personality that he made me believe it, too.

Life seemed one long round of pleasure with him; I suppose it was that side of his nature which made me love him. It was impossible to be unhappy long in his company; he had the gift of shrugging off the unpleasant and making the most of what was delightful.

I had asked him not to gamble again. I said: 'You see what it has brought you to.'

He put on a mock-penitent expression and said he would do anything in the world to please me. I took it that meant he would restrain himself from the habit which had already wrought such havoc in our lives.

I was young; I was adventurous by nature and I could not help throwing myself into the excitement of the moment. I began to accept Gervaise's optimism. We *were* going to strike gold. In a very short time we should come back rich and all debts would be paid to Uncle Peter. We should live happily ever after in our dear little house in which I had taken such pride. And having acquired a fortune, Gervaise would lose the desire to make another. The present and the future were always good in Gervaise's eyes; it was only the past, if that were unpleasant, which should be forgotten.

And so I began to enjoy the voyage. We made a few friends

on the ship. We liked Captain Gregory. He knew Australia well. His father had settled there forty years before and had a property outside Melbourne. The Captain had come to England to study navigation. He visited his family when his ship called at Australia. We often dined with him and the Chief Officer – a very pleasant young man who told us a great deal about the ship.

We looked forward to arriving at the ports. Morwenna said that one of the most delightful experiences was being at sea and waking up one morning to find oneself in port. The four of us would go out together; we revelled in strange places and marvelled at the scenery and the customs of the people, which were different from our own; life was amusing and full of pleasure.

It was wonderful to see places which hitherto had been only names on the map; it was exciting to take a horse-drawn carriage in Tenerife and visit that spot where our own Lord Nelson had fought and lost his right arm. I could have lingered there. I should have enjoyed going up to the sunken crater of Las Canadas and to have mounted even higher up Pico de Teide which dominated the island.

But our stay was brief. I told the Captain that was a matter of great regret. He smiled at me and said: 'The object, my dear young lady, is to get you to Melbourne as fast as we can. We stop at these places only to load stores.'

Gervaise said: 'It is probably as well that our stays are brief. It makes us appreciate it all the more.'

He was determined to enjoy every moment and I wondered briefly whether in his heart he doubted whether we would come out with the gold which would change our fortunes and how he would adapt to the life of a miner. If he did, he never showed it. I had learned a great deal about him since our marriage but there was still a great deal to discover.

I remember Durban – the capital of Natal – which had recently become a British Colony. It was a very beautiful town right on the coast and there was something very exciting in the sight of the waves breaking on the shore.

But perhaps what makes that time stand out so vividly in my memory was what happened aboard.

I had thought Morwenna looked a little tired and when we

205

returned to our cabins she said she would lie down. I had a feeling that there was something on her mind and I sought an early opportunity of talking to her.

That opportunity came after we had left Durban, from which we sailed at midnight. We were sitting on deck together. The sea was calm; there was not even a ripple on the water; it was the colour of translucent jade with here and there a touch of aquamarine.

I glanced at her sideways; she was pale and there were shadows under her eyes.

'Morwenna,' I said, 'is something wrong?'

'No, no,' she replied sharply. 'What should be?'

'I thought you looked a little . . . strained.'

'Strained? You mean tired?'

'Yes . . . as if something is worrying you.'

She was silent for a few moments, then she said: 'I'm very happy, Angelet. I don't think I have ever been so happy. The only thing that makes it less than perfect is that Ma and Pa are not here. I think they were very worried about my going.'

'Naturally they would be uneasy. They have adored you all your life. But it is always like that with families. The children grow up and marry and lead their own lives. I dare say my parents felt the same as yours.'

'I know.'

'That isn't what is worrying you.'

'I'm not worried, Angelet, I'm very happy.'

'Then what are you trying to tell me?'

'I thought you might guess. I am going to have a baby.'

'Morwenna!'

'Yes.' She was smiling. 'I think it is what I have always wanted. A little baby . . . all my own . . . and Justin's too.'

'What does Justin say?'

'He doesn't know. That's what makes me a little worried. That strain you detected. I am a little anxious. He is so enjoying all this. I didn't want to spoil it for him.'

'Do you think he would not want a child?'

'Oh no . . . He hasn't said anything like that. But you see, we are going to this new country and we don't know what we are going to find. He would be worried about me . . . and the baby.'

'That will be all right. They have midwives there and doctors, surely.'

'Yes, I suppose so.'

'It's wonderful. Oh Morwenna, I can't imagine you with a baby. You make me feel envious.'

'I suppose you'll have a baby one day.'

'Yes, I suppose so. And Justin doesn't know?'

'Not yet. You see, *I* knew before we left. At least I suspected. I thought if I told anyone it might spoil things. Mother and Pa would have put their foot down firmly and my father can be very persistent when he wants to. They would never have let me come away if they had known. They would have wanted me to go back to Pencarron and have the child.'

'Well, I can understand that.'

'Justin would have been worried. He had to go on this venture. I knew it. He is so enthusiastic . . . so sure that it is going to make our fortunes.'

'Just like Gervaise.'

'You would have done the same if you had been in my position, Angelet.'

'Yes, I suppose I might. But there is no need to keep it secret any longer. You're here on this ship. It isn't going to make any difference now. We are going on.'

'Yes,' she said. 'But I don't want to worry Justin.'

'He has got to share in this. Besides, you ought to be taking special care, oughtn't you? We shall have to cosset you a bit now.'

'I'm so glad you know.'

'I reckon we should tell the men.'

'All right. Let's do that. I'll tell Justin first . . . when we are alone.'

'And have I your permission to tell Gervaise?'

'Of course.'

When I told him he was amused. 'Well, fancy that,' he said. 'She's stolen a march on us.'

'She is very happy about the baby. She is so good and

207

unselfish. She doesn't think about going into what might well prove to be a primitive place. All she thought about was spoiling Justin's pleasure in all this.'

'Yes, she's a good girl. Justin is lucky. We are both lucky.'

That evening we celebrated. Justin was delighted; and I had never seen Morwenna so happy. Her first thought was that no one at home should know until the baby was born, for she was sure her parents would be very worried at the thought of her far from home at such a time.

There was another occasion during that voyage that I remembered well. It was after we had left Bombay. We had had only one day ashore but we had made the most of it. The heat had been intense, but we had been enchanted by the city, yet depressed by the multitude of beggars who surrounded us. Gervaise had quickly given away all the money he had brought out with him and for the rest of the day he cheerfully borrowed from the rest of us. We bought some beautiful silk materials and ebony elephants and some exquisite carved ivory.

It had been a most exciting day and that evening we dined with the Captain.

He loved to talk and was something of a raconteur. He had a pleasant custom of dining with most of the passengers during the voyage, and always at his table there was a great deal of gossip and laughter. Gervaise said he probably told the same stories over and over again; and that was why he liked to change the company.

That night he was in a reminiscent mood.

He said: 'Well, we shall not be so very long now. Soon we shall be reaching our destination and I shall have to say goodbye to all you charming people.'

We all said how we had enjoyed the voyage.

'It is an adventure in itself . . . the first time. Of course when I consider the number of times I have sailed between the Old Country and Australia . . . well, to tell the truth, I find it hard to remember how many.'

'It must have made you somewhat blasé,' I commented.

'Not as far as people are concerned. It is amazing how different people are. No voyage is ever like another . . . and it is all because of the people. I know you don't intend to settle in Australia. We get quite a number of passengers who are doing just that. I supose it is just a visit for you. Are you visiting relations?'

Gervaise said: 'We shall have a look at the goldfields.'

'Ah yes. We have had many coming out for that. Only of course the fever has died down a little lately. To what part are you going?'

'It's some miles north of Melbourne. A place called Golden Creek.'

'Oh, that's Lansdon country.'

'Lansdon country?' I stammered.

'That's what they call it. Chap named Benedict Lansdon made a bit of a stir there a few years back. He's a sort of big white chief in the neighbourhood.'

'We are going to see him. He's a . . . connection of mine.'

'Oh well, you'll be in the best company with Ben Lansdon. Couldn't be in better hands.'

'Do you know him?'

'Everyone thereabouts knows Ben Lansdon.'

'Why?'

'Well, he's made a bit of a name for himself. They think a great deal of him out there. It was rather like the Eureka Stockade affair all over again.'

'What was that all about?' asked Gervaise.

'I suppose that sort of news wouldn't get to the Old Country. Or if it did, it would just be a few lines on the back page of the newspaper. It was all over Melbourne. Peter Lalor was a sort of hero in that affair. It was miners against the government and it was the miners who really won in the end. Well, Ben Lansdon is another Peter Lalor. He's one of those natural leaders. He took charge and things got sorted out . . . so to speak. He's quite a name in the district.'

I felt a certain glow of pride. I was remembering him as he had been when he arrived at Cador. He had been different then from anyone I had ever known. I had admired him so much, adored him would be a more apt way of putting it. But in those days of my youth I had set up idols: my father: Jonnie: Ben. Yes, I was an idol-worshipper. But then that affair at the pool had changed everything and Ben had gone and I had been left to face it alone.

The Captain settled down to tell the tale. He loved an audience and on this occasion he had a very attentive one.

'You see,' he said, 'men were rushing out to find gold. People had been finding it for years and then – when would it be? – must have been in the early 'fifties, I think, when they found gold in New South Wales. Then at Ballarat near Melbourne someone found six hundred ounces in a couple of days . . . and that was it. People were scrabbling frantically for gold. Some found it. All over Victoria they were coming across gold. My father's place was nearby. He's often told me how the place changed overnight. All over the country little townships were springing up. They even had the odd hotel. Not the classy establishments they have at home, but good enough for miners who weren't looking for fancy living. They had one thing in mind: gold. Men were coming out by the thousands. When you've mined a certain spot for a few years the gold can run out. There is not an inexhaustible supply. There was a lot of hardship. Some would be working for weeks and months and finding nothing. To my mind, the government wanted to put a stop to the fever so they started to charge people a licence to dig. The more hardships there seemed to be, the higher were the fees. You see, what was wanted was to get people back to the towns, to put a stop to this search for gold which was not there.'

'But they wouldn't accept that,' said Gervaise. 'They had come out for gold and naturally that was what they were going to try for.'

'All very well,' went on the Captain, 'if it is there, but that was what the government was thinking. But if they were finding nothing how could they pay this money to the government? They got together and this Peter Lalor . . . he was a sort of leader.'

'Like Ben Lansdon,' I said.

'Oh, it was before he was around. I'm taking you back ten

years or more. All I said was that Ben was another like Lalor. They always come out when the time is ripe. Well, the government sent an order. There was to be an inspection of licences and all those who hadn't got them would have to leave the goldfields. You can imagine what they said to that!'

'But how could they fight the government?' asked Justin.

'I'll tell you how. Lalor rallied the men. They knew that the officials were coming to inspect licences, so they built a stockade. You must have heard of the Eureka Stockade. So they were ready and when the government men came for the inspection all those who had licences, for which they had paid much less than was now being asked, threw them out before the stockade and burned them.'

'I suppose,' said Justin, 'the licences had to be renewed and it was the expensive renewal that they objected to.'

'That must have been about it,' said the Captain. 'Well, you know how these things go. The action of a little group of miners became a great rebellion. The government had to bring in the army. The miners stood firm by the stockade and over it they flew their flag. You'll be seeing that flag a good deal, I should imagine. It's flown on every goldfield in Victoria. It has a blue background showing the stars of the Southern Cross in white. We call it the Eureka Flag.'

'Who won?' asked Gervaise.

'The miners were outnumbered, as you can guess . . . three to one in fact, so the tale goes. There were seventy men, but they were brave men and they were fighting for what they thought was right. They were quickly subdued but there were losses on both sides.'

'So the rising was in vain,' said Justin.

'Not really. The government naturally had to show the miners that they couldn't make their own laws, but on the other hand they did not want people rising up like that all over the country. You could say that the men of the Eureka Stockade won in the long run. Before the year was out the law was changed. There was no inspection of licences. The Victoria government decided that it would dissociate itself from the miners. It was victory really because it was what they had been fighting for. Lalor, the

211

leader of the revolt, went into the Victoria parliament. He is now one of its most respected members. What started all this was your mention of Ben Lansdon. He is just such another as Peter Lalor.'

'He was a great man,' I said.

'He was a leader,' went on the Captain. 'There are men born to be such.'

'And Ben Lansdon is another?'

'I'd say that and no one could say otherwise . . . after the way he's taken over Golden Creek.'

'Has he found lots of gold?'

'My dear young lady, nobody – not even Ben Lansdon – can find gold where it is not.'

Justin put in: 'Do you mean to say there is no more gold in Golden Creek?'

'Who can say? When the Rush started men were finding it day after day, but, as I've told you, the supply ran out . . . or they are looking in the wrong place. I don't think there have been any big finds in Golden Creek in the last ten years or so.'

'And you say it is Ben Lansdon's country,' I persisted.

'Well, he's got his men working for him. You see, there are some who would rather work for a weekly wage than have nothing but hope for the odd find. That's men with families mostly. You can't feed a family on hope. So Lansdon . . . well, he's not the sort who would want to do hard labour – and believe me working a mine is just that – so he gets other people to do it for him.'

'But what does he do?'

'He's right at the heart of things. He's at his mine every day. He watches how everything is going. True, there is a yield. But it is just about enough to keep things going. He did have some luck earlier on . . . enough to build a house for himself and bring a little of Old Country-type comfort into his life. He's done a lot for the place. He keeps a sort of law and order. Men out there can get a bit rough with each other when day after day they are looking for luck which doesn't come. Somebody said, "Hope deferred makes the heart sick" and that's true enough. Oh yes, Ben's done a lot for Golden Creek. He's the

212

King of the place, that's what. It suits him. He's a born leader, and leaders like to lead . . . to rule, if you like.'

I felt a great longing to see him. Forgotten memories of the times we had spent together came back to me; those occasions which had been overshadowed by the incident of the pool, so that for a long time I had failed to remember all the interesting talks we had had; and how important it had been to me then.

Gervaise said: 'I can't wait to see this hero.'

When we were alone that night, he said: 'The Captain is obviously a great admirer of your Ben, who is evidently a very forceful character. How do you feel about seeing him again?'

'I don't know.'

'Will it bring it all back . . . that time?'

'I expect so. But, Gervaise, you have made me see that we couldn't have done anything else.'

'I expect this leader of men has long realized that. I feel pretty sure that he will have forgotten all about it long ago.'

'Does one ever forget such a thing?'

He took my face in his hands and kissed it tenderly.

'You might not, Angelet, but I'd bet that Ben has.'

I nodded.

And I thought: Perhaps I shall soon find out.

I recognized him on the quay as soon as we arrived.

He was very tall and he seemed leaner than I remembered. His hair was so bleached by the sun that it seemed almost white against his bronzed skin; and his eyes were a brilliant blue; they were creased at the corners as though against the sun; and he had an authoritative air about him.

He saw us at once and came striding towards us.

'It's Angel,' he cried. 'I'd have known you anywhere. You've grown up, though, since I last saw you.'

I was laughing. I said: 'You too, Ben.'

He put his arms round me and hugged me. He grinned at Gervaise, whom he had decided must be my husband. 'We're old friends,' he said, as though apologizing for his exuberant and familiar welcome.

213

'I know,' replied Gervaise with his charming smile. 'I've heard a great deal about you from Angelet, and this is Justin Cartwright and his wife Morwenna.'

'Pleased you've come,' said Ben. 'I reckon you'll need a day or so in Melbourne before you come out to the Creek. I've booked you in at the Lord Melbourne. The baggage can go to the hotel. I expect you have brought quite a bit. I can arrange to have it all sent on to the Creek.'

'Oh Ben,' I said, 'you are so good to us.'

The others agreed.

'It's nothing,' he answered. 'I'm glad you've joined the company. I can tell you we're starved of news of Home. The whole community is looking forward to your arrival. But now let's get you to the hotel and I'll tell you what arrangements have been made.'

We were put in what I learned was called a buggy, and passing through streets where I glimpsed some pleasant-looking houses we had soon arrived at the hotel.

We were taken to a reception desk where a lady in black presided. I caught a glimpse of men sitting at tables drinking and others at a bar.

We were at length led up a wide staircase and along a corridor to rooms which looked out on the street below. Our room had an alcove in which were washing necessities, and we were agreeably surprised.

When the door shut on us, Gervaise turned to me and, picking me up, danced round the room.

'We're here,' he cried. 'Now . . . to fortune!'

'Oh Gervaise,' I said, 'I do hope it turns out that way.'

'Of course it will. We'll make it.'

'Can we?' I asked.

He nodded with certainty.

Ben had told us that he was staying at the hotel for one night to settle us in. Then he would return to Golden Creek and we were to follow later.

Over dinner that first evening in Melbourne he explained a great deal to us.

He said: 'You will find life down at the Creek somewhat

214

rough, although it has improved a great deal since I came here. I expect you are a little surprised by what you have seen of this town. Is it not a little more civilized than you were expecting?'

We all said that Melbourne appeared to be a very fine city indeed.

'Stretch your imagination a little and you might be in a provincial town in England, eh? Well, almost. They've worked wonders here. It's all been happening since we got self-government.'

'But surely this is a colony?' said Gervaise.

'What I mean is separation from the rest of Australia. When you talk of us you say "The Colony of Victoria". That's how we like it. The Queen of England granted us the right to separate ourselves and because of that we do her the honour of calling the colony after her. We're Victoria and she is pleased. One day I'll show you a cutting I have. I've kept it. It is a bit of history really. It's from the *Melbourne Herald*. "Glorious news," it states, "Separation at last. We are an independent Colony."'

'I should have thought,' I said, 'that it would be better if you all stood together.'

Ben shook his head. 'They are an independent people out here. 1851. That was the great year in the history of Victoria.'

'It's the year we must have met,' I said involuntarily.

He smiled at me. 'That is absolutely right. There was the Great Exhibition going on in Hyde Park. And I appeared out of the blue. Quite a shock for my grandfather.'

'Your grandfather is shock-proof.'

'He is a little like his grandson, perhaps.'

The blue eyes were on me. Some understanding flashed between us. I knew he was thinking, as I was, of the man we had dragged into the pool.

He changed the subject abruptly.

'There's a good deal of wealth round about Melbourne. You'll see some really fine houses here. They've grown up since the Gold Rush. Those who got in first were the lucky ones.'

'What of you?' asked Justin.

'I've had a small share of the pickings, I'd say; but I haven't struck the rich veins.'

215

'Do you think,' said Justin in some alarm, 'that it has been worked out?'

Ben was silent for a moment. Then he said: 'One can't tell. There is no doubt that we have had gold in this part of the world. Whether it has been worked out is something we can't be sure of. One thing we do know: it is not as easy as it was.'

'We did hear that you had a mine,' I said. 'The Captain of the *Royal Albert* seemed to know a great deal about you.'

'Fame travels,' said Ben lightly. 'What did he tell you about me?'

'That you were a sort of Peter Lalor.'

'Oh . . . our respected member of Parliament and the hero of the Eureka Stockade. I shouldn't have thought we were alike. I have no intention of going into politics here.'

'He said you were a leader.'

Ben burst out laughing. 'Lalor was a noble fellow. I don't think I'd match him in that. He worked for the good of the community.'

'And for whose good do you work?'

'For the good of myself, of course.'

We all laughed.

He said: 'I have arranged for places for you with Cobb's. It'll make travelling out to the Creek a little more comfortable than it would have been in the past.'

'Who are Cobb's?'

'Mr Cobb is from California. He came out here when there were so many people who wanted to get from the goldfields to the towns. His business extends all over Australia now. We are grateful to Mr Cobb of California. He is a great boon to us all, I can assure you; and when you travel in one of his coaches and ask yourself how, without him, you would get from one place to another, you will be ready to sing his praises, too.'

'I don't know what we should have done without you, Ben,' I said.

'You'd have managed. But you might have found it a bit rough going. It is better to have someone who knows the ropes to help you along.'

'Uncle Peter said you would do all you could for us.'

'Naturally I will,' he said, his blue eyes holding mine for a moment. He went on: 'I shall be leaving tomorrow, so I shall be there when you arrive. I did think the ladies would want a little time to shop in Melbourne. There will be certain things you want to get. We've got one shop in the Creek. It sells most things, but there is not much choice. I've arranged places for you to live in . . . close to where the work goes on. You'll have to stake your claim. I should advise you to go in together if that would suit you. You'll be needing each other. It's hard going, you know. But you'll learn.' He looked at me intently. 'You won't find the place like Cador or my grandfather's London residence.'

'We are prepared for inconveniences,' I said.

'That's a good thing because you'll get them.'

Gervaise said: 'You have been most kind. We don't know how to thank you.'

'When you strike gold you can give me a commission,' said Ben lightly.

'We certainly shall,' said Gervaise. 'I'll drink to that.'

'Very well, partner, but first find the gold.'

'We were told you have a mine and people work for you,' I said.

'That's true.'

'Do you not . . . do the mining yourself?' asked Morwenna.

'I'm there every day. I know exactly what's going on. I just have a few men to do the donkey work.'

I thought it was very exciting to be with him. He had that immense vitality which made one feel alive. I wondered if he had married. No one had said anything about a wife. I supposed there were not many women at Golden Creek. I might have asked him – but I did not.

We returned fairly early, for it had been an exhausting day. Gervaise was elated.

He said: 'It is all working out beautifully. This relation of yours . . . he really is quite a character.'

'Yes,' I said.

'One can believe all one has heard of him.'

'Do you like him, Gervaise?'

217

Gervaise was thoughtful. 'I'm not sure,' he said at length. 'He'd be a good friend, but I imagine he could be quite ruthless. He must have been to have done what he did.'

'You mean the pool?'

'It would take some courage to do that . . . a cool sort of courage. Yes, I think he would be a good friend, but I should not care to provoke him.'

'Why?'

'As I said, I think he could be ruthless. But we're here. Isn't it wonderful?'

'Yes, it is, Gervaise. It's exciting. I like this place. I am sure they must have some good midwives here.'

He stared at me.

'I was thinking of Morwenna,' I said.

We had three days in Melbourne. Morwenna and I explored the town together. We shopped and bought clothes for the baby. There was a good supply and we were delighted. We discovered a hospital. I wanted to make enquiries about it but Morwenna said it was too soon.

Everywhere we went we were welcomed. The people here seemed to enjoy having visitors from Home, which was how they regarded England. All the time they wanted to hear news of what was happening there and they told us how they lapped up everything they could hear and how irked they were because they could not get enough news. They were proud of their town but there was a certain detectable nostalgia in their voices when they talked of Home.

It is exciting to be in a city which is almost growing under one's eyes. At home everything was so old. London had been the Londinium of the Romans; antiquity lurked in every corner; and Cornwall, with its legends and stories, memories of before the coming of Christianity to our islands, seemed ageless. But a few years ago there had been no buildings here. I tried to imagine what it would have looked like then, and failed. But after I had listened to some of the people, who were very ready to talk, and had read accounts of the first settlers, a picture

218

began to form in my mind. I could see those settlers coming over from Van Diemen's Land and how they must have been struck by the beauty of the scenery – the wild bushland and the oaks and eucalypts and the river, its banks covered with bright yellow flowers, flowing into the sea. That was in the year 1835 before I was born, but to these people it did not seem so long. There had been some aborigines here – dark men who regarded them with wonder and from whom they learned that the name of the river was the Yarra Yarra.

I could see myself arriving with those people, marvelling at the colourful birds – red-crested black cockatoos, yellow-crested white ones, the gallahs and the laughing kookaburras – all of which I was looking forward to discovering.

I was excited, wondering what my life here would be like. Ben was never far from my thoughts. I wanted to talk to him, to hear of his adventures. I wanted to hear everything about this new country from him.

There were some fine houses. Gold had made the town rich. We were amused to find that the name of one of the nicest parts of the town was Richmond, so reminiscent of our own Richmond on the Thames. When I had been to London to visit the Exhibition and had first met Benedict we had been to Richmond together. We had gone down the river from Westminster Stairs. Jonnie had been with us, but what I remembered most was laughing with Ben, talking with Ben and the pleasure of being with him.

Although I was on the other side of the world I felt at home. I could love this place; it excited me because it was different and yet not alien. People talked to us in shops over the baby linen about the stores which we thought we should take with us. Morwenna and I had agreed, though, that we should have to see what we needed first, which we could only do when we settled in; then we should have to pay other visits to Melbourne. These people were very anxious to tell us what a fine town they had; we heard of the theatre which had been built; the fine shops which were springing up everywhere; the grand houses, and how the settlers had brought with them English manners and customs. They played cricket just as in England and a short while ago, in 1861 to be precise, the All-England Eleven match had been played on the Melbourne Cricket Ground. Two thousand people had come to welcome the players from Home, and the match had gone on for four days.

It was just like home.

The men were impatient to be on the move, and although I felt there was so much more I wanted to see in Melbourne, I was eager to take the coach and set out for Golden Creek.

We took the Cobb's Coach on the appointed day. It was a smart-looking vehicle, made in America, drawn by six sturdy horses and it carried seventy passengers.

Our purchases and baggage had been sent on to Golden Creek, so we had nothing to worry about.

It was a very interesting journey. We had a chance to see some of the fine houses which had been built in the environs of the town. Most of the builders had endeavoured to produce an English country mansion.

At length we were out in the country. There were miles and miles of bush broken only by the occasional tall eucalyptus trees.

The days seemed long. I was rather anxious about Morwenna, who was beginning to show signs of fatigue. There could be no possible doubt that she was fairly well advanced in her state. I prayed that all would go well with her. Whatever she said, as soon as we arrived, I was going to make enquiries as to what arrangements could be made for bringing children into the world.

There were two nights when we stayed at inns which were prepared for the periodic visits of the travellers and were referred to by some people as Cobb's Houses. Conditions were primitive; the comforts of the city did not extend to these places.

'Never mind,' said Gervaise. 'It is only for two nights. We didn't expect luxury, did we?'

We were all eager now to reach Golden Creek.

Several people got off the coach. The rest were going on to other fields further on.

220

Ben was waiting for us.

He said: 'I think you had better come first to my place. Then in the morning you can get down to business.'

I looked round me.

We had alighted in what could be called a street. There were a few buildings, mostly primitive. There was a shop. I supposed that was the one which sold everything; and about it the dwelling-places were like shacks. The pavement was a raised wooden platform. A number of people came running out of the shacks and the buildings at the arrival of the coach. There were several children, all shrieking and shouting, greeting some of the people who alighted.

'It's a red letter day when the coach comes in,' Ben explained.

'Where are the goldfields?' asked Gervaise.

Ben waved his arm. 'All about the town,' he said.

'You mean this place?'

'I'm sorry. I'm flattering it . . . calling it a town. The town of Golden Creek.'

'Is there a creek?'

'Certainly there is a creek. That is where it got its name.'

'Golden Creek,' murmured Justin.

'It deserved it once,' said Ben. 'Let's hope it will again. Come this way. It's just along here . . . away from the street. You can't see the house because it is surrounded by bush. I kept it that way. Privacy, you know.'

He led the way. 'You'll need horses,' he went on. 'Can't get on without them here. I have a biggish stable.'

'You are so good to us, Ben,' I said gratefully.

He laid his hand on my shoulder. 'Now, whom should I be good to if not to my own little cousin Angel? I'm not sure if it is cousin but that seems to be a term used for these vague relationships.'

We walked with him and in a short time we came to a spot where the bushes grew thick. He led us through them and before us was a lawn and then . . . the house.

It was of white stone and looked elegant and dignified and, perhaps because it seemed so out of place, imperious.

'Behold Golden Hall,' said Ben.

221

'Is that what you called it?' I cried.

He nodded. 'It was built out of gold. It's here because of gold. So what more appropriate?'

'It is really amazing,' I said.

'You will find a lot to amaze you out here, I hope.'

'I'm looking forward to that.'

'Well, come along in. They are prepared for you.'

'Who?' I asked quickly, and I felt a sudden fear that he was going to introduce us to his wife. I shouldn't have minded, but I did.

'I have two people working for me with their family,' he explained. 'Thomas and his wife Meg; they have a son Jacob and a girl Minnie. That is my staff. Thomas sold up everything to come out here to find gold. A familiar story.'

'So he didn't find gold. He found the Golden Hall instead?' said Gervaise.

'That's right. Many of them come out here with gold fever. They work frantically and perhaps they never have a find . . . and then they turn against it. They don't want to hear another word about gold. They want to settle down to the steady life they had before they came. Thomas is like that. And his wife agrees with him. I don't know about Jacob. He's young yet. Perhaps he'll catch gold fever one day and be off.'

'You seem to have found a pleasant niche for yourself here,' said Justin.

'The best of both worlds is the way I see it. I live like a squire but I have my mine and my hopes linger. One day I am going to find that rich vein of gold . . . and it will be such as was never found before.'

'And if you don't?' I asked.

'I shall go on trying until I find it or they carry me off in my coffin . . . whichever comes first.'

'There is determination,' said Gervaise.

'A lesson to you,' I replied.

'Well, come along in. Meg will have a meal cooking and I'll show you your rooms for the night. Then tomorrow . . . sharp . . . we'll get down to business.'

The house was a replica of an English manor house. There were high ceilings and heavy oak beams.

Ben said to me: 'I've tried to make it look like home.'

'It does,' I assured him.

We were taken into a drawing-room. It had french windows opening on to a garden.

'Jacob tends that,' said Ben. 'Thomas helps a little and Meg picks the flowers.'

'You must have thought of home often,' I mused, 'to make it so like . . .'

'Often,' he assured me. 'You should see your rooms now. Ah, here is Meg.'

She was a rotund, comfortable-looking woman with rosy cheeks and rather wispy brown hair.

'Our visitors, Meg,' he said.

She nodded to us and said she would take us to our rooms. She hoped we'd be comfortable and if there was anything we wanted we should ask.

She took us up the wide staircase and there were our rooms. Gervaise and I gave a little gasp of pleasure as we went into ours. The light filtering through the blinds showed us the blue carpet and the covers to match, the cosy armchair, the writing-desk and the alcove in which was a basin and ewer; there was a wardrobe and a dressing-table with a swing-mirror on it.

'I'll bring you hot water,' said Meg. 'Dinner will be in about twenty minutes if you can make it.'

We assured her we could.

Gervaise looked at me. 'This is more like it,' he said. 'I haven't seen anything like this since leaving home. I will say that Ben knows how to look after himself.'

Very soon we had washed and changed from our travelling clothes. We went down to the pleasant dining-room, which had windows similar to those in the drawing-room but these looked out on a well-kept garden to fields beyond.

I stood there looking out and Ben came to stand very close to me.

'That's Morley country,' he said.

'Morley country?'

223

'My neighbour, James Morley. He owns a lot of land round here. I bought this patch from him to build my house on.'

'Did he make a fortune out of gold?'

'No. He's been here for years. He came before the Rush and bought the land for next to nothing. He's a farmer . . . a grazier . . . cattle and sheep. That's his business and he has never deserted it for gold. He has done very well for himself, I can tell you. You'll be sure to meet him sometime. Now we mustn't let the food get cold or you will be in Meg's bad books right at the start, I can tell you.'

It was a wonderful evening, to sit there listening to Ben. He did most of the talking. We just plied him with questions.

There was hot soup followed by thick steaks.

'People here have big appetites,' Ben told us. 'It is the outdoor life.'

We made the acquaintance of Minnie, who came in to help her mother.

Ben talked about what lay ahead of us.

The following day he would take us to see the accommodation he had found for us.

'I don't know how you ladies are going to like it,' he said. 'It is primitive. But it is what they all have.'

'Except you,' I reminded him.

'Well, I decided to put my earnings into this house. That's reasonable. They thought it was a bit crazy, I don't doubt. The general idea is to strike it rich and move out.'

'And your intention was to stay?' asked Justin.

'Not I. When I have made the fortune I came out to find I shall go home. But it has to be a fortune. No little pickings for me. But in the meantime I want to make it comfortably. I have been thinking that you ladies ought to stay here.'

'Tell us about these places you have found for us,' said Morwenna.

'They are shacks really. It's a shanty town. You saw some of them coming in.'

'It is good of you to suggest we stay here,' I said. 'Thank you, Ben. But we shall have to be together . . . and do as the others do.'

He looked at me ruefully.

'So we are to live in two of those shacks . . .'

'The very same. At one time they were just in tents . . . and then they put up these shacks. They are in demand. I had to arrange a few details to get even them for you. There are two side by side. I thought you would like that. They are furnished with a bed, a few chairs and a table. There is a small rental. There is a division making a bedroom and a living-room and there is a little wash-house at the back. You have to get your water from the well. Water is rather precious here. The man who owns the places is another retired from the gold hunt. He finds this business of letting more profitable.'

I looked anxiously at Morwenna and thought of her condition.

'I am sure we shall be all right,'she said bravely.

'Well, you ladies are welcome to stay here whenever you like.'

'It is so kind and thoughtful of you,' said Morwenna, 'but we should want to be with our husbands.'

'Somehow I thought you might. It is what they would expect of you here.'

'Who?' I asked.

'The rest of the community.' Ben frowned. 'You see, you are all living close together. They would want you to be as they are. They're a mixed lot . . . all sorts and conditions. Some are quite aristocratic . . . others . . . well, definitely not. You have to mix with them. There is a certain code. We don't want trouble in the township. We have to keep a sharp lookout for that sort of thing.'

'What is there?' asked Gervaise. 'Some sort of vigilante?'

'You could say that. Well, you will see soon enough how it works. Now tomorrow you will want to see about your claim. What you buy will be your piece of land. I dare say you will want to work it together. I should think that was the best thing to do. The Mandeville-Cartwright Plot. You'll need two of you in any case. Well, we shall see.'

'I can't wait to start digging,' said Gervaise.

Ben gave him a strange look. I knew he was finding it difficult to imagine Gervaise as a miner.

225

That night I slept peacefully in the luxurious bed and I awoke early. I could not stay in bed, so I left Gervaise there and went into the alcove and washed; and then went downstairs.

I found my way to the dining-room, opened the french windows and stepped out.

The early morning air was delightfully fresh. I stood there looking out over the garden to what Ben had called Morley country.

I was thinking of a man who had come out here and bought up the land cheaply and started by grazing his sheep and cattle, unperturbed by the desire to make an easy fortune.

There was a step beside me and I was startled out of my reverie.

It was Ben.

'Taking the air?' he asked.

I nodded.

'Good, eh?'

I agreed that it was.

'Are you going to like it here, Angel?'

'Isn't it rather too soon to say?'

'Yes. You are going to find it rough, you know. Perhaps I should have given you more warning.'

'We didn't think we were coming out to a place with myriads of servants to wait on us, you know.'

'Even so . . . Well, remember, there is always room for you at the Hall here if it gets too much for you.'

'We shall have to live like the others.'

'Just at the moment, perhaps.'

Justin came out to join us. He looked fresh and rested. Ben asked him if he had had a good night and he replied that he had indeed. He was all ready now to start on the enterprise.

We went in to breakfast.

That day was one of great activity and discovery. In spite of Ben's warnings, Morwenna and I were a little taken aback at the sight of our new homes. Shack was an apt description. I could not quite see my elegant Gervaise fitting into such surroundings; but with the lust for gold on him, he made no complaint. This was going to be the greatest gamble of all.

There was a great deal of business to be done; and the men went off to choose their plot, which they did with Ben's help; and then they staked their claim. This took some time and while they were doing it, Morwenna and I made a minute examination of our new homes. When we had recovered from the initial dismay, we began to make plans for them. We decided that we could make them more attractive with perhaps a pretty curtain at the window and a few cushions. We looked at the township, which did not take us very long for it was just one street with its wooden platform serving as a sidewalk, and the rest was scattered shacks rather like our own. We discovered the wells. There were two. We went to the store and were helped by a certain Mrs Bowles, who ran it with her husband – two more who, I gathered, had given up the search for gold and settled for work which, while it might not bring the ultimate reward, gave them a steady living. She was very friendly and advised us as to what we should need. She was talkative and, as with most people, she was more interested in herself than in others: and once she had satisfied herself as to what part of the Old Country we had come from – no need to ask for what purpose – she was satisfied. She told us that her husband, Arthur, had come out to find gold.

She gave me a little nudge. 'These nuggets the size of your fist don't grow on trees. It's one in a million that finds them. After we'd gone three months without finding more than a few specks, I said to Arthur, "Enough's enough. What they want here is a good store . . . and that's what we are giving them."'

She told us that at home she had been a midwife. I was delighted. I looked significantly at Morwenna.

'Not enough babies born here to make it a profession,' she said. 'So I do it in between, like. When I'm called Arthur or one of the women will see to the shop. It works.'

We said nothing about Morwenna's condition then, but at least we knew there was an experienced woman close by. It was comforting.

During the next few days I learned a little about what life would be like here for Morwenna and me. We should be busy in the house. We had to cook, which meant keeping a fire going in the outhouse-type kitchen. We had to get water from the well. We had to be ready to buy meat early in the morning, so that we got it before the flies did. We could not keep it but had to cook it immediately. It seemed that we – who had never done any domestic work in our lives – had a good deal to learn.

So had the men.

Ben explained to us that much of the gold to be found now was deep in the earth. That near the surface had already been mined. It would be found in channels which they called leads – and we must follow them. This could mean digging down to perhaps one hundred feet. It had been easier in the beginning when the leads had been close to the surface of the earth.

Shafts had to be sunk through the clay and gravel; and these shafts had to be timbered as there was a danger of the earth's falling in and burying the miners alive.

Great heaps of what they called mullock – the earth which had been dug up – made hillocks at the sides of the mine shafts.

'Windlasses used to be placed on top of these,' said Ben, 'but that was simply not good enough for deep sinking. There have to be men down in the mine digging and filling buckets with earth; these are drawn up by winding the windlasses. Then the soil has to be panned in the stream to see if it contains the magic metal.'

Neither Gervaise nor Justin lost any of their enthusiasm at the prospect of so much hard work. This was a gamble, and I had come to realize that for Gervaise there was nothing in life which he found so irresistible.

They were out all day and came back to the shacks exhausted. Morwenna and I cooked the steaks for them over the open fire in our kitchens and we learned how to make dampers. There was beer to drink, for we had a saloon run by another of the disillusioned miners.

A week passed and I was surprised how much had been accomplished and how quickly we accepted our way of life.

I had glimpsed Ben now and then. He always seemed pleased to see me. He called at the shack one day and asked if Morwenna and I would ride with him. He thought we ought to see something of the countryside. He had seen Gervaise and Justin that morning and they were hard at it. He grinned.

'They can't stop working,' he said. 'It's always the way when people first come out. They are afraid to lose a minute because that might be the one minute when they find the six-hundred-ounce nugget. I told them I was going to call on you ladies and suggest I take you for a ride round.'

I said I should enjoy it and I thought Morwenna would too.

We found Morwenna lying down. She was having one of her bouts of sickness.

'Then it will be just the two of us,' said Ben. 'Come on. I'll find a horse for you.'

He had a sizeable stable; he chose a mare which he thought would be suitable for me and saddled her.

'She's yours,' he said, 'for as long as you are here.'

'You are so generous.'

'What! To my old friend?'

I smiled at him. 'I'm glad you're here, Ben. I think I should be a little uneasy if you weren't.'

'No need to think of that. I'm here. And here I stay.'

'Till you find your fortune.'

'That's right. How's that? Comfortable?'

'Very.'

'She's a good old stager, aren't you, Foxey?'

'Foxey! Is that her name?'

'Yes. She's that reddish colour and there's a look of a fox about her . . . or there was when she was born. She's a nice easy-going old thing.'

'You mean she's sober and suitable for a greenhorn?'

'Exactly. You don't want a wild thing when you are new to a country. This isn't like home, you know. It's all shrub for miles and miles. You could lose yourself here and wander round and round in circles. Now Foxey likes her home here in the stables and I wouldn't mind taking a bet that if you were lost, she'd bring you back.'

We rode away from the township.

'This is like old times,' he said. 'Remember how we used to ride together when I came to Cador?'

229

'Yes. Ben . . . do you ever think of . . .'

'You mean all that by the pool?'

'Yes,' I said. 'It haunts me even now.'

'It is all over and done with.'

'I can't forget what we did, Ben.'

'I know.'

'Does it still haunt you?'

'Not much.'

'In a way we killed him.'

He looked at me in amazement. 'He fell and hit his head on a stone. That was what killed him. It was a good thing. He wouldn't be able to murder any more innocent little girls.'

'But we . . . disposed of him.'

'H'm. Perhaps we should have left him there on the grass and reported it. That would have been the right thing to do, I suppose.'

'Yes, Ben, I wish we had.'

'There would have been a lot of questions. It would have been horrible for you . . . for me, too. No, what happened was best. He would have been hanged in any case.'

'I tell myself that.'

'My dear Angelet, I believe it has worried you terribly.'

'And you?'

'I don't think about it. It happened. I knocked him down and he struck his head on a stone. It killed him. We put him in that pool. That finished it.'

'I wish I had felt like that.'

'My dear Angel, it was easier for me. I was not nearly raped and murdered. You were the one who suffered that nightmare.'

He had pulled up and was looking at me.

'It has been on your mind all this time. Oh, you poor little Angel.' He took my hand and kissed it. 'I wish I'd known. I would have come to comfort you and made you see it as I did.'

'All the way from Australia?'

He looked at me solemnly. 'From the ends of the earth,' he said.

'Well, it would have been from the other side.'

We laughed and he said: 'You don't still feel guilty, do you?'

230

'I feel better and better. Seeing you helps.'

'I'm so glad you have come, Angel. I've thought a lot about you.'

'You mean because of that man?'

'No . . . not only that . . . though it was quite something to share together, wasn't it? But there were other things . . . our rides . . . our talks. Do you remember how we used to go to the moor, tie up our horses and lie on the grass and talk?'

'Yes, I remember.'

'Such happy times. Memorable times. I shall never forget them. We must go riding like this . . . often, Angel.'

'We shall both have work to do.'

'We'll find time. Come on.'

He started to gallop and I went after him.

Suddenly he pulled up. 'Look at all this,' he said. 'Fine grazing land. Morley territory . . . miles and miles of it.'

'He doesn't put fences round to keep people out.'

That made Ben laugh. 'My dear Angelet, he couldn't do it if he wanted to. It's too vast. As long as we don't steal his sheep we're welcome here. Look at this place. We could tie up our horses on that bush, and we could sit and talk as we used to. It brings back our youth, doesn't it?'

'A good idea.'

And it was just as it had been all those years ago on Bodmin Moor.

'I always remembered the tale you told me of the men who found gold in the tin mine and how they left a portion of the profits to those weird little men . . . who were they?'

'The knackers.'

'I remembered that when I heard there was gold here . . . in Australia. Well, I shan't be looking for gold in a tin mine, but in a far more likely place.'

He plucked a blade of grass and looked at it. 'Not as green as the variety we get at home,' he said. 'Are you homesick?'

'For Cador perhaps and my parents. But this is a new life and Gervaise is here . . . and Morwenna . . .'

'So you feel you have a little bit of home around you?'

'I suppose that's so. Tell me about the Morleys and the man I had heard called Bruin.'

He laughed. 'Bruin? That's Robin Bears, actually. We're lucky to have him here. He's invaluable to me . . . and to all here. I think they know it. He is always called Bruin . . . due to his name, of course. And he looks like a bear.'

'Is he one of the diggers?'

'Yes. But he has other duties. He was a prize fighter back home . . . quite a renowned one. He killed a man in the ring and after that he never wanted to box again. So he came out here to make his fortune. There was some difficulty about his claim and I was able to sort it out for him. I did very little really, but he thought it was a great deal. He is a simple man and the sight of that piece of paper with writing on it terrified him. I showed him where to put his mark and he thought I was some sort of magician. He now has his stake here; and I had an idea that he could help to keep order. You'll have to understand about that, Angel . . . all of you will. This isn't home. We have some rough characters here and we have to make the laws.'

'I know. You did tell me that.'

'You see, here we have this closely-knit community . . . most of us bent on one thing: finding that amount of gold which is going to make us rich overnight. It's a dangerous situation.'

'You mean theft?'

'I mean that among other things. There are some women here . . . but more men. When I see some of the men's eyes on the women, I am watchful. I have to be. We can't have trouble in the township. We have to make sure of some law and order.'

'Why you, Ben?'

'Because I have a lot to lose, I dare say. In any case, all of those who want peace while they get on with their work are with me. We can't set up courts of law. We'd have the government after us . . . and the government doesn't want to be troubled with petty squabbles on a gold-mining estate. They would like to see the whole thing dispersed and the men going back to working in the towns . . . and then perhaps the government would organize a search for gold. We don't want that. But we have to keep law and order going. This is where Bruin comes

232

in. If any man is found guilty of a sin against the community, Bruin issues a challenge. He demands they come and meet him in the ring. He then proceeds to punish them in accordance with their sin. It works. No one wants to face up to a pummelling from Bruin.'

'What an extraordinary way of meting out justice!'

'It works. Things have to be a bit unconventional here, you know. But you'll like Bruin. He's quite . . . unusual. He is well over six feet tall; his nose was broken in a fight and it has flattened it somewhat; he's got what they call a cauliflower ear; but he has the most innocent pair of wide blue eyes that you ever saw. They reflect his innocence. He is naïve; he is almost childlike. But you must like Bruin.'

'I feel sure I shall. Now tell me about the Morleys.'

'I am arranging for you to meet them very soon. I have told James about you. He wants you to go up to the house. He's glad you're here. He thinks Lizzie might find suitable friends in you and Mrs Cartwright.'

'Lizzie? It's the first time I've heard of her.'

'Lizzie is his daughter . . . the apple of his eye.'

'Is there a Mrs Morley?'

'Not now. She died. There are only old Morley and Lizzie. I'll show you their house. It's quite grand in its way. You see, we do have some beautiful houses here.'

'I know. I saw some in Melbourne.'

'Built by the gold millionaires mostly.'

'It is amazing how everyone wants to be rich.'

'Of course they do. Riches mean power, and power I suppose is one of the most desirable objects on earth . . . men being what they are.'

'You want that don't you, Ben?'

He nodded. 'Yes, I do.'

'And when you have it what will you do with it?'

'I shall see what my immediate needs are.'

'And then you will gratify them?'

'If it is possible, yes.'

'Power . . . money . . . they cannot give you everything.'

He looked at me steadily and said: 'There are things above

233

them, I know. But you must admit they provide a good deal. Are you happy, Angel?'

'Happy . . . why, yes.'

'Your Gervaise . . . he is a charming fellow.'

'Yes, he is. He was so wonderful when I told him . . . about the pool. He made me see it differently. I haven't worried so much since then.'

'Good. Sounds sensible. And Justin Cartwright? What of him?'

'Oh, he and Morwenna had a romantic match. She ran away with him to Gretna Green. They gave us a shock at the time but that's over now. I am worried about her though, Ben. She is going to have a baby.'

'Good heavens! When?'

'In about three months or so, I should think. I am anxious about her being here.'

'There is a midwife. She runs the store.'

'I know. I've met her. Is she good?'

'I think so. It is a pity Mrs Cartwright came out. It would have been better for her to have had the child at home . . . and perhaps come out later.'

'Oh, she wouldn't have wanted to do that. She knew she was going to have the child before she came . . . or at least she suspected it. But she didn't say anything because she thought it would upset everyone. Morwenna is like that. She is completely unselfish.'

'Well, Mrs Bowles is quite good.'

'I do hope it will be all right.'

'Lizzie Morley was born out here. And there have been others. From what I gathered it was touch and go with Lizzie. Old Morley had been a farmer at home and was down on his luck when he heard how cheap land was going out here . . . some of it given away. He was obsessed by the idea. He's told me the story many times. He was a tenant farmer and he had always wanted his own place. He and Alice had been married for some years. There were no children. She was about forty at the time and had given up hope of ever having any. So they sold up and came out here. Alice wasn't so keen to come. She

234

was a home-lover and home to her was England. Some people are like that, you know. They pine away for the sight of home. They hate the droughts here and they hate the heat; and it can be cold in this part, too. They hate the glare of the sun and they think of misty days and cool sunshine and the blessed rain. They pine away. Alice wasn't as bad as that and naturally she wanted to be where her husband was and she made a home for him in this country.'

'What of Lizzie?'

'Oh, Lizze wasn't born then. I don't know what it was . . . the Australian air . . . the change of everything . . . who can say? They settled in, bought their bit of land with their savings. It was true, the government here was almost giving it away. They wanted settlers of James Morley's kind . . . good, steady, hard-working people, mingling with the convict stock which had come out in the first place. Everything seemed to be working well . . . and then Alice was going to have a child.'

'They must have been delighted.'

'They were. It was just what they needed.'

'What happened?'

'Alice was no longer young, as I told you. She was turned forty, actually. There was misgiving. Everyone was saying she was too old to have children. But she came through, and there was general rejoicing when Lizzie was born. They adored the child. I heard all this when I came here. You can't keep secrets living close as we do. I think Alice had a fall when she was holding the child. I don't know whether it was that or not. No one does. But Lizzie didn't grow up quite like other girls.'

'You mean she is crippled?'

'Oh no . . . not crippled. It's just that she is a little . . . simple. She's practical enough. She nursed her mother when she was ill. But there is a kind of innocence about her as though she hasn't really grown up. She is a sweet girl. People are fond of her. She is good and gentle . . . but a little childish. She was wonderful looking after her mother. That was very sad. Alice was very ill for some months. This happened when Lizzie was in her early teens. It was some sort of growth. There was no hope, really. There wouldn't have been even if they had been

235

at home, but you can imagine what it was like here. It was a very painful death and Lizzie nursed her mother throughout. She died and there was only the two of them. Poor James. He was heartbroken. He turned all his affection to Lizzie. He was already doing very well at that time. He had worked hard and it was beginning to show results. Lizzie was a good housekeeper. It was just that she was slow. He sent to England for a governess for her who taught her to read and write. The governess said she was a dear girl but she just could not teach her much beyond that. But she could sew, do the garden and she looked after her father's comforts wonderfully. If you are kind to Lizzie she repays you with genuine affection.'

'She sounds a very nice person.'

'Nice, yes, that's Lizzie. It's a shame that she is as she is.'

'I look forward to meeting her.'

'It will be arranged. What about now? Why don't we call on our way back?'

'I'd like that.'

'It's pleasant here. I'd like to stay for a long time . . . talking to you.'

'I like it too, Ben.'

He looked at me and smiled and for a time neither of us spoke.

I felt a little uneasy. Ben was so often in my thoughts. I rose and said: 'Yes, I do want to see Lizzie and her father and if we are going to do that today we should be going now.'

I went to Foxey and mounted her. We rode off in silence, for Ben was thoughtful, too.

The Morley house was quite large. It had been built in the mock-Gothic style so fashionable at home. It gave an impression of solidity. It was surrounded by gardens which had obviously been very carefully tended, and as we rode up to the house I saw a girl with a basket on her arm; she had been snipping the dead flowers from the bushes.

'It's Lizzie,' cried Ben. 'Lizzie, come and meet Mrs Mandeville.'

Lizzie gave a little cry of pleasure and came towards us. Some of the dead flowerheads fell from the basket. She stopped and

236

looked at them as though puzzling as to whether she should stop and pick them up or come on to us.

'You can pick those up later,' said Ben. 'First come and meet our new friend.'

She nodded as though pleased to have the problem solved for her; she came towards us smiling.

She had the face of a young child, quite unlined, wide blue eyes, and sleek fair hair in a plait which was wound round her head.

Ben took her hand and she gave him a smile of contentment as though she were very glad to see him.

'Mrs Mandeville . . . Angelet,' he said.

'Angelet,' she repeated after him.

'And, Angelet, this is Lizzie about whom I have told you.'

I took her hand and she gave me that rather lovely innocent smile.

'Is your father at home, Lizzie?' asked Ben.

She nodded.

'Perhaps we could all go and see him, eh? Ah, here is Mrs Wilder.'

Mrs Wilder, a rather stern-faced woman in, I imagined, her late thirties, had emerged from the house and was coming towards us.

'Good day, Mrs Wilder,' said Ben. 'This is Mrs Mandeville. I was telling you and Mr Morley about the new arrivals, you remember.'

'Of course, Mr Lansdon,' said Mrs Wilder. 'Welcome to Golden Creek, Mrs Mandeville. Mr Morley will be delighted to see you. Do come in.'

I had not heard of Mrs Wilder before but I guessed by the manner in which she went to Lizzie and took her arm that she was a sort of housekeeper or companion to Lizzie.

'Lizzie has been wanting to meet you,' said Mrs Wilder. 'Haven't you, Lizzie?'

'Oh yes . . . yes,' said Lizzie.

Her candid gaze met mine and I returned her smile.

We were taken into a hall. It was hung with prints of horses mostly. There was a heavy oak chest over which was an ornate

237

mirror in a heavy brass frame. Mrs Wilder knocked at a door and called out: 'Visitors, Mr Morley. Mr Lansdon has brought Mrs Mandeville.'

'Come along in,' called a voice.

We went into a room which seemed full of heavy furniture. On the mantelshelf where there were many ornaments was a daguerreotype picture of a woman in a tight black bodice and a voluminous skirt. Her hair was drawn down at the sides of her face to a knot at the back and I could see in her a faint resemblance to Lizzie. I guessed this was Alice Morley, for the picture had pride of place among the vases.

In a big armchair, a table beside him on which stood a glass of ale, sat James Morley.

'Hello, James,' said Ben. 'I've brought one of our newcomers to meet you. This is Mrs Mandeville.'

He was about to make a great effort and rise, but Ben stopped him. 'Don't get up, James. Mrs Mandeville understands.'

'I'm a bit stiff in my joints these days,' said James Morley. 'But welcome to Golden Creek. I'm glad to see you.'

'Do sit down,' said Mrs Wilder. 'I dare say you would like some refreshment. Wine . . . or ale . . .'

We agreed that we would like a little wine and Mrs Wilder went away to get it.

'Now,' said James Morley. 'What do you think of Golden Creek?'

Ben laughed.

'A difficult question for Mrs Mandeville to answer politely, James. She has just come from fashionable London.'

'A little different here, eh?'

I said that indeed it was but that I was finding Golden Creek very interesting.

'People come and go. I should never have come . . .' He looked at the picture on the mantelshelf.

Ben said quickly: 'We could all say that at times.' He turned to me. 'Mr Morley has one of the most prosperous properties in Victoria.'

His eyes brightened a little at that. 'Good grazing land,' he said. 'I was one of the lucky ones. I was here before the others came. Why, when I first came here there wasn't a homestead for a good many miles.'

The wine had arrived and Mrs Wilder served it.

'We met Lizzie doing something with the flowers,' said Ben.

'Lizzie's always doing something with the flowers,' said her father indulgently. 'Aren't you, Lizzie?'

The girl nodded, smiling happily.

'And she's done wonders with them, too, hasn't she, Mrs Wilder?'

'I never thought,' said Mrs Wilder,' to see them grow as they do. You have green fingers, Lizzie.'

Lizzie laughed happily.

'So you're out here to find gold, Mrs Mandeville,' said James Morley.

'Yes,' I said, 'and that seems to be the usual reason why people are here.'

'A wild goose chase, I reckon.'

'But some people catch the goose,' added Ben.

James Morley looked at him and cocked his eye on one side. 'And if anyone's going to do that, I'll lay a sovereign it'll be you, Ben Lansdon.'

'It is what I intend,' said Ben.

'The quest for gold,' said the old man. 'If only we were content with what we've got and didn't go stretching out for more.'

'The world would just stand still,' said Ben. 'Now, James, we've had this argument before.' He turned to me. 'James thinks I ought to go in for grazing. He reckons it's the sensible thing to do.'

'Well, look how it's turned out for me. Look at my land . . . and who's to say I've finished yet. There's money in sheep. There's money in cattle. I reckon I've got the finest house here . . . barring none.'

'Well, mine is not exactly a hovel,' said Ben. 'Bear me out, Angel, Mrs Wilder, Lizzie . . .'

Lizzie laughed. 'It is a lovely house,' she said. I saw her father's eyes on her. They were fond and a little sad.

239

'Tell me,' went on James Morley, 'what is happening in London. We don't get much news out here.'

I tried to think of what had happened. England seemed far away. I told him of the death of the Prince Consort and how sad the Queen was; then I wished I hadn't because I saw him look at the picture on the mantelshelf.

I searched my mind. There had been trouble with the cotton workers in Lancashire. Not a very pleasant topic. The Prince of Wales was going to marry Princess Alexandra of Denmark and there was Civil War in America.

It all sounded very remote. So I told them about our journey and the ports we had visited. Then I said: 'Morwenna, Mrs Cartwright, would love to visit you. She would have been with me this morning but in fact she was not feeling very well. She is going to have a baby.'

Lizzie's eyes sparkled. 'Oh, I love little babies.'

'Well,' I said, 'you will be able to see Morwenna's.'

Mrs Wilder said: 'Not very many babies are born out here. Has Mrs Cartwright seen Mrs Bowles yet?'

'No . . . not yet.'

'I think she should. I know a little about nursing . . . not very much. But I did look after my husband for several years. Babies are not my line. It's more general nursing.'

'I'll tell Morwenna. You will like her.'

'Morwenna . . .' repeated Lizzie.

'Yes. Isn't it a pretty name, Lizzie? Is it Cornish?' asked Mrs Wilder.

'Yes. Morwenna is Cornish. So am I, partly. My grandfather was Cornish. We have a house there.'

'A wonderful place,' said Ben. 'It has stood there for hundreds of years. You must tell Lizzie all about it.'

'Oh yes, please,' said Lizzie, clasping her hands and smiling.

I noticed how pleased her father looked and when we rose to go he took my hand and pressed it warmly.

'Come again,' he said. 'There will be a welcome for you at Morley House.'

'Thank you,' I replied. 'I am so pleased we called in.'

240

Mrs Wilder and Lizzie walked with us to the stables to get our horses. They stood waving as we rode away.

Ben said: 'You see how it is with Lizzie.'

'They seemed to treat her like a child.'

'She is a child in a way. She is not dull. It is just that she has never really grown up.'

'Who is Mrs Wilder?'

'She is the indispensable one. She came to the place when her husband died. Another casualty of the mines. He was half-suffocated down there and after they brought him up he was never the same again. When James's wife died he was always looking round for someone to look after the servants and to be a surrogate mother to Lizzie. Mrs Wilder came . . . She's been there ever since.'

'She seems very efficient.'

'Morley is lucky. So is Mrs Wilder. It is a good post for her and she fills it admirably. She gets on wonderfully well with Lizzie.'

'I could see that Lizzie is fond of her.'

'My dear Angelet, Lizzie loves the whole world. She thinks everyone is as good and kind as herself. Sometimes I think people like Lizzie are the lucky ones. They think the world is a beautiful place. They are happy.' He looked at me steadily. 'It is because they never reach out for the impossible.'

I felt there was some deep meaning behind his words and they made me uneasy.

After the first two or three weeks at Golden Creek time began to fly past. The days were so full. We had to clean the shacks and try to bring a little homely comfort to them, which was not easy. Neither Morwenna nor I were accustomed to housework; moreover, we had to cook. We took this in turns – sometimes the four of us eating in their shack, at others in ours.

Both Gervaise and Justin – perhaps even less accustomed to the sort of work they were doing than we were – were exhausted at the end of the day. I used to wonder how long they would stay here. I could sense a growing disillusionment. I mentioned this to Gervaise when we lay in our narrow uncomfortable bed, too tired almost even to talk and just doing so in sleepy sentences.

'Gervaise,' I said, 'why don't we go home?'

'To all those debts?'

'We'd do something. How can you go on digging . . . endlessly tipping those cradles into the stream . . . looking in vain.'

'It won't always be in vain. If I left . . . and the very next day they found gold I should never forgive myself.'

I understood what kept all these men going. Not yesterday . . . not today . . . but tomorrow.

There was a similarity between Gervaise, Justin and all these men around us. It was the lust for gold. Ben had it, too. It was only a few like Arthur Bowles and James Morley who had turned their backs on what I thought of as the Golden Goddess, and when I considered those two I sensed a certain serenity about them which the others lacked.

When I became used to this way of life, I found I could do what I had to in the house and enjoy a little leisure. I began to know the people. Ben had been right when he said there were all sorts and conditions. There was Peter Callender, of whom it was whispered that he sported a title back in the Old Country. He never used it here; that would have been frowned on; but his manners and speech betrayed him as what they called 'one of the nobs'. He was always gallant to the women and displayed an easy-going nonchalance, but he worked on his patch as fervently as the rest.

In contrast there was David Skellington, a weasel-like cockney, who, it was said, had worked his term and settled. What crime he had committed no one knew. There were several like him. Backgrounds were never enquired into. There were certain conventions in the township and that was one of them.

There was the Higgins family – father, mother and two sons; they worked like maniacs and I heard that a year ago they had struck quite a little haul. They ought to have left when they did, but they wanted more.

And of course I made the acquaintance of Bruin. I liked him. As with Lizzie, there was something childlike and trusting about

242

him. He had the gold fever too. I was surprised really because I should never have thought he was an ambitious man.

He was not a great talker. Almost everything I learned about him had to be squeezed out of him by relentless questioning.

'Do you never miss England, Bruin?' I asked.

His battered face creased into an almost tender smile. 'Well, Missus, I wouldn't say yes and I wouldn't say no.'

'Well, what would you say, Bruin?'

Then he laughed and said: 'You are a caution.'

It was a favourite saying of his. I believe he had quickly summed me up as being that, whatever it was, and he was going to stick to his deduction. I hoped it was meant to be some sort of compliment.

'When did you discover you were a fighter, Bruin?' I asked.

'Oh . . . er . . . a long time ago.'

'When you were eight . . . ten?'

'Aye,' he said. 'Aye.'

'And did someone find out and make you start?'

'Reckon.'

'You had to learn, of course.'

He grinned, looking down at his fist, clenching it and taking a punch at an imaginary opponent.

'I believe it is a sport enjoyed by royalty. The Prince Regent, I have heard, was very enthusiastic about it in his day.'

He was silent. I was sure he was looking back in the past. Then suddenly his face puckered and I guessed he was thinking of the man he had killed in the ring. It was easy to sense his emotions because he was too guileless to hide them.

'Tell me how you came out to Australia, Bruin,' I asked, changing the subject and I hoped diverting his thoughts.

'On a ship.'

'Of course. But why?'

'Gold,' he said. 'Mr Ben . . . he was good to me.' His face expressed a kind of adoration. He looked upon Ben as above ordinary mortals.

Ben came into our conversation quite frequently. I realized that was one of the reasons why I liked talking to Bruin.

Gradually I drew from him how Ben had sorted out his

243

papers. He could not make head nor tail of them. He had thought he would have to go back home because he could never understand the papers.

'Then just like that,' he said snapping his fingers, 'Mr Ben . . . he said "You put a cross here, Bruin," he said, and I staked me claim . . . just like that.'

I liked to see his face light up with appreciation for Ben. In fact Ben was hardly ever out of my thoughts. That was understandable. He stood out in the community. He was different from the rest; and oddly enough, although they insisted on a certain conformity and Peter Callender with his title was supposed to mean no more to them than David Skellington with his questionable background, they did realize that Ben was different.

Ben had acted unconventionally. He had had a good strike. It was not a major one but it had made him comparatively rich; it had been enough for him to build a grand house in Melbourne and live like the gentleman he obviously was . . . or go Home. But what did he do? He built a house here . . . near the township; he had his own mine with men to work for him. Moreover, he had set himself up as a sort of guardian of the township. Yes, there was something different about Ben.

They respected him. Moreover, they felt he was necessary to the smooth running of the township. He kept a certain order and with such a motley crowd that was no small matter.

Morwenna's time was getting near. Mrs Bowles had seen her and had told her that she seemed to be in good health and she was sure that everything would go as it should.

'Mind you,' she said to me, 'she's a lady and having children's not so easy with them sort.'

'Why ever not?' I demanded.

'Don't ask me. I'm not the Almighty. I reckon it's because they've been too well looked after all their lives.'

'You do think she'll be all right?'

'Right as a trivet. I'll see to that.'

I was growing anxious and I spoke to Ben about it. He said: 'When the time arrives she must stay at Golden Hall.'

'Oh, thanks, Ben. I'll tell her.'

'I shall insist. At least she will be comfortable there. And, Angel, you'd better come with her. She'll want you nearby, I dare say.'

I felt excited at the prospect. Naturally I wanted to be with Morwenna, and at the same time I should enjoy being in Ben's house.

It was summer and the days were very hot, although the temperature could change abruptly – and even though it would be what we called warm in England, it seemed cool after the excessive heat. The flies were a pest. They seemed to take a malicious delight in tormenting us and the more one brushed them away the more persistently they came back. I thought longingly of home. It would be winter there now. I remembered evenings at Uncle Peter's, those dinner parties with Matthew and his political acquaintances, talking interestedly of affairs round the dinner table. I pictured my parents at Cador and an almost unbearable nostalgia beset me.

I think at that time I was beginning to fall out of love with Gervaise. He had changed, and although he was easy-going and never lost his temper, I could no longer see the elegant young man whom I had married; he was often unkempt – he who had always been so elegantly attired; this arduous labour was something he had never done before. I believe he had fancied he could come out, dig up a little soil and then . . . Eureka! there was the precious shining fortune in his panning cradle.

It was not like that.

But I still saw the gleam in his eyes . . . that feverish desire to gamble which had already cost us our comfortable and civilized existence.

And there was Ben. He worked as hard as any of them. He was at his mine most of the day . . . supervising, watching, organizing, giving orders. But he retained the calm reassurance which I had noticed when he first came to Cador. He did not change.

When I saw the conditions in which most of them lived, I realized what he had done for us. We had thought our shacks very humble dwellings, but they were a great improvement on most of the others. He had put rugs on the wooden floors; he

245

had had adequate bed linen sent for us. We owed a great deal to him.

He called in frequently at the shack. He would look at me anxiously and ask if I was all right. We were lucky to have him as our friend.

Gervaise and Justin were working hard, spurred on by the thought that one day they were going to find, what was called in the township a 'jeweller's shop'. They did have one or two small finds which made them hilariously merry, because it was an indication that there was a possibility of finding more in that spot. Some diggers had found not a sign of the precious metal in their land, which must have been very depressing.

There had been great rejoicing the first night they had found their ounce of gold. There were a few men in the township who played cards, sometimes in one of the shacks, but mostly in the saloon. Gervaise, of course, had joined them; and I felt that he had learned nothing from all that had happened. He quickly lost all that little find had brought him. Not so Justin; he played and won a little. I began to think that Justin was as confirmed a gambler as Gervaise, but a luckier one.

I did not understand Justin very much. Morwenna was devoted to him and she talked frequently of his virtues. She was so lucky that he had chosen her, she said. She often marvelled at it. But then she had been one of the most self-effacing people I had ever known. She had come to believe that she was not attractive and her coming out had seemed to confirm this. I had always tried to tell her that if she cast off that feeling of inferiority and behaved as though she were not so concerned as to whether people liked her or not, they would certainly realize that she was a very charming girl indeed. However, Justin had apparently seen her worth and she was eternally grateful to him for that.

I did get the impression sometimes that there was a certain secretiveness about his past. All we knew of him was that he had been in America and had come to England to 'see what he would do': he had a small private income which enabled him to 'look around'. Well, he had cast his eyes on the goldfields of Australia. I wondered whether he was already regretting that.

246

One day when I was alone in our shack I was surprised to see him, for usually he was working at the mine at this time.

He said: 'I'm on my way to the Bowles' to get some stores. But I wanted to have a word with you, Angelet. Are you busy?'

'Of course not. What did you want to say to me? Do sit down.'

He sat on one of the stout wooden chairs which had come to us through Ben's generosity.

'I'm worried about Morwenna,' he said.

'You mean having the baby . . . here?'

He nodded. 'I don't think she is very strong.'

'She's stronger than she appears to be,' I soothed him. 'And Mrs Bowles who is supposed to know about these things says everything is all right.'

'Angelet, you will be with her?'

'Of course. It is good of Ben Lansdon to have offered us rooms in his house. It will be much more comfortable there.'

'Oh yes,' he said. 'Oh, Angelet, I want it to be over . . . I long for our son to be born.'

'It may not be a son.'

'No, I hope it will but what I want is for Morwenna to be all right. If she comes through this I shall think very seriously about taking her and the child home.'

'I think it may be in Gervaise's mind too,' I said.

'You are always hoping . . . Next day will come the big find . . . and if you went back, for the rest of your life you'd be thinking, "What did I miss?"'

'I know. But you could go on through your life thinking of missed opportunities.'

'It's true. But when the child is born . . . I shall seriously think of leaving. I feel this is not the place in which a child should be brought up. Do you agree, Angelet?'

'Yes,' I said. 'I do.'

'And all that housework you and Morwenna do . . . It is not what you are accustomed to.'

'We are getting accustomed.'

He was thoughtful. Then he said: 'If this works out, I'll go and do something. I'll change, Angelet, I will, I will.'

247

I looked at him questioningly. He saw my intentness and he laughed suddenly. 'I'm a bit overwrought,' he said. 'I'm worried about Morwenna. Angelet, promise me you will be with her.'

'All the time . . . if they'll let me. Don't worry, Justin. Babies have been born in places like this before.'

'I know.'

'The sooner we get her to Ben's house the better.'

'It is good of him.'

'We owe a great deal to him, Justin. It would have been even more primitive without him.'

'Yes . . . we owe a lot to him.'

'Don't worry. Morwenna is so happy. You have made her happy, Justin. And this baby . . . well, it just means that with you both she will have everything she wants.'

He stood up abruptly.

'I'm afraid I've talked too much.'

'Of course not. I'm glad you came. She has good friends around her, Justin.'

He nodded agreement and gave me a rather uncertain smile as he went out.

I thought a good deal about how fervently he wanted a son. Most men did. He really cared for Morwenna. I felt my distrust of him slipping away and I realized that I had not before been aware how deep that distrust went.

Mrs Bowles had predicted the time the baby was due to arrive. Ben suggested that a week before we should move into Golden Hall where rooms had been prepared for us.

I was very glad, for Morwenna was experiencing the usual discomforts and a little luxury was what she needed.

Meg was delighted at the prospect of having a baby in the house even though it would be only a temporary arrangement. Gervaise and Justin would go back to the shacks after their day's work, change there and come on to Golden Hall to dine.

This seemed to work well.

'This is the life,' said Gervaise. 'What a good thing it is to have friends in high places.'

He was not envious. That was not in Gervaise's nature. In

248

fact he was a very good man. If only he had not had that one overwhelming weakness, how different our lives would have been!

The day which had been calculated for the baby's arrival came and went. Morwenna seemed quite well but there was no indication that the baby was ready.

Two days passed and when the third came we began to get anxious.

Mrs Bowles said: 'Nothing to worry about . . . yet. Babies are funny things. No use telling them to hurry. They come in their own good time.'

Morwenna was very tired. She was longing for the ordeal to be over. She slept a good deal.

One afternoon when I was by her bed and she was dozing, there was a gentle knock on the door. I went out to find Ben standing outside. He drew me into the corridor.

'Angel, you ought to get out for a while. Come now.'

'Suppose it happens while I'm away?'

'There's no sign. Meg's here. She'll send Jacob for Mrs Bowles. I'll warn her. Come on. You need a little change or you will be ill. Just for an hour or so.'

I looked at Morwenna. She was sleeping.

'All right,' I said. 'But we must put Meg on the alert.'

'We'll tell her.'

'Perhaps she could come up and sit here.'

'All right. She shall.'

Meg was only too delighted.

'I'll see she's all right . . . and at the first sign Jacob or Thomas will be off. You get out, Mrs Mandeville. You'll be the one who's ill if you don't. You look as if you need a bit of fresh air.'

So I rode out on Foxey, with Ben beside me.

We came to that spot where we had sat before. It was quite pleasant. One could see the flat land right to the horizon. We tied our horses to a bush and sat watching the dappled sunlight in the creek close by.

Ben said: 'I worry about you, Angel.'

'About me? Whatever for?'

'This life out here. This township . . . those little shacks . . . You're nothing but a housemaid.'

'It's no different for me than for any of the others here.'

'You must long for home.'

I was silent. I couldn't deny it.

'How long can you stand it, Angel?'

'I suppose for as long as it has to be.'

'You're a stoic.'

'No. I am very impatient sometimes.'

'Morwenna ought not to be here either.'

'You don't think anything will go wrong?'

'I wasn't thinking of that. But this is no place for women.'

'Nor for men either.'

'Tell them that and they won't believe you.'

'You live comfortably enough.'

'When I first came out here I lived the same as the rest of them.'

'But you found your way out of it.'

'I do find my way out of difficult situations. Some people are like that. I find it a little uncomfortable to live here as I do . . . so close to the others and yet different.'

'Well, your place is a refuge to those in need . . . like Morwenna at the moment.'

'And you, Angel?'

'I am sharing in the luxury.'

'I wish you would share it . . . always.'

I was startled yet not really surprised. I had tried to hide from myself my feelings which were becoming more and more difficult to suppress. I loved Gervaise, I kept telling myself; but something had happened on our honeymoon. I had thought so often of Madame Bougerie sitting at her reception desk . . . trusting us . . . liking us . . . and then he had been able to go off like that without a great deal of compunction. He had said he was going to pay later, but would he have done so? Yes, that was when my feelings for him had begun to change.

And then seeing that feverish look in his eyes . . . that need always to gamble . . . irritated me and made me impatient. It was like a disease.

250

I tried to pass it off lightly. 'I shall enjoy it while it lasts,' I said.

'I should never have come here in the first place,' he went on. 'I should have gone back to Cornwall. Perhaps I should have stayed there, had an estate nearby. We should have seen each other . . . often.'

'Well, that would have been very pleasant, I am sure.'

He took my hand suddenly and gripped it hard. 'It ought to have worked out that way. It might, but for . . .'

'The man in the pool?' I said.

'You were so ill. They said it was fever. I knew it was due to all that . . . They were afraid you were going to die. I came to see you lying there . . . flushed. You looked so vulnerable lying there with your cropped hair and eyes wild and you looked at me and you cried, "No . . . no." They thought my visits disturbed you and they sent me away. I knew that I should always remind you . . . and you couldn't get better while you were reminded. So as soon as I convinced myself that you were beginning to recover I went away.'

'Everything would have been different if I hadn't gone to the pool that day. That's life, isn't it? One little incident can spark off a train of events . . . changing people's lives for generations. It's an awesome thought.'

'*I'd* like to change the course of my life, Angel.'

'Most of us would.'

'What I mean is, I don't want events to push me this way and that, because I believe I am the master of my own life. I will push aside those things that threaten me . . . I will go where I want to. But if only I could live that particular time of my life again . . .'

'It's an old complaint, Ben. But when something happens it is there indelibly. For ever.'

'It is too late . . . all those wasted years too late, but I love you, Angel, and I shall never love anyone else as I love you.'

'Please don't say that, Ben.'

'Why not? It's the truth. Do you believe me?'

'I am not sure.'

'Do you *want* to believe me?'

251

I was silent. I was not sure, and I thought: Yes, I do. Because I love you, too.

Neither of us spoke after that for some little time. I listened to the murmur of the light breeze ruffling the grass near the creek.

Then at length he said: 'Tell me truthfully, Angel. Are you happy?'

'Well . . . I think I could be if I were at home. Everything seemed all right there.'

'With Gervaise, you mean?'

'Gervaise is one of the kindest people I have ever met.'

He nodded. 'I know about the debts. He told me himself. He's indebted to my grandfather. I understand that.'

'It doesn't seem so bad as it is Uncle Peter. We know he won't suddenly descend on us and demand payment or else face the consequences.'

'If he found gold . . .'

'We could go home.'

'He might want to stay for more.'

'As you did.'

'It would be different. I vowed I would not return until I had my fortune. I found some wealth and it gave me this . . . But it was not what I had set out for. I couldn't settle for less. It would be weakness and to a certain extent failure.'

'And you could not be seen to be weak. You have found enough to come home and perhaps start some enterprise. But you vowed to come back immensely rich . . . because that was the task you set yourself.'

'I do not care to be beaten, Angel.'

'So you will stay here until your goal has been reached . . . and if you do not hit the target that will be for ever.'

'There are two things I want, Angel. That fortune, you know of. I want to find it in my mine. I want to have one of those discoveries which men had in the beginning, which brought them out here in their hundreds. That is one thing. But what I want more than that is you.'

'I wish you would not talk in that way.'

'I want to be absolutely frank with you.'

252

'It is impossible, Ben. I am married to Gervaise.'

'And you don't love him.'

'I do.'

'Not entirely. He has disappointed you. I can see that.'

He had turned to me and I was in his arms. He kissed me wildly. I was so taken aback that I could not think clearly. All I knew was that I wanted to stay with him, close . . , like this. I was accepting that which I had refused to face for some time . . . ever since I had seen Ben again.

Gervaise had been good to me, a kind and tender husband. I had thought I was in love with him. I had been too young and inexperienced to know my true feelings. I had not really known Gervaise. I had only begun to on our honeymoon when I had first discovered his weakness – not only his obsession with gambling, but a certain amoral attitude to life which could allow him to go off without paying the money he owed to people who trusted him, and gambling with money which was not really his.

I was closely bound to Ben. I always should be because of what we had endured together. I began to think about what might have been but for that man in the pool. It all came back to that. I had thought of it ever since it happened as the most momentous event in my life; and I saw now that it had certainly been so. But for it everything would have been different.

I withdrew myself.

'We must not meet like this, Ben,' I said.

'We must,' he replied, 'often. I must have something of you, Angel.'

'No,' I said.

He looked at me intently and replied: 'Yes.'

'What good can it do?'

'It can make me happy for a while. You too perhaps.'

I shook my head.

'You love me,' he said. It was a statement rather than a question.

'Ben, I have not seen you for years . . . and then I come out here . . .'

'And you knew at once. Don't let's waste time denying the truth, Angel. Let's think what we can do.'

253

'There is nothing. We shall go away from here. You will stay in your comfortable house until you have made that vast fortune. It will probably take years and years and then we shall both be old enough and wise enough to laugh at this folly.'

'I don't see it that way.'

'What else?'

'I never accept defeat.'

'I can't imagine what you mean.'

'I am in love with you and you with me. You are married to a nice, decent man. He's a gambler. He's a loser, Angel. I know one when I see one. Your life with him will be a continual running away from creditors. You feel you can live with that now. It has brought you to this primitive society because you had to run away. Leave him now. I shall be waiting for you.'

'You can't really mean that.'

'What I mean is that we should not sit down meekly and accept what life deals out. You have married this man. I admit he has charm. He is gracious and courteous, the perfect English gentleman. But I will tell you what your life with him will be. I can see it clearly. I know men. He's a loser, I tell you. He's different from your friend Justin Cartwright.'

'What do you mean?'

'He is a man who knows how to win.'

'To win?'

'I've heard things. He has good luck at the tables. Every time he plays he walks off with some winnings. He's more likely to make his fortune at the tables than in the mines.'

'How do you know this.'

'They play at the saloon. Old Featherstone runs a profitable business with his saloon. He's one of those who has a way of making money and it isn't winding up the windlasses either. There are all sorts of ways to fortune and your friend Justin is not too bad at one of them.'

'Perhaps he'll want to go home. He is worried about Morwenna.'

'I think that's likely. The London clubs would be more profitable than a township in the outback. Prospecting for gold by day and winning at the tables by night . . . well, it's a pity for

Gervaise's sake that a little of Justin's luck doesn't rub off on him. Angel, you've got to leave him. Tell him. If we talked to him and told him how things were he would understand. He is that sort.'

'I think you are mad, Ben.'

'Yes . . . mad for you, Angel. I knew it would be like this between us as soon as you stepped off that ship. I thought of you often . . . but as a little girl. I was attracted then . . . I knew there was something between us . . . and when I saw you again I was sure of it.'

'We should not be talking like this.'

'My dear Angel, you are not in your parents' drawing-room now. Are you going to let life buffet you which way it wants to?'

'I am married to Gervaise. I love Gervaise. I will never leave him. He is a good man. He is kind and he has been good to me.'

'You will always be at the mercy of his obsession with gambling. Believe me, I know. I have seen this sort of situation before. It mustn't happen to you, Angel.'

'And you? Are you not obsessed? You vowed to make a fortune and you say you will not leave here until you do. Isn't that rather the same?'

'No. I am going to. He never will.'

'How do you know? He might strike gold tomorrow.'

'Suppose he does? Suppose he goes home? I guarantee that he would lose the lot in a very short time. A couple of years . . . perhaps three. That's the pattern of a gambler's life.'

'I do not want to talk like this, Ben.'

'I never sit down and accept defeat,' he told me vehemently. 'We were meant for each other. Never forget that.'

'It is foolish to talk in this way.'

'It is truthful. I love you. I want you. One day we shall be together.'

As he spoke he picked up a handful of earth and let it slip through his fingers. 'I'll find what I seek in this land,' he went on. 'And one day you and I will be together.'

I said: 'We must go back now. I don't want to leave Morwenna too long. Look at your hands. What do you expect, playing with the soil like that?'

He looked towards the creek and said: 'I'll wash them in there.'

I watched him, as he knelt by the creek and I tried hard to subdue the disturbance he had created in me.

He was right. I loved him. I knew that full well now. I doubted his faults were any less than those of Gervaise; but his would be the faults of strength, Gervaise's those of weakness. Gervaise acted not because he wanted to but because the weakness in him made him submit to his obsession; Ben acted through strength and the certainty that the world was made for him. What was there to choose? From a point of view of morality . . . nothing. It was a matter of strength and weakness. But what sense was there in making comparisons? Love came without being bidden. One did not really love for that sort of reason.

He was a long time at the creek. I saw him dabbling his hands in the water. I rose and, going to my horse, untethered it and mounted. I must get back to Morwenna.

He seemed reluctant to leave the creek.

'I'm going now,' I called.

He rubbed his hands on his coat as he turned.

He was very quiet and seemed to be deep in thought as we rode back to the house.

He is regretting his outspokenness, I thought. He is realizing that he should never have said what he did.

I was glad he had, though. It was a warning to me. In view of those feelings he had expressed for me and mine for him. I should have to take care.

The next day there was excitement throughout the township.

One-Eye Thompson and Tom Cassidy had found gold – not just a speck or two but the real thing.

One-Eye – so called for obvious reasons, but no one seemed to know how he had lost his right eye – was a man who did not mingle very much with his fellows. He lived in a shack which he shared with his partner, Tom Cassidy; they were usually a taciturn pair, and they were rarely at the saloon unless it was to drink a mug of ale and then depart immediately afterwards.

They had worked steadily and, until this time, without success.

The news spread rapidly. If someone had found gold in any quantity it could mean that there were still rich alluvial deposits in the neighbourhood. Hope ran like a fire through the settlement.

One-Eye had little to say but Cassidy could not contain his joy.

'It's come at last,' he said. 'We're made. Soon it will be Home for us . . . millionaires.'

Feverishly they worked, raising the wash-dirt from the bottom of their shaft, then taking it to the stream to be panned that the dross might be separated from the precious gold.

Everyone was talking of One-Eye's and Cassidy's luck. There was no other topic of conversation.

For three days they worked furiously turning out the gold. But it did not last. It ceased as suddenly as it had begun.

'Never mind,' said Cassidy. 'Our fortunes are made.'

It was going to be Home for them.

The gold was in bags ready to be taken to Melbourne. There it would be valued; and there was no doubt that they had become rich men overnight.

As was the custom when anyone, as they said, 'struck it rich', there was a celebration throughout the town.

The successful partners would be hosts to the entire community. There would be a roasted sheep; it would be out of doors. There would be dancing and singing, for when one man experienced such luck it stressed the fact that this could happen to any of them. It was the whole meaning of the life; it brought fresh optimism to the site, for everyone knew that if someone had found leads to a 'jeweller's shop' there must be others.

'Gold will be as plentiful as it was in '51,' they said. 'It is just that it is farther down and more difficult to find.'

I remember that occasion well. The excitement was intense. It was impossible not to be part of it. Even One-Eye expressed his jubilation; Cassidy was obviously in a state of bliss.

Gervaise was delighted. 'Theirs today and ours tomorrow,' he said. 'Soon we'll be out of this place. There's gold there. You can smell it.'

'I have a feeling that we shall soon be lucky,' said Justin.

'Everyone has that feeling,' I told them. 'I only hope it is true.'

The heat of the day was over; the night was pleasantly warm and the stars brilliant in the velvety sky . . . the Southern Cross to remind us that we were far from home. Fires were lighted for roasting the meat. Dampers were cooking in the ashes. It seemed that everyone in the town was assembled.

'You will see,' Ben told us, 'how a really big find is celebrated here. After months of depression when people begin to feel that the good days have gone forever, someone has a find like this and hope springs up.'

I could see that there was a change in him. He too was deeply affected by this find. He had the gold fever as intensely as any of them.

Gervaise was in specially high spirits.

'Just think,' he said. 'It could have been us.'

'If only it had,' I sighed.

'If only . . .' repeated Justin.

They were two words which seemed to be in my mind a great deal lately. Ben's confession had had a profound effect on me. I told myself I ought to get away. I felt unsure of myself.

Some of the men and women had begun to dance. Two of the men had brought violins with them and they were always in great demand. One of them had a very good singing voice.

It was a strange sight. The light from the fires sent a glow over the shacks, endowing them with a mysterious quality they lacked by daylight.

Morwenna was of course not with us. She was not well enough and hourly we were expecting – and hoping – for the child to be born. We never left her alone. Always one of us was within call, holding herself in readiness. Meg was on duty at this moment and her husband with her. He would fetch Mrs Bowles immediately if there was any sign of the child.

I was seated on the grass, Justin and Gervaise with me.

258

Gervaise was talking enthusiastically of the find. I knew that his desire to go home and his need to find gold were grappling with each other. I do believe that had it not been for the debt he owed Uncle Peter he would have wanted to leave by now. As Ben had said, it was easier to make money at the card tables in London's clubland than in the goldfields of Australia.

This find had probably made him change his view. 'There must be more,' he kept saying. 'It is like that. If you find traces it must mean that there is more not far off. It could be anywhere under this ground. We are going to find it. I know we are.'

'Soon, I hope,' I said.

'I heard a rumour,' said Justin, 'that Ben Lansdon wants to buy land from James Morley. What do you think he plans to do? To graze sheep?'

Gervaise said: 'He doesn't seem like a grazier to me.'

'To open up another mine?'

'Why on Morley's land?'

'Who knows? Do you think he has come to the conclusion that the present one is worked out?'

'There have been poor yields for some time.'

I thought: Yes, he has the gold fever as much as any of them. He will never give up, any more than the others will.

I saw Ben among the crowd. With him was James Morley and Lizzie. Ben was talking animatedly to them. James was laughing and Lizzie smiling happily. She looked quite beautiful in the firelight with that lovely serene expression which seemed to indicate complete contentment.

They came over to us.

Ben took my hand and pressed it firmly.

'Well, what do you think of our jamboree?' he asked.

'Exciting,' I said. 'The township looks different in the fire and starlight.'

'It casts a rosy glow. I think One-Eye and Cassidy are very happy men tonight.'

'We shall miss them,' said Gervaise.

'Others will take their places, never fear.'

'And there will be more disappointments,' said James Morley.

259

'I reckon it would do most of them more good to get hold of a piece of land and raise sheep and cattle.'

'They might not all have your success, James,' said Ben.

'They would if they worked. All this dig . . . dig . . . dig and perhaps there is just nothing at the end of it. It's making a mess of good grazing land.'

'You have one aim in mind, James,' said Ben with a laugh. 'Return to the land.'

'Yes, and give up this gimcrack notion. Gold there might be . . . but there is not enough to go round . . . and I say leave it be.'

'Yours certainly seems to be a happier way of life,' I said.

'You see before you one of the most successful graziers in Victoria,' said Ben. 'Not all are so successful. And show me two happier men tonight than One-Eye and Cassidy.'

'They are happy,' I said, 'because they are getting away from it.'

'But darling,' put in Gervaise, 'think of the joy of tilting your pan and seeing it there . . . and realizing that you have stumbled on it at last.'

'Yes,' I told him, 'I can imagine how they feel. But how often does it happen?'

'Angelet is homesick,' said Gervaise.

'Aren't we all?' asked Ben.

James Morley said; 'Well, I'm not. I like to see my grassland. I like to see my sheep and my cattle. I wouldn't want any of my land disturbed . . . and that's a plain fact.'

'Not even if there were nuggets the size of your fists underneath it?' asked Gervaise.

'You'd have to show 'em to me first before I'd have one square foot of my land disturbed.'

'How would you know unless you looked?' I asked.

'That's good reasoning. You wouldn't, would you? Well, as far as I'm concerned it could stay there. I'm happy as I am. I don't want anything to do with this gold rush. Look at all those people . . . dancing . . . singing. It's like a scene from the Bible. Remember when they were all worshipping the golden calf.'

I went over to stand beside Lizzie.

She said: 'Isn't it pretty in this light? You can't see how ugly it is in daylight.'

I agreed.

Someone started to sing. They were the old songs from Home which we knew so well: 'Come Lasses and Lads', 'The Mermaid' and 'Rule, Britannia'.

I saw many of them wipe a surreptitious tear from their eyes. They were songs which reminded them of Home.

Then Cassidy sang a song which I had never heard before. It was the song of the goldfield:

> 'Gold, Gold, Gold
> Bright and yellow, hard and cold,
> Molten, graven, hammered and rolled,
> Heavy to get and light to hold.
> Price of many a crime untold . . .'

There was silence among the crowd as his voice rang out clear on the night air. It had a sobering effect, coming after the songs which most of them had sung in their childhood. 'Heavy to get and light to hold, Price of many a crime untold . . .'

Those words kept ringing in my ears.

I said to Gervaise: 'I think I will go now. I don't like leaving Morwenna.'

'There are people there to look after her.'

'Yes, but I am thinking of her all the time. I wish this baby would come.'

'I believe there are often delays like this.'

'Perhaps. We ought to have taken her to Melbourne. There is a hospital there.'

Gervaise said soothingly: 'It will be all right. Don't fret.'

'I'll try not to, but I do want to see her.'

'I'll take you back to the house.'

Ben had come up. 'Are you going?' he asked.

'I keep thinking of Morwenna. I'm going to see her.'

'Can't you trust Meg?'

'Yes, of course, but I'd like to be there.'

'I'll walk you back. I was going anyway. Come on.'

'Goodnight, Gervaise,' I said.

He put his arms round me and kissed me.

'It will be nice when you are back,' he said.

'It will be soon, I hope. This can't go on.'

The walk to Golden Hall was not very long. Ben said: 'I wanted to talk to you.'

I waited.

'Something has to happen,' he went on. 'Soon.'

'Such as what?'

'About everything. The way we are going. I want you to leave Gervaise and come to me.'

'What are you suggesting?'

'Just that. You love me. You were never really in love with Gervaise.'

'You are talking nonsense, Ben. We met long ago and now we have met again briefly. How much do we know of each other?'

'A great deal. We shared an experience . . . once. I have thought of you ever since. Have you thought of me?'

'After that experience you went away. You left me.'

'If I had thought you needed me I should never have gone.'

'After that terrible thing . . . I was a child. I needed help.'

'I thought you were too young for it to have a great impact.'

'You must have thought I could take it as easily as you did.'

'I believed you understood that it was not our fault. We harmed nobody. But it is in the past. It's the future I'm thinking of. I love you, Angel. It is important for me to know now that you love me . . . that you will come back to England with me.'

'This has all happened too quickly.'

'It has been happening over the years.'

'Well then, why did you stay in Australia? Why didn't you come and find me . . . before I married Gervaise?'

'Because I did not know until I saw you again. It all fell into place then. I knew you were the only one.'

'And what of Gervaise?'

'What of him?'

'He is my husband. We are happy together. Do you think I can just say to him, "It was nice knowing you but I have finished with you now"?'

'Gervaise will recover from the loss in time.'

'How do you know?'

'Because I have met many like him. He is kind, gentle, loving and weak. He would be the same with any woman as he is with you. You are not first in his life. What is most important to him is gambling. That is what he really cares about. If he lost you and won at roulette or found gold . . . he would recover. If I lose you I never shall. Nor will you. We are different. Our feelings go deep. We were meant for each other from the day we met. Angel, I must know . . .'

'What must you know?'

'That you will come to me. We will explain to Gervaise together. He would not stand in our way.'

'Do you mean he would simply pass me on to you?'

'He would want you to be happy. I would compensate him. I would make over my gold mine to him, and you and I could return to England.'

'What a preposterous suggestion.'

'I suppose I am rather preposterous.'

'I can't think you are serious.'

'I am deadly serious. He would agree to a divorce. We could marry and settle in England.'

'How do you think we should be received at home? Your grandfather . . .'

'My grandfather is a man of the world. I am very like him in many respects. He would understand. I do not anticipate any trouble there . . . and if there was I should overcome it. I am not dependent on him or anyone.'

'Oh, Ben,' I said, 'you make everything sound so easy.'

'Be honest with me. Do you enjoy being with me?'

'Of course I do.'

'More than with anyone else?'

I did not answer.

'Silence is construed as yes,' he said.

I was thinking of it . . . being with Ben all the time . . . and going home. It seemed like paradise to me. It was the first time that I had admitted to myself that I had been so uneasy and apprehensive ever since I had met him again. I had tried to convince myself that it was due to the adventure we had shared – but it was not that. I wanted to be with Ben. If I were free . . . if only I were free!

But I did love Gervaise. Who could help loving Gervaise? He had always been so good to me, and because of the weakness I saw in him, I wanted to protect him. Surely that was love. Perhaps it was possible to love two men at the same time.

Gervaise's love for me was tender and patient. That of Ben fiercely possessive and passionate. I knew in my heart that it was Ben I wanted. I also knew that I would never leave Gervaise.

Yet I allowed myself to indulge in fantasies. Going home with Ben . . . I could imagine him facing them all . . . making them see it his way. Ben would always win.

As we approached the house, he gripped my arm. 'Please, Angel, you must realize this. If you don't, you will spend all your life regretting.'

'I am sure that if I did what you suggest I should do the same. No, Ben, I could not. I think you have not given this enough thought.'

'I have thought of little else since you came here. I can't be happy without you, Angel. Can you . . . without me?'

'I am going to try, Ben. I was happy enough before . . .'

'Before you realized you had made a mistake?'

'I did not think of it as a mistake.'

'When you knew that there would be no serenity in your life? There never will be, you know. This will always be there . . . like a shadow over everything. There will be debts . . . always debts. There is no other way.'

'I am going to try and change it.'

'You can't change people, Angel. They are as they are.'

'I think one can overcome disabilities.'

'Some, perhaps. But not this one . . . not when it has such a firm hold, when it is part of that person. I have seen it often.'

'I dare say we all have our faults.'

'I more than any.'

'Well then . . .'

We went into the house. It was silent. Jacob and Minnie

would be with the revellers. Thomas was probably in bed and Meg would be dozing at Morwenna's bedside.

We stood in the hall and he put his arms round me.

'I want you here with me,' he said, 'now. I want reassurance. Angel, I will give up everything – everything here, I swear – if you will be with me tonight.'

'Oh . . . no, I couldn't do that, Ben.'

He held me tightly.

'It's important. Dearest Angel. I want to be sure. I must be sure . . . tonight. I will give up everything if you will say yes. We will go home . . . we will be together always.'

He was kissing me and a terrible longing possessed me – not only for home but for him. I had made a mistake. I had taken good looks, courtly manners, kindliness, tenderness for love. It was not like that. Love was a wild thing that came to you when you least expected it . . . suddenly; and then once it had taken hold of you, you were captured.

Life is strange. One must be in the right place at the right moment. And that was where it had failed me. Gervaise had been there when it should have been Ben; and I had mistaken the shadow for the substance, the dross for the gold.

It was too late. Too late. Those words kept echoing in my ears.

But was it too late? Living life to the full was taking opportunities. Nobody knew that better than Ben.

He was now saying: It is *not* too late. We do not have to accept this. We can change it all.

I was afraid. I felt my resistance weakening. I loved Ben. I wanted Ben. My reasoning told me that this was impossible and what he was suggesting was wrong, very wrong. One could not throw aside morality just because one had made a mistake and realized it.

I was calling on all my powers of resistance; but with Ben's arms about me and his face close to mine, I was afraid . . . desperately afraid that my passionate need of him would rise above my scruples.

Perhaps it might have done. We were in this house . . . all but alone . . . together.

There was a sound above us. I heard a call. The spell was broken.

Thomas stood at the top of the stairs.

'It's Mrs Cartwright,' he said. 'Meg thinks it's the baby at last.'

The ordeal had begun. I hastened to Morwenna's room. Meg was very anxious and Morwenna was in great pain.

'I hope Mrs Bowles won't be long,' Meg said. 'Thomas has gone for her. She is all ready and waiting so she must be here soon. Everything's ready. I'll go and get the water hot. They always seem to need that. If you'll sit with her . . .'

Morwenna looked very pale and every now and then she writhed in pain. She was trying not to cry out. I did not know what to do. I prayed that Mrs Bowles would arrive soon.

It seemed a long time before she came but it was, of course, not really so. She was prepared for this. Had we not been waiting more than two weeks for the arrival of the baby?

Mrs Bowles turned us out of the room, keeping only Meg with her. Meg had helped bring another baby into the world only recently and Mrs Bowles had found her useful.

Justin and Gervaise had arrived at the house. Minnie and Jacob had come too, to see if there was anything they could do.

And the vigil began.

We sat silently, waiting . . . fearfully.

The time dragged on and it must have been just after midnight when Mrs Bowles came down to us.

She said: 'There's something not quite right. I want a doctor. You'll have to get Dr Field.'

'Dr Field!' cried Ben. 'He's ten miles from here.'

Mrs Bowles replied tersely: 'It's necessary.'

'I'll go at once,' replied Ben.

He left immediately.

After he had gone we sat on in fear. I was sorry for Justin. He looked quite unlike the man I had known. He just sat staring ahead of him.

266

'It'll be all right,' said Gervaise. 'There are often these little complications.'

I wanted to shout at him: What do you know of these things? Why do you always say everything will be all right? I felt irritated with him. I think it was because I had, in my thoughts, been unfaithful to him. I despised myself for this and when one does that, one likes to blame the person one has wronged. Then I was desperately worried . . . and there was no room for any feeling but concern about Morwenna.

That was the most wretched period I had ever lived through. We sat waiting fearfully, wondering what was happening in the room above, starting at every sound, waiting for Mrs Bowles to come and tell us what was happening, longing for a sight of her and fearing what news she would bring.

Meg was with Mrs Bowles. I wanted to help but they thought that there would be too many people in the room. There was little I could do in any case, said Mrs Bowles. If she needed me she would call. But we must wait for the doctor and pray that he would come soon.

I shall never forget poor Justin. I had not really thought he cared so much. Secretly I had wondered a great deal about his motive in marrying Morwenna and I had sometimes felt it was due to her expectations, for it seemed certain that Morwenna would one day be a considerable heiress. The Pencarrons were very wealthy apart from their mine, which was a most profitable concern. And everything would be for her. But it seemed now that he was genuinely distressed.

He had so longed for a son.

The hours were slipping by. It was not until morning that Ben arrived with Dr Field. The doctor had made himself available and they had ridden hard through the night.

He went to Morwenna at once and the waiting began again. We sat there tense and expectant.

Then Meg came down. 'The doctor wants a word with Mr Cartwright,' she said.

Justin rose at once and followed her out of the room.

And we sat on . . . waiting.

Gervaise said: 'What's happening, do you think?'

'I'm frightened,' I told him.

'It'll be all right,' he replied. 'It's bound to be all right.'

There was silence and the waiting went on. The tension was unendurable.

I said: 'I am going to see what is happening.'

Gervaise laid a hand on my arm. 'You mustn't distress yourself, Angelet.'

I turned away and ran out of the room.

I found Justin. He was sitting on the stairs outside the room in which Morwenna lay. His head was in his hands. I went and sat beside him.

'Justin,' I said, 'what is it?'

'The doctor asked me. It's all going wrong, Angelet. He said he can save the child but it could cost Morwenna her life . . .'

'Oh no,' I said.

He nodded. 'It could be a matter of the mother or the child . . . and he said that we could never have another child.'

'Oh Justin . . . how terrible.'

'I said he must save Morwenna.'

'I know how much you wanted this child, Justin.'

'The doctor said . . . they were both in danger . . . but he thought he might be able to save one.'

We were silent. I thought of how Morwenna had longed for this child. She was going to be very unhappy.

I felt a great tenderness towards Justin. I was almost on the point of asking him to forgive me for mistrusting him.

And as we sat there we heard the sudden cry of a child.

Justin started up and we looked at each other.

Justin's lips formed the word: 'Morwenna.'

Oh no . . . no . . . I thought. It could not be. Justin had said save the mother.

I had heard of such choices before. Why had we come to this benighted spot! If Morwenna had been in London all the care possible would have been hers; she would have had the most practised doctors and the best nurses would have been attending her.

We sat on. I could think of nothing to say to him, but my

268

silent sympathy must have been as clear to him as words would have been.

I don't know how long we sat there. We heard the child cry again. Justin put his hand over his eyes. He just sat there . . . in silence.

Then the door opened and the doctor came out.

'Mr Cartwright,' he said.

Justin sprang to his feet.

'Your wife is sleeping. She will sleep for several hours. She will need nursing for a while. Mrs Bowles is quite experienced. She will know what to do. You have a son.'

'But I thought . . .'

'I admit to my surprise. I did not think it would be possible to save them both. I believe your son is going to be a tenacious young fellow.'

Justin and I just stared at each other. Then he put his arms round me and hugged me.

That day stands out in my memory as one of perfect happiness.

There was no place for anything but rejoicing. That which we had thought lost was restored to us. Morwenna was weak but all she needed was careful nursing. As for her son, he was a lusty baby. The little difficulty in arriving was not going to upset him.

Mrs Bowles preened herself; she was the heroine of the hour in her own opinion; she it was who had presided; she had known when to send for the doctor; she had known all along that everything was going to be all right.

I saw Morwenna later that day. She lay there, her eyes shining: she was beautiful in her complete contentment; and when Mrs Bowles laid the baby in her arms she looked like the Madonna.

'I never thought to be so happy,' she said. 'Angelet, you must write at once to Mother and Pa and tell them they have a grandson.'

I was too emotional to speak. As I had sat on the stairs I had said to myself over and over again: How am I going to tell the

269

Pencarrons? And now there was only joyful news to impart.

Justin was there, smiling at Morwenna, marvelling at the perfection of his new son. Everyone wanted to see and touch the baby, but Mrs Bowles stood over him like a stern sentinel protecting him from invaders.

There was great rejoicing everywhere.

That was a perfect day.

The first thing I did next morning was to go to Morwenna's room. Mrs Bowles was sleeping at the house; she was going to look after Morwenna for as long as she considered it necessary. She was sleeping in a room next to what was now called the nursery.

I said that when Morwenna was well enough we would go to Melbourne and buy a cot and perambulator for the baby. I wanted to buy some toys.

Morwenna laughed at me. 'He won't be playing with many toys yet. He would like a nice furry thing to cuddle, perhaps.'

I sat by her bed for most of that morning telling her how frightened we had been . . . how we had waited all through the night.

'You are all so wonderful to me,' she said.

'Ben Lansdon rode ten miles all through the night . . . and ten more bringing back Dr Field.'

'I shall never forget what he did.'

'Heaven knows what would have happened without the doctor, Morwenna. You *would* have all those complications.'

She laughed. 'Justin is delighted with the baby,' she said softly.

'He is even more delighted with you,' I told her. 'There was a choice, you know . . . at one stage the doctor said he could save your life or the child's . . .'

'I didn't know that.'

'Justin said, save you. You see, you are loved, Morwenna.'

There were tears in her eyes. 'Did he really say that, Angelet?'

'Yes, he did.'

'I . . . sometimes wondered . . .'

'What?'

'Whether he truly loved me.'

270

'Why? Did he ever seem not to?'

'Oh no. He always said he did. But I couldn't really believe that anyone could care like that for me.'

'You are a silly creature, Morwenna. Well, now you know.'

'I am so happy. Fancy! Here, in this place, I am happier than I have ever been in my life. Isn't it odd? And isn't it wonderful?'

I agreed that it was.

The news spread through the town. One-Eye's and Cassidy's gold had disappeared, and David Skellington with it. He must have stolen it and gone off during the revelries. No one had noticed him go and neither One-Eye nor Cassidy had missed the gold for twenty-four hours. It had taken them all day to sleep off the effects of the celebrations.

The next day there was no talk of anything but the robbery; and then when it seemed that One-eye and Cassidy had lost their fortunes and that David Skellington was obviously the thief, the arrival of the new baby and the difficult birth with its final happy conclusion turned their minds temporarily from the terrible fate of the two miners.

There was a great deal of marvelling at the skill of the doctor and Mrs Bowles. It was the latter's finest hour. She was staying at Golden Hall where Morwenna was with the baby; and when she came into the town people would gather round her to hear the tale.

'It was touch and go,' she told them. 'Dr Field, he said to me, "Mrs Bowles, what do you think of this?" And I told him straight. I said, "It's either her or the baby." And he said, "That's what I'm afraid, Mrs Bowles. But we'll do our best." And we did. The Lord alone knows how we did it. We pulled them both through. I never thought we could but we did.'

I guessed the tale would be told for years to come as she weighed out the sugar and sliced the bacon.

We were all in a state of euphoria that week. Morwenna was getting better every day. Happiness was a great restorer. Mrs Bowles was growing prouder and the baby stronger.

Morwenna had discussed the baby's name and she decided

271

on Pedrek. It was a good old Cornish name and it had belonged to her great-grandfather. She remembered that when she was a child she had seen it on a tombstone. She had always liked it.

There would be a christening at Walloo, where Dr Field had his practice. There was a church there and a parson. He had come over once or twice, Mrs Bowles told us, for funerals and weddings; and he could come for a christening.

'We'll have a christening, then, when he is a little older,' said Morwenna.

It had been arranged that she should stay in Ben's house until she was stronger. Mrs Bowles was to remain for a week or so to look after her and the baby. She darkly hinted to me that although she and the doctor had performed their miracle, there must be no going back.

I thought this wise. As for Mrs Bowles, she was delighted, for while still living in a haze of glory – and she knew how quickly that could fade in spite of her efforts to keep it going – she also enjoyed living in what she called the lap of luxury.

Much to Ben's chagrin, I returned to the shack. I said there was no excuse for me to remain longer; in fact I was desperately afraid of the emotion which Ben aroused in me.

This was a time of discovery. I was learning to know people. One received an impression and judged them on that, and later was proved wrong. The fact was that people were complex beings; one could not divide them into categories – the bad and the righteous. One should never make hasty judgements or assess people on what one saw superficially.

In my innocence I had endowed Gervaise with all the knightly qualities and then I had found the feet of clay – that obsession which had changed our lives and would one day, I felt sure, ruin us.

Each day I fell more and more out of love with Gervaise and this was largely because I was falling more and more in love with Ben.

At the moment I was happy because, during those moments on the stairs with Justin, I had vowed that I would give everything I had or had hoped for, if Morwenna could live and have her baby. She had her baby and she was getting stronger every

272

day; and I was already forgetting my vow. Not only did I want happiness for her but for myself too.

I was tired of this place, of the perpetual grime, the rough living, the four walls of my dismal shed . . . trying to clean the place, building the fire which had to be kept going in the excessive heat because we must cook, the ration of water, insects which I had never before known existed, the ubiquitous flies. I wanted to go home . . . for many reasons. I wanted to see my family; I wanted to live in comfort; and I was afraid of what would happen between Ben and me if I stayed here.

He was always there. He made a point of being where I was. He was always urging me, if not with words with looks. I think he, too, wanted to go home. He seemed to be grappling with himself.

I said to him one day: 'You could go home. Why do you not just leave?'

He said he had vowed not to return until he had found gold in such quantities as he knew existed somewhere under this soil.

I replied that it was folly to make such vows. He could return now. He had enough money to go back and engage in some profitable enterprise.

'If you will come with me, I will go,' he said. 'Otherwise I stay. Everything is tied up here. What would my grandfather think of me if I went back without what I came for?'

'He would understand.'

'If you came back with me . . . yes. He would understand then.'

'Ben, I cannot go back with you. I shall always be faithful to Gervaise. I married him. I took my vows.'

'Tell me,' he said, 'do you mean it?'

'I mean it absolutely.'

'Will you change your mind?'

'Never, never . . .'

He looked at me sadly.

'Then,' he said, 'it looks as though I shall have to go ahead . . . here.'

'You are important here. A sort of head man.'

273

He laughed at that, but his laughter was hollow.

'You actually employ these people in the mine. You have your house with servants. Your life is different from all the others. Only the Morleys can compare with you.'

'I know what I want. It is to go home . . . to go home with you. If I cannot have that . . .'

'You can't, Ben.'

'Never?'

'I have vowed to be true to Gervaise. I shall never break that vow.'

'Then,' he said, 'I must make the best of what I have. Is that what you are telling me?'

'Yes, Ben, it is. You are a very ambitious man, Ben. You can be content with what you have and what you might find here. That would console you . . . for us.'

'Nothing would console me,' he said. 'But you are right, I must take what I can get. I will be lucky in everything . . . but love.'

'You will have to consider yourself fortunate to be lucky in something.'

'It is not what I want. Always remember this, Angel. It was not what I wanted.'

I felt my resistance weakening and I fought it with all my strength.

It was true that I was falling deeper and deeper in love with him. Not as I had with Gervaise, which was a matter of a young girl eager to experience love and imagining it would come from the first charming man she met.

This was different. I had been drawn to Ben from the first. I had a feeling that we belonged together. I had loved Gervaise until I had discovered his weakness, but I believed that whatever fresh weakness I discovered in Ben I should continue to love him. Perhaps that was the difference.

I had a suspicion that I might be going to have a baby. I thought at first that this might be because I had become so obsessed with young Pedrek.

It would surely not be surprising. I was young and healthy; so was Gervaise. Why should we not produce a child?

If we had been at home and I was still in love with Gervaise, I should have been delighted at the prospect. I could imagine the fuss there would have been. My mother . . . Amaryllis . . . taking care of me . . . and my child born into comfortable surroundings.

But here! This was no place to bring a child to. I had been wondering how we were going to manage when Morwenna left Golden Hall, which she would have to do soon. She would not want to be Ben's guest forever, although he would raise no objections. How could we manage in the little shack with the baby in his cradle and the difficulty of getting fresh milk and all that was needed? I thought of all the work which would have to be done.

Women had done it before, but Morwenna had to rest and I was not used to hard labour.

So . . . the prospect of having a child here was very different from what it would have been at home.

Ben said it was impossible for Morwenna to take the child back to the shack. She must stay where she was. Meg and Minnie were all for it. They loved having a baby in the house.

'It is only reasonable,' said Ben. 'Besides, you will have to come here every day to visit her. I insist that she stay, if only a little longer.'

I talked it over with Justin and Gervaise.

'It's an excellent idea,' said Gervaise. 'And why not? There are all those rooms at Golden Hall. What a lucky fellow Ben is to have got himself into such a comfortable spot!'

'He worked for it,' I said a little tartly. 'He did not gamble everything away as soon as he got it.'

Justin was disappointed that Morwenna was staying on, but he knew it was best for her.

So she stayed and the baby flourished.

I was now certain that I was pregnant.

When I told Gervaise he expressed great pleasure.

'Gervaise,' I said. 'I think we ought to make plans for going home.'

'Now?' he said. 'After One-Eye's and Cassidy's find?'

'I can't bring up a child here.'

'That's months away. We'll have found gold and left by the time the child comes.'

'It's seven months, Gervaise.'

'Loads of time.'

'I don't think so.'

He ruffled my hair and gave me his charming smile. 'I promise you. We'll go in good time.'

I sighed. As Mrs Penlock used to say, 'Some people's promises are like piecrust. Made to be broken.' Gervaise's promises were like that.

Beneath the charm there was selfishness. He would do what he wanted and smile affably while he did so, murmuring words of tenderness. I think I completely fell out of love with Gervaise then.

I did not tell Morwenna that I was going to have a child. I thought it would upset her. She would remember her ordeal and how she had come through it by a miracle. She would be fearful for me and I did not want any difficulties to impinge on this bout of perfect happiness she was enjoying now.

One-Eye and Cassidy had gone, on the day after the celebrations, in search of David Skellington, vowing revenge on him when they found him. They had been explicit about what they would do to him.

I talked about it with Gervaise. I said: 'You see how this lust for gold arouses the evil in people. It has made a thief of David Skellington.'

'He was a thief before that . . . and an ex-convict, you know.'

'And if they find him, they will kill him. It will make murderers of them. Don't you see, Gervaise? It is wrong. I feel it in this place. When I see the look in those men's eyes . . . I can't bear it. They are all looking for gold which will make them rich overnight.'

'Overnight!' he cried. 'Think of the months of hard work!'

'It's wrong, Gervaise. I just know it. It's worshipping the Golden Calf.'

'Ha!' he said, taking my chin in his hands and kissing me – a gesture which used to charm me and did so no longer.

'Yes, it is like worshipping a goddess . . . a golden goddess,

276

which is fundamentally evil because the obsession makes men do evil things to earn her favours.'

'You were always fanciful, darling.'

'Gervaise,' I pleaded, 'let's go home. Let's leave all this. Let us face what we left behind. Let us try to live within our income. I am sure Uncle Peter will not be hard on us. He will give us time to pay back what we owe him. I might ask my father to help us. I could explain the situation to him . . . if only I could be sure that you were not going to squander everything in this perpetual gambling.'

'Everything is going to be all right,' he said soothingly. 'We are going to find gold. I'm convinced of it. It might even be tomorrow . . . Then we'll go home. Our little one will be born into riches. We are going to live happily ever after.'

'Let's not wait for the gold, Gervaise.'

'Just think what we should feel if we packed up and went and as soon as we left they came up with the richest find ever known. We'd never forgive ourselves.'

'I feel in my bones that we must go . . . before it is too late.'

'I know what's wrong. It's the baby. Women get fancies when they are going to have babies.'

'I have had this feeling for a long time.'

He kissed me lightly: and I knew that I could never make him understand.

I went to see Morwenna. She was able to take the baby into the garden now. She was still weak, however, and in no condition to return to the shack.

She said: 'I shall always be grateful to Ben for allowing me to stay here. I don't know how I could have coped with living in that little place.'

'Yes,' I said. 'Ben has been very helpful.'

'Meg and Minnie are wonderful and even Thomas and Jacob come out and look at him. It is rather funny to see them. They are just a bit awkward and feel it is not manly to be interested in babies. I have written to Mother and Pa and told them all about him . . . how bright he is. He already knows me.'

'Does he?'

'Well, he stops crying when I pick him up.'

'That means he is going to be a genius.'

It was wonderful to see her so happy. I thought: Happiness is transient . . . a moment here and another there . . . and then it is gone. One should savour it when it comes and never miss an opportunity of seizing it when it is offered.

'Yes,' said Morwenna. 'I owe a lot to Ben. The way he rode through the night to Dr Field. I should have lost my baby but for that.' Her eyes closed with horror at the thought. 'But he went . . . all that way . . . all through the night. And then letting me stay here. When I try to thank him he won't listen. He says it was nothing. Anyone would have done it. I wish I could repay him.'

'His repayment is to see you and the baby well and happy here.'

'I wish he could get that land he is trying to buy.'

'You mean Morley's land?'

'Morley is obstinate. He's afraid Ben would start mining there and he just wants it for cattle. Justin told me about it. Morley is an obstinate man.'

'Yes,' I agreed. 'I wonder if Ben will get it in the end.'

'Ben is determined and so is Morley. When you get two men like that you never know what will happen . . . except that it is Mr Morley who owns the land, and if he won't give it up then Ben can't succeed in getting it. Mr Morley thinks that everyone ought to go back to the towns and earn what he calls a decent living and stop scrabbling in the dust for what isn't there.'

'But, you see, once it was and some found it. Think of all those lovely houses in Melbourne.'

'Yes,' said Morwenna. 'Wouldn't it be lovely to go home?'

'Yes,' I said fervently, 'it would.'

After leaving Morwenna in her comfortable surroundings, the shack seemed particularly uninviting. No matter how one tried it was impossible to keep the place clean. The dust blew in and covered everything.

I thought that the men at least had the excitement of hope with every shovelful that was brought up and washed in the stream because it might contain what they sought. That would keep them going. For the women there was nothing but the daily chores – the unpalatable food to prepare, the preservation of the precious water.

I said to myself: I will not endure this any longer. There were times when I felt like going to Ben and saying: You promised to take me away from this. Take me home and I will come with you.

No. That would make it seem like a bargain. But it was not only the prospect of going home; I wanted to be with Ben. I knew he had this ambition, this lust for gold which I deplored; and yet it made no difference to my feelings for him.

Then One-Eye and Cassidy came back to the township.

They rode in at midday; the men were all working on their patches; the women were in the shacks. There was a certain midday peace over the town.

And then they came. A shout went up. The men left their work; the women came out of the shacks. They crowded round to hear the news.

One-Eye and Cassidy were triumphant. They had found their gold. They had it with them. And they had found David Skellingon, too. With him was his horse – a skeleton of a horse.

'He was lying out there where we found him,' said Cassidy. 'Not more than fifty miles from here. His horse was still alive . . . wouldn't leave him.'

One-Eye patted the animal. 'We'll feed him. We'll put him to rights,' he said. 'It was through him we found Skellington.'

Everyone was firing questions at them and they were only too ready to tell their story. But the horse had to be fed. One-Eye and Cassidy wanted him looked after before they would sit down. They owed their find to him and they were men who paid their debts. The horse was going to be given royal treatment. He was theirs from now on.

We crowded into the saloon. One-Eye and Cassidy sat down and ate meat pies and drank ale with relish.

And then they told their story.

They had gone off in search of Skellington. 'Like looking for a needle in a haystack,' said Cassidy. 'We was hopping mad, wasn't we, One-Eye? There was one thing we had in mind . . . what we was going to do to that cheating little thief. There wasn't nothing too bad for him. We was going to string him up. We was going to let him die by inches. All this time it took . . . and him not more than fifty miles away. He was always a fool, Skellington was. I don't know where he was trying to make for . . . Walloo, perhaps . . . and get on from there. He thought the first place we'd look was Melbourne. He was right there. We did. Made enquiries. No one had seen him. So we knew he hadn't gone there to try to place the nuggets. So we came back. We'd almost given up hope, hadn't we, One-Eye?'

One-Eye said they had.

'Then,' went on Cassidy, 'when we was almost back and reckoned we'd have to start digging again, we saw the horse. There he was standing by the body of Skellington. Know what had happened? He was just starved to death. He'd tried eating grass. There was stains on his face. The buzzards would soon have made short work of him, I reckon . . . when they got wind of him. But there he was. So we didn't get him alive.'

One-Eye nodded.

Arthur Bowles said: 'And he's still lying there?'

'Yes,' said One-Eye.

Cassidy added: 'Seeing him like that . . . made us sort of glad that we wasn't the ones to have to take revenge. We was glad it had been done for us. I don't know . . . funny how you change. We found our gold on him . . . some in his belt . . . some in his pockets . . . We've found every single bit . . . haven't we, One-Eye?'

'Yes,' affirmed One-Eye, 'every single bit.'

'It makes you think,' went on Cassidy. 'A man's dead and gone for good, ain't he? And once he's gone you feel different about what you're going to do. Me and One-Eye wants to get a coffin made for him and we're going out to get him and bring him back. We're going to give him a burial here . . . and then we're going home. And we're never going to let that gold leave our sight again, are we, One-Eye? Not till we get to Melbourne, get it weighed up and all that has to be done.'

There was little work done that day. Everyone was talking

about the way they had found poor old Skellington who was now dead.

Poor old Skellington, they said. He had never had a chance. They sent him out for seven years when he was little more than a boy and he had lived hard ever since. He hadn't even had that little bit of luck which had come to most people at some time. Poor old Skellington.

True to their word, One-Eye and Cassidy made their coffin. They took the buggy with them and went out and brought Skellington home.

The parson was summoned from Walloo and there was a burial service; and outside the town where a few graves already existed, old Skellington was laid to rest.

The entire incident made me feel more eager than ever to go home.

It was just after the funeral when Ben asked me to ride with him because he must talk to me.

We went out to that spot near the creek, and we tethered our horses and sat down.

He said: 'How long are we going on like this?'

I replied: 'I suppose something will happen. It usually does.'

'It won't unless we make it. Listen to me, Angel. Are you going to spend your life in this place?'

'God forbid.'

'Do you think Gervaise is ever going to find gold? Enough to make him give up?'

'No . . . not really. I don't think anyone will. I know somebody did and started all this. It was a pity. I wish the gold had stayed where it was and nobody knew about it.'

'You can't go on living like this, Angel.'

'I have felt that.'

'Have you told Gervaise how you feel about it?'

I nodded.

'And he said, "We'll strike gold soon and then we'll go home," eh? Is that what he said?'

'Yes.'

'He won't find it.'

'Why not? One-Eye and Cassidy did.'

281

'And suppose he did? What would he do? Go home? It would be gone in a few weeks. Then would you be persuaded to come out and start all over again?'

'Once I was home, I would never come back.'

'I'll take you home. I'll give you my word. Come with me . . . and we'll go home. We could leave in a few weeks. Say yes, Angel. You don't know how important it is for you to say yes . . . now.'

I closed my eyes. It was like having the kingdoms of the world spread before my eyes and being told: This will be yours. Ben . . . and Home. I would be freed from the perpetual worry of how many debts would be mounting. I should be home . . . I should see my family. Yet I must say: 'Get thee behind me, Satan.'

'Angel . . .' His arms were about me.

'No, Ben, no. I can't.'

'You want to.'

I did not answer.

He kissed me and said: 'We can't go on like this . . . either of us. I know your feelings. You know mine. Look, Angel, I came here to find gold. I vowed I wouldn't go back until I did. I'd give that up for you. Doesn't that tell you . . . ?'

'Why did this have to happen now? Why did you come here in the first place? Why didn't you come back to Cador?'

'It's no use saying that. It's too late. You know very well you can't go back and change things.'

'Oh Ben . . . if only I could.'

'We could start from now on. We can make our own way. All we need is the courage to leave this place . . . to go home and start afresh.'

'What of our families?'

'They would be shocked. We'd live that down. You are too important to your family for them to want to lose you. There would be a fuss at first. But people get used to these things. They always do.'

'I can't do it, Ben.'

'You could.'

'I can't. I'm going to have a child.'

282

'A child! Gervaise's child!'

'Who else's? He is my husband. It makes a difference, doesn't it?'

'It's a complication certainly, but we'd get over that.'

'I couldn't, Ben.'

'But for this child you would have said yes?'

'I don't know. I couldn't leave Gervaise.'

'Why not? He is perpetually in debt. He's playing now . . . if not in the saloon, in one of the shacks. Justin Cartwright is such another, but he seems to know what he is about. Gervaise is a loser. I happen to know he is in debt at the saloon.'

'Oh no!'

'Yes. It will go on like that all your life. Are you going to endure that? Come away with me. We'll go home. There'll be a scandal. My grandfather won't like it, but he has come through worse, I believe. One thing about him: he is no saint, but like most sinners, he is not hard on his own kind. It would be all right in time. It would be as it was meant to be from the moment we met. Oh, Angel, don't turn away from our second chance.'

'There is the child,' I said.

'We'll look after the child together.'

'But Gervaise will be its father. How could I explain that?'

'You wouldn't have to. There is no reason why it should know.'

'Secrets. Deception. Oh, I know it would be wrong. Ben, I couldn't do it. Gervaise would be so hurt. He thinks everything is right between us.'

'He is happy as long as he has the cards in his hands. He's a gambler, Angel.'

'If he could only find the gold . . . if we could go home . . . it would make a difference. I believe I could . . .'

'You can't change people, Angel. I can't change you and you can't change me. This is important. This is important. Today. Now. Angel, I have to know. We belong together. I have to make plans. This is very serious. I must have your answer . . . now.'

'My answer can only be no.'

283

'Because you don't love me? Because you haven't faith enough in me?'

'You know it is not that. It is just that I cannot do this. I cannot leave Gervaise. Particularly now there is to be a baby.'

'You must go home for the child's sake. Remember Morwenna.'

'It wouldn't happen to me. I'm stronger than Morwenna.'

'I must have your answer, Angel. You don't understand why I must have it now.'

'Ben, I can't. I can't.'

He had turned away. He was staring at the creek.

'There is little time,' he said. 'I must have your answer, Angel. I must, I must.'

'It has to be no. I have married Gervaise. I have made my vows. They are sacred to me. And there is the child. Don't you see? I could never be happy . . . either way I cannot be happy. I'll be frank. I do love you, Ben. It should have been us. But it didn't work out that way. We were unlucky. Things . . . got in the way. And here we are. I suppose it has happened to many people before us.'

'We are not concerned with what happens to others. I am offering you happiness. For the last time, Angel . . . will you take it?'

'I must go home. There is a meal to cook. I have to think of things like that.'

'You should never have been brought to this.'

'I am here and things are as they are.'

'So you have decided.'

'I have to, Ben. I have to.'

His mouth set firmly. I thought he was angry; but he was very gentle as he helped me into the saddle.

I had the news from Mrs Bowles.

I had gone into the shop to buy a few stores. She greeted me warmly.

'And how is that little darling?' she asked.

She was referring to Pedrek in whom she had established proprietorial rights.

I said he was well.

'Should be, living up there off the fat of the land. It will be nice for Mr Lansdon to have a mistress in the house. It's not good for men to live alone. Mind you, I'm saying nothing against that Meg and Minnie. He couldn't have better to look after him than them. But a wife's a wife and there's no gainsaying that.'

'I think he is very well cared for,' I said.

'Meg will still be there with the others. *She*'ll want all their help in running the house, that's for certain.'

'Meg?' I said. 'Why . . . ? What . . . ?'

Mrs Bowles burst out laughing. 'I was thinking about that Miss Morley.'

'What about her?'

'It's clear you haven't heard about the engagement. They say the wedding will be in a few weeks. That's how things go out here . . . and Mr Morley being not in the best of health, like . . . I reckon he'll be glad to pass his daughter into good hands.'

'I'm afraid I'm rather mystified, Mrs Bowles.'

'You're not up to date with the news. You could have knocked me down with a feather. I've often said it was a pity he didn't have a wife up there . . . but I wouldn't have thought of Miss Lizzie.'

I began to feel a coldness take possession of me. I could not believe what I was beginning to realize. I must be mistaken.

I said slowly: 'Do you mean that Mr Lansdon is going to marry Miss Lizzie Morley?'

'That's about it. Well, she's a dear, sweet thing . . . no harm in her. It's just that she's a little simple. Something went wrong soon after her birth. It was before my day,' she added regretfully, as though, if she had been there, Lizzie would have been as bright as the rest of us.

'Are you sure?' I heard myself stammering. 'It's rather . . . unexpected.'

'I'm sure enough. Congratulated him myself, I did. He smiled and thanked me.'

Everyone in the town was talking about the engagement.

Gervaise said: 'It will please old Morley. He's devoted to that girl; and it must have been a worry to him as to what would become of her when he was gone. It's just that she's hardly the sort for Ben. Attraction of opposites, I suppose.'

I could not face Ben. I avoided him as far as possible. Nor did he seek me out. But I had to go to Golden Hall to see Morwenna, for I could not abruptly stop doing that. Every time I went I was afraid I should see him. I had no idea what I should say to him.

I felt his avowal of love for me had been meaningless. I had been duped into thinking it was something else. What had been his motive? The quick seduction of another man's wife?

I realized I had led a sheltered life. I did not understand people. I made quick judgements. I had with Gervaise and consequently I had suffered because of this.

Morwenna was eager to talk of the news.

She said: 'I hope he will be happy. I think he will. Lizzie is such a dear girl. She is happy . . . blissfully. She's always adored him. I think perhaps she is the right sort for him. He is a man who will want his own way and Lizzie would never dream of questioning anything he did. She truly loves him. I have rarely seen anyone so happy. And Mr Morley, too, he is delighted. I think he has worried a lot about leaving her. I happen to know that he is not in the best of health. He had a slight stroke some little time ago and just before we arrived Dr Field told him he would have to go very carefully. He came here, you know, with Lizzie and we had a long discussion. It may be that he was so overjoyed by the engagement that he was off his guard. He said: "I'm so glad to see my Liz settled. Ben will know how to look after her. It's a great relief because, you know, I could pop off at any minute." So you see.'

'Yes, I see.'

'The wedding is going to be very soon. There is no point in waiting.'

'No point at all.'

'I expect Mr Morley will see to that. You can understand a man in his state of health and caring as he does for his daughter

. . . he wants to make sure everything is all right for her before he goes.'

'Yes,' I said. 'He is a very good father.'

'When you are a parent you understand these things,' said Morwenna with a certain pride.

All I could think of was: How could he? He must have been contemplating this when he was attempting to become my lover.

I would never trust anyone again.

I don't know how I lived through the next few weeks. Everything seemed unreal. Each day I awoke in the dreary little shack, Gervaise beside me. He never lost his cheerfulness. I supposed the gambler is a natural optimist and it is an indication of his nature that he can go on saying: 'Perhaps this will be the day. Perhaps tonight I shall be a rich man.' And perhaps I should have applauded it. Instead, it made me impatient.

On rare occasions he won at cards. Then he would say his luck had turned and it was the beginning of change. He was going to be lucky at the mine as well as at the card table.

I knew that Justin was gambling with him and I wanted to talk of this to Morwenna, but I could never bring myself to do so. In my heart I believed that Justin was every bit the gambler that Gervaise was; but it seemed to affect him differently. He never seemed to be in those financial difficulties which were always hanging over Gervaise.

No one would have suspected this. It was only those to whom Gervaise owed money who were aware of it. He treated all with that nonchalance which I had once called charm.

Perhaps I was finding fault with Gervaise because I was in love with Ben and I was telling myelf that all men were deceivers. I had been deceived by Gervaise and, being the fool I was, I had allowed myself to be deceived by Ben.

Now that I had lost him I realized how much he had meant to me . . . how I had somehow managed to keep my spirits up by looking to Ben as a means of escape . . . escape to happiness. Had he really meant he would give all this up if I would go back to England with him? How could he? When he immediately turned to someone else?

But Lizzie Morley! Oh, she was pretty enough . . . but how could a lively-minded man like Ben marry a girl like Lizzie?

I was in due course to learn the reason.

In the meantime there were those terrible weeks to live through, while the inhabitants of the township talked of little else but the coming wedding.

It was to be held at the Morley house and everyone was invited.

The parson from Walloo would come and perform the official ceremony. It was to take place in the garden before the house. They said that Mr Morley had sent to Melbourne for the finest caterers and arrangers of weddings to see to everything.

There had never been such an occasion in the memory of the township.

Mrs Bowles had her comment: 'A funeral and then a wedding. I don't know. That seems a bit funny to me. One coming so close on the heels of another. I wonder what'll be next. Funeral, most like. Can't expect another wedding, can we? Whose would that be? Well, you never know. I mean to say, who would have thought of this?'

'Ben's property will be joined up with Morley's now,' said Gervaise. 'Well, they are adjoining.'

Justin's remark was: 'Ben will be pleased to get a stake in Morley's land at last. He's been trying to buy it for some time.'

I told myself that that was why he was marrying Lizzie. It must be. He wanted the land. The thought only increased my anger against him.

During the weeks before the wedding I felt convinced that something must happen to stop it. I simply could not believe it would happen. Sometimes I thought I had dreamed the whole thing.

The day came. The weather was perfect, slightly less hot than we had been having. There was great excitement; the mines were deserted. Nobody was going to work on Ben and Lizzie's wedding day.

Mr Morley had engaged fiddlers to come and play. Everyone

said it was the perfect wedding. Chairs had been set up in the garden in front of the house; there weren't enough for everyone so some stood about, others squatted on the grass. There was a hushed silence when the parson from Walloo appeared and took his stand at the table which had been set up and Mr Morley appeared with a radiant Lizzie clad in white and orange blossom. Arthur Bowles came in with Ben; and I closed my eyes as Lizzie and Ben stood together and took their vows.

I wished that I were anywhere but there; but of course I had had to come. If I had stayed away people would have wondered why. And I could not feign an illness. Part of me wanted to torment myself. I wanted to see what I had been telling myself up to that moment could never be.

And so Ben and Lizzie were married.

How I longed to go home! I wanted to put this entire episode out of my life. I had been so foolish. I had believed Ben loved me: I feared that on one or two occasions I had come near to surrender. I had been childish. But I felt this betrayal had sent me hurtling into womanhood. I would never trust anyone again.

I pleaded with Gervaise: 'Do let us go home.'

'I have a feeling it will not be long now,' he said.

'You always say that. Gervaise, I cannot live this life.'

'I know. It's not pleasant, is it? But be patient, darling . . . just for a little longer.'

'How long?'

'Till I'm lucky.'

'I somehow feel you are never going to be.'

'How can you say that? Look at Cassidy and One-Eye. They must be on their way home by now.'

'But who else, Gervaise? They are the only ones . . . after all this time.'

'Tomorrow it will be us.'

'You don't believe that.'

'Oh, but I do. I know that one day . . . You'll be surprised. It will all have been worth while.'

'I want to go home in time for the baby.'

'We'll be home long before it comes.'

What was the use? The lure of gold held him so firmly that it would never let him go. It would always be thus. And if we were at home he would gamble as he had before we came. There was no way out.

I had married a gambler and I was no longer in love with him. I loved someone else – again unwisely and this time too well.

I wished I could have confided in Morwenna but I could not. She would never have understood. Besides, it would make her unhappy, and she was so contented now.

Lizzie had become mistress of Golden Hall. She begged Morwenna to stay.

'I suggested leaving,' Morwenna told me. 'It is different now. I ought to go. I am quite well and the baby is strong and healthy. I ought to be in my own home. Lizzie flung her arms round me. She is a most affectionate creature. One can't help loving her. It's good to be with her, Angelet. Ben is so gentle with her, and as for old Mr Morley, he has slipped into a sort of contentment.'

So Morwenna stayed on at the Hall. Justin went often to dine there. I had not been since the wedding. I supposed I should have to go one day. But not yet. The betrayal was too recent.

Then Mr Morley died.

His servants went into his bedroom one morning and found that he had died peacefully in his sleep. It was as though, now that he was assured that Lizzie would be cared for, he had quietly departed from this life.

So Mrs Bowles was right. There was another funeral. Poor Lizzie! She had been all in white and now she was all in black. She had been devoted to her father and now, from complete bliss, she had been dashed into sorrow.

'I am so glad Ben is with her,' said Morwenna. 'He is a great comfort to her.'

A message came to me from Ben by way of Morwenna.

She said to me: 'Ben asked how you were. He said he had not seen you for some time.'

'Oh . . . no, I suppose not,' I replied.

'He said that it was a long time since you had ridden. He wants you to know that Foxey is always at your disposal.'

'I don't get time,' I said shortly.

Morwenna said: 'I feel so guilty living here. I ought to come home.'

'Home! Oh, you mean the shack. Don't be a fool, Morwenna. How could Pedrek live in such a place? You have to stay there for his sake.'

'That's what I tell myself, but I feel I'm cheating, really. Angelet, I don't know how you stand it. I wish you could come to Golden Hall.'

'How could I?'

'I am sure Lizzie would love to have you.'

'What? As a permanent guest?'

'It just makes me feel guilty. And there is Justin . . . I should be with him.'

'He is glad you are there. He knows it is best for you.'

'How I wish they could find enough gold to satisfy them and we could go home.'

'Home!' I said wistfully. But I was beginning to believe that I should be no happier there than here. I had been foolish. I had believed him. I had allowed myself to be caught in a snare and now I was trapped.

Then suddenly it all became clear to me.

I received the news, as usual, through Mrs Bowles.

'You've heard, of course.'

'Heard what?' I asked.

'The find.'

'Find? Whose?'

'Gold. On Morley's land. Well, it's Ben's and Lizzie's now. They say that it's already something bigger than anything that's been known before throughout the length and breadth of Australia.'

'On Morley's land?' I stammered.

'Yes. Do you know that creek . . . not so far from the house . . .'

The creek on Morley's land. Memories came back . . . sitting

291

there talking to Ben . . . listening to his avowal of love, watching the sunlight playing on the water of the creek.

'I . . . yes, I know.'

'Well, that's where it is. Mr Ben found it. It's like that time in 'fifty-one when that man found six hundred ounces in a day in Ballarat. It was there in the creek . . . right on the surface . . . clear as daylight and no one seeing it till Mr Ben came along. Trust him. Well, it's a fortune for him now. I don't reckon he'll be here long. He'll be off home, that's what.'

It was all becoming clear to me. This was why he had married Lizzie. He had discovered gold in the creek and from then on he had determined it should be his, no matter how he acquired it. What was there to choose between him and Gervaise? They were both the slaves of their Golden Goddess.

It eased my anger against myself, although it increased it towards him. I had been foolish but I could tell myself I had been fortunate in a way. Suppose I had succumbed – and only now I knew how near I had been to doing so – and then I had learned that I had linked my life with another gambler; a different kind it was true, a ruthless, successful one – but the motive was the same.

These men cared first for gold. Everything else came after that.

I heard myself saying to Mrs Bowles that it was great good fortune.

I could not resist strolling up to the creek.

There were signs of activity there. Shafts had already been set up. The peaceful scene was no more. It seemed a long time ago that I had sat there and he had told me he loved me.

I met him as I was coming away.

'Angel,' he said softly. 'It's ages since I've seen you.'

'The last time was at your wedding.'

He nodded.

'I hope you'll be happy.'

'You know I won't be.'

I raised my eyebrows. 'I've heard to the contrary.'

He looked at me with longing and although it should not have, it raised my spirits.

I tried to pass him but he put out a hand and caught my arm. 'I'd like to talk to you, Angel,' he said.

'Well, talk. But is there anything you have to say to me?'

'I didn't want it to work out this way.'

'I thought your way was to make things go the way you wanted them to.'

'This marriage . . .'

'You weren't forced into it, were you?' I asked, I hoped ironically.

He was silent for a while, then he said: 'You know I wanted you. I shall always want you.'

'Hardly what one expects to hear from the newly-wedded husband.'

I was pleased with myself. I was doing well, acting flippantly when my heart was leaden, feigning indifference when I was more unhappy than I had ever been in my life before.

'You refused me.'

'How could I have done anything else? I am married and now you are . . . so that makes two of us. Why don't we stop this senseless talk, and if that is all you have to say to me . . .'

'Wait a minute. I must tell you . . .'

'Let me say Congratulations. The whole town is talking of your discovery. You are the lucky one. That is what you came out for, isn't it? You must feel gratified. You have achieved your purpose. I hear this discovery is one of the biggest ever.'

'Let me explain to you.'

'What is there to explain? You discovered there was gold on the land. That was why you were so eager to buy.'

'That's true.'

'That day we talked . . . I remember your washing your hands in the creek. Something happened . . . I know it now. Was it then?'

He nodded. 'I saw gold then . . . actually in the creek. If one could see it like that I knew there was a rich store.'

'You didn't tell Mr Morley.'

'He wouldn't have done a thing. He hated the coming of the miners. He wanted to keep the land as it was.'

'It was his land.'

293

'If you had come to me . . . I begged you to . . . I would have abandoned all this . . .'

'I don't believe you, Ben. You're like the rest of them. You're suffering from the same fever . . . gold fever. You would never have given up the search for it, especially when you had this evidence.'

'You remember when we sat here. You remember the day I discovered there was gold in the creek. It was after that day that I asked you to come home with me. I would have gone home with you then.'

'After you had helped yourself to the gold here.'

'Listen to me, Angel. I came out here to find it. I vowed I would not go home until I had made my fortune. But I would have gone . . . if you had come with me.'

'After you had bought this land . . . After you had unearthed its treasure.'

'Well, I should have been a fool not to.'

'Yes, you would have been a fool, and you would never be that, Ben. There was only one way you could get that land, wasn't there? By marrying for it.'

'If you had come with me I should never have married Lizzie. I should never have got this land. I'll be honest. I want the gold . . . but I wanted you more. I still do. I'd give it all up for you.'

I laughed at him. 'I'm not a gullible girl any more, Ben. I understand your ways . . . and all those of the men here . . . or most of them. This is an obsession. It's a fever that takes possession of you all. You can't break away from it.'

'I tell you this,' he said. 'When I have what is on this land . . .'

'The land you bought through your marriage?'

'I mean this land . . . I will go home and never want to see another piece of gold.'

'There is no need to tell me all this. I know you, Ben, now. I didn't before. It is my fault for being so naïve.'

'Angel . . .'

'Goodbye, Ben. There is nothing we have to say to each other now.'

'Angel,' he called as I turned away. 'I must see you sometimes.'

'I don't think you should.'

'You are afraid of your feelings for me.'

I turned on him angrily. 'This is a small community. I should hate there to be gossip. It would hurt Lizzie. She is the innocent one in all this, isn't she? The lamb delivered up for slaughter.'

'Lizzie is very happy now,' he said. 'And I intend that she shall remain so.'

'Let us hope she never discovers she was married for a gold mine. Goodbye.'

'If you care to ride Foxey . . . she is always at your disposal.'

'Thank you,' I said coldly and turned away.

My emotions were in a turmoil.

I wondered how all this would end.

The weeks were passing. There were only five months to go before my child was born. I thought that already it was getting rather late to leave. Even in my present condition I should not fancy the jostling of the Cobb's coach to Melbourne and the long sea voyage.

I consulted Mrs Bowles.

'Another little baby!' she cried. 'Well, that *is* good news. I'll guarantee yours will be easy. I know just by looking at a girl. Now, Mrs Cartwright, I knew as soon as I saw her that she was going to have a bit of trouble. But you . . . you'll be right as rain.'

That optimism which I had noticed when One-Eye and Cassidy had had their find settled on the township. One person's luck must mean that others could share in it, because if there were alluvial deposits so near the surface on neighbouring land it must mean that there were others nearby. It was a reminder that this was indeed gold country.

Gervaise and Justin were working feverishly; at the end of each day the story was the same. Maybe tomorrow will be our lucky day.

'Trust Ben Lansdon,' said Justin enviously. 'He hasn't done too badly in the past and then he alights on this.'

'He had to marry Lizzie Morley to get it,' I said waspishly.

'Well, never mind how he got it,' replied Justin. 'He knew the gold was there. That's what everyone says. That's why he took on Lizzie. I've heard it said that Morley made a bargain with him before he died. Take Lizzie and you get the land.'

'Do you believe that?' I asked.

'Well, it seems to have worked out that way, doesn't it? He was desperately trying to buy the land . . . offering a fantastic price, so I understand. Then he gets it through marriage and, hey presto, gold.'

'Well, I suppose it does seem rather obvious.'

'Ben won't mind. As long as he achieves his object he'll be ready to pay the price.'

There was more talk about gold than ever in the past. The men were constantly discussing veins and placers. Veins, Gervaise told me, were like other deposits of metals. In the alluvial deposits – the placers – the metal was found embedded in the soil, usually in chambers worn away by water. The fact that it was actually discovered in the creek must show that it was very plentiful in that spot. That was what had aroused Ben's excitement.

I had watched the men panning many times. There was a special method of doing it – a certain shaking and twisting and gyrating movement, and great care had to be taken to wash away the soil and lose none of the precious metal which might be there.

There were what they called cradles for treating larger quantities of soil; and there was another complicated one called a Tom.

Ben had all methods working. He paid some of the miners to help him and several of them were glad to earn money that way.

More than ever I wanted to get away. I felt there was something evil in this search for gold. I often thought of David Skellington who could not resist the temptation to steal gold which had been found by others, and how he had met his wretched end because of this.

Sometimes I went to the graveyards and looked at the rough stones which had been set up. James Morley. David Skellington. Two who had died since I had come. I shuddered to think that

Morwenna or her baby might have been here but for the grace of God, and the skill of Dr Field . . . not forgetting Mrs Bowles.

Then came the night when Justin was in our shack for a game of cards with Gervaise. More frequently they joined other players in the saloon but this was an evening when it was to be just a friendly game of poker between the two of them.

Before Pedrek's birth when they had played in one of the shacks, Morwenna and I would be together. We usually went into the bedroom and talked while they played.

On this occasion I was alone as Morwenna was still sleeping at Golden Hall.

I left them and went into the bedroom. I wanted to get away. I found the scene sordid – not so much the shabby room with the candles guttering in their iron sticks, as the intent looks on the faces of the two. It sickened me. It was an outward sign of all that had brought us here away from our families, our homes and a gracious way of life.

Suddenly I heard a shout from the other side of the partition, the sound of a chair being pushed back, raised voices.

I ran into the next room. The two men were on their feet glaring at each other across the table.

'Cheat!' Gervaise was shouting. 'I saw that. You can't deny it.'

Justin's face was very white. He said nothing. I saw the cards on the table. The ace and King of Hearts were uppermost.

Gervaise said in a cold voice: 'So this is it. This is the reason for your winnings. You're a cheat, Cartwright. A card-sharper . . .'

Justin stammered: 'It was . . . a mistake . . .'

'A mistake to get caught.' Gervaise walked round the table. He pulled up Justin by his coat. He was several inches taller than Justin. He lifted him and shook him as though he were a dog. Then he threw him from him. Justin stumbled and went sprawling against the wall.

He stood up slowly. I thought he was going to run at Gervaise, who stood there waiting for him.

I put myself between them. 'Stop it!' I cried. 'Stop it! I won't have fighting here.'

'He's a cheat and a liar,' said Gervaise. I had never seen him

297

cold like that before. He was a different man. Never had I seen him so furiously angry. But this was because I had never been present when the rules of this sacred matter had been violated.

I said: 'Justin, I think it would be better if you left . . . now.'

'I shall never play with him again,' declared Gervaise. And I had never heard such coldness in his voice as I did then.

Justin did not speak. He was deflated. I thought: It's true, then. He cheats at cards. It is why he has the luck. Oh, poor Morwenna. Gervaise was a gambler but at least he was an honest one.

Justin slunk out. The door shut behind him.

'This,' I said, 'is very upsetting.' I scooped up the cards on the table and put them into a drawer. 'I don't suppose you will want to play again in a hurry,' I said.

'Not with that card-sharper. He will not play again in this place. Nobody will play with him when they know.'

Gervaise sat down and stared ahead of him. I sat opposite him. I said: 'Shall you tell them?'

'What else can I do? How can I let him sit down at a table knowing what I do?'

'Perhaps he only did it once . . . in sudden temptation.'

He shook his head. 'He was too practised for that. I wondered some days ago. His luck was almost too good to be true. I think he has been doing it for years. He's too good at it. It must be long practice. I wondered the other night when he kept coming up with the right cards. Then I watched. He's clever. You have to be sharp. Well, tonight I was sharp.'

I was silent for a while. I thought: How I hate this gambling. How I hate this place. I want to leave and never see it again.

I said: 'What will this mean? You will tell?'

'What else can I do?'

'What of Morwenna?'

'What has she to do with this?'

'She is his wife. Does this mean that it is the end of friendship between you and Justin?'

'You can't expect me to be friends with a man like this, can you? I've caught him red-handed.'

'What shall we tell Morwenna?'

'She'll know the truth, that's all.'

'She can't. She will be too upset.'

Gervaise stared at me incredulously.

'You don't mean that I should let this pass? Go on as though nothing has happened because Morwenna will be upset?'

'She has not entirely recovered from the birth of Pedrek. Don't you understand? It was a terrible ordeal. She nearly died. She mustn't be upset. If she is, the baby will be upset. Remember, it was touch and go. They both still need care.'

'I can't let Justin Cartwright play with others, knowing what I know. At home he would be drummed out of any club. There would be a scandal if anyone was caught cheating as he has been.'

'For the sake of your precious game you would run the risk of harming Morwenna and her baby!'

Gervaise looked at me in bewilderment.

I said: 'I know what we'll do. I'll go and see Justin. I'll make him promise not to play for a while. And if he does promise, will you give me your word not to say anything about what happened tonight to anyone . . . just for a while?'

'You don't understand, Angelet.'

'I do understand all too well. This wretched gambling means more to you than anything. Everything can be thrust aside for it. Look at what it has brought us to. There are debts at home and debts here . . . and all because you have followed this urge. Always you lose today and will win tomorrow. And now you are going to tell all those gamblers what Justin has done. Justin is Morwenna's husband. She loves him. I will not have her upset. Gervaise, you have to promise me that you will say nothing of what happened tonight to anyone.'

'I cannot let him play . . . knowing this.'

'It's against the gamblers' ethics, I know. It is all right to risk money they haven't got . . . to plunge deeper and deeper into debt . . . to bring misery to their families . . . but to break their silly rules is a mortal sin.'

Gervaise was fast becoming his old self. His choler had disappeared. He was tender and gentle. 'You are so vehement, Angelet,' he said soothingly.

299

'I won't have Morwenna upset. She could so easily be now. She is getting on so well, living in comfort at Golden Hall. Lizzie is so good to her and loves to have her and the baby there. Gervaise, she must not know about this.'

'I won't let him sit down and play with others, knowing what I do,' he said.

'If he promised not to play . . .'

'He wouldn't.'

'He would. He's got to.'

'Where are you going?'

'To see him. No . . . don't come with me. I'm going alone.'

I ran out to the nearby shack. Justin was sitting at the table, his head in his hands.

'Justin,' I said.

He looked up and saw me.

'Angelet . . .'

'I want to talk to you.'

I went to the table and sat on the other side so that we were facing each other.

'I'm sorry it happened,' he said.

'Do you always cheat?' I asked.

He nodded.

'Is it . . . your profession?'

'I had to do something,' he said. 'I'm not much good at anything else.'

'Morwenna's father offered you a job working with him.'

He looked at me ruefully. 'Not much in my line.'

'Justin, what are you going to do?'

'What can I do? I'm ruined.'

'Gervaise has promised me that he will tell no one for a while.'

'What?'

'Providing you don't play.'

'He will tell.'

'No, he won't. He's promised me not to. It mustn't be known. Morwenna must not know.'

He looked frightened.

I went on: 'I can't imagine what she would think. It would

300

break her heart. She is so proud of you. And there is the baby. I won't have Morwenna knowing.'

'No,' he murmured. 'She mustn't know.'

'Gervaise will do nothing for a while at least if you will promise not to play.'

He looked at me piteously.

I said: 'You live by it, don't you? Is that what you do in London?'

He did not speak and that told me enough. What had we done, Morwenna and I? It seemed that she had made a greater mistake than I had. Gervaise was weak but at least he was not a cheat.

'It's got to stop, Justin,' I said. 'You were bound to get caught sooner or later.'

He said: 'If I could only strike gold I'd never touch another card. Why does it always go to those who have enough already? Look at Ben Lansdon.'

'He didn't gamble away what he won, did he? He put it to a useful purpose.'

'Yes . . . and now he's married to a gold mine.'

'Don't be bitter, Justin. It seems to me that there is little to chose between any of you. But I want your promise that you will not play again until it is decided what we shall do. I'll talk to Gervaise again. I want everything to go on as though this hasn't happened. But you will not play cards again. As soon as you do, Gervaise will tell. He believes it is a matter of honour to do so.'

'There is nothing I can do but agree.'

'It is better not to rush into anything. Both you and Gervaise will feel differently about all this tomorrow. You can't be enemies. After all, you are working together.'

'I'll do it. I'll promise.'

I stood up.

'You must . . . for Morwenna's sake.'

He nodded and as I went out, he murmured: 'Thank you, Angelet.'

*

301

There was an uneasy truce between the two men. I wondered how long it could last. They scarcely addressed a word to each other which was not in connection with their work. One would be deep down in the earth digging, the other winding up the pails of earth to bring them to the surface.

I had ceased to be interested in the methods of working; my revulsion to the whole matter was growing daily. The frantic desire for gold I saw in the faces of those men repelled me; the greed and, after the first exultation at someone's find – simply because they thought the same thing could happen to them – the bitter envy. Lust for gold . . . envy of others . . . I could see why they were two of the most deadly sins.

I longed more than ever to be away from the place, to go home, to the excitement of London, the peace of Cador; they seemed like heavenly bliss to me.

I was growing listless. I supposed that was because of my condition. I thought constantly of the baby. How happy I could be if I were at home and my child could be brought up as I and all my family had been . . . in comfortable surroundings. But to have a child here! How could I bring up a child in this squalor?

Everywhere I looked there was disaster. I was anxious about the situation with Justin, although I confess I had little sympathy with him. My thoughts were all for Morwenna, who might discover in due course that her husband was a cheat. Poor Morwenna, she was less worldly than I. How would she take it?

I longed for something to happen, something which would take me away from this increasingly unpleasant situation in which I found myself.

My prayers were answered . . . but not in the way I had expected.

Afterwards I learned a little about the methods which were used in the mines. When gold had first been discovered here in the early 'fifties, mining had been comparatively simple. That was when the presence of gold had been found to exist in the valleys . . . the deposit formed in dried-up streams. It was near the surface of the earth. That was soon discovered and mined. But now the men had to dig deeper down into the earth and that was why deep shafts had to be sunk. After one or two fatal accidents, it was realized that the clay, gravel and sand had to be shored up with wood.

When the earth which might contain gold was brought to the surface it was put into wheelbarrows and taken to water to be what they called puddled and washed by means of the cradle, to separate the soil from the gold.

It was a disheartening process; and again and again the results of their efforts were fruitless. Now and again there was the tiny speck . . . nothing much in itself, but a reason for hope.

As the shaft grew deeper and deeper, naturally the danger increased. There were poisons from rotting vegetation. There was one young man in the township who was a permanent invalid. He had worked with his father and had been down below when there had been a slight fall of earth, which meant it was some hours before they could dig him out. As a result, he had a perpetual cough and it was obvious that he was slowly dying.

So it was very necessary that the timber which propped up the sides of the shaft was strong enough to hold back the earth.

It was early afternoon. I was on my way to the store. I knew Mrs Bowles would want to know how little Pedrek was faring: she would listen to accounts of his actions, head on one side, lips pursed, sparkling with self-congratulatory pleasure. Her child, the one who might never have been brought into the world but for her skill.

Just as I was about to enter the shop, I heard the shouts. I stood listening. Mrs Bowles came out of the shop and stood beside me, her eyes grave.

Men had left their work and were running to a certain spot.

'There's trouble,' said Mrs Bowles. 'Arthur! Quick!'

Arthur joined us and we ran with the crowd. I felt a fearful apprehension, for they were running in the direction of our shaft.

I was on the edge of the crowd.

I saw Gervaise. Men were crowding round him. I tried to push towards him.

I heard a man say: 'Someone's down there.'

303

'It's Cartwright. It must be,' said another.

'Gervaise!' I called. 'Gervaise.'

He did not hear me.

'What's happening?' I said.

One of the men turned and looked at me. 'Timber must have given way.'

I came a little nearer. It was not easy to force my way through.

Gervaise said: 'He's down there. I'm going to get him.'

'You're a fool, man,' said Bill Merrywether, one of the oldest and most experienced of the miners. 'You'd never do it.'

'I'm going,' repeated Gervaise.

'Gervaise! Gervaise!' I cried.

He turned briefly and gave me a smile of tenderness.

Bill Merrywether attempted to restrain him but he pushed him aside. I watched him disappear down the shaft.

Someone turned and looked at me. It was one of the miners.

'It's all right, me dear,' he said.

Someone else said: 'He's crazy. It'll be the two of 'em now.'

'What's going on?' I begged. 'Tell me.'

Mrs Bowles was beside me. She put an arm round me. 'It's a fall,' she said. 'It will be all right.'

'My God,' said someone. 'He's got guts.'

'Gone in to save his mate.'

'Madness. Suicide.'

Nobody answered.

I tried to fight my way to the head of the mine, but several of them held me back.

'You can't do nothing,' said one of the miners. 'We've just got to wait, me dear, to be ready if . . .'

I don't know how long it was. Time stood still. The silence was intense. All that sky . . . the scene which had become so repugnant to me . . . and all these people now joined together as though in silent prayer.

How long? I do not know. Seconds . . . minutes . . . hours. I kept thinking of them in that room, Gervaise glaring at Justin. Gervaise the gambler, Justin the cheat . . . and they were down in the mine together . . . the mine I had always subconsciously feared and hated.

304

There was a sudden shout.

Something was happening. As one person we moved towards the mine.

I saw Justin then. He was unconscious. Gervaise was holding him, pushing him upwards. Several men had rushed forward. They had Justin now. They had dragged him out. For a moment I glimpsed Gervaise. I saw his face triumphant . . . grimed with dirt. I saw the flash of his white teeth.

And then there was a rumbling sound. Someone reached out to seize him . . . but he was no longer there.

We heard the terrible sound of falling earth. The shaft had collapsed . . . taking Gervaise with it.

It took them four hours to dig him out. There was mourning throughout the township for a brave man. And I had become a widow.

Justin was carried to the shack. Morwenna left Golden Hall and came to him. He was shaken and bruised but there was nothing from which he could not recover.

My emotions were in too much turmoil for me to think clearly. I believed many of them were concerned for me. There was I, six months pregnant, having lost my husband in dramatic circumstances.

Morwenna insisted on looking after me, as well as Justin.

She could not speak of Gervaise's heroic deed, but I knew it was uppermost in her mind.

The whole of the township wanted to take care of me. They did all they could to help – each in his or her own way. I was deeply touched and I thought how disaster brought out the best in people. The good and the evil, they were there in us all. Recently I had thought a great deal about the lust for gold, the greed and the envy. I had seen it in this place so clearly where now I saw the caring compassion.

I thought often of Gervaise, remembering the happy times – how kind he had been on our wedding night; how gentle he had always been to me. I forgot that incident at the *auberge*; I forgot the debts. When one has lost someone one has loved one remembers only the good things.

I had a great deal to think about; my future had changed.

Ben came to see me.

He sat in the shack and looked at me sorrowfully.

'Oh, Angel, what can I say? If there is anything I can do to help . . .'

I smiled. 'That is what everyone is saying to me.'

'If only . . .'

I looked at him pleadingly. I knew what he was going to say and I could not bear it.

'I suppose you will go home now,' he said.

I nodded. 'I shall have to wait until the child is born.'

He looked round the shack. 'I hate to think of you in this place.'

'I'll be all right. It has happened to others.'

'And only Mrs Bowles. I shall have Dr Field here. He shall stay at the Hall.'

I smiled wanly. 'You are forgetting, Ben. This is nothing to do with you.'

'Every concern of yours is mine, too.'

'How is the mine going?'

He did not answer. He looked very sad.

I said: 'Everyone here is so kind to me.'

'I shall make sure everything is done . . . everything possible.'

'Thank you, Ben. It was good of you to call.'

'You speak as though I am just one of the others.'

'That, Ben, is really what you have become.'

'I'll talk to you later. At the moment you are too shocked.'

I said, 'Thank you,' and he left me.

Gervaise was buried in the graveyard. They gave him a hero's funeral. The parson came from Walloo to preside.

It was very moving. I was there, Morwenna on one side of me, Justin on the other. I was a pathetic figure, the widow soon to bear the dead man's child – the man who had died a most heroic death and had won the admiration of every single one of them.

The parson spoke of him most movingly.

'His death is an example of the supreme sacrifice. His friend was in danger. No one could have expected him to take such a terrible risk. But he did not hesitate. They had come out together; they had worked together in amity; they were friends.'

Visions of them, facing each other across the card table, came to me. Gervaise, departed from his usual nonchalance, blazing with anger; Justin crouching before him: Gervaise seizing Justin and shaking him as though he were a dog.

'Greater love hath no man than he who layeth down his life for his friend,' said the parson.

I saw that many of those present were openly weeping.

And so they laid Gervaise to rest not far from the remains of David Skellington.

I thought: He will never go home now. He will never find that fortune which he was so sure would be his.

Poor Gervaise. He had always lost.

Morwenna had left Golden Hall, much to Lizzie's sorrow. She visited us frequently and was constantly bringing gifts for the baby. She was worried about me, too.

'Angelet,' she said, 'you must come and stay at the Hall. Your baby must be born there.'

'Oh no,' I said. 'Thank you, but that is not possible. You are so good to us all and it is so kind . . .'

'But I want you to come,' she insisted, her eyes filling with tears. 'I love little babies.'

'We have to be in our own homes, Lizzie,' I said. 'We just cannot go into other people's.'

'Ben wants you to come.' She smiled triumphantly. 'He says he is going to insist.'

'I couldn't, Lizzie.'

She thrust that aside. I could see she thought Ben's wish must be law.

I had long talks with Justin and Morwenna.

'We're going home,' said Morwenna with delight. 'We have decided that, haven't we, Justin? I have written to Pa and Mother. They'll be so very pleased. They've hated our being so far away. We are going to take you with us, Angelet.'

I looked down at my spreading figure.

'We're going to wait,' said Morwenna. 'We've worked it all out. We won't go before the baby is born. You couldn't travel yet and then you wouldn't want to until the baby is, say, six months old.'

'That will be nearly nine months. You wouldn't want to wait all that time. You'd better go now. I'll make my own way home.'

'Of course we wouldn't do that, would we, Justin? You see, if you know that you are going, it is not so bad. You count the days. You tick them off as they pass and you know it's getting nearer. What is so dreadful is not knowing when it is going to end. We want to wait for nine months, don't we, Justin?'

Justin answered: 'Yes, we do and we shall. We're not going to leave you here, Angelet. We shall all go back together. After all, even if we weren't going to wait for you, we couldn't just walk out. In the meantime I shall get someone to help me work the mine.'

'Oh Justin, you can't go down there again . . . after what happened.'

'I think I know where it went wrong. There was so much damp down there that the wood rotted. You get to learn these things, you know. You don't make the same mistakes twice.'

'I know you are longing to get away after all you went through . . . particularly Justin. Please don't worry about me. I'll manage.'

But they would not hear of it.

Later I talked to Justin alone.

He said: 'I feel so ashamed. Only you in this place can know how ashamed I feel.'

'It's all over,' I said. 'Gervaise is dead. Only the three of us know what happened on that night. You can't go on thinking of it for ever.'

'We had not spoken in friendship . . . since it happened,' he

308

went on. 'He despised me, I know he did. I saw it in his eyes . . .'

'Yes,' I said. 'Cheating at cards. It was the ultimate sin. Gervaise was obsessed by gambling.'

'So many of us are.'

'Are you going to give it up?'

He looked helplessly into space.

I said: 'You could go home. There would be a place for you with Morwenna's father.'

'I know. I'm going to try. I feel I can never forget this. It was so noble of him.'

'There was a lot of nobility in Gervaise.'

'Oh yes. He hated me. He despised me. There was no need for him to come down like that. If he had not, he would be here today. I should be lying where he is. Why did he do it? He knew what a risk he was taking.'

'He liked to take risks. He was a gambler right to the end. He thought he could win . . . always. He was betting then against the biggest odds ever. But this time he was betting for a different reason. Not for gain . . . for another man's life.'

'And he lost,' said Justin.

'No, he won. He saved your life, Justin. That was his aim.'

I turned away to hide my emotion.

'Oh, Angelet, I'm sorry. I should have been the one. I'm the unworthy one.'

I said: 'You have made Morwenna happy. That is wonderful. You have your son. You will love him and care for him. Justin, we have to forget what we have done in the past. We have to grow better for our experiences. We have to learn from them.'

He looked at me very seriously and said: 'I shall do all I can for you, Angelet. I shall try to repay Gervaise through you.'

The weeks passed. Everyone in the township wanted to show their appreciation to the widow of a hero.

Morwenna was my constant companion. She was very happy at the prospect of going home. She talked of it most of the time. 'Eight more months . . . the time will soon be gone.'

Justin had taken a partner with whom he worked – John

Higgs, who would take over the claim when he left. They had shored up the mine afresh and everyone declared it was as 'safe as houses' now – however safe they were.

I believe it must have been something of an ordeal to descend the mine after what had happened to him; but he did. I dare say he was spurred on by the hope that he would find gold after all. What a wonderful conclusion to his life at Golden Creek that would be . . . to have escaped death to find a fortune.

Nothing so spectacular happened; there were the trivial finds now and then – just enough to raise hopes. He played cards occasionally. I wondered if he cheated. I did not ask. I did not want to know.

I no longer wanted to make hasty judgements of people. One could not know them . . . ever, it seemed. I thought often of Gervaise, sadly, nostalgically, remembering so much of him that I had loved. Whenever I thought of our escape from the *auberge* I would supplant that image with one of the hero and remember the last glimpse I had had of him, the dirt caking his hair and streaking down his face – Gervaise, the elegant man about town as I had first seen him. I would always remember the look of triumph on his face when he had brought up Justin. He had gambled his life and lost it, but he had won in the end because his goal had been to save Justin, the man whom he despised as a cheat.

My thoughts were now centred on my baby which was the best thing that could happen to me.

I did not want to dwell on the past. I wanted to put all that behind me. I did not want to think of Ben and Lizzie. I did not want to remember how I might so easily have been unfaithful to Gervaise; I did not want to think of the disappointment and disillusion I had suffered from Gervaise. It was all over. The new life with the baby was about to begin.

One day when I was in the store Mrs Bowles said to me: 'I've arranged everything. We're going to have the rooms Mrs Cartwright had when young Pedrek was born.'

'What!' I said.

'Now, now, this is a time when *you* don't have to think at all. You leave everything to me. I'm to have the room next to yours

310

and we'll go there a week before the baby is due. It's all been fixed.'

'*I* haven't fixed it, Mrs Bowles.'

'I have . . . with Mr Lansdon and Miss Lizzie. We're going to send for Dr Field. He'll be staying for a night or two at the Hall. The first signs of the baby and Jacob will ride over to fetch him.'

'I can't . . . have all these arrangements made for me, Mrs Bowles.'

'Here, don't you get into a fratchett. Not good for the little 'un, that sort of thing. We don't want him poking his nose out to see what all the fuss is about, do we . . . not before we're ready for him.'

'But I want to be in my own place.'

'No place for a baby. What could have happened to Mrs Cartwright, do you think, if she hadn't been in the right place with the right people there on the spot?'

'I'm different.'

'No, you're not. Women is all one and the same all the world over . . . especially at times like this. Now you stop worrying. It's all fixed. Why, if you go on like this folks'll think you've got something against them there up at the Hall.'

Then I realized that I had to give in – for the baby's sake as well as for 'what folks would think'.

I have to admit I did so with a certain relief. Morwenna had been extremely worried at the prospect of my having the baby here – and so had I.

I would forget from whom the hospitality came. After all, my child's life was more important than my pride.

My time was near. I was greatly looking forward to having my child. And soon we should be leaving. I longed for the time to pass.

I heard a good deal of talk about Morley's Mine. Presumably it was more productive even than had been thought in the first place. Ben had always been the most respected man in the town; now he assumed an almost godlike aura. He had found gold;

he had contrived to make it his. It was something they all admired.

They knew, of course, that he had married Lizzie for it. Lizzie must have known, too. But as they were both satisfied with the bargain, I remarked to Morwenna, what did it matter what was the motive behind it?

Morwenna was romantic. 'I would rather think that he had fallen in love with Lizzie and married her for that reason . . . and then discovered gold on the land. After all, she is pretty and appealing and so sweet-natured. I don't think she has ever had an evil thought against anyone in her life. And he would want to protect her. Strong men like to have someone to protect.'

I smiled at her. She was so innocent. I rejoiced that we had managed to keep Justin's disgrace from her.

In due course I went to Golden Hall. Ben was there with Lizzie when I arrived in the company of Mrs Bowles.

'I'm glad you have come,' said Ben.

'It was not really necessary. It was all arranged for me.'

He just put a hand on my shoulder and said, 'Lizzie insisted.'

'Yes, I did,' said Lizzie delightedly. 'And Ben said you must come, too, didn't you, Ben?'

I was taken to the room I was to occupy. How different from the shanty! No, I could not have let my baby be born there.

Mrs Bowles bustled round in profound appreciation of her own efficiency. In due course Dr Field arrived.

It was a simple and uncomplicated birth and I experienced a thrill of joy when they laid my little girl in my arms.

I said that what I had wanted more than anything was a little girl.

'It is so nice,' said Morwenna, 'because Pedrek is a boy. Perhaps when they grow up they'll marry.'

'I insist that you allow my child time to get out of her cradle before you plunge her into matrimony,' I said.

We talked of names.

Morwenna wanted her to be called Bennath, which was Cornish, she told me, for blessing.

312

'And that,' she added, 'is what this child is going to be for you, Angelet.'

Bennath. I thought: People will call her Ben or Bennie. I could not have that. It would remind me of him.

What I wanted to do was to take my child away and forget this place . . . and all that had happened in it.

I would go home where perhaps it would be possible to start afresh.

I finally decided on Annora Rebecca – Annora after my mother and Rebecca because I liked it. 'But we shall call her Rebecca,' I said, 'because it is always awkward to call two in one family by the same name.'

So Rebecca she became.

She flourished. I stayed on at Golden Hall. I said it was for the baby's sake; but I wanted to be there, too.

I could not face going back to the shack.

Mrs Bowles stayed with me and taught me all the things one has to learn about babies. And I found myself happier than I had been for a long time.

I wrote to my parents and told them about Rebecca and that I should be with them as soon as my baby was old enough to travel. I had written in detail of Gervaise's death and I had had letters from them urging me to come home as soon as possible.

We were ready to leave. Justin had been to Melbourne to book our passages on the *Southern Cross*, and all being well, we should arrive in England in about three months' time.

It would be spring there and here the winter would be starting. Winter in the township was hard to bear, although the heat of the summer could perhaps be equally trying. I noticed the envious looks which were cast in my direction. We were the lucky ones, even if we had not found gold. We were going home.

I was in the shack one day packing up the last of my things when Ben came in. In two days we were to take the Cobb's coach to Melbourne.

He shut the door and stood against it looking at me.

'So soon,' he said, 'you will be gone. Oh, Angel, what a mess we have made of everything.'

313

'What? You . . . the envy not only of Golden Creek but of the whole of Australia!'

'It wasn't the way I wanted it to be.'

'It was the way you made it be.'

'It is going to be very dull here when you have gone.'

I tried to laugh and said: 'I have hardly been the life and soul of the party.'

'You know what you have been to me.'

'I remember what you have told me . . . in the past,' I replied.

'I shall always love you, Angel. Everything was against us. When I was free you were not, and now . . . Who would have thought . . . ?'

I wanted to be flippant. I felt I had to be before I broke down and betrayed my true feelings. That, above all, I must not do. 'Are you implying,' I said, 'that Gervaise might have timed his exit more conveniently to suit you?'

He looked aghast.

I went on: 'Perhaps you should be grateful. Just suppose I had listened to you. Suppose I had left with you as you suggested . . . I should still be a woman without a husband and you a man without a gold mine.'

'You were more important to me than the mine.'

'Remember your vow. You weren't coming back until you found gold . . . a lot of it. Well, now you have.'

'I shall come back,' he said. 'Soon.'

'Not while the mine yields up such rewards, Ben.'

He came towards me but I held back.

'No, it is over,' I said. 'Over? Well, it never was, was it?'

'I should never have come to this place. I should have come back to Cador. I should never have left Cador. I should have insisted on staying with you.'

'It is all in the past, Ben. I shall leave here and everything will seem different when I get home. I have my child. I shall begin a new life. This is over. Finished. It is going to be as though it never was.'

'You won't forget. You did care for me.'

I said: 'I shall try to forget, and if I ever do look back and

314

feel the slightest bit sad, I shall say to myself: He married Lizzie. He married her because he knew there was a gold mine on her father's land and that was the only way he could get his hands on it.'

'It is not a flattering picture, is it, Angel?'

'Oh, I'm not judging. It has made Lizzie happy. It has given you what you want. Lizzie's father died contented because of it. I suppose there is good in everything. I have my child now. You have your mine. You see, we both have a great deal to be thankful for.'

'It is not goodbye, you know. I shall soon be in England.'

'Oh no, Ben. There must be more gold in that mine . . . yet.'

'Gold! Gold! You think of nothing but gold.'

'No, Ben, I only talk of it. You live for it.'

'You don't understand.'

'I do . . . absolutely. Enjoy what you have and don't reach for the impossible. That is what I am going to do. You must go now.'

He went to the door and looked back at me.

'Angel, please don't forget me.'

He was gone. I went to the door and leaned against it. A terrible desolation swept over me.

Then I went to Rebecca's cot. She was awake. She looked at me wonderingly and then I saw recognition in her eyes. I saw what seemed to me a smile of contentment.

I thanked God for Rebecca.

Two days later we left. It seemed that everyone in the township had come to see us off.

Our baggage had been sent to the docks a week before and now we ourselves were ready to board the coach.

There were handshakes and good wishes, signs of envy and the nostalgia for home was more evident than usual.

Ben was there with Lizzie. He looked very sad; so did she.

'Both the little babies going,' sighed Lizzie.

Ben took my hand.

'Don't forget us. Don't forget me.'

I looked at him intently and I said: 'Do you think I ever could?'

The words would have seemed normal enough to any listener, but both of us knew they meant something special.

Then we were off. I looked out of the window until we had passed through the town. I had longed to go and now I could only think: I may never see him again.

But Rebecca was in my arms; and as I held her warm body against my own I knew I had a great deal to live for.

The Return

The voyage was uneventful. There were warm days on deck when we sat and dreamily talked. We could not help comparing this with the last voyage and memories of Gervaise were ever present. He had been full of optimism, so certain was he that he would come home a rich man. It had never occurred to him that he might not come home at all.

There was rough weather in the Tasman Sea and, sailing round the Cape, Morwenna kept to her cabin. Justin and I sat on deck and, because we were alone, we could refer to matters which we had kept secret from Morwenna.

He was amazingly frank. I think he could not forget that Gervaise had saved his life and it seemed incredible that he could have lost his own in doing so when only a short time ago he had clearly shown that he despised him.

I had a notion that Justin wished to look after me as a kind of compensation for not being able to express his gratitude to Gervaise.

'He was the one who should have been saved,' he said. 'He was a better man than I. I do not believe I should have gone down to save him. I have thought a lot about it, Angelet. They brought him up dead and my first thought was: No one will know now what happened. Only Angelet knows and I am safe with her.'

'I should not reproach yourself on that score, Justin,' I said. 'I suppose it would be a natural reaction.'

'But that he should have died saving me . . .'

'Yes, that was significant. But it was typical of Gervaise. He would always act nobly automatically . . . in ordinary life. It was only when he was at the card table that he changed.'

'But he would never have cheated.'

'No . . . not at cards. But it is cheating in a way to gamble with money you haven't got.' I was thinking, too, of Madame Bougerie. 'Gervaise did that.' I went on: 'He was noble in a way; he was wonderfully kind, self-sacrificing too, as he showed so clearly . . . but no one is perfect. Justin, you've got to forget all this. It's all behind you.'

'I haven't cheated at cards since,' he said.

'And you will give all that up?'

He was silent for a while. Then he said: 'It was my living, Angelet.'

'You mean . . . you lived on your winnings . . . those which came to you through your way of playing!'

'It's polite of you to put it that way. It's what is called living by your wits. One can win large sums of money in the London clubs. What I did in the township was . . . trivial. It's exciting because once you are caught it is over for ever. But I was very good at it. I must have been very slack to have been caught like that by Gervaise.'

'Poor Morwenna,' I said. 'She has such a high opinion of you.'

'I promised myself that if I found gold I'd give it all up. I was longing for that. Since I married Morwenna, I've battled with my conscience. She thinks I have a private income. The only income I have is . . . from this.'

'You could have gone to work at Pencarron Mine.'

'I couldn't face it. Life in that remote spot far away from everything I was used to . . .'

'And now?'

'I've changed. All that has happened has changed me. I'm trying to be honest. I was caught by Gervaise. That means I'm slipping. I was not so good. It's ever since I married Morwenna. And now there is the baby. It's made a lot of difference to me. If Morwenna's father offered me something down there, I'd take it, Angelet . . . and I'd do my best to make a good thing of it.'

'Oh, Justin, I'm so glad. You'll have to forget all that has gone before.'

'You've been a good friend to me, Angelet. I feel safe with you. You'd not betray me.'

I laughed. 'My dear Justin, I don't think you are so very wicked. I suppose you only took from the rich.'

'Well, perhaps not in the township . . .'

'If you give it up – if you live honourably from now on – I think you can be very happy. It must have been a terrible strain, fearing all the time that you might be caught.'

'Yes, but there was a sort of excitement which was irresistible.'

'But you have Morwenna and Pedrek to think of now. Can you give all that up, Justin?'

'Yes, I can do it,' he said.

I was glad for Morwenna's sake. She at least could be happy.

And so the days passed and the ship was taking us nearer and nearer to home.

At last the great day arrived.

What a bustle of preparation! What a mass of emotion! We were all on deck to catch the first glimpse of the white cliffs.

And at last I saw my parents and those of Morwenna eagerly scanning the passengers as they disembarked. Then the cry of joy and my parents side by side staring at me in wonder, for there was I with their granddaughter in my arms.

We seemed to be in a huddle. My father and mother were trying to embrace me at the same time; and it was happening like that with Morwenna. Justin stood by smiling.

'My dearest child,' cried my mother. 'Oh . . . Angelet . . .' There were tears in her eyes. 'And this is Rebecca. Oh, what a beautiful child! She is just like you were. Look, Rolf . . .'

They were both ecstatic.

'Thank God you've come home,' said my father.

We were all going to London first to spend a few days there before returning to Cador.

'Everyone in London wants to see you,' said my mother, 'so that has all been arranged. Let me take the baby, Angelet. My goodness, you are thin. We'll have to remedy that.'

My father took the light luggage. The rest was to be sent direct to Cornwall.

319

And so we arrived in London.

We stayed at the house in the square, which was the most convenient. The whole family was there to greet us – Uncle Peter and Aunt Amaryllis, Matthew and Helena with Geoffrey, and Peterkin and Frances: Grace Gilmore came too.

They all kissed me fondly and marvelled at the baby.

'I hope you don't mind my intrusion at this very special occasion,' said Grace. 'But everyone is so kind to me that I really feel I am one of the family.'

'It is wonderful to see you, Grace,' I said,

'You must come and stay with us in Cornwall now that Angelet is home,' added my mother.

Amaryllis was cooing over the babies. They were being put together in the old nursery and the servants were vying with each other for the privilege of looking after them.

To sleep in a luxurious bed, to eat graciously, to be back in this world of ease and comfort, was wonderful. But one soon grew accustomed to such things and the dull ache returned.

I thought of Gervaise . . . dead, and Ben far away . . . and I felt incredibly lonely.

During the days we were in London my mother was very concerned for me.

She said: 'Do you want to talk about it? My poor darling, it must have been terrible for you. He was so very noble. There was a piece in the papers about it. When he heard what had happened Uncle Peter arranged that.' She smiled ruefully. 'You know how he likes to squeeze a little advantage out of everything that happens.'

I could visualize the caption: 'Relative of Matthew Hume in valiant rescue. The hero who lost his life saving a friend is related to Matthew Hume, the well-known politician . . .' And I could imagine his thought: This will be worth a few votes.

I said I could talk about it.

'If only you had never gone out there,' said my mother.

'Gervaise wanted it.'

'Yes . . . I heard about the debts.'

'He thought if he found gold he would pay it all back.'

320

'Gambling, wasn't it? So many young men fall foul of that. They have to learn their lesson.'

I did not tell her that Gervaise would never have learned the lesson. He was a born gambler and would have remained so. I wanted her to keep the picture of the gallant hero.

'And he never saw Rebecca!'

'No. But he knew she was coming.'

'Poor Gervaise. My dearest, you will get over it. You are young. At the time these things happen they seem overwhelming.'

'Yes,' I agreed. 'I have to get over it.'

'And you have the adorable Rebecca. We are going to take you home. We're going to take care of you. I don't know whether you will want to stay in Cornwall . . . but you need time to sort things out. You have the house here . . . the one you had when you married.'

'It's not mine really,' I said. 'Uncle Peter has it as a security against the money he lent to Gervaise so that he could pay his debts and go to Australia. That house will belong to Uncle Peter now.'

'He has told us about this and has said that he will waive the debts so that the house should be yours when you returned.'

'Oh no! The debts should be paid . . . to him.'

'Well, your father wouldn't have it. He has insisted on paying Peter what was owed to him and the house is now yours. You need have no qualms because it is part of the money which would have been yours in any case. But it was generous of Peter to offer. He is a strange man. He has always been kind to me. My mother hated him. There are shady aspects of his life, but he has good points.'

'Most people have two sides to their natures. No one is entirely good . . . no one entirely bad, it seems to me.'

'Perhaps so. I thought you would like to know about the house. I think Morwenna will probably be coming to Cornwall. The Pencarrons have been talking to us about the future. They have been so wretched, . . . missing Morwenna so much. Mr Pencarron will make a very tempting offer to keep Justin down there.'

'You mean to work with him?'

'After all, it seems sensible. All they have will pass ·to

321

Morwenna one day and that will mean Justin. I am sure Mr Pencarron wants it all for the generations to come and young Pedrek to take over in due course. That's the sort of man he is. I thought it would be nice for you to have Morwenna near. It will be like old times. Oh, Angelet, I am so happy to have you back. It is desperately sad that Gervaise is not with you . . . but let's be thankful for what we have.'

Thankful for what we had! That was what I intended to be.

Morwenna told me that Justin had agreed to go to Cornwall and work for her father.

'It has made me so happy,' she said. 'I hated being away from Pa and Mother . . . and they adore Pedrek. It has all worked out so well for me. If only it could have for you, Angelet.'

'I'll be all right,' I said. 'I have my family around me . . . and wasn't it a wonderful welcome home? And there is always Rebecca.'

So I came back to Cador.

Everything had been done to make me happy. There was my old room looking as though I had never left it.

There was a cradle in it. 'I thought at first,' said my mother, 'that you would like to have Rebecca with you. We'll get busy whenever you like, fitting up the nursery. Several of the girls are hoping to be the one selected to look after her. I thought about getting in touch with Nanny Crossley. She was very good with you and Jack.'

'Could we have a little time for a while to think about it?' I asked. 'Rebecca is very young yet. I looked after her in Australia . . . with the help of the local midwife at first . . . and with all the assistance I get here, I can manage. And later on, we'll decide.'

'You feel unsettled as yet, I know,' said my mother. 'It's natural. Your father says you need time to settle after all you have gone through in Australia.'

My brother Jack seemed to have grown up while I was away. His welcome was no less warm, if less emotional, than that of my parents. He was now helping a great deal on the Cador estate which would one day be his.

He was very interested in Australia and asked all sorts of

questions while my parents listened anxiously, afraid that so much talk would open up old wounds.

Morwenna came to Cador often and I went over to Pencarron. She was very happy. Justin was settling in and her father thought that he was quite an astute businessman. Pedrek was an adorable two-year-old . . . a year older than Rebecca; and they played together happily.

I could not resist going to the pool. It still seemed eerie and the memory of what had happened there was as vivid as ever. I stood on the brink of those dark waters and tried to probe their mystery. All this time he had lain down there at the bottom of the pool which was said to be bottomless.

I rode along the shore to the old boathouse; I went to the town and down to the quay. Nothing seemed to have changed much. The fishing smacks were dancing on the waves; the men were gutting fish and one of the older men was sitting on the stones mending his nets. Mrs Fenny was at her door. 'Good day to 'ee, Miss Angel. So you be back, eh? And brought a little 'un with 'ee. It were a terrible thing what 'appened to that 'usband of yours. Don't 'ee fret, me dear. 'Tis well you'm back. Going to foreign parts never done no one no good.' There was Miss Grant, crocheting away in the wool shop, coming to call a greeting as I passed. 'Nice to see 'ee back, Miss Angelet.' There was old Pennyleg and his barman rolling barrels down to his cellar. 'Welcome 'ome, Miss Angelet.' There were furtive looks of commiseration for the widow who had lost her young husband so tragically, and nobly.

I said to my mother; 'Nothing changes in the Poldoreys. Here it seems just the same as it ever was.'

'Yes. People die and get born . . . You remember old Reuben Stubbs in the cottage near Branok Pool?'

I started as I always did at the mention of that place.

'Old Reuben, of course. He was quite a character, and what of his daughter? Jenny, wasn't it?'

'That's what I am going to tell you. Reuben died before you were married.'

I remembered him. An unkempt old man who always seemed to be collecting the wood or beachcombing. I had always felt

323

there was something uncanny about him. He glared at all who came near his cottage as though he feared they would take something from him. Jenny, his daughter, was what they called in these parts 'piskymazed'.

'I was going to tell you about Jenny,' went on my mother. 'She was always a little strange, remember . . . going round talking to herself . . . singing, too. If you spoke to her she'd look scared and turn away. Well, she went very strange after her father died. She lived on in the cottage. Your father said we should just leave her alone. She was harmless. She kept her place clean. She always had, and after her father died it was quite sparkling. She does a little work at the farms when they want extra help. She'll give a hand at anything. There was nothing wrong with anything she did. It was just that she was a little strange. Well, what do you think? She had a baby.'

'She married?'

'Oh no. Nobody knows who the father was. There was a man who came to do hedging and helped the farmers. He was one of those itinerant labourers . . . so useful at haymaking and harvest and planting and so on. He used to talk to her and she didn't seem to be scared of him. We think it must have been this man. Well, he went off and later she had the baby. Born about the same time as Rebecca. We all wondered what would happen, but we need not have done. It changed her completely. It brought her back to normality. No mother could care more for a child than she does for hers. The change is miraculous. Did you see her cottage when you went to the pool?'

'I . . . I don't go down there very much.'

'You might see her about the town . . . always with the baby.'

'I'm glad she's happy,' I said. 'What was the verdict of the town? I can guess Mrs Fenny's.'

My mother laughed. 'Sitting in the Seat of Judgement, of course. Well, that's her way. And it doesn't make much difference to Jenny.'

I could understand how Jenny's life had changed. I had my own child.

The summer passed; it was autumn. Christmas came. The Pencarrons spent it with us.

324

My parents tried to make it a very special Christmas because I was back and there was now a new member of the family and it would be the first Christmas she was really aware of.

She was nearly two years old now. I could hardly believe it was so long since I had seen Ben. I still thought of him constantly. In fact, more than ever. There had been the excitement of coming home and being reunited with my family; and now that I had settled into this routine, memory was more acute. I had judged him harshly. He was ambitious. I had always known that. He wanted money and power. It was a very common masculine trait. He had to win. My refusal of him must have been the first real defeat he had ever suffered. I could see it all so clearly now. He was determined to fail in nothing else. His search for gold would be successful, for he had already found it on another man's land. And because of Lizzie that land was not out of reach. I could understand it all so well. I knew that I could never be really happy without him. I should always be haunted by the thought of what I had missed. I accepted what he had done, for when one loved one loved for weakness as well as strength. I tried to throw myself into the Christmas spirit.

Rebecca was talking now. She called herself Becca and everyone took up the name.

It was touching to see her eyes alight with wonder when the Yule log was brought in and the house decorated with holly, box and bay. Red-faced and flustered, Mrs Penlock was busy in the kitchen. Rebecca was a special favourite with her and the child seized every opportunity of going down to the kitchen. I did not encourage this because Mrs Penlock could never resist popping things into Rebecca's mouth, for she had a conviction that what everyone needed was 'feeding up'.

My mother and I decorated the Christmas tree with the fairy doll on top which was to be Rebecca's, and the jester in cap and bells beside her which was for Pedrek.

We still made the Christmas Bush, which had been part of the decorations before the coming of the tree. It was two wooden hoops fastened to each other at right angles and the frame was covered in evergreens and apples. It was hung up and any pair of the opposite sex meeting under it were allowed to kiss. We had mistletoe as well as the Kissing Bush in the kitchen, which I believe gave great delight to them all, and the stablemen often came in to try to catch the young maids, while Mrs Penlock looked on, purring and not objecting to a kiss for her own august self, because of the time of the year, she said.

There were the carol singers and the poor who came begging with their Christmas bowls. There was the wassail. We kept up the old Cornish customs because my father – though he himself was not Cornish – took a great interest in the old Celtic ways, and as a matter of fact knew far more about the ancient laws of the Duchy than the Cornish themselves.

He encouraged the Guise Dancers because they had existed before the coming of Christianity, and consequently we had dancers in the neighbourhood who visited all the big houses in turn and gave performances during the year. The children clapped their hands with glee to watch them and to see the conflict between St George and the dragon.

In the morning we went to church and came home to the traditional goose and plum pudding; the tree was stripped of its gifts and there was something for everyone. It was wonderful because of the children and I had rarely seen such contentment as that on the faces of the Pencarron parents and their daughter.

Justin was, as they said, 'settling in', but I guessed it was not easy for him to fit in with the quiet country life. It was expecting too much. Gervaise could never have done it. I hoped fervently that it would always remain as it was now for Morwenna and her parents.

When the children, exhausted by the joys of Christmas, could no longer keep their eyes open they went to bed, and Rebecca's last words before she fell into a deep sleep were: 'Mama, may we have Christmas tomorrow?' And I knew that it had been a success.

So the time passed.

During the winter Jenny Stubbs's baby died. It was a calamity which touched the whole neighbourhood. Even Mrs Fenny was sorry. It always amazed me how people who deprecated others, largely because they were not liked themselves, and who have little sympathy with their minor predicaments, will suddenly change when real tragedy strikes. Everyone was sorry for Jenny Stubbs. It was so tragic. Her baby had developed a sore throat and in a few days was dead.

Poor Jenny! She was dazed and heartbroken. My mother went to the cottage with a basket of special food for her and to offer comfort.

She took me with her.

Jenny seemed hardly aware of us. Because of Rebecca I could feel deeply, especially deeply, for her in her sorrow. I wished I could do something to help her.

She changed after that; the new sensible Jenny retreated; the poor dazed creature emerged. It was very sad. Everyone tried to help. Those for whom she had worked offered her more work. They wanted her to know how they sympathized with her.

'She'll get over it,' said Mrs Penlock. 'It takes time.'

Mrs Fenny thought it was the wages of sin. 'When all's said and done she was born out of wedlock and that ain't going to please the Lord.'

I felt so angry with her that I retorted: 'Perhaps He was pleased to see the difference the child made to Jenny.'

She gave me one of her sour looks and I knew she would tell the next person who came along that that Miss Angelet should never have gone to foreign parts because if people live among heathens they start to take after them.

There was nothing we could do to help poor Jenny over her sorrow; but everyone continued to be gentle with her and whenever she appeared would call a greeting to her, as they had never done before.

It was spring, the best time of the year in the Duchy, where the land is caressed by the south-west wind bringing the warm rain from the mighty Atlantic Ocean. Flowers were blooming in abundance – bright yellow celandines, golden dandelions, red campion and purple ground ivy. The woods were full of colour; the songs of the blackbirds and thrushes filled the air; and the wind which blew off the sea was fresh and invigorating.

Time was passing. Was I becoming reconciled? How often were my thoughts in that shanty township? Winter would be

327

coming on now. I thought of Mr and Mrs Bowles in their store. How many babies had been born? I thought of the graveyard, Gervaise and David Skellington lying not very far from each other. I tried to shut out the memory of Golden Hall. How had they spent Christmas? How was Ben faring? How was his marriage? Was the mine as profitable as ever? It must be, or he would have come back. I could not believe that he was happy. How could he be? He was a man who liked lively conversation. He had always enjoyed discussion. There were one or two educated men in the township to whom he could talk. But Lizzie? Lizzie was gentle and kind and loving . . . but could she give him what he wanted? Perhaps she could. Perhaps a dominating man like Ben was happiest with a docile wife.

And so my thoughts went on. I tried to forget, but although I was in Cador where everything was done to make me happy, and although I had a beloved daughter with me, still I hankered for a crude Australian township . . . for the dust, for the dirt, for the flies . . . and the discomforts of a two-roomed shack.

You must be crazy, I said to myself.

Then I would play with Rebecca; we would walk in the gardens; I would listen to her amusing comments; I would talk with my mother and father. I read a great deal. My father was making me more interested in the distant past, the history of the Duchy and its quaint customs; he had done quite a lot of research on these subjects and we had some lively discussions. I should be happy.

It was April when there was a letter from Grace. It was so long since she had seen us. Might she come and visit us for a few weeks.

My mother replied enthusiastically that we should be delighted to see her.

Aunt Amaryllis was a constant letter-writer and she kept us up to date with what was going on in London. Her letters were usually full of Uncle Peter's clever projects and Matthew's wonderful performance in the House and what good work Peterkin and Frances were doing at the Mission.

So we had learned that Grace gave quite a lot of parties in her house. True, it was not very large but people seemed to

328

find that amusing. Grace was invited out frequently and Peter made sure she was always at their parties. 'Peter says she is a born hostess,' wrote Aunt Amaryllis. 'He feels that she ought to get married again. After all, it is a long time since Jonnie died. One cannot go on grieving for ever. Sometimes I think Grace herself would like to marry. Perhaps one day some nice man will come along.'

I said: 'Do you think Aunt Amaryllis is doing a little match-making?'

'That could well be,' answered my mother.

Grace arrived. She had always had a look of distinction although she was not what could be called handsome, beautiful or even pretty. But she was certainly soignée and elegant.

Jack drove to the station to meet her and I was with him.

She was effusively affectionate.

'It is just wonderful to see you, Angelet,' she said. 'And I can't wait to see Rebecca.'

'She calls herself Becca,' I told her. 'I suppose Rebecca was a little difficult for her to pronounce.'

'Becca. I like that. It is more unusual. I expect your child to be unusual, Angelet. You are rather, yourself, you know.'

'If that is a compliment, thanks.'

'It is wonderful to be here again. I shall never forget all that your family have done for me.'

'It is your family now,' I said. 'You married into it and before that you seemed to be a member of it.'

'It's like coming home.'

My mother greeted her with pleasure.

'Do you remember how you used to make our dresses? I shall be tempted to make use of you while you are here.'

'I should love that,' declared Grace. 'It would make me feel so much at home.'

'You must feel that all the time,' said my mother.

Grace was impressed with Rebecca's beauty, charm and intelligence, which endeared her further to me. Rebecca liked her, too.

It was wonderful to have news from London.

'In our circle,' she told us, 'it is politics all the time. There

329

was a great to-do when Palmerston died. We never thought he'd go. There he was almost eighty . . . and no one would have guessed it. He was jaunty till the end. People used to pause outside Cambridge House in Piccadilly to see him come out in his natty clothes and ride his grey horse out to the Row. The people all loved the old sinner. He always had an eye for the women right till the last. It was just the sort of thing to appeal to them. He was Good Old Pam to the end. He remained witty and when he was dying he was supposed to have said, "Die? Me? That's the last thing I shall do!" The Queen was upset, though he was never a favourite of hers. John Russell had to step in . . . but not for long. Once Pam had gone the Liberals were out of favour and Lord Derby is back now. That is good for Matthew, of course.'

'Politics,' said my mother, 'is an uneasy game. One is in one day and out the next.'

'That is what makes it so exciting,' said Grace.

'We hear quite a bit . . . even down here . . . of Benjamin Disraeli.'

'Oh yes, the coming man,' said Grace. 'Perhaps not coming, though. He's arrived. We shall be hearing a great deal about him. He has somehow managed to charm the Queen, which is amazing. One would hardly have thought she would have approved of those dyed greasy black curls.'

'The Prince Consort would have been most displeased, I imagine,' I said.

'How is she getting on after his death?' asked my father.

I saw my mother flash a glance at him. She meant: Don't talk of dead husbands in front of Angelet.

He saw the point at once and looked abashed.

'It seems that she revels in her mourning,' said Grace and changed the subject.

Rebecca had shown a fondness for one of the parlourmaids. She was young and quite clearly had a way with children. Her name was Annie.

My mother had said that she thought Annie might help to look after Rebecca until we came to a decision about a nanny. We had not yet asked Nanny Crossley to return. I remembered

330

her – excellent at her job but a little domineering in the nursery; and I wanted no one to take my daughter from me.

It seemed, therefore, an ideal arrangement that Annie should help, particularly as Rebecca had taken a fancy to her.

I shall never forget that afternoon. During it I experienced some of the most harrowing hours I have ever known.

Grace and I had gone for a ride. Grace wanted to go up to the moors. It was beautiful up there at this time of the year. The gorse was plentiful and the air so pure.

Annie was looking after Rebecca and had said she would take her for a little walk.

When Grace and I returned to the house it was to find it in a tumult. When I heard what had happened, I was cold with fear. Rebecca was lost.

'Lost!' I screamed. 'What do you mean?'

Annie was in tears. They had been walking along laughing and talking when Annie suddenly tripped over a stone. She had gone down flat on her head. She showed us her arms which were grazed and had bled a little.

'It knocked me out for a bit,' she said, 'and when I come to . . . she'd gone.'

'Where?' I cried.

My mother put her arm round me. 'They're out looking for her. She can't have gone far.'

'How long ago did this happen?'

'An hour or so . . .'

'Where? Where?'

'Along the road . . . not far from Cherry Cottage.'

'They are looking there,' said my mother. 'They are looking everywhere.'

Grace said: 'We will go and look. Come on, Angelet. She can't have wandered far.'

'All alone! She's only a baby.'

'She's very bright. She'll probably find her way home.'

'That's what we thought,' said my mother. 'That's why I'm waiting here.'

331

'Come along,' said Grace.

'Yes, you go,' added my mother. 'She'll be here soon . . . Don't worry.'

We rode off towards Cherry Cottage. On the way I saw my father. He gave me a look of despair. I felt sick with fear.

'We're going on,' I said.

'We have been up there. No sign . . .'

'Never mind,' said Grace. 'We'll look again.'

So we went on and with every moment my fear increased. Hundreds of images crowded into my mind. Where could she have gone? She had never been told not to wander off, simply because she had never been out on her own.

Suppose someone had taken her. Gypsies? There were none in the neighbourhood. And then the fear struck me. The pool!

I said to Grace, 'Turn here.'

'Where are you going?'

I murmured: 'The pool . . .'

'The pool!' she echoed and I heard the fear in her voice.

She did not speak. My horse broke into a canter. We had turned off the road and there was the pool . . . glittering, evil. I walked my horse down to the edge and there, as though mocking me, was a little blue silk bag. It was on a gilt frame and had a chain handle. I recognized it. It had been one of the presents on the Christmas tree. Rebecca had received it and she took it everywhere with her.

I cannot describe my terror as I held that little purse in my hands.

I looked at the pool. It was retribution, I thought hysterically. We had hidden the body of the man here . . . and now it had taken my child.

I think I would have waded in, but Grace restrained me.

'What's this?' she said.

'It's Rebecca's purse.'

'Are you sure?'

I nodded. 'I know it well. It can only mean . . .'

I looked at those dark sinister waters.

Grace said: 'Let's get back to the house quickly. We'll tell them what we've found.'

332

'Becca,' I called senselessly. 'Come to me, Becca.'

My voice echoed mockingly, it seemed, through the willows which hung over the pool . . . the weeping willows, I thought, weeping for Rebecca.

But Grace was right. There was nothing we could do. We must get help. They could drag the pool, but whatever they did it would be too late.

I was dazed. I heard Grace explaining. There was consternation. My father went off, several of the men with him. I heard them talking. They were going to drag the pool.

Night came. They were out there. I was there, my mother and Grace beside me. I shall never forget the sight of their faces in the torchlight – devoid of hope.

I was conscious of a great heaviness of heart. Somewhere in my mind I thought: Will they find her? How can we be sure? But they will find him.

They did not find Rebecca; but there was a result of that operation. On a ledge just below the water they found a man's gold watch and chain. There were threads of cloth clinging to it. They also found the remains of a man. He had been too long in the water for him to be identified; but officials came and what was left of him was taken away, with the watch which seemed to have aroused some interest.

I was only half aware of this. I was thinking of my child. There was a hope. At least she was not drowned.

My mother's arms were about me. Grace was at my side looking at me pityingly.

'She'll come back,' said my mother.

'She could have wandered off and fallen asleep somewhere.'

The thought of her alone and frightened, perhaps unable to find her way home, was terrible, but less so than that she should be lying at the bottom of that treacherous pool.

I could not stay in the house. I had to go out searching; and inevitably, it seemed, my footsteps led me to the pool. Grace insisted on coming with me.

'She must have come here,' I said. 'We found her purse.

333

Becca!' I called and my voice echoed back to me on the silent air.

And then I heard it. It was distinctly the sound of bells and they appeared to be coming from the pool. I must be dreaming. They heralded disaster and I could only think of my child.

I looked at Grace. She had heard them too. She was looking about her, startled. Then suddenly she darted away from me; she had run round the side of the pool towards a clump of bushes. I heard her shout. She was dragging someone with her. It was Jenny Stubbs. In her hand was a child's toy . . . two bells on a stick to be shaken in order to make them ring.

Grace called: 'Here are the bells.'

Jenny tried to run away but Grace held her firmly.

I went over and said: 'So it is you who have been playing tricks with the bells, Jenny.'

She looked at me from under her lids. 'My dad never got caught, he didn't. He played 'em when people came round and he didn't want them there.'

Grace had taken the toy from Jenny.

She shook the stick. 'So much for the bells of St Branok,' she said.

'Why did you want to drive us away, Jenny?' I asked.

'There's been a lot of them here,' she said. 'All round the pool . . . And now you've come . . . I thought you'd come to take her away from me.'

My heart leaped in sudden hope.

'Take her, Jenny? Whom did you think we should take?'

'Her. Daisy.'

'Your little girl.'

She nodded. 'She came back.'

'Where is she?' I asked breathlessly.

She looked crafty.

I did not wait for more. I started to run towards her cottage. The door was locked. I banged on it. I heard the footsteps of a child and relief flooded over me, for I knew whose they were.

'Becca!' I shouted.

'Mama! Mama! I want to come home. I don't want to be here any more.'

334

I said: 'Open the door, Jenny. Give me the key.'

She was docile now. She handed it to me. I opened the door and Rebecca was in my arms.

We had a rather disjointed story from Rebecca. When Annie sat down in the road she walked on. She saw Jenny and Jenny took her hand and said she would take her home. She said she was Daisy and not Becca and her home wasn't where home was. It was somewhere else.

She had not been frightened. Jenny was nice. She gave her milk and said she must lie in the bed with Jenny. She hadn't minded until she didn't want to play that game any more.

Everyone joined in the rejoicing, but my mother and I were very sorry for Jenny.

'Poor girl,' said my mother. 'She wouldn't have harmed the child. She thought she had found her daughter. She is very sick, really. I am going to ask the Grendalls to keep her there for a bit. Mrs Grendall is a good sort and Jenny has worked quite a bit for her. I'll go along to see her. That poor creature is in a daze.'

The Grendalls were tenant farmers on the Cador estate – good, honest, hardworking people and we were sure they would help.

'She couldn't be in better hands,' said my mother. 'She mustn't be reproached for what she has done. She meant no harm and she cared well for Rebecca all the time she was with her. She needs to be treated very gently.'

That night I had Rebecca's little bed brought into my room. She had suffered no harm from her adventure but she wanted to be close to me; and I wanted her there so that I could reassure myself through the night that she was safe and well.

The Bodmin newspapers were full of the discovery at the pool.

The watch and chain which had been found bore initials on it: M.D. and W.B. They were not engraved but appeared to have been scratched on. Readers would be reminded of a case

335

some years ago. A man had been on trial for a particularly dastardly murder; he had sexually assaulted and murdered a young girl. He had been about to stand trial when he had escaped from jail. He had been traced to the Poldoreys area and although there had been an extensive search he had never been found. At length it had been assumed that he had escaped from the country.

He had been in the water so long that it was not easy to identify the body but certain evidence pointed to the fact that it could have been he. The watch bore the initials M.D. His name was Mervyn Duncarry. Those of W.B. might well belong to someone for whom he had a sentimental attachment. It was difficult to imagine how an escaped prisoner could have had such a watch. He certainly would not have been wearing it in prison; but his prison clothes had been discovered on Bodmin Moor, so it seemed obvious that he had had help from somewhere. It could have been said that he had stolen the clothes and the watch with them and perhaps scratched on it the initials of himself and this person. The police were reading it as a clue to his identity. It could have been caught in the rocky ledge when he fell into the pool and so remained there near the surface. It was a mystery; but the police were almost convinced that the man discovered in St Branok Pool was Mervyn Duncarry – though they were not closing the files on the murder case yet.

Grace looked rather shaken, I thought. I guessed she was thinking of Rebecca wandering out on her own when there were such people in the world.

A few days later when we were riding together she wanted to go down to the shore. We galloped along the beach to the boathouse. She paused there and said: 'Let's tie up the horses and walk a little.'

We did and as we went along she said: 'I can't help thinking of that man in the pool.'

I did not want to speak of him. I had not been able to get him out of my mind since the discovery in the pool.

I said: 'I don't think we should be back too late. I really don't entirely trust Annie with Rebecca.'

'She's bound to be doubly careful now. The others are very watchful. Are you thinking about that man? I remember so well when it happened. There was a young man staying here.'

'Ben . . . you mean?'

'Yes, Ben. Do you remember you had a ring . . . ?'

'Yes,' I said faintly.

'There were initials on it. M.D. and there were two more besides.'

'I think it was W.B.'

'They were on the watch,' she said. 'You found the ring, didn't you?'

I nodded.

'Where Angelet?'

'It . . . it was when I had my accident.'

'On the beach here . . . near the boathouse?'

I did not speak.

'It's odd,' she said. 'The watch was in the pool and the ring . . . here by the boathouse. Why did he come here and lose his ring and then go and drown himself in the pool? What do you make of it, Angelet?'

'It's very mysterious.'

'Show me the spot where you found the ring.'

'I can't remember . . . quite. Grace, we must go back.'

She laid a hand on my arm. 'Angelet.' Her grip was very firm and her eyes looked straight into mine. 'You know something . . . don't you?'

'What do you mean? Know what?'

'Something about this man. You remember. You had an accident. You were on the beach. You found the ring . . .'

'It's so long ago. I don't remember.'

'Angelet, I think you do remember. It wasn't like that, was it?'

I felt trapped and again there came that impulse which I had had with Gervaise, to talk and explain.

I heard myself saying: 'No, it wasn't like that.'

'You've always felt something about the pool, haven't you?'

'How did you know?'

'I've watched you. Something happens when it's mentioned.

337

What is it about the pool? Did you know they would find him?'

'Yes,' I cried. 'I did know . . . because . . .'

She came closer, her eyes were glittering with curiosity; she kept a firm grip on my arm.

'Tell me about it. Tell me, Angelet. It will help you to tell.'

I closed my eyes and saw it all. 'We shouldn't have done it,' I said. 'We should have called people. Let them know that he was dead.'

'Dead? Who?'

'That man. That murderer.'

'You saw him?'

'Yes, I saw him. He was going to do to me what he had done to that other girl. Ben came in time . . . and they fought. He fell and knocked his head on that bit of wall. You could not see it very much before it was excavated. It was just a sharp piece of flint sticking up in the grass. He cut his head on it. It killed him. Ben and I threw him into the pool.'

She was staring at me. I hardly recognized her, her eyes were brilliant in her very pale face.

'And the ring?' she said.

'It was by the pool. I picked it up without thinking. I put it in the drawer. I didn't remember putting it there. I didn't think it was his ring. Then you said you liked it and I gave it to you.'

'I see,' said Grace slowly. 'And all the time they were hunting for him you knew he was lying at the bottom of the pool.'

I did not speak.

'I can see clearly how it happened,' she said. 'Who else knows? Have you told anyone?'

'Only Gervaise.'

'Gervaise,' she said slowly.

'Grace, do you think we were wrong?'

'I think you should not have tried to hide the body.'

'I believe that to be so now. Then, it seemed the best thing. We were afraid there would be trouble. We thought they would say we killed him . . . and it was rather like what happened to my grandfather. You know, he killed a man who was attempting to assault a girl. It was called manslaughter and he was sent to Australia as a convict for seven years.'

338

'That was a long time ago.'

'Not so very long. Perhaps we were impulsive. We didn't know what would be best. He was dead and he would have been hanged anyway. We told ourselves that it was better for him to die the way he did.'

'But it has been on your conscience, hasn't it? All these years?'

'It's something you never forget. I'm glad I've told you, Grace.'

'Yes, I am, too.'

As we rode home neither of us said very much. We were both thinking of the man who for all those years had lain at the bottom of St Branok Pool.

Grace went back to London. I missed her very much. I was beginning to feel restive. I felt as though I were lying in a great feather bed, over-protected. I think at times my parents forgot I was no longer a child. I was sinking deeper and deeper into a sort of limbo where everyone contrived to stop anything ever happening to me in case it should be harmful. They forgot I had been married; I had travelled to Australia and lived a very unconventional life there. I found it hard to settle down to the quiet life of an English country gentlewoman in a remote corner of England – even though it was the home of my childhood.

My mother knew how I was feeling. I was sure that there were long consultations between her and my father. There were several dinner parties to which young men were invited – at least, they were not very young and most of them I had known since childhood. I knew what they were trying to do. They felt I should marry again and they were trying to find a suitable husband for me.

I did imply that I did not want a husband, and if I did I should prefer to find my own; they knew I saw through their little ruses. Their great desire was for my happiness, but I felt restricted, shut in, with too much loving care. I wished I could have told them about Ben and my feelings for him. But there seemed no one to whom I could talk of that.

339

One day Mrs Pencarron came over to tea. She liked to visit us and did so fairly frequently. Then, of course, we were invited to dinner parties at Pencarron Manor and they came to us at Cador.

Morwenna and the Pencarrons were in the conspiracy which was to find a husband for Angelet. I was half amused, half impatient with them.

On this occasion Mrs Pencarron had news.

Sitting in the drawing-room, slowly stirring her tea, she said; 'We've been talking, Josiah and I. It's about Justin.'

'Oh?' said my mother.

I was alert. I thought: What has he been doing? I had visions of a card table in the Pencarron drawing-room. They never played cards, by the way. But I imagined Justin, red-faced and guilty, with the ace of hearts up his sleeve.

'He's a very good young man . . . very clever,' said Mrs Pencarron. 'We're so grateful to him. He's made our Morwenna so happy.'

'She is certainly that,' agreed my mother.

'He truly loves her and he adores young Pedrek.'

'Well, Pedrek is a charming little fellow. Our Rebecca dotes on him and she has very good taste.'

Mrs Pencarron smiled. 'I was all against it at the first. So was Josiah, really. But he said we mustn't be selfish and he's right. For a long time . . . before Morwenna's marriage . . . he said we ought to have an office in London. From the point of view of business it would be a good thing . . . marketing and export and things like that . . . which Jos says is too much to be done down here. So he's thinking of opening up this office and putting Justin in charge of it. He's told Justin . . . in a vague sort of way. You see, they could go to London . . . after all, though it is a long way from here, there's the railways and everything. And Justin says how they could come down here often and perhaps we could have little Pedrek here from time to time, for they'd be very busy in London and the country air would be good for him. It's going to be a bit of a wrench. But it'll be good for business . . . and now there's someone in the family who could take on this office.'

340

'I see,' said my mother. 'We shall miss Morwenna, shan't we, Angelet?'

She was looking at me intently; and after Mrs Pencarron left she said: 'I believe you are envying Morwenna . . . going to London.'

'Justin will be pleased,' I said.

My mother made no other comment on that occasion, but I knew she and my father had many discussions, and I began to guess what was in their minds.

At length it came. 'Angelet, I think you would like to go to London. You must find it a little dull here.'

'Of course not. It's just that . . .'

'I know.' She was thinking of Gervaise. 'It was a tragic thing that happened to you, darling. And you so newly married. It has been a great worry to us. But you know your father and I want the best for you and we have both come to the conclusion that if you felt you would like a little stay in London we wouldn't want you to think about leaving us. You have the house there. There are Uncle Peter and Aunt Amaryllis and Helen and Matthew . . . Well, the family.'

I felt my spirits lift a little. It would be a change and there was always an element of excitement in that.

My mother, who was quick to notice my moods, realized this.

'That's settled, then,' she said. 'You could go up with Morwenna and Justin. I'll write to Amaryllis. I expect you could stay with them until you get settled into your own house. Would you like to take Annie with you for Rebecca? We shall miss you very much but we'll come and visit you and you'll come back here.'

I put my arms round her and hugged her. 'You are so good to me,' I said.

She laughed and replied: 'What else did you expect? There is nothing your father and I – and Jack – want so much as to see you happy again.'

Morwenna came over. She was so pleased because I was going with them.

'I wasn't looking forward to it, Angelet,' she told me. 'I love it here. And I think the country air is so good for Pedrek.'

'There are wonderful parks in London,' I reminded her.

'Yes, but it's not the same. On the other hand, Justin is so pleased. He's not really a country man. It's an excellent idea, this office in London, you know.'

Dear Morwenna. She was disturbed; she wanted to go on with the easy country life just as much as I wanted to escape from it. However, there was no doubt that she felt relieved because I should be with them.

A few days before we left there was a letter from Amaryllis.

I am so looking forward to seeing Angelet and dear little Rebecca . . . Morwenna and Justin, too, of course. It will be lovely to have them close. We are having her house made ready for Angelet but of course she must stay here as long as she likes . . . as she must know.

What do you think? Ben has come home. He is very rich now. Peter is so amused . . . and I think proud of him. He said he wouldn't come home until he struck gold and my goodness, he has kept his word. Peter says you can trust Ben to do everything in a big way. He's sold the mine now. I think he has probably had the best from it and he intends to stay at home! 'No more roaming,' he says. 'I've had enough.' He has bought a beautiful house, not far from this one – but his is more grand. There will be a lot of entertaining done, for what do you think? He is going in for politics. Peter thinks that is highly amusing. I wish they were on the same side. You know Peter supports the Conservatives and Matthew is a highly respected member of government in that party when it is in power. Ben is ranging himself with the Liberals. We have some lively conversation here, as you can imagine. I must say it has all been very exciting since he came back. Ben is that sort of person. One can't be dull in his company.

I am rather sorry for his poor little wife. Dear Lizzie, she is such a pleasant creature . . . so good really, but not in the least suited to all this. She is a little simple. I don't think she can be very happy although she adores Ben and is very proud of him. But how she'll stand up to what he's planning, I don't know. Helena will tell you what it is like being a parliamentary wife. But Helena has managed to throw herself into it . . . and Peter of course has done a great deal to further Matthew's career. He would for Ben but it will be difficult, their being on opposite sides of the fence as it were.

One thing I'm glad of is that Grace has taken to Lizzie and Lizzie to her. It's a very good thing. Grace has made herself into a sort of chaperone . . . helps her choose her clothes and things, bolsters her up. In fact, I think she is making herself invaluable to both Lizzie and Ben. I think Ben is grateful to her. It's good for Grace, too. I think she is a little lonely sometimes. It has always been my opinion that she would like to marry again. After all, it is so long since Jonnie died. She has mourned long enough. But no one has turned up yet. So this looking after Lizzie has been a blessing to Grace as well as to Lizzie herself.

I am so looking forward to seeing Angelet and Rebecca.

My love to you all.

While my mother was reading the letter I was thinking of Ben . . . back in London, his mission accomplished.

I was a little apprehensive at the prospect of seeing him again but that feeling was quickly suppressed by an immense excitement.

Arriving in London, we went first to the house in the square where we were greeted warmly by Aunt Amaryllis. Rebecca and Pedrek were duly admired and put to bed in the old nursery. There were two little beds side by side, for Amaryllis thought that as they were in a strange house they should be together in case they woke up in the night and were frightened.

We had brought Annie with us and Morwenna had May, Pedrek's nursemaid. They would probably go back to Cornwall in due course when the nannies were engaged.

Justin and Morwenna were staying for the night. I was to remain until I was ready to go into my house.

It was wonderful to see them all and I was feeling better already. Helena and Matthew arrived with Geoffrey; Peterkin

343

and Frances came too, and just as we were going into dinner Ben came with Lizzie.

As soon as I saw him, looking taller and extremely healthy, his eyes against his bronzed skin even more blue than I remembered, I told myself that, knowing he was here, I should not have come. In Cornwall I had tried to put him out of my mind; but I should be quite unable to here.

'Angel,' he said. 'How marvellous to see you!'

'Thank you, Ben. And Lizzie, too! It is good to see you, Lizzie.'

She smiled at me shyly and I kissed her.

'I did not expect you to be home so soon,' I said.

'I intended to come at the first possible moment,' he answered.

'Aunt Amaryllis did tell us that you would be here.'

'So you decided to come and take a look at me?'

'Well, actually I had already decided to come. It was only a few days ago that I heard you were here.'

'Well, here we are together at last.'

We went in to dinner. Uncle Peter, a little more silvery at the temples, but as distinguished as ever and looking extremely young for his years, was at one end of the table, beaming at us all; Aunt Amaryllis with her gentle unlined face at the other.

'So you are going to set up an office here,' said Uncle Peter to Justin.

'Yes,' replied Justin. 'I shall get busy tomorrow.'

'I can introduce you to a few people who might be useful.'

Dear Uncle Peter, someone had once said he had a finger in every pie, and that was true. I thought of what he had done for Gervaise and me, and even if he was a wicked old sinner, I was fond of him. I was sure he would be of considerable help to Justin, and if ever he discovered Justin's weakness he would not be censorious. One of the most lovable things about sinners like Uncle Peter was that they were lenient with other people's foibles.

Peterkin and Frances talked a little about their Mission, and Geoffrey about the law which was going to be his profession;

344

but the conversation was dominated by Uncle Peter and Ben, and politics was the chief topic.

I was very interested to hear them. Matthew had slavishly agreed with his father-in-law; Ben had no intention of agreeing with his grandfather. They were on opposing sides. Uncle Peter extolled the virtues of Disraeli who had just become Prime Minister on the retirement from office of Lord Derby. But William Gladstone's was the star to which Ben was hitching his wagon.

'Disraeli may have the ear of the Queen,' Ben was saying, 'but Gladstone is the strong man. He will be Prime Minister, mark my words, and before long. And then he will be with us for a long time. Who is this man, Disraeli?'

'The cleverest politician on the scene at this moment,' retorted Uncle Peter. 'The Queen realizes this and gives him her support.'

'But the government of this country does not rest with the Queen. It is an elected government and it is the people who decide. They'll stand solid behind a strong man like Gladstone – not a fly-by-night like Disraeli.'

'This new Reform Bill will put nearly a million voters on the roll. Gladstone's bill would have had only half that number.'

'Then,' said Ben, 'we must see that the new voters vote for us.'

'No,' cried Uncle Peter. 'We shall see that they vote for *us*.'

And so they went on, fiercely arguing, but with the utmost respect for each other throughout.

I found it stimulating even on that first day, and when I lay in bed that night I was still thinking of Ben in his splendid house, with Lizzie who had hardly spoken a word throughout the entire evening; and I did wonder what the future would hold.

Within a week I was settled in my house. Amaryllis and Helena helped me choose a few servants and there was a nanny to help with Rebecca. My daughter was enchanted by London. She loved the parks. Rebecca had great charm. She believed that everyone loved her and consequently she loved everybody; she enjoyed life and could not help sharing that enjoyment. Each day I thanked God for her. She was remarkably like Gervaise; she had his nature, too, which had been a delightful one flawed only by that obsession which I was determined to see never took possession of Rebecca.

Morwenna, too, had settled in. Justin was happy and that was good enough for her; and the children were always eager to see each other.

One day, very soon after I had settled in, Ben came to see me. It was mid-morning, Annie had taken Rebecca to Morwenna's house. She was going to spend the morning with Pedrek; and as I had planned to do some shopping, I was almost ready to go when Maggie, my new maid, came to tell me a gentleman had called to see me.

'Did he give his name?' I asked.

'Yes, Madam. Mr Lansdon.'

I expected to see Uncle Peter.

'Ben!' I gasped.

'Well, don't look so surprised. You knew I'd come to see you. It is wonderful that you are here.'

'Why?'

'What a question! Because what I want more than anything is to see you, is the answer.'

'Would you like some refreshment? Tea? Coffee? Wine?'

'No, thanks. To see you is refreshment enough for me.'

I laughed with an attempt at lightness.

'So the gold ran out and you came back.'

'I never intended to stay. No, it has not run out. There is a certain amount left.'

'But all the certainty has gone. Now it is more or less like any of the others, I suppose.'

'Better than that. I've left some for the others.'

'And sold at a good price?'

'A price the buyer thought it worth paying. But I didn't come here to talk business.'

'What did you come to talk about?'

'I just wanted to be with you.'

346

As he approached me I stepped back. 'Nothing has changed,' I said.

'No, I suppose not,' he answered ruefully. 'I have missed you so much. I think of you constantly. You remembered me perhaps?'

'There has been a lot to think of.'

'And now we are both in London.'

'I did not know you were here until I had made my plans to come.'

'Would it have made any difference if you had known before?'

'I don't know.'

'Let's stop talking around all this, shall we? I love you, Angel. I have from the first. When you were a little girl . . . Oh, why were you only ten years old when we first met? If only it could have been different.'

'What are you complaining of? You got your mine. If you had married me, you wouldn't have had that.'

'I know. You should have come to me before . . . We would have come home. Gervaise would have divorced you . . .'

'You are very glib about other people's divorces.'

'I know now,' he said, 'that being with you, loving you . . . would have been more important to me than anything.'

'More so than the gold mine?'

'Yes. I'd have found some other way to fortune . . . just as my grandfather did. I am very like him. We think alike.'

'In politics?'

'Yes, in politics. It doesn't matter if we are on different sides, I don't mean opinions. I mean aims . . . the way we set about everything. There is no doubt that I am his grandson. And about us, Angel. Things haven't worked out as we wanted them to. We were both in the wrong place when we should have been together. That's how life goes. But if you don't get exactly what you want you have to take something.'

'What are you suggesting?'

'That we love each other. We are here. It can't be quite as we wished . . . but why shouldn't we have something?'

'You mean some clandestine love-affair?'

'I mean . . . something. We can't just give everything up

347

because one of us isn't free. First it was you . . . and now I am the one.'

'And Lizzie?'

'Ah, Lizzie. She is a good girl and very innocent. I could never leave Lizzie. I feel I have a duty to her. I promised her father that I would always care for her. She needs care.'

'Your promise was a part of the price you paid for your gold mine.'

'Do you remember long ago . . . when we were on the moor together and you told me the story of the men in the tin mine who found gold? Those little people showed it them and the men made a bargain always to leave part of their findings to them. And they did.'

'Yes, I remember. It's a well-known legend.'

'And when the sons failed . . . the gold failed, too.'

'Are you afraid that if you deserted Lizzie, the gold would fail? But you have finished with the gold. You have your fortune.'

'I mean that if I hurt her in any way I should lose something of myself . . . my self-respect, shall we say?'

'Oh, Ben, you have suddenly become very noble.'

'I have never been that, as you know. But try to understand my feelings for Lizzie.'

'You regard her as some sort of talisman . . . like the knackers in the mine; she could make some evil befall you if you deserted her . . . But you don't love her so deeply that you would not be prepared to have a degrading love-affair with someone else . . . degrading to you . . . to me . . . and to Lizzie.'

'You are being over-dramatic.'

'No, Ben, I am not.'

'You love me, do you not?'

I hesitated.

'I know that you don't want to answer because the answer is yes. You have never forgotten me.'

I said: 'We did share a shattering experience. You know what happened a little while ago?'

'Yes, I heard of it. They found a watch or something with his initials on it. That must have been a shock for you.'

348

'I felt nothing more than relief at first. I had feared they would find Rebecca. She was lost and it was for that reason that they dragged the pool.'

'My poor Angel! What a terrible thing for you.'

'And all the time she was well. She had been taken by a woman who had lost her child and thought Rebecca was hers.'

He put his arms about me and for a few moments I allowed myself the luxury of laying my head against him.

Quickly I drew away.

I said: 'I think, Ben, it would be better if we did not see each other . . . alone. We shall meet at the family gatherings, of course. That must be enough.'

'It will not be enough for me,' he said.

I shrugged my shoulders.

'We are having a dinner party next Wednesday. You have not seen my house yet. Do come.'

'Who will be there?'

'My grandfather and Amaryllis, of course, Helena and Matthew and friends. I am hoping to be adopted as candidate for Manorleigh which is in Essex. There are people I should get to know.'

I smiled knowledgeably.

He added: 'Peterkin and Frances I hope will be there. They are, I fear, not very interested in these occasions.'

'But they are good for you,' I said. 'Connections devoted to good works and all that.'

He smiled.

'Yes,' I said. 'You are very like Uncle Peter.'

'Grace Hume has been very helpful. She has been very good on several occasions. Lizzie clings to her. Poor Lizzie, she loses her head and is sure everything is going wrong . . . and she is no good as a hostess . . . but with Grace there beside her she doesn't do too badly.'

'Grace has always been a help in the family ever since she came . . . years ago. Do you remember?'

'That never-to-be-forgotten time.'

'She was there when . . .'

'Yes, I remember. Well, she helps Lizzie with clothes and

349

things and it is really amazing how she does it. She is often at our place – as a matter of fact, when there is something special on she comes and stays.'

'I am glad she is of use. In time Lizzie will get accustomed to it and she'll make a good Prime Minister's wife. I suppose that is the office for which you are aiming.'

'It is always a good plan in life to aim high. You may not get right there but you get somewhere.'

'I am sure you are right.'

'So we shall see you on Wednesday?'

'I shall be there.'

'I thought I had better ask Justin and Morwenna. They can escort you.'

'You think of everything.'

He came to me suddenly and took both my hands.

'I am not going to let you go, you know. I'll find some way.'

'There is no way,' I replied. 'There can be no way.'

'There is always something,' he said firmly.

Grace visited me.

There was a subtle change in her; her step was more springy and there was a certain radiance about her.

I thought: Can it be that she is in love?

I remembered what Aunt Amaryllis had written of her. She believed she wanted a husband. It was just a matter of the right one's coming along. One could not expect her to go on grieving for Jonnie for ever.

I waited for confidences, but none came.

Instead she wanted to talk about Lizzie.

'She is such a dear creature,' she said. 'I was drawn to her the moment I saw her.'

'Ben told me how good you have been to her.'

'Oh, have you seen Ben?'

I did not want to tell her that he had come to see me. I said: 'He was at dinner the night I arrived.'

'Of course. He is so kind and patient. It is a little trying for him at times.'

'Do you mean . . . Lizzie?'

She nodded.

'He married her,' I reminded Grace.

'Yes, I know. I believe he was very sorry for her.'

I smiled. 'She brought him a good deal.'

'I know her father owned the land on which Ben found gold. He has often told us that. Lizzie is delighted about it. She has told me how much. She hasn't an idea what is expected of her. But she is getting on . . . a little. I'm doing all I can for her.'

'And that is a great deal, I gather.'

'Did Ben say so?'

'Yes.'

She smiled, well pleased. 'She tries so hard. It's rather pathetic. She wants to be a credit to him.'

'Of course. He is going far.'

'In politics, you mean.'

'He is one of those men who will always succeed. But he had luck in marrying Lizzie.'

'You're referring to the land that came with her . . . and the gold.'

'That's exactly what I mean.'

'Don't you like Ben, Angelet?'

I felt my face twist into a wry smile. 'Oh,' I said, trying to speak lightly, 'he is clever and amusing and all that.'

'You speak as though you don't approve.'

'It's not for me to approve or disapprove. He is happy, presumably. I believe he has a splendid house and brilliant prospects. What more can he want? Lizzie, of course, is another matter.'

She wrinkled her brows and looked intently at me. 'You are rather vehement.'

'Am I? I didn't realize it. Tell me, how are things with you? What do you do all the time?'

'I have so little time to spare. I have entertained a little. Of course, my house is rather small. I have some amusing dinner parties. The Lansdons senior have always been good to me and so have Helena and Matthew. They invite me to their houses and there I meet interesting people and ask a few of them to

351

my place. But since Ben and Lizzie came I seem to have much more to do.'

'Ben says you have acted as a sort of duenna to Lizzie.'

'Does he?' She smiled rather complacently. 'Well, I couldn't let the poor innnocent little thing loose in the jungle, could I?'

'You call the social circle a jungle?'

'It is in a way. She is such an innocent lamb, and as to clothes, she has no idea how to dress.'

'I thought she looked very charming the other night.'

'My guidance, my dear. I steer her through. I tell her to talk to people . . . what to say . . . what they are interested in. She is doing quite well. By the way, there was no more news about that man and the watch, was there?'

'No,' I told her, 'nothing at all.'

'I don't suppose we shall hear any more of it. That's as well, don't you agree?'

I did agree.

And I thought to myself: Something has happened. I wonder what.

I was amazed at the grandeur of Ben's house. Uncle Peter's had always seemed splendid, but this was more so.

There were chandeliers in the hall and at the top of the wide staircase where Ben and Lizzie stood receiving their guests. Grace was standing a little to the side – like a lady-in-waiting.

There were about thirty guests, many of them well known in political circles. Uncle Peter came up to me. He took my hand and kissed it.

'What do you think of this establishment?' he asked.

'Quite glorious,' I replied.

'To tell the truth, I'm a little envious. It took Ben to outdo me.'

'People say he is a chip off the old block.'

'I often regret it took us so long to get together. Irregularities in family life cause so many regrets. I suppose that was why the conventions were thought of in the first place. If you obey them, you sail peacefully through life.'

352

'Wouldn't that be a little dull for someone of your temperament?'

'Perhaps,' he said. 'But I should not advise anyone embarking on life to fly in the face of them.'

'To be different from you . . . and Ben . . . who have been so successful?'

'We are of a kind. We shouldn't founder. Some would. I once heard a story about Walter Raleigh and the Queen. He scratched on the glass of a window with a diamond, "Fain would I climb, but fear I to fall". The Queen took the diamond from him and scratched underneath, "If your heart fails you, climb not at all". They were very careless with their property. Fancy disfiguring a beautiful window in that way! But perhaps for such sound good sense it was worth it.'

'You were never afraid to climb.'

'Oh no, I suppose not, and I have done some dangerous mountaineering in my time. Ben is like me. Far more than Peterkin is . . . or Helena for that matter.'

'Yes,' I mused. 'You must have been a very attractive man when you were young, Uncle Peter.'

He laughed. 'That suggests that you think Ben is very attractive and I am no longer so.'

'I didn't mean that. You'll always be attractive . . . both of you.'

'That reminds me of another quotation. This is our honoured friend, Disraeli. "Everyone likes flattery but when you come to royalty you must lay it on with a trowel." Is that what you are doing now, my dear, laying it on with a trowel?'

'Indeed not . . . but I do always think of you as King of the family, so you are royalty in a way. But what I said is true and has nothing to do with your status.'

'You are a dear girl. You remind me of your grandmother. I was very sad when she died. It seemed such a terrible end for someone so bright and attractive . . . and so young. Oh dear, you are making me morbid. And here is my noble daughter-in-law Frances coming towards us. I shall leave you with her, for she is such a righteous lady who always reminds me of the sinner I am.'

353

'Dear Uncle Peter, it is so good to be with you.'

'Ah, Frances,' he said. 'Where is Peterkin? Oh, I see . . . over there. I dare say you are longing to have a talk with Angelet. I shall leave you together. I must have a word with some of the guests.'

Peterkin joined us. He and Frances told me how pleased they were to see me, and they asked if I intended to stay long in London.

'It depends,' I said. 'I haven't made up my mind. I have the house here and I can be completely independent, which is very pleasant. Not that I haven't been given wonderful hospitality by Uncle Peter and Aunt Amaryllis.'

'I understand that you like your independence,' said Frances. 'You might like to come to see us at the Mission.'

'I intended to invite myself if you didn't ask me,' I said.

'My dear, there is no need to wait for invitations, is there, Peterkin?'

'Of course there is not. We'd love to see you there. We might even make use of you.'

'There is always a great deal to do,' explained Frances, 'especially now we have enlarged the place considerably. We have the house next door now which has made us almost double the size. We have big kitchens. We make gallons of soup each day, don't we, Peterkin? Good nourishing stuff. We're always looking for someone to give a hand.'

'Most of our workers,' Peterkin explained, 'work because they believe in what we are doing. So we have to have mostly people of independent means. We can't afford to pay many people. We need all the money we can get for the work.'

'I know you have done wonders.'

'A lot has been due to my generous father-in-law,' said Frances. 'He is very helpful, particularly when there is some political crisis and he wants to call attention to the family's good works. Matthew benefits from it. And all he asks is that it is known where the help comes from. A small price to pay for the goods, as I always say.'

Frances was a little cynical about Uncle Peter. I knew there was always a motive behind almost everything he did – but he did give the money to the Mission, which had made a great deal of difference to it.

'Well, do come along, soon,' said Frances.

And I promised I would.

Dinner was a sparkling occasion. Ben, from the top of the table, led the conversation, which was amusing, witty and topical, and there were many references to what was going on in the political field. Many of them seemed to be on intimate terms with 'Dizzy' and Mr Gladstone and Her Majesty herself. There were references to the Queen's gillie, John Brown, who, some thought, was more than her gillie; they talked of the rather scandalous cartoons appearing in the press, and speculated as to whether the sly gossip would bring the Queen out of her retirement.

I noticed that Grace joined in the conversation and seemed to be as knowledgeable as any of them. Lizzie said hardly a word. She sat at the end of the table, opposite Ben, an unwilling hostess. She looked at times as though she were going to burst into tears and I noticed how often her eyes strayed to Grace, who was seated a place or two away from her. But Grace was engaged in animated conversation and did not look poor Lizzie's way.

I wished I was nearer to her so that I could talk to her.

I was very much aware of Ben. There he sat at the head of the table so assured, certain that very soon he would be in Parliament. All he needed was an election. I felt he was certain to win.

Once or twice he caught my eye and smiled at me. I think he guessed what was in my thoughts. I had a stupid impression that he was doing all this for my benefit . . . reminding me that he was the kind of person who always won.

After dinner the ladies went to the drawing-room, leaving the men at the table with the port.

I saw Lizzie then and I said: 'It was a most successful party, Lizzie.'

'Yes,' she said.

Then Grace came up.

'You were very good, Lizzie,' she said.

355

'Was I?' asked Lizzie.

'Oh yes. It's getting easier, isn't it? Isn't it lovely to have Angelet here?'

'You've been living in the country, haven't you?' said Lizzie.

'Yes, with my parents.'

'That must have been nice.'

'Very nice.'

'I hope I shall see the dear little baby.'

'Oh, you mustn't call Rebecca a baby. She wouldn't like that. She's a little girl now and wants everyone to know it.'

Lizzie laughed delightedly and the furrow disappeared from her brow.

I said: 'Pedrek is the same. He's quite a little man. They play together. They love the parks. I'll bring them to see you some time. May I?'

'Oh, please do.'

Before the men returned Lizzie took me up to her bedroom. There was a special room set aside for the ladies, but she took me to hers. I fancied she wanted to speak to me alone.

I could see that this was not in any sense Ben's room. So they occupied separate rooms, I thought.

She said: 'It's nearly over now, isn't it?'

'Nearly over?'

'This evening.'

'Oh yes. We shall soon be gone and you will have your lovely house all to yourselves.'

'I didn't mean that.'

She looked at me and suddenly flung her arms about me, starting to cry.

'Oh Lizzie, Lizzie,' I said, 'what is it? Don't cry, there's a dear. It will make your eyes red . . . and you wouldn't want people to see.'

'Oh no . . . no . . .' She began to tremble.

I helped her dry her eyes. 'What's wrong, Lizzie?' I asked gently.

'I . . . I want to go home . . . I'm no good at this. I shouldn't have come.'

'You mean meeting all these people?'

356

'I don't know what to say to them. Grace tells me . . . and I say something . . . but I don't know what to do next. I'll never know. I'm just not clever like they are. I know Ben wishes he hadn't married me.'

'Has he said so?' I demanded sharply.

She shook her head. 'But I know.'

'Isn't he . . . kind to you?'

'Oh, he's very kind . . . he's always kind . . . He's patient . . . You see, he has to be patient. He ought to have married Grace.'

I wanted to say: But she could not bring him a gold mine. But what I did say was: 'He married *you*, Lizzie, because he wanted to.'

'I think my father persuaded him.'

Poor Lizzie. I was overcome with pity for her. I felt I hated Ben then. He had found the gold in the creek that day . . . kept it secret, tried to buy the land, and when he couldn't he had married Lizzie and thrust her into a life for which she was most unsuited.

'All this, Lizzie, this entertaining and meeting people . . . It's not important, really.'

'Oh, it is . . . It is to Ben. It's because he's going into Parliament. Then it will be worse. I'll never be able to do that. I try . . .'

'You do very well.'

'I'm not clever . . . I'm not clever enough for Ben.'

'Men don't like clever women, you know.'

She stared at me.

'No,' I elaborated. 'They like to think they are the clever ones. I know some clever women who pretend to be less clever . . . so that the men like them.'

She shook her head. 'You're trying to comfort me,' she said. 'Oh, Angelet, it's so hard. I worry.'

'You mustn't, Lizzie.'

'Grace has been so good. But she is not there all the time. She helps me. She tells me what to wear and what to say . . . but I still don't do it right. I can't sleep at night. I lie awake thinking about it and wishing I was back and Dad was alive and nothing had changed.'

357

'Oh, Lizzie, you mustn't feel that. You are married to Ben and you can see how highly thought of he is.'

'That's what troubles me. I ought not to have married Ben.'

'But, Lizzie, you *are* married to him. Think: without you he would not have all this. You brought him the mine, didn't you? He owes a great deal to you. I am sure he knows that. You see, you are not looking at this clearly. Do you love him?'

She nodded.

'Well then, everything will be all right.'

'I have Grace . . . and now you. I can't sleep, though. I feel better when I do. Grace got something for me to make me sleep.'

'Oh, what was it?'

'I've forgotten the name. It's on the bottle. I'll show you.'

She opened a drawer and took out a bottle.

'Laudanum,' I said, aghast.

'It's good, Angelet. It makes me sleep. You mustn't take more than it says or you would get too sleepy.'

'Perhaps you should see a doctor. Ask his advice about taking this stuff.'

She shrank. 'I couldn't do that. I'm not ill. I just get worried and then I can't sleep. I feel better when I take this. I sleep and sleep. Then I wake up and feel better. Things always seem different in the mornings.'

'I don't know whether you should be taking that, Lizzie. Does Ben know?'

She shook her head. 'You won't tell him, will you? I wouldn't want him to know I was worried.'

'No, I won't tell him. But will you see a doctor? I know you have to be careful with laudanum and things like that . . .'

'Grace says people have it for all sorts of things. It stops toothache. Though I haven't got that . . . but it makes you sleep. It really does.'

'Do see a doctor, Lizzie, and make sure it is all right. He might give you something else to take for sleeplessness.'

'Yes,' she said.

'Look, Lizzie, you and I are going to see each other . . .

358

often. We have so much to talk about, and I shall bring Rebecca to see you. Morwenna will bring Pedrek.'

'Promise,' she said.

'I promise, and you will see a doctor. Now I think we ought to go down.'

When we returned to the drawing-room the men were already there.

We talked for a while in little groups. I saw Justin in earnest conversation with Grace. Ben came over to me. He sat close to me and asked if I had enjoyed the evening.

'Very interesting,' I replied.

'And you approve of my house?'

'I think it is very suitable for your purposes.'

'I take it that means approval. It is wonderful for me to see you here. You won't try to avoid me, will you?'

'I don't know. It depends on what happens.'

'If I can see you sometimes life will be a great deal more tolerable to me.'

'I thought it was highly tolerable. Here you are the epitome of success.'

'It's rather an empty sort of success.'

'Did you think of that when you were weighing up the carats? And now here you are poised to take parliamentary England by storm.'

'How dramatic you are! You always were.' He moved a little nearer to me. He was looking at me quizzically, I thought.

I said: 'Don't be too effusive. People will notice.'

'I don't see how I am going to hide my feelings for you.'

'Then in the circumstances it would be better if we did not meet.'

'Perhaps not in public. But somewhere . . . alone.'

'I have no intention of indulging in a clandestine adventure.'

'We will meet somewhere. Let's go up the river . . . somewhere where we can talk.'

I ignored that. I said: 'I have been talking to Lizzie. She is not very happy,' I added.

He was silent.

359

I said: 'Is it fair to take her gold mine and with the proceeds thrust her into a life she hates?'

'We share the mine,' he said.

'I thought a married woman's property became her husband's. What a pernicious law!'

'I would not dream of taking from Lizzie what is hers,' he said. 'I try very hard to give her what she wants.'

'I think what she wants is a quiet life in the country . . . something like that which she enjoyed before her marriage.'

'She will grow to like this. She was so pleased when she heard you were coming.'

Grace had come over and taken the seat on the other side of Ben.

'It has been a most successful evening,' she said. 'I do congratulate you, Ben.'

'It's not over yet,' he reminded her.

'I thought it went very well indeed. I noticed Lord Lazenby was most amused by the cartoons of HM.'

'He would be. He is very anti-monarchy. I can't think why, with his background, he should be, except that he has always been perverse.'

'It was great fun. Oh, look at poor Lizzie. She's all alone. Do come with me, Angelet. I must look after her.'

'Yes,' I said, and we rose. Ben gave me a regretful look which I ignored; and we went and talked to Lizzie.

She was grateful and we stayed with her for the rest of the evening.

When I returned home I felt elated but melancholy. I was completely fascinated by Ben. I should have so much enjoyed helping him in his political battles. They said Mary Anne Disraeli was a wonderful wife to her husband. She herself had stated that he had married her for her money but if he had to do it again he would marry her for love. Perhaps it would be like that with Lizzie. Mrs Disraeli always waited up for her husband to come home from the House and however late, she would have a cold supper waiting for him. 'My dear,' he was reputed to have said, 'you are more like a mistress than a wife.' Charming in its cynicism. But Lizzie was no Mary Anne Disraeli.

360

I felt very sad about the situation I had witnessed that night; and it was not only because I had had brought home to me all that I had missed.

Poor Lizzie, she would never change. When I looked into her clear blue eyes I could see her struggling with herself. Grace had been good to her but Grace could not be beside her all the time . . . as had been seen tonight.

I wondered what would happen. There was no doubt that Ben would succeed and when he was high up the greasy pole – another Disraeli allusion – how could she help him stay up there? How would an eminent politician feel when his wife would be more at home on the Australian goldfields than in her husband's luxurious home?

Fanny

The children liked to be together, and we arranged that one day Rebecca would go to the Cartwright house and on the next Pedrek should come to mine. This gave Morwenna and me time to shop and do many things which would otherwise have been difficult, for neither of us wished to leave our children entirely to servants.

It was on one of these days when I decided to take up the invitation Frances and Peterkin had given me to visit their Mission.

When I told Helena of this she said I would find it interesting and perhaps a little heart-rending, for people had no idea of the suffering which was endured by others. Matthew was deeply aware of and had talked to her about it. He had discovered a great deal when he was gathering material for his books, and Frances and Peterkin could tell some very sad stories.

She said she would have me driven down there in the morning and send the carriage to pick me up.

There was no need, I told her, I would get a cab.

'You might get one to take you there, but I doubt you would pick up one to bring you back.'

So I set off in the middle of the morning and as I was driven eastwards I was struck by the change. The streets of London had always interested me; they were so full of life; in that area which I knew best the houses were large and elegant; there were many garden squares and the parks added a delightful suggestion of the countryside. The Row, the Serpentine, the Palace where the Queen had spent her childhood – they were all delightful to the eyes. But what a contrast when we came to the mean steets.

The vitality had increased. There was noise everywhere.

People seemed to talk at the top of their voices. We kept to the main road but I glimpsed side streets. I saw grim-looking children, barefooted; I saw stalls on to which seemed to have been crowded every commodity one could think of . . . from chests of drawers to fly-papers. There were women selling pins and needles, and men selling hot pies; there were men sitting on the pavements doing something with counters which I presumed was some sort of game; there were ballad-singers who gave demonstrations of their goods. There was noise and bustle everywhere.

The Mission was a tall square building which had, at one time, been two houses built at a time when there had been a certain affluence in the district.

The door was open and I stepped into a large hall. It was lofty and there was no furniture apart from a table and a chair. On the table there was a bell so I rang this. Almost at once a young woman appeared. She was tall, large-boned, with untidy hair, and wearing a coat-like overall.

I thought she was a servant until she spoke.

She said: 'Oh, hello. You're Mrs Mandeville. Frances said you would be coming. She's in the kitchen. It will be open shortly and we are running a bit late. I'll take you to her. By the way, I'm Jessica Carey. How do you do?'

I said How do you do and thanked her.

She smiled at me and started off, so I followed her.

I could smell something savoury.

We went down a flight of stairs to a large room in which was a big fire. There were several large cauldrons on this and on a table a pile of wooden bowls.

And there was Frances herself in a coat-like overall, rather flushed, giving orders in that precise way which I had come to know. When she saw me she smiled.

'Welcome,' she said. 'We're running late. They'll be here in half an hour. We have to get these bowls up. You could help carry them.'

'Yes. Where?'

Jessica Carey picked up a handful of the bowls and said: 'I'll show you.'

I did the same and followed her.

363

We went up a short staircase. We were in a room with a long wooden table on which were several iron stands. I gathered they put the cauldrons on these. Beside them were laid several large ladles.

'We serve it here,' Jessica told me. 'It's convenient. The door is right on the street . . . and they can just come in. It's a busy time of the morning, this. Feeding time. Frances says it is one of the most important. We have to look after their bodies as well as their souls.' She laughed. 'I'm glad you've come. We need all the help we can get.'

We put the bowls on the table and went down to get more.

'I'll leave you to it,' said Jessica Carey. 'It will be a great help. There are one or two things I have to see to. If you'll get these bowls up and help dish out . . . They'll be here at eleven-thirty. We have to be ready by then or there is chaos. There seem to be more of them every day. And we've had to make extra. Frances gets really upset if we run out and have to send some of them away.'

I thought this was a strange welcome. Frances had been so earnest in her desire that I should come. But I did realize that her work here was most sincere. Amaryllis had always said that she and Peterkin worked as hard as anyone she knew.

I toiled up and down with the wooden bowls and had set up quite a pile of them on the table when the door opened and a man came in from the street.

I was about to say that we were not quite ready yet when I realized he could not possibly have come for soup.

He was neatly dressed and there was an air of distinction about him. I noticed that he had a rather sad face which changed when he smiled.

'Good morning,' he said.

'Good morning,' I replied.

'We haven't met before.'

I wondered why he should think we had. Then it occurred to me that he must be a frequent visitor to the Mission and there would be quite a number of helpers doing brief spells of duty.

'I'm Timothy Ransome,' he said.

'How do you do? I'm Angelet Mandeville.'

364

'Oh,' he said, 'Frances mentioned you. You're related to Peterkin, I believe.'

'Yes, that's right. It's rather a complicated relationship but it exists.'

'Have you been here before?'

'This is the first time.'

'And they've put you on to the bowls, have they?'

'They all seemed so busy, and these things had to be brought up here.'

'Oh yes, for the morning soup. I'll give you a hand.'

He took off his coat and set to work.

When we went into the kitchen several of them called; 'Hello, Tim. Running late.'

'I'm helping with the bowls,' he said.

'Good.'

Soon we had brought up all the bowls. He said: 'Many hands make light work.'

'It seems so. Are you a frequent helper?'

'I come quite often. I think Frances and Peterkin are doing a wonderful job here.'

'Yes, I have always heard so.'

'And now you have come to see for yourself.'

Someone was calling. 'Tim! Tim! Strong man wanted for the cauldrons.'

'Right,' he answered. 'Coming.' And to me: 'Excuse me.'

That was a strange morning. I stood behind the table with several others, Timothy Ransome among them – ladling out soup. It was a sobering exercise . . . to see those eager hands stretched out for the bowl, to watch the ravenous manner in which they devoured the soup. They were ragged, unkempt and hungry. It made me both sad and angry. It was the children who touched me most. I thought of our own children . . . of Pedrek who sometimes had to be coaxed to eat with stories like 'And the fisherman caught another little fish to feed his family and he popped it into the mouth of the youngest, and then the second youngest . . .' and so on until he had eaten it all.

At last it was over. The morning's supplies were diminished and everyone had had their share.

365

Timothy Ransome said to me: 'You mustn't get too upset. At least we are trying to do something about it here. It's a gruelling experience at first.'

'I suppose you have done it many times.'

'Oh yes . . . There are many things that you will find upsetting here . . . things you didn't dream of.'

'I know I have to be prepared.'

'After this, there is a little refreshment for us. Humble fare. Bread and cheese and a glass of cider.'

'It sounds good to me.'

'I'll show you. If we are lucky we can help ourselves and have half an hour's respite.'

I saw Frances then. She came hurrying towards us. 'Hello, Angelet, lovely to see you. Sorry I was so busy when you came. What a morning! I thought we shouldn't be ready in time for the hungry hordes. Tim . . . you're looking after Angelet. Showing her the ropes. Good.' She grinned at me. 'You soon get used to it. In the evenings we have a supper when we all get together and talk about the day. That is when you ought to be here. I'll see you later. I'm having a little trouble with Fanny . . .'

'Can I do something?' asked Timothy.

'No. I've got someone on it. I don't know what we going to do about that child. We'll see. I'll be with you later, Angelet . . . if I can.'

Then she was off again.

Timothy Ransome said: 'Let's see about that food.'

It was a strange experience sitting in a small room with a man whom I had never met before, eating hot crusty bread and cheese with a tankard of cider beside me.

'I have to admit I know something about you,' he told me. 'I heard about your husband. It was in the papers at the time. That's when I learned you were related to Peterkin. I am so sorry. It was a terrible tragedy.'

'It is over now,' I said.

'Your husband was a hero.'

'Yes,' I said. 'He died saving another man's life.'

'You must be very proud.'

366

I nodded.

'Forgive me,' he went on. 'I'm sorry. I shouldn't have spoken of it. Do you intend to work here?'

'Oh no. I couldn't. I have a daughter. She is four years old. I am here today because she is with friends.'

He looked disappointed.

'But I shall come again,' I said, 'when I have the opportunity.'

'It can be very distressing,' he said. 'It's so strange and upsetting at first. One gets over that. One realizes that there is no virtue in being upset and shaking one's head in pity and doing nothing about it. The place grows on you. Frances is one of the most wonderful women I have ever met. She never sits down and groans about inequality . . . she does something practical. Of course, everyone could not do it, I know. Frances has her private income . . . so has Peterkin. They are a good team. Theirs is a good marriage – perfect, I should say – except that they have no children. Yet if they had I suppose this work would suffer. On the whole I would say theirs is one of the few perfect unions.'

'You admire them very much, don't you?'

'I do. Everyone must . . . Once they get used to Frances's rather stringent manner they must know that beneath it lies the proverbial heart of gold.'

The very mention of the word gold always took me back to Golden Creek . . . Ben washing his hands in the stream and discovering the presence of the precious metal. But for that he might be free now.

I said: 'I think she is wonderful, too.'

'You'll come again. You'll get caught up in it. I come two or three days during the week. I'm what Frances calls one of her casual labourers. What she likes is full-timers like the Honourable Jessica. You know her?'

'I met her when I arrived.'

'Oh yes, Jessica is the right-hand woman. She's dedicated, and we should all like to be but for commitments.'

'Have you many commitments?'

'An estate to run. Fortunately close to London . . . which makes it easy for me. It is just outside Hampton. I have a son

367

and daughter. So you see I cannot give myself entirely to the cause.'

'I understand.'

'Your daughter must be a great compensation.'

'Oh yes.'

'I find that with Alec and Fiona. I lost my wife, you see.'

'Oh, I am sorry.'

'It was some four years ago. A riding accident. It was so sudden. She was there in the morning . . . and by night-time she was gone.'

'What a terrible tragedy!'

'Well, these things happen all the time. It is just that one doesn't expect them to happen to oneself!'

'How old are the children?'

'Alec is ten, Fiona is eight.'

'So they remember.'

He nodded sadly. Then he smiled. 'Well, this is gloomy talk. Would you like some more cider? I am sure I could find some.'

'No, thanks,' I said.

When we took back our plates and tankards and washed them in the kitchen we saw Frances.

'There's trouble,' she said. 'Billings is up to his tricks again.' She turned to me. 'We get cases like this all the time. But this kind makes me mad. It's where young people are concerned.'

'Fanny again?' asked Timothy Ransome.

'Yes. I don't know what we can do. I'd like to get Fanny away . . . but there's the mother. She doesn't want to leave him.' She wrinkled her brows. 'Billings drinks. He's not so bad when he's not drinking, but he can't resist the gin palaces. You know what they say: "Drunk for a penny and dead drunk for tuppence." Well, he's dead drunk most of the time. Emily Billings is a silly woman. She should leave him. But she won't. He's the second husband and seems to have her completely under his spell. Fanny was the daughter of the first marriage,' she explained to me. 'He was a builder and fell from the scaffolding. There was no compensation. That's one of the things we're working on. In the meantime Emily married Billings and her troubles really started.'

368

'There are so many similar cases,' said Timothy Ransome.

'True. As far as Emily's concerned, I'd say all right, if you won't leave him take the consequences. It's the child . . . Fanny. She's a bright little thing. I could do something for her. But I can't take a girl of fifteen away from her home. Emily would stand by him in a court of law. She'd deny anything. He could almost kill her and she'd say she had fallen down the stairs. But it is Fanny. From what I hear there is danger of sexual abuse. Emily knows it and tries to hide it. It was something Fanny said that gave me the clue. I just can't put it on one side. I have to do something because of Fanny.'

'It's a problem,' agreed Timothy Ransome. 'If there is anything I can do . . .'

'I'll call on you, never fear. Angelet, you have been thrown in at the deep end, as they say. If it hadn't been for all this blowing up this morning, I could have shown you round properly.'

'Don't worry about that. I want to see how everything works. I'm getting a real insight.'

'The carriage is coming for you at four, I believe.'

'Yes, they insisted.'

'Quite right, too. You'd never get a cab here.'

'Had I known I would have taken you home,' said Timothy Ransome.

Frances answered for me. 'Another time, Tim. I feel sure Angelet will come again.'

'I shall,' I said. 'Perhaps on Friday if Rebecca goes to Morwenna.'

Timothy Ransome said: 'And on Friday I shall be here. I'll see that you are returned safely to your home.'

Frances beamed on us both.

'Very well. I shall see you on Friday. I promise I shall find plenty for you to do.'

I had been going to Frances's Mission twice a week – on Wednesdays and Fridays. Frances was delighted and I always found plenty to do. I learned things about other people's lives which were so different from my own; I was appalled, shocked, and at the same time exhilarated because I felt I was doing something worthwhile.

I was becoming very friendly with Tim Ransome, who also appeared on Wednesdays and Fridays. The carriage would take me there and he would bring me home.

Aunt Amaryllis said how delighted she was that I was helping Frances and Peterkin. Frances had told her all about it and how useful I was making myself.

'It's such good work,' said Aunt Amaryllis. 'Uncle Peter says it is just what you are needing. He gives a lot of money to the Mission.'

I nodded, remembering Frances's comments that he made sure that his gifts were noted, but that she was grateful for them all the same.

I heard from the servants that Ben had called on one or two occasions. 'He seemed most put out, Madam, that you were not at home.'

Frances made a point of sending Timothy and me on errands of mercy. She would not let me go out alone and he was always my escort. We took clothes and food to the sick and needy, and I became fairly familiar with the neighbourhood. We would be sent to shop in the markets for the stores needed in the Mission and this I greatly enjoyed. The stalls would be piled up with merchandise of all descriptions and the noisy costermongers would shout their wares in audacious cockney . . . often using the rhyming slang which was quite unintelligible to me without Timothy's translation.

It was natural that our friendship grew quickly in such circumstances.

I knew him for a man who had never really recovered from the loss of his wife; he was fond of his children but they could not compensate him completely. He was fortunate, he told me: his elder sister was unmarried and devoted to him and the children; she lived in his country house and looked after his home.

'I should be lost without her,' he said. 'And the children are very fond of her.'

Frances must have told Amaryllis of my friendship with Timothy and as a result he was asked to dine at the house in the square.

This he did on one or two occasions and it was clear that they liked him.

Grace was a guest on one occasion. She said what a charming man he was, and smiled significantly. It was the first indication that it might seem there was something serious and special about our relationship.

I had seen Ben once or twice – usually when others were present. There had been few opportunities of speaking together alone. I did not seek them, but I believe he did.

He said to me once: 'I hear that you are devoting yourself to good works.'

'You mean the Mission.'

'Yes. They tell me you attend regularly.'

'I like to feel I am doing something.'

'I wish I could see you sometime.'

We were at a dinner party at Matthew's and Helena's and the men had just rejoined us after dinner. It was only a snatched conversation.

I did not answer. I looked across the room to where Lizzie was sitting trying to make conversation with the middle-aged gentleman seated beside her; and the effort was making her miserable. Grace was there, talking brightly to a young man. She looked over and saw us, and in a few moments she was making her way towards us.

She talked brightly to Ben of the constituency to which he had been elected as candidate. I was surprised how well informed she was.

I took the opportunity of slipping away.

There were a great many dinner parties – either at the house in the square or Matthew's and Helena's house.

Helena said: 'There is a feverish expectancy in the air. I call it the electoral disease.'

'Do you really think there is going to be an election soon?'

She nodded vigorously. 'I can see the signs. Disraeli can't hold out. He'll have to go to the country.'

371

'And then?'

'Who can say? We're hoping he'll get back. But, of course, Ben has other views.'

'It is strange to have such divergence in a family.'

'Oh, it is all very friendly. It is, you know, in the House. It has often struck me that members of the same party are more venomous towards each other than to those of the Opposition.'

'I suppose that is because they are reaching for the same prize. With the other side . . . well, they are not rivals in the same way.'

'Exactly.'

'Well, it is rather exciting.'

'Yes, if it doesn't get too serious.'

She was right about the electoral fever.

It was October. Cool winds were blowing across the parks and the ground was carpeted with red and bronze leaves. Excitement was in the air and people were saying that Disraeli's ministry could not carry on as they were. They must go to the country.

I was often at the house in the square. Ben was there, too, so we saw each other frequently . . . but never alone. Timothy was often asked. Frances and Peterkin came rarely. They pleaded too much work.

I found the conversation stimulating.

There were discussions between Uncle Peter and Ben which I thought must be worthy of the House itself – Uncle Peter supporting Disraeli and Ben Gladstone. The rest of us joined in but those two were the main speakers.

'You'll have to get busy down at Manorleigh, Ben,' said Uncle Peter. 'How is it going?'

'Very well indeed.'

'You think you're going to manage it?'

'I know I'm going to manage it.'

'Voters are unpredictable creatures, Ben. You're going to find it hard to convince them that Gladstone's a better bet than Disraeli.'

'I happen to think otherwise and I shall persuade my constituents to do the same.'

Grace addressed Uncle Peter. 'I think, Mr Lansdon, that the

372

voters of Manorleigh are beginning to like their new candidate.'

She looked at Ben with an almost proprietorial air.

'So you have inspected the territory, have you, Grace?' said Aunt Amaryllis.

'Oh yes. I went down with Ben and Lizzie last weekend. Lizzie and I went to some shops and talked to them, didn't we, Lizzie?'

Lizzie mumbled that they had.

'It was so exciting. I think we made some impression.'

'That's what gets the voters,' commented Uncle Peter. 'Never mind the policies. Just show them that you are a good family man, your wife beside you, and they'll put their crosses by your name.'

'That's exactly what I thought,' said Grace. 'Lizzie is going to be a great help.'

'I . . . I . . . Grace helped me,' said Lizzie.

'Oh come, Lizzie, you did your part.'

They talked about the chances of both sides but I rather thought Uncle Peter was of the opinion that it would be a victory for the Liberals – which he was certainly not hoping for. But I saw him glance often at Ben with something like pride and amusement.

After dinner I had a word with Uncle Peter.

'I find all this parliamentary talk very interesting,' I told him.

'Fascinating, isn't it?'

'Do you really want the Conservatives to win?'

'My dear Angelet, I'm a staunch supporter of the Party.'

'But there is Ben.'

He sighed. 'Oh, he's set himself on the other side of the fence.'

'Do you think he'll get in?'

'Of course he'll get in. They won't be able to resist him. I wish . . .'

I wanted to hear what he wished. But he said: 'She's right, you know . . . Grace. It's the happily married man they like. Helena's always been an asset to Matthew . . . and then of course her brother marrying Frances and that Mission. Good stuff.'

'It's good for a lot of people as well as Matthew, Uncle Peter.'

'Oh yes. You're one of them now, aren't you? Nice fellow . . . that Timothy Ransome. Seems steady : . . and comfortably off.'

'Have you been investigating?'

'Naturally I investigate all friends of my family.'

'Uncle Peter, you are incorrigible.'

'Yes, I am. Always was and always will be. Never mind. Put up with me, will you, my dear?'

I smiled at him. 'Willingly,' I said.

It was about a week later when Fanny came into our lives.

Timothy and I had done our usual stint at the soup counter; the empty bowls and cauldrons had been taken back to the kitchen; everyone seemed to be intent on something or other. We were in the little room next to that where the soup was dispensed, and we were talking, as we usually did, about certain cases which had struck us as particularly sad or interesting, and a little about ourselves, when we heard the door being opened. We paused to listen. Then we heard stealthy footsteps.

We rose and hurried to the room from which they came and there she stood.

She was half poised for flight.

I said: 'Can we help you?'

'Where's Mrs Frances?' she asked.

'She's not here at the moment. What can we do?'

She hesitated. I saw how thin she was; she looked cold, too; the threadbare dress she was wearing was not adequate protection against the autumn dampness.

'I . . . I've run away,' she said.

'Come and tell us all about it,' answered Timothy. 'Would you like something to eat?'

She licked her lips.

'Come along,' said Timothy.

There was no soup left but we found some bread and cheese which she devoured ravenously; we found some milk for her, too.

She said defensively: 'I know Mrs Frances.'

'What's your name?' I asked.

'Fanny,' she told me.

I felt excited. This was the Fanny who had caused Frances so much concern, and here she was with us!

'She will be in soon,' I said. 'You must wait and see her. Tell us what it is that is bothering you. Perhaps we can help till she comes. We work here with Mrs Frances. She tells us what to do and we do it. I know she wants to help you.'

The child, for she was little more, said: 'I couldn't 'ave stood it no more. Last night he nearly killed me Mum. And when I tried to stop him he turned on me. There won't half be a carry-on when he knows I've gone.' She looked frightened. 'He'll blame me Mum. I've got to go back.'

'Don't go yet,' I begged. 'Wait till you have seen Mrs Frances.'

'We know she wouldn't want you to go back . . . yet,' added Timothy.

She nodded. 'Mrs Frances . . . she's a good lady . . .'

'That's why you should listen to her,' I said.

'It's me Mum. It's what he'd do to her.'

'We'll find some way of stopping him,' promised Timothy.

She looked at him scornfully. 'What, you? How? No one can't. I'm frightened of him. See, he wants my money . . . Every day he takes it off of me . . . all I've got, every penny. Then he's off. It's good when he goes. He's in the gin shop . . . and he stays there. I wish he'd stay all night. I wish he'd never come back.'

'Where do you get your money?' I asked.

'I works, I does. I goes to old Felberg and he gives me a tray . . . sometimes it's flowers . . . sometimes it's pins and needles . . . sometimes it's apples. You never know with old Felberg. Then I brings back what I've took and he takes it and gives me tuppence back . . . and that's my money, I reckon. But *he* don't. He takes it off of me and he's off round the gin shop. I'm frightened of him when he hits me, but more when . . .'

She faltered and I put my hand on her shoulder. I said: 'We can stop this, you know. Mrs Frances wants you to stay here. She can do something . . .'

375

'It's me Mum,' she said piteously.

When Frances came in her face lighted up with joy.

'Fanny!' she cried. 'So you've come. Good girl.'

'Oh, Mrs Frances, I was so frightened of him last night. You said come.'

'Of course I did and at last you are a wise girl. Now then. This is your home for a while. We're going to look after you. No harm can come to you here.'

'I could bring me money back from Mr Felberg.'

'You can forget Mr Felberg. You're going to be here while we put our heads together and come up with something. You're not going back, Fanny, not again.'

Frances was a wonderful woman. I have said that many times, I suppose, and will continue to say it. I imagine that Timothy and I were rather sentimental in our approach; we wanted to fuss over Fanny, to make much of her, to compensate for the terrible life she had; but Frances was different – brisk and businesslike. I could see that was what Fanny needed. She would despise our attitude. To her it would seem 'soft'.

Frances said: 'We'll get you out of those clothes . . . fast. We'll get Mrs Hope to put them on the fire. We'll find something for you. And a good bath is what you need and your hair thoroughly washed. Then we'll give you something to do, eh? What are you good at, Fanny? You'd like to help in the kitchen. There are lots of things to be done there.'

I could see that that was the way to treat her.

Timothy and I were amazed. We saw Fanny change overnight. The frightened waif became a self-important person. Fanny belonged to the streets. There was nothing soft about Fanny. Her stepfather must have been an ogre to have frightened one of her spirit. She was a cockney – shrewd, quick-witted, full of what Mrs Penlock would have called 'sauce' or 'lip'.

She adored Frances, looking upon her as some superior being. For Timothy and me she had a certain affectionate contempt, but she thought we were 'soft'. 'Nobs', she called us, which meant that we spoke differently and acted in a manner unlike that of the people she had known before she came to the Mission. For some reason we had been born into soft living and

376

we lacked the knowledge of how to protect ourselves. We had got by because we had never had to face up to what to her was real life. I am sure she felt we were more in need of her protection than she was of ours.

But our special place in her affections was due to the fact that when she had decided to come to the Mission we were the first ones she had seen, and I do believe that we had somehow persuaded her to wait for Frances and that was at the root of her affection.

Frances was a special person. Born a 'nob', she was for all her fancy voice and high class ways one of them.

Fanny changed the Mission for us. She was the first one we looked for when we arrived. She would give us that rather casual greeting and smile secretly as though we amused her.

Timothy and I talked of her a great deal when we were alone and wondered what Frances would decide about her future. Frances had said that, so far, she was unprepared to make a decision.

'The girl's still frightened of that terrible man,' she said. 'She's aggressive, isn't she? I know what that means. She's telling herself she's strong. She's got to be because somewhere in her mind she is afraid she is not finished with him yet. She is trying to tell herself she can stand up to him. She must never go back.'

'Good heavens no!' said Timothy.

'It's risky. I suppose he's legally in the place of father. He will know where she is. He'd guess. I've tried to get her away from them before . . . We'll have to watch for him. I expected to hear from the mother. Strange I haven't.'

'Do you mean she will try to get her back?' I asked.

'She wouldn't want to. She knows it's best for the girl to get away. But he wants the pennies she earns. He can get drunk at the gin shop on Fanny's few pennies. There is something else. The mother hinted . . . You know what I mean.'

'You did mention it,' said Timothy quietly.

'I've got to stop that. These people are capable of descending to the very depths of depravity. Their lives are so empty. They go to the bottle and then they lose all sense of decency. You get someone like Billings . . . no sense . . . no morals . . .

377

nothing. I'm sorry for him in a way. I don't know what his life
has been. How can one judge? But I know I've got to keep
Fanny here. I'll find something for her soon. I'd like to get her
into a nice home. She'd make a good parlourmaid . . . with
training. But just now she isn't ready. I want her to stay here
for a while.'

'She'll stay. She adores you,' I said.

'I hope she will. I can't hold her against her will . . . yet I
want to fight for her.'

'Why should she want to go?'

'Who knows what Fanny thinks? She has this feeling that she
has to protect her mother. That's what has kept her in this
wretched hovel so long. I should have had her here weeks ago.
Well, at the moment I'm holding everything as it is . . . It all
depends on what happens. You two have done a good job with
her. She's quite fond of you.'

'I think she despises us sometimes. She thinks we're soft.'

'That's her way. She's fond of you all right. And she trusts
you. That means a lot with Fanny.'

As the weeks passed the change in Fanny was miraculous. She
did odd jobs about the Mission. Frances gave her a small wage
which she hoarded with delight. I believe she felt she was rich.
Her hair, now that it was washed, was glossy and fell in soft
curls about her face; her small dark eyes were clear and alert;
they darted everywhere as though she were afraid she was
going to miss something; her skin had lost that pasty look, and
although she was still pale she looked far from unhealthy. I gave
her a ribbon for her hair. She treasured it and said she would
save it for Sundays.

Timothy and I looked upon her as our protégée. We talked
of her constantly; we watched her progress, marvelling. One
day we went out and bought a dress for her. When we brought
it back to the Mission she stared at us in amazement.

'It's not for me,' she said. 'It can't be.'

We assured her it was.

'I ain't never had nothing like that in my life before,' she said.

378

'Well, it's time you did,' Timothy told her.

She looked at us and said; 'Well, I dunno . . . You two . . . I reckon you are a pair of old softies.'

That was thanks enough.

One of the jobs which gave her most pleasure was to go to the market and buy provisions for the Mission. This had been one of the tasks allotted to Timothy and me and we had always enjoyed it. She accompanied us once or twice and was scornful of our achievement.

'Tell you what,' she said when we returned to the Mission. 'They see you two coming and up goes the price.'

'Surely not,' I said.

She looked at me derisively. 'You don't know nothing,' she said.

She told Frances that she could shop cheaper than we could and Frances, who was always eager to help Fanny prove herself, immediately complied with her request that she should do the shopping herself; and from that moment Fanny brought in the bargains. It was a great game to her.

'I got him to knock three-farthings off that for you,' she would announce proudly. We always marvelled at her bargaining skills.

'You're saving us pounds, Fanny,' Frances told her.

This state of affairs went on for three weeks and during that time Fanny emerged as herself.

Then, one day, she disappeared.

She had dressed herself in her blue merino and tied the red ribbon in her hair, and gone off to the market as she did every morning.

At first we thought the shopping had taken her a little longer than usual and we were not unduly concerned; but as the time began to pass we grew anxious. Then we found the shopping-bag which she usually took with her and with it the money she had been given to shop with; so we knew her departure was intentional.

Frances was bitterly disappointed.

'What did we *do*?' I cried.

'I think it must be her mother,' said Frances. 'She's gone back to her.'

379

'But the stepfather . . .'

'Fanny is a girl who has a strong sense of right and wrong. She may have got that from her own father. You see, she takes the dress and the ribbon – they are hers. She has taken the wages she has earned; but she leaves the shopping money. How many girls in her postion would have done that?'

'But what are we going to do?' asked Timothy.

'There is nothing we can do. I can't storm her home and take her away. She's gone back to them of her own accord. I'm sorry. It's disheartening, but there is nothing we can do. It is just another of those cases which didn't work out the way we wanted it to. There are many of them.'

I realized how much our concern for Fanny had drawn Timothy and me together. We had shared our delight in her progress and now our sorrow and disappointment at her departure.

I was trying not to think of Ben, working hard in Manorleigh for the coming election.

Timothy came again to dine at the house in the square. He was about as different from Uncle Peter as a man could be, but they liked each other. I knew what Uncle Peter and Aunt Amaryllis were thinking. They were fond of me, concerned for me, and they were weighing up Timothy as a possible husband for me. Aunt Amaryllis in particular believed that the married state was ideal for every woman. Uncle Peter took a more practical view. He would like to see me settled and he had obviously decided that Timothy's background, financial standing and character fitted him for the role of husband.

I saw through them, of course. But I did not want to think beyond the present which Timothy was making tolerable for me. Yet again and again my thoughts went back to Ben.

I heard from the family that his campaign was being successful and he was making a very good impression on the voters.

One evening when I was having a talk with Uncle Peter, Ben was mentioned.

'I feel sure he is going to win,' he said. 'It'll be an achievement. It's been a Tory stronghold for a hundred years. I don't think it will be a big majority . . . but comfortable enough. It will be a feather in his cap.'

'Do you really think he'll win?'

Uncle Peter looked at me and smiled. 'I have reason to say that I think his opponent is getting rather rattled.'

'How is he doing it?'

'Oh, you know Ben. It's that vitality. A certain power. A determination. He believes he's going to win and he gets everyone else believing it too. I flatter myself that he gets that from me. His grandmother was a fighter too. She was a milliner.' He smiled, looking back. 'I came near to marrying her. I couldn't, though. It wouldn't have done.'

'You mean . . .'

'Just not quite right.'

'Yet you were in love with her.'

'I have always been able to regulate my emotions.'

'They didn't stop your having an illegitimate son.'

'That's not what I mean. I set her up in her own shop in Sydney. I sent her money. She got on very well. We were in a way two of a kind. She understood how it was. What I am telling you is that Ben gets his fighting spirit from both sides.'

'You must have had a very eventful life, Uncle Peter.'

'I think life should be eventful. Ben will make his so and I am pretty certain that before long he'll have a place in the House.' He was thoughtful for a moment. Then he said: 'It's a pity he married Lizzie. She's not the wife a politician needs.'

'I think she appears with him, doesn't she?'

'Yes, but there is more to it than that. Grace is with them. Now she knows it all. I believe she is quite an asset. But it is not the same. It should be the wife who is there.'

'I know Grace helps Lizzie quite a lot. Lizzie herself said so.'

'That's what I'm saying. Lizzie should be doing all this. She shouldn't need prompting. It doesn't go down so well. No, I'm afraid Lizzie is a bit of a handicap for a man like Ben.'

'A handicap!' I cried. 'Where would he be without her? She brought him the gold mine, didn't she? Without her help he would still be scrabbling for gold in Golden Creek.'

'You are very vehement, my dear.'

'Well, it is true. I hate all this talk about Lizzie's being a handicap when it is only because of her that he has become in a position to do all he is doing.'

Then he said a strange thing. He put his arm about me. 'I, too, wish it had been otherwise.'

'What do you mean?' I stammered.

But he just smiled rather sadly at me and I knew that Uncle Peter was aware of my feelings for Ben . . . and his for me.

We had betrayed ourselves in some way.

There was a letter from my mother.

My darling Angelet,

Amaryllis tells me how hard you are working at Frances's Mission and finding it so rewarding. I am glad. I told your father that you needed something like that. It must be interesting and harrowing too, but Amaryllis tells me that Frances is delighted to have you there and what a great help you are to her.

We miss you very much and I have written to Amaryllis telling her that I should love to come up . . . just for a few weeks. Your father can't leave the place at this time, nor can Jack. But I feel I want to see you. I want to hear all about the work you are doing and see for myself that you are well and getting happier.

Everything here goes on much as usual. And how is darling Rebecca? It is wonderful for her to have Pedrek to play with. And Morwenna is so close and you help each other with the children, so giving you those opportunities to go to the Mission.

Josiah Pencarron tells me that Justin is doing a fine job in London and he wonders why he did not think of opening the office up there years ago.

So everything seems to be going well.

I shall see you soon.

Much love,
Mother

I knew what this meant. Aunt Amaryllis had reported my growing friendship with Timothy Ransome, and my mother wanted to know how far it had progressed.

I wished that they were not so interested in my affairs. Of course, it was all for my benefit. There *was* a hint of seriousness in my friendship with Timothy. I was aware of that in Timothy's manner.

But I did not want to think of it. I liked him. I enjoyed his company; but I did not want to go farther than that. My heart was in Manorleigh. There was nothing I should have liked better than to take part in that campaign and everything else seemed only a makeshift and a poor consolation.

Now that Fanny had gone, Timothy and I returned to our old task of shopping in the markets for the provisions. We did so in a somewhat disenchanted mood having been told by Fanny that we were not much good at it.

We had lost the excitement we used to have in the project, perhaps because it reminded us of Fanny.

One day we set out. I was telling him that my mother was coming to London for a short stay and he was saying how pleased he would be to meet her.

'I am sure you will be invited to,' I told him.

He pressed my arm and said: 'I'm glad of that.'

We stopped at one of the stalls to buy fruit. I chose it and while Timothy was paying for it, I turned suddenly and stared. There among the crowd was Fanny.

'Fanny!' I called and started after her.

She must have heard me but she began to run.

'Fanny! Fanny!' I called.

But she ran on, pushing her way through the crowds.

Perhaps I should have let her go, but some impulse would not allow me to. I had to talk to her. I had to ask her why she had run away.

We had left the market behind. But she was still ahead of me.

'Fanny!' I shouted. 'Come back. I want to talk to you.'

She did not glance back but sped on. I followed without

thinking where I was. On she went. We were in a maze of little streets where I had never been before and still Fanny was running. She darted round a corner and I nearly lost sight of her. I rushed on.

I was only vaguely aware of my surroundings. The houses were nothing more than hovels and I noticed an unpleasant odour of old clothes and unwashed bodies. There was a gin shop on the corner of the street into which Fanny had turned; and as I dashed past, I caught a glimpse of people in there. Outside one man sprawled on the pavement.

Someone called out: ''Ello, Missus,' as I passed. I went on blindly. I saw Fanny turn into one of the hovels and disappear from sight.

Suddenly the folly of what I had done dawned on me. I was lost. Timothy would wonder what had happened. He had been paying for the goods we had bought and suddenly I had darted away. And here I was . . . in this place alone . . .

Children were squatting on the pavement playing some game; they stopped to stare at me. There was a woman on a doorstep. She pushed the greasy hair back from her face and laughed at me.

Two men . . . little more than boys . . . were coming towards me.

'Can we 'elp yer, Miss?'

As I stepped back and they came forward, one slipped behind me, the other faced me.

I was filled with terror.

'Fanny!' I called.

But what was the use? She had disappeared. She could not hear me and she had taken no heed of me when she had.

One of the men seized my arm. He was leering at me.

'Good-looking gal,' he said meaningfully.

I shouted: 'Go away. How dare you!'

And then I heard a voice.

'Angelet!'

It was Timothy. He took hold of the young man who was touching me and threw him to the ground. The other came at him but Timothy was too quick for him. They were spindly youths, ill-nourished, I could see. They were no match for Timothy.

'Angelet . . . what on earth . . .' he began.

I pointed to the house. 'Fanny,' I said. 'She has gone in there.'

Timothy hesitated for only a second. Then he said: 'Come on. We'll go in.'

His face was grim. He took a firm hold of my arm and we went towards the hovel which I presumed was Fanny's home.

We were in a dark passage which smelt of damp and decay. A door opened and a woman with a baby in her arms came out and said: 'What do you want?'

'Fanny . . .'

She jerked her head. 'Upstairs.'

We mounted the rickety staircase. The banister was broken and water was dripping through the ceiling.

There was a door at the top of the stairs. We opened it and were in a room. A piece of torn cloth had been put up across the window to serve as a curtain. There was a couch from which the springs protruded and which I presumed was used as a bed. But I hardly noticed the room because there was Fanny and with her the woman I judged to be her mother.

Fanny was wearing the blue merino which had lost its pristine freshness. She wore the ribbon in her hair. She looked ashamed and very unhappy.

'Fanny,' I said, 'why didn't you speak to me?'

'You didn't ought to have come,' she snapped.

'Of course I had to come.'

'Likes of you shouldn't be here.' It was the old aggression.

'We had to come,' said Timothy gently.

'Fan,' said her mother, 'you ought to go with 'em. You oughtn't to of run away. I told yer.'

'I had to, didn't I? 'Cause of 'im.'

Poor Mrs Billings. I could see the wretchedness in her face.

I realized with a rush of gratitude to fate that he was not here and that raised my hopes.

Timothy said: 'We want to take you back, Fanny. You were getting on so well.'

'That's what I tole her,' said her mother.

385

But Fanny looked at us and scowled. I knew instinctively that it was because she was afraid she would cry and that would be the ultimate weakness.

'I tole her,' said Mrs Billings. 'Time after time I tole her. I said, "You go back to that Mrs Frances, Fan. It's best for you. You gotter get away." But she won't. She's always hoping he'll kill hisself . . . fall down stairs or something. He did once.'

'Mrs Billings,' said Timothy, 'we want to take Fanny back. We were getting on so well. You can always come and see her at the Mission . . . or wherever she is. Mrs Frances would like you to come with her, too.'

She shook her head. 'I couldn't leave 'im,' she said. 'Not that.'

'And what of Fanny?'

'Fanny should go. I tole her . . . time after time . . .'

'There you are, Fanny,' I said. 'Your mother wants you to come with us.'

'What about him?' said Fanny.

'Leave him to me,' said her mother.

'Mum, you come too. It's ever so nice. They're kind. Mrs Frances and these two . . .'

'I can't leave 'im, Fan, you know that.'

'But what he does! He's a beast.'

'I know . . . but I can't leave him.'

'But Fanny is coming with us,' said Timothy. 'We won't go without Fanny.'

'He mustn't come back and find you two here,' said Fanny, aghast.

'So, let's go now,' I said. 'Come on. Mrs Billings, you understand. We want to help. Fanny was so happy with us. Please . . . it is important for her. Come and see for yourself. Mrs Frances would find work for you. Come with us . . . both of you.'

Fanny was looking pleadingly at her mother.

There were tears in the woman's eyes. She shook her head. 'I'd never leave him. He's me 'usband when all's said and done.'

'Then we will take Fanny,' said Timothy firmly.

386

'Yes, Fan, you go,' begged her mother. 'Go, girl. It's what I want. It's better you're not 'ere. It's better then. Strike me pink if it ain't. I fret over you, I do. I'm all right on me own. Go, Fan. It's what I want. It's best for you.'

'Oh Mum . . .'

'Come on,' said Timothy. 'Mrs Billings, thank you. Do remember, there will always be a welcome for you at the Mission.'

She nodded. 'Take Fanny. It's what I want for her. It's a blessed relief to me . . . if she goes.'

'He'll knock you about, Mum,' said Fanny hesitantly.

'You go. It's what I want. It's best for you . . . best for us all.'

Fanny was still wavering.

'It's all right, Fanny,' I said. 'You can do no good here. Your mother will come and see you and perhaps one day you can be together.'

I held her hand firmly and drew her to the door.

'I dunno . . .' she began.

'Oh yes, your mother is right. Mrs Frances is right. She is always right, isn't she? Come on.'

At last we took her away.

The journey back was horrifying. I had not realized how far I had come. I saw the old clothes shop with the second-hand clothes hanging outside the door, the undernourished children, the cursed gin shops. People called after us. At one stage Fanny turned and stuck her tongue out at them. They laughed at us jeeringly. I think it might have been difficult if they had not known that we came from the Mission; and they had a certain respect for that place.

I wondered where the beast was drinking . . . In the gin shop on the corner? What if we came across him? But we were safely past the shop now.

After a long walk we came to the Mission.

Frances's joy at seeing us was great. But at first she gave her attention to Fanny, who went through the same washing process as before. The merino dress and ribbon were sacrificed to the flames and I promised that I would find another exactly like it. The red ribbon could be easily replaced.

387

While this was in progress we told Frances what had happened.

Timothy said: 'I was paying the woman at the stall when I realized that Angelet had gone. I saw her running off. I left everything and hurried after her. I was just in time to see where she was going. I had no idea what it was all about at first because I didn't see Fanny. Unfortunately Angelet had a fair start of me.'

'You should never have gone into those streets alone,' said Frances, 'but I'm glad you did. God knows what might have happened to you.'

'Something might if Timothy hadn't come up in time.'

'I arrived panting, to see her being accosted by two very unsavoury-looking youths.'

'Just in time,' I said, smiling at him. 'He played the gallant knight and saved me. Then together we went into the house . . . if you can call it a house.'

'The living conditions are appalling. I hope we shall be able to do something about that in time. And you saw Mrs Billings?'

'Poor woman. How can she? She should have come with Fanny. Why does she stay with the brute?' said Timothy.

'The answer to that,' replied Frances, 'is involved with the complexity of human nature. Some people call it love. I've seen it happen again and again. They come to us almost battered to death. They ask for refuge. We give it to them. We nurse them back to health. We set them on the road to a decent life . . . and then . . . they go back to be battered all over again. It's disheartening. But it is something in a certain type of female. While that exists we shall always be the weaker sex . . . because somewhere inside these women . . . they want to be dominated. It maddens me. Well, I can do nothing for Mrs Billings. What we have to concentrate on is Fanny . . . and that, my dear, is what you are going to do. Bless you for bringing her back. I've vowed to myself that I am going to give Fanny a chance of a good life . . . and you have helped me more than I can say.'

She did a rare thing. She kissed us both and we kissed each other, Timothy and I. He took my hands and looked earnestly into my eyes. I believed then that he loved me.

There was a dramatic sequence to that adventure.

The next day the papers were full of it.

HORRIBLE MURDER IN SWAN STREET.

I read it over breakfast and as I did so the significance of what had happened dawned on me.

Jack Billings returned home after a drunken spree and battered his wife Mary to death in their home. Mrs Billings's daughter by her first marriage was by good fortune staying at the Mission run by Peter and Frances Lansdon, son and daughter-in-law of the well known philanthropist, Peter Lansdon.

That was all.

I went at once to see Frances. She had heard the news.

'Thank God you brought Fanny here,' she said.

'I think Mrs Billings's death is probably due to the fact that Fanny left,' I said.

'It might have been, but there was bound to be something like this sooner or later.'

'What of Fanny? Does she know?'

'Not yet. I'm wondering what's best to be done.'

Timothy arrived, having heard the news

His first words were: 'What of Fanny?'

'She doesn't know yet,' said Frances. 'I am considering what to do.'

'Would it be a good idea to get her away?'

'I think it might.'

'I could take her down to Hampton.'

'Oh, Tim . . . would you?'

'I don't see why not. I've told my sister and the children about her. They'd be pleased.'

'I think that is an exciting idea. There will be lots in the paper. Fanny can't read . . . but there'll be talk. She's very sharp. I want the shock to be cushioned when it comes.'

'Do you think Fanny would agree to come?' asked Timothy.

'I think she would with you. We'll ask her. She is fond of you and you have won her confidence . . . particularly after the way you two went down there and brought her away.'

It was a new Fanny we saw – washed and shining. Her dress was a little too big for her but it was the best Frances could find among the clothes which had been donated to the Mission from time to time.

'Fanny,' said Frances, 'Mr Ransome wants to take you to his house in the country. Would you like to go?'

'I ain't never been to the country.'

'Well, now is your chance to see it.'

'With 'im?' she said, pointing to Timothy.

'That's right. It's his home. He's got two children . . . a girl and a boy. They've heard of you. You could help look after them.'

I could see that she liked the idea of looking after children.

'What about 'er?' she said nodding in my direction.

'I don't live there, you see, Fanny.'

'Oh.' I felt flattered that she looked disappointed.

'Perhaps we could persuade Mrs Mandeville to come and stay with us,' said Timothy.

'All right,' she said.

'I'll tell you what we'll do,' I said. 'We'll go out today and buy another merino dress . . . a blue one as like the other as we can find.'

'And a red hair ribbon?' she said.

'That too,' I promised.

And that was settled.

The next day Timothy took Fanny down to Hampton. I missed them very much and was surprised that some savour seemed to have gone out of my life.

But there was a letter from my mother. She was coming to London immediately and would be with us in two days' time.

My mother was eager to know all that had been happening in London. I noticed how she kept studying me intently. I knew what she meant. She wanted to know how far my friendship with Timothy had progressed and whether I was happy.

I could not tell her because I did not know myself.

I thought increasingly of Ben and wished more than ever that I were at Manorleigh helping with the campaign.

390

I had enjoyed working at the Mission and little could be as worthwhile as that, but how I should have enjoyed doing all the things which Lizzie hated so much and which, presumably, Grace was helping her to do.

I thought it must be a most exciting life – but perhaps that was because it was Ben's.

One of the first things Amaryllis did when my mother arrived was to invite Timothy to dinner.

'I know,' said Aunt Amaryllis, 'that your mother is eager to hear how you helped that young girl.'

Then my mother had to hear the story of Fanny.

'You went into that dreadful place alone!' was her first comment.

'I didn't think of it. I just followed Fanny.'

My mother shivered. 'It was foolish of you.'

'But if I hadn't what would have happened? It was all for the best. And Timothy was not far behind.'

'What a terrible thing! That poor woman . . . murdered.'

'It will at least be the end of that . . . monster,' said Aunt Amaryllis. 'He's guilty and everyone knows it. He admits it himelf. He'll hang.'

'And that poor child?'

'She's with Timothy's family at the moment.'

'Oh yes . . .'

It was clear that my mother had had a full report on Timothy's family from Aunt Amaryllis.

'It was good of him to take her in,' said my mother. 'I must say he seems to me to be a very kind person . . . working for the Mission and all that.'

'Oh, you know Frances. She insists that people come and then she makes them work.'

'Frances is wonderful.'

'Peterkin is a great help to all those people, too.'

'They are a wonderful pair.'

'I am so glad Timothy's coming to dine. I do look forward to meeting him.'

When Timothy came it was obvious from the first that they took an instant liking to each other.

'I've heard so much about you,' said my mother, 'and all that you have been doing at the Mission. There is so much I want to know about the poor child you rescued. I do think it was wonderful.'

We were at the dinner table with, as usual, Uncle Peter at one end and Aunt Amaryllis at the other. They were beaming like two benign gods who have settled the troubles of the world. I could see that they had decided that I should marry Timothy Ransome and live happily ever after. Why is it that other people's problems are so easy to solve? It is only one's own which are fraught with difficulty.

They talked of little but politics. It would not have been a dinner party at that house without that. My mother wanted to know how Ben was getting on and I noticed the pride with which Uncle Peter told her that he had a fair chance of beating his opponent.

'It is rather amusing,' said my mother. 'You and Matthew on one side and Ben on the other.'

'It adds spice to the contest,' agreed Uncle Peter.

'Grace is being so useful,' said Aunt Amaryllis.

'She is a clever woman,' replied my mother. 'I always thought that . . . from the day she came to us. Do you remember that day, Angelet?'

I said I did.

'And I gather she is looking after Lizzie . . . which is good of her. Poor Lizzie!'

'She ought to have married someone not quite so demanding,' said Aunt Amaryllis. 'Well, at least she has Grace.'

'What about this poor child you rescued? Isn't it dreadful about her mother and stepfather? What will happen, do you think?'

'He will get his deserts,' replied Uncle Peter. 'It's a plain case of murder. It's good publicity for the Mission, though, because the young girl was there when it happened. She might have shared her mother's fate if she had been in her home.'

'How is she taking it, poor child?' said my mother.

'We haven't told her yet,' explained Timothy. 'She's settling in quite happily. I don't know what will happen when she hears. She was devoted to her mother.'

392

'Poor, poor girl,' said my mother.

'We didn't want her to think that her mother died because she, Fanny, left home.'

'She didn't, did she?'

'Well, the stepfather didn't want Fanny to go. He wanted the few pence she earned as a salesgirl to buy himself gin. Coming home drunk and finding Fanny gone, he apparently attacked his wife and killed her.'

'We can't be sure it was quite like that,' I said.

'In any case,' went on Timothy, 'it would have happened sooner or later. He had ill-treated the poor woman often enough before. Fanny is liking the country.' He turned to me and smiled. 'She looks quite different. The children like her. They think she is quaint. She was with their governess when I left them to come to town. I think she is a little put out because Fiona, who is so much younger than she is, can read and write. Fanny herself would like to do that.'

'So you will have her taught?' asked my mother.

'If she wants to. I am not quite sure what we should do for her. My sister Janet would train her as a parlourmaid or something. I want to do the best for Fanny. She is unusually bright and intelligent. I was hoping to ask your advice.' He looked at me. 'You understand her . . . you always did. I wish you would come down to Hampton and see her there.' He glanced at my mother. 'Perhaps you would come with Angelet, Mrs Hanson. My sister Janet would enjoy that.'

'I don't see why not,' answered my mother. 'I think it is an excellent idea.'

'It is not very far out of London.'

'We should enjoy it so much, shouldn't we, Angelet?' said my mother.

I smiled and said we should.

Everyone was satisfied. The evening was going according to plan.

And so my mother, Rebecca and I went to Hampton, Timothy escorting us there. Rebecca was very excited. She already knew

393

Timothy well and in her usual affectionate manner accepted him as a friend. She was elated at the prospect of visiting him, but a little sad because Pedrek was not one of the party.

Riverside Manor was a beautiful old Tudor house and, as its name implied, close to the river. It was the black and white type of building so typical of the period, with black beams and whitewashed plaster panels in between. The upper floors projected over the ground floor and in front of the house was a garden now full of chrysanthemums and dahlias. It must have been very colourful in the spring.

We stepped right into a typical Tudor hall with high vaulted ceiling, thick oak beams and panelled walls, where Janet Ransome was waiting to receive us. She was a tall woman with a spare figure and a certain severity of countenance. Crisp, neat and rather taciturn, I thought; but I was to discover that this exterior hid a kind and sentimental heart.

She looked at me keenly and I think very soon decided to like me; and I was very pleased that she did.

My mother was effusively complimentary about the house, said that houses fascinated her and that our own had been in the family for generations.

While we were introducing ourselves, there was a patter of feet overhead and the children came down – Fanny hovering in the background.

'Fanny,' I cried.

She came hurriedly to me and then stopped. ''Ello,' she said. 'So you've come.'

'Fanny likes Hampton, don't you, Fanny?' said Timothy.

'It's all right,' said Fanny grudgingly.

'Oh, and this is Fiona.'

The bright-eyed little girl gave me a smile of welcome.

'And here's Alec.'

Alec, a rather tall and gangling youth shook hands rather awkwardly; and I felt I was going to like Timothy's family. This was quickly confirmed.

Fiona immediately decided that it was her place to look after Rebecca. This greatly pleased her father, and Janet Ransome looked on approvingly.

394

Janet and Timothy showed us the house from top to bottom: the buttery, the laundry house, the great kitchens with their stone floors, big ovens and roasting spits.

'We don't use these much now,' said Janet. 'Thank goodness we don't eat the gigantic meals our forefathers did.'

We went on our tour of inspection; the hall, the dining-room with the delightful linenfold panelling, the long gallery with the portraits of the family, the tapestries on the dining-room walls and the chair seats of needlepoint in rich shades of blue worked by some ancestress who had lived more than a hundred years before. There was the crown post room, the attics, and all the bedrooms, many with their fourposter beds which had been in the family for generations.

From the windows were views of the river and the gardens running down to it. There were a few stone steps leading to the water which they called the privy stairs: there were two boats, attached to posts there, in which one could row oneself up and down the river.

From the topmost rooms one could see Hampton Court, the famous palace which had once been Wolsey's before he was compelled to make a present of it to his king.

It was a delightful place.

'I wonder you can bear to leave it,' I said to Timothy.

He looked a little sad. I supposed the place was full of memories. This was where he had lived with his wife. From these stables she had gone out one morning and had been carried back to this house on a stretcher – gone forever.

There was a portrait of her in the gallery – a pretty woman with a pleasant smile. I had guessed who she was before I was told.

My mother was delighted with our visit. She thought the place enchanting and the family delightful. I could see that she had decided that I could do far worse than settle down here.

In a few days I was feeling that I knew the house and its inhabitants very well indeed. Rebecca had settled in and her new playmates compensated for the loss of Pedrek. She was delighted with Fiona but I think she was especially fascinated by Fanny.

Fanny was obviously pleased by Rebecca's preference; and when I saw Fanny with my daughter I believed she looked happier than I had seen her before.

'I like it here,' said Rebecca. 'Are we going to live here?'

Her words startled me. I knew my family thought that marriage with Timothy would be the best possible solution for me, and now that I had met Timothy's sister, I was sure that she too was not averse to the idea. Her home was in this house and she had been mistress of it, but I could see that kind of authority did not mean a great deal to her. She was absolutely devoted to Timothy and she firmly believed that he needed to marry again to enable him to recover from that devasting blow which the death of his wife had obviously dealt him.

I had not realized until I came to the house how deeply he had suffered and still was suffering, I believed. In my heart I guessed that no one could ever take the place of his first love, the mother of his children. But it would not surprise me if he asked me to marry him.

We went riding together. It was the only way to be by ourselves without interruption from some member of the family. I was not exactly taken aback when he pulled up his horse and suggested that we walk a little. He took my arm and we went down to the brink of the river.

It was November, but warm for the time of the year, and the bluish mist gave an air of mystery to the river and the big houses on the other side.

He said: 'I expect you know what I am going to say, Angelet? It has been in my mind for some time. Will you marry me?'

I hesitated.

He went on: 'I love you, you know. I felt drawn to you from the moment we met and when you went chasing Fanny I was in such a state of panic and I saw how lonely I should be if I lost you.'

'Marriage is too serious a step to rush into,' I said.

'I agree. I have thought a lot about this. Have you?'

'I haven't thought of marriage. I am not sure that I want to . . . yet.'

'Of course, we have not known each other very long, but we

have been through some adventures together. When I saw how you cared about Fanny . . .'

'You cared very much, too. You have brought her here.'

'Yes, I do care about her. I think we could have a good life together.'

'Perhaps,' I said.

'I can see no reason why not. We know each other well. I admire you so much. The children are already fond of you. So is Janet. Rebecca has settled in. Your mother feels friendly towards me. It seems to me that it would be ideal.'

'Yes, it would be ideal from their point of view. But there is more to it than that, Tim. I think you are still in love with your wife.'

'She has been dead a long time.'

'She is the one . . . she will always be the one.'

'I can care for you, too. And you? You remember your husband. He must have been a wonderful character . . . just as my wife was. We were both lucky in our marriages . . . until we lost them, and both violently. That in itself draws us together. We can't go on mourning all our lives, Angelet.'

'No,' I said. 'But I am not sure yet, Tim.'

'That means you want more time to think.'

'Perhaps I do. You haven't forgotten her . . . and I . . .'

'You mean we both really love someone else more . . .'

I nodded.

'It is hard to live up to the hero Gervaise was.'

I did not answer. When I had agreed that we each loved someone more I was not thinking of Gervaise but of Ben, which was absurd. I had an obsession with the man. He was continually cropping up in my thoughts. I was a fool to go on thinking of him. I should take this offer. It was second best for both of us. Surely it was a unique situation. I could wean him from his regrets for the loss of his wife; he would show me that there was no hope of a happy future for me while I thought of Ben.

It was sensible. It was reasonable. I contemplated the life we should have together in this gracious house. We could make a happy future for Fanny and the children. He would be a good and kind father for Rebecca. Our families approved. We would continue with our work at the Mission. I was a fool to turn away from it.

But I had not turned away. I knew that I would be foolish to. I saw so clearly that Timothy and I could make a good life together. But I wanted time to think . . . time to come face to face with myself and this obsession with Ben. How could I be so foolish? There was a man who had married for the sake of gold, who was ruthless, determined to succeed. How could such a man be capable of the love and devotion I could expect from Timothy? Besides, Ben was married.

I knew them both well enough to know that I could find a quiet and peaceful happiness with Timothy and nothing but storm and stress from Ben. Ben's passion would be fierce. I did believe that he loved me, but he loved gold . . . and power more. Timothy loved me, too, but he loved his first wife more. In time, Timothy and I could grow close together; I was sure of that; we could lay the ghosts of the past . . . perhaps. But can one ever compete with the dead?

I was in a quandary.

I fell back on the excuse. 'I need time to think.'

He understood perfectly. He always would.

'We'll wait,' he said. 'Let things ride for a while and then I think you will come to see, Angelet, that we have much to offer each other.'

We rode thoughtfully home.

I sensed their disappointment because they had been expecting an announcement.

The very next day I said to Timothy: 'I think we should speak to Fanny. There was something in the papers about the murder. Her stepmother is going on trial. The result is a foregone conclusion. I know she can't read, but someone might say something to her.'

So we decided to tell her . . . together.

My mother and Janet knew what we intended and promised to make sure that we were not interrupted.

'We want to speak to you, Fanny,' I said seriously.

398

She looked from one of us to the other and I saw panic in her eyes. 'You're going to send me away,' she said.

'We'll never do that,' said Timothy. 'This is your home for as long as you want it to be.'

'Then what is it?' she asked.

'Your mother,' I told her. 'She's . . . dead.'

She stared at us. 'When?' she said. ''E done it. It was 'im, wasn't it?'

'Yes,' I told her.

Her face was contorted with grief. I went to her and put my arms round her.

'I'll kill 'im,' she cried. 'I will, I'll kill 'im.'

'There will be no need for that, Fanny. The law will do it.'

She smiled. 'Then they've got 'im?'

'They've got him,' I repeated.

'I wasn't there,' she murmured. 'If I had of been . . .'

I held her head against me. 'No, Fanny. It was as well you weren't there. She should have come to us.'

'She *would* stay with 'im.'

'It was what she wanted.'

'She shouldn't 'ave.'

'People have to make their own choices in life. She knew this could happen and she stayed with him.'

Timothy had moved closer to us. He put his arms round us both.

'It'll be all right, Fanny,' he said. 'You'll be here. Ours . . . completely now.'

'You won't want me.'

'Oh yes we shall.'

'You got yer own . . . both of you.'

'We can always do with more,' I told her. 'We're greedy, Fanny, and we want you.'

'Do you reely?'

'We do indeed,' said Timothy fervently. 'We want you to stay with us . . . we want that very much.'

'Why?' she asked.

'Because we love you,' I said.

'Garn,' she said. 'Nobody never said that to me before.'

'We're saying it now.'

Then suddenly she was crying – the first tears I had ever seen her shed. She clung to me . . . and then she reached out and included Timothy in the embrace.

At length she withdrew herself and dabbed angrily at her face. 'Look at me. You'll think I'm daft.'

'We think you are a very nice girl,' said Timothy.

Then I could see the tears coming again.

'It's all right, Fanny,' I said. 'We all cry sometimes, you know. They say it's good for you.'

She just lay against me while the tears rolled down her cheeks. I wiped them gently away.

'I love her,' she said. 'She was good to me. She was my Mum.'

'I know.'

'I 'ate 'im. I always 'ated 'im. Why did she 'ave to? My Dad was all right, he was.'

'Life is like that sometimes,' I said. 'We have to take it and make what we can of it.'

'I like it 'ere,' she said. 'I never thought you'd keep me. You're funny, you two. I ought to be scrubbing floors or something. I wouldn't mind. But I like being with the little 'uns. I like that Rebecca. She going to live here?'

Timothy pressed my hand.

'No, we live in London,' I said. 'We're just visiting.'

'But you will live here, won't you? The two of you . . .'

She was almost pleading.

'You together . . . both of you. You're all right. I like you . . . better even than Mrs Frances. She's some sort of angel, ain't she . . . but you two . . . well, you're just . . . people. That's what I like, see? I want to be with you both . . . and the children . . . and that little Rebecca.'

'It may well turn out that way,' said Timothy, looking at me.

She said slowly: 'I'll never see me Mum again. I can't believe it.'

'It is terribly sad,' I said. 'If only she had come away . . .'

'Will they hang him?' she asked.

'It seems likely.'

400

'I'm glad of that,' she said vehemently. 'It makes me feel a lot better. He won't be able to 'urt nobody no more.'

Then suddenly she turned to us and hugged us, first me and then Timothy.

He said: 'We'll work it out, Fanny. Don't worry. I think we are all going to be very happy together.'

He took her hand and then mine; he held them in his own.

I felt then that, in time, I should be here with them both.

The Diary

We were at breakfast next morning – my mother, Timothy, Janet and I. My mother had been glancing through the morning papers.

'Here is something that will interest you,' she said. 'This is a real scandal sheet. It's about Benedict Lansdon. It could mean that he is getting on so well in Manorleigh that he has got some people worried. It is scandalous the way they are allowed to print such things.'

'What do they say about him?'

She took up the paper and read: 'Benedict Lansdon, charismatic candidate for Manorleigh, is creating quite an impression. It seems he is leaping ahead of his rivals. He is indefatigable . . . here, there and everywhere, dispensing charm in exchange for the promise of votes. It is prophesied that for the first time in many, many years the seat will change hands. Benedict Lansdon has had a spectacular career before taking up politics. He is a golden millionaire – one of the few who struck lucky in Australia. Benedict's luck came to him through his marriage which brought him the mine containing rich veins of gold. Mrs Elizabeth Lansdon appears at all functions with her husband, but who is the elegant third? I can tell you. It is Mrs Grace Hume, daughter-in-law of Matthew Hume, Cabinet Minister in the last Tory administration. Mrs Grace is a staunch supporter of the party in opposition to her father-in-law. Rather a storm in the family teacup? Perhaps, but Mrs Grace gives her fervent loyalty to candidate Benedict. It is Mrs Grace who speaks to the press. Mrs Elizabeth's lips are sealed. Why does she appear with the sad look on her face? Is she worried about her husband's chances with the Manorleigh voters? That seems to be rather unnecessary as things are going. Or is it because the elegant and ardent supporter of her husband should be such an intimate member of the household?'

I felt myself growing more and more angry as my mother read on.

'What a horrible suggestion!' she said, laying down the paper. 'Grace is only trying to help Lizzie. Poor Lizzie, what must she think?'

'I wonder what Ben thinks about it,' I said.

'Oh, he'd shrug it off. But it is very hurtful to Lizzie and Grace.'

'I always thought,' said Janet, 'from what I have heard of Benedict Lansdon that he must be a very attractive man.'

'Did you know he is some sort of distant relation of ours?' asked my mother. 'You've met Amaryllis and Peter, Timothy. Well, Benedict is Peter's grandson. It was a love-affair before his marriage. Aparently Peter always looked after the family.'

Janet looked disapproving.

'Yes,' went on my mother. 'It was irregular. Somehow people forgive Peter his indiscretions, don't they, Angelet?'

I nodded.

'And he has done so much for the Mission. They wouldn't have been half as successful there without him. Their activities could not have been so widespread. I'd like to know what Peter thinks of these paragraphs.'

'So you think they will affect Ben's chances of getting the seat?' I asked.

Timothy said: 'No. I shouldn't think so for a moment. There is a good deal of this sort of thing going on at election time. I think people don't take too much notice of it.'

I was thoughtful. I was shocked at the suggestion and scarcely listened to their comment. I was thinking of Lizzie, so inadequate, so scared of what had been thrust upon her, trying to face all those people; and of Grace who was able to talk to them with charm and efficiency.

Grace and Ben! Could there really be anything in the suggestion? Most women would admire Ben and it was a long time since Grace had become a widow. Lizzie had turned to Grace. Had Ben, too?

403

I thought then how foolish I was. I had had an offer of marriage and a peaceful life from a man whom I could trust and I was refusing it because of my feelings for someone who was out of reach and in any case of whom I should always be unsure.

My mother and I returned to London with Rebecca. The Ransomes were very reluctant for us to go. They came to the door to say goodbye as the carriage arrived to take us to the station. Fiona and Alec waved frantically. Janet said: 'You must come again . . . soon.' Timothy was coming to the station with us and Fanny stood looking at me reproachfully. Rebecca burst into tears, which was the most effective way of saying she had enjoyed the visit. We could only pacify her by telling her that we should be coming again soon.

At the station Timothy pressed my hand and said: 'I shall see you at the Mission on Wednesday.' And we said goodbye.

On the way home my mother eulogized about their being such a charming family and how pleased my father would be to hear the result of our visit. She did look at me with slight reproach, I knew, because there had not been an announcement of my engagement to Timothy and they had all gleaned that it was my fault.

So I travelled back to London between a tearful daughter and a rather disappointed mother; and I told myself once more that I had been foolish not to fall in with what everyone seemed to think was an excellent plan.

But there was still time.

The next night we were invited to the house in the square; and to my surprise Ben was there. Lizzie was not with him. She was resting, he said. Grace was with her.

I said: 'I did not expect to see you. Shouldn't you be charming votes out of the voters of Manorleigh?'

'There is time before polling day,' he said.

At dinner Uncle Peter talked about the piece in the paper. He waved it aside. 'Just malicious gossip,' he said. 'It shows they're rattled, Ben, looking for stuff like that.'

After dinner when the men joined us in the drawing-room, Ben made a point of coming over to me.

'I must talk to you, Angel,' he said.

'Well? Talk.'

'Not here. Could we meet somewhere?'

'What is it you have to tell me, Ben?'

'Let's meet. Shall we say in the Park? Kensington Gardens . . . in the flower garden.'

'Do you think we should?'

'We must. Tomorrow, ten-thirty.'

'But . . .'

'Please, Angel. I shall expect you.'

I slept little that night. I lay awake wondering what he would say to me.

I found him waiting impatiently. He rose as I approached and, taking both my hands firmly in his, drew me to a seat.

'What is it Ben? What's happened?'

'It's this Timothy Ransome.'

'What of him?'

'You have been visiting his house . . . with your mother.'

'Well, what of it?'

'It is rather significant that he should invite you with your mother. It seems to me that it is for one purpose. Have you promised to marry him?'

'No, I have not and, Ben, I don't see . . .'

'That it is my business? It *is* my business, Angel. I love you. You and I were meant for each other.'

'But you are married to Lizzie.'

'That was because . . .'

'You don't have to explain. I know only too well. You didn't love Lizzie, but you loved what she could bring you. You knew there was gold on her father's land and that was the only way you could get it. You did try to buy it at first, I know . . . I grant you that.'

'Stop it,' he said. 'You don't understand.'

'I understand, too well. I was there, remember.'

'It is all in the past.'

'But the effect is with us still.'

405

'I love you. I want you . . . you only. More than anything I want you. You were married to Gervaise. Life was cruel to us both. It was always too late. And now you are proposing to marry again. First you were married to Gervaise. Then I was married to Lizzie . . .'

'You are still married to Lizzie.'

'She might divorce me.'

'Divorce you? On what grounds? I remember you suggested that Gervaise and I might divorce. It seems to be a ready solution for you.'

'It is a solution.'

'Never. Think of your political career. Would you stifle it at birth?'

'I would do anything if we could be together.'

'Ben, you are being rather rash.'

'What I want to say to you is . . . wait. Don't rush into this. Oh, I know he is a worthy man . . . full of virtue and good works . . . as I could never be. But could he love you as I do?'

'I really don't think you should be talking like this.'

'I'm telling you the truth. I know that we are meant for each other. We shared that . . . incident together. It bound us to each other in some way. I should never have gone away. Oh . . . isn't it illuminating? One can look back and see where one has gone wrong all along the line. I should have stayed with you then . . . until you were well. I should never have gone back to London. I should never have gone to Australia. I think it was something to do with that which made me want to go. It was on my conscience too, Angel. I thought I would get right away. You see, you were only a child then. Had you been older, I should have known . . . and then, as soon as you came back, I *did* know but you were married to Gervaise then.'

'It is no use going over it. We are where we are today and that means that you are married to Lizzie. I am sure she loves you devotedly. She brought you what you wanted . . . the mine . . . money . . . power. It was what you had always aimed for. People have to pay for the things they want.'

'But such a price, Angel.'

'Remember the miners . . . the story you liked so much. They thought they need not go on paying and look what happened to them.'

'That is a legend. It has nothing to do with our case.'

'You can compare them,' I said. 'Listen to me, Ben. You have a great deal. You have a career which you will enjoy. It stretches out ahead of you. Perhaps it is not everything you want . . . but it is a great deal.'

And I was thinking: I have Timothy. It is not everything I want . . . because I want Ben; but it is a great deal.

'I'll never give up hope,' he said. 'Have you promised to marry him?'

'No,' I answered.

'I thank God for that.'

'You have become very pious suddenly, Ben.'

'Don't joke. This is too serious a matter.'

'How can it change, Ben?'

'I never give up hope.'

'I must go.'

'Wait a while.'

'I really shouldn't have met you here. What about all this talk?'

'What talk?'

'That piece in the paper about you and Lizzie and Grace?'

'Oh, that. That was just the enemy getting rattled.'

'Could it spoil your chances?'

'Sensible people will take it for what it is.'

'How does Grace feel about it?'

'Rather put out, I'm afraid.'

'It seems . . . so horrible . . . just because she helps Lizzie.'

'I know. But most people take it for what it is.'

'So you are going to get in?'

'I hope so.'

'The first step along a dazzling career?'

'That is what you think of me, is it?'

'I know you, Ben.'

'Don't give up hope, Angel. Something will be done.'

'I must go.'

'I have to get back to Manorleigh this afternoon.'

'I suppose you will be there until the election?'

'It looks like it.'

'Well, good luck, Ben.'

'There is one thing that matters to me more than anything else.'

I smiled at him ruefully and left him.

When I returned to the house Grace was there with my mother.

'I had to come and see you,' she said. 'It is just a flying visit.' She smiled at my mother. 'I heard you were in London and I told myself I must see you.'

'I was just saying to Grace how nice it is to be here and that I hope she will come to Cornwall when this election is over.'

'Thank you,' said Grace. 'I should like to. But you can imagine how it is in Manorleigh just now. There is very little respite.'

'How is Lizzie?' I asked.

'Oh . . .' She frowned. 'She is always tired. She doesn't really like all this public life.'

'It must be a terrible trial to her.'

'I help her all I can and she manages.'

'It's a change from Golden Creek.'

'Indeed yes. I hear you have been doing wonderful things at the Mission. Your mother has been telling me about the poor girl whose stepfather is on trial for murder.'

'It's a very sad case.'

'And Timothy Ransome has taken her in?'

'He is a wonderful man,' said my mother.

'He must be. And you have just returned from a visit to his place. Frances thinks a great deal of him, I gather. I always admire those people who give up so much of their time to good works.'

'Angelet has been doing her share lately.'

'So I heard. You're rather friendly with Mr Ransome, I believe.'

'Oh yes . . . we're good friends.'

My mother was smiling a little complacently.

'I am lucky to have this work,' went on Grace. 'It's done a lot for me. I suppose you feel the same about the Mission. It can be lonely for a widow . . . on her own.'

'Well,' said my mother, 'perhaps life will change for both of you.'

I did get a few words alone with Grace before she went.

She said: 'Is it true that you are going to marry Timothy Ransome?'

'No. Who told you that?'

'I gathered it from the way they were talking . . . Amaryllis and your mother. They seemed to think that an engagement was imminent.'

'No, not imminent.'

She nodded. 'It's a big step, marriage. One needs time to consider it, particularly when one has already experienced it. You realize how easily things can go wrong. It makes you cautious.'

'Yes,' I agreed.

'Well, Angelet, I wish you every happiness. I hope it works out well for you. I do know that Timothy Ransome is a very good man. People talk. And . . . good men are rare.'

Another, I thought, who wants to see me married.

She left that afternoon with Ben and Lizzie for Manorleigh; and the next day my mother went back to Cornwall.

I had just had breakfast and was in the nursery with Rebecca when one of the maids came round with a message from Aunt Amaryllis. Would I go to them at once.

Uncle Peter was there. He was preparing to leave. He looked white-faced and shocked – quite unlike himself.

'Oh, Angelet,' cried Aunt Amaryllis, embracing me, 'I wanted to tell you before you heard elsewhere. The papers are full of it. Uncle Peter is going straight away to Manorleigh. He knows Ben will need his support.'

'What is it, Aunt Amaryllis?'

'It's Lizzie . . .'

'Lizzie? Is she ill?'

'She's . . . dead.'

'Dead!' I cried. 'How? Why?'

'It looks like an overdose of laudanum.'

I clutched a chair. I felt I was going to faint.

Aunt Amaryllis was beside me, putting an arm round me.

'I'm sorry. I should have broken it more gently. We're all so terribly shocked.'

'Tell me. Tell me all about it.'

'They found her . . . this morning . . . It was Grace who was the first. She went into her room and found her . . . dead.'

'Where was Ben?'

'He was in his room, I suppose. They had separate rooms, you know. There was the bottle beside her bed. Poor Lizzie . . .'

'I'm going down to see what can be done,' said Uncle Peter. 'I'll be in touch as soon as possible.'

He left us and Aunt Amaryllis said to me: 'I'm going to get you some brandy. You look so shocked.'

'No, thanks, Aunt Amaryllis. It's just . . .'

'I know how you feel . . . I do the same. It's so awful. That poor child . . . I don't know what it means.'

She made me drink a little brandy, but I knew that nothing could stop the terrible thoughts which were crowding into my mind.

We sat there. Aunt Amaryllis was talking. Grace had gone in and found her . . . Ben had sent a message to his grandfather at once.

'Peter will sort things out,' said Aunt Amaryllis.

How did one sort out death in such circumstances? I wondered. Surely that was beyond even Uncle Peter's powers.

I don't remember the next few days in detail. It was like living in a nightmare.

I went back to my house. Morwenna and Justin came to see me.

'This is terrible,' said Morwenna.

'The papers will have a field day,' added Justin.

'Yes,' I said. 'They will.'

'This is a little different from the snippets of scandal we've had so far,' said Justin. 'Is Grace still there?'

'Well, she was with them. She and Lizzie were great friends. She was such a help to her. Oh, poor Lizzie, she never wanted to leave Golden Creek.'

'I wonder if Grace will stay there,' said Justin.

'She's been helping with the campaign. I suppose that has to go on.'

'It will be a hopeless cause now.'

'You mean . . .'

'Why, Angelet, you don't think they would elect a man whose wife has just died in mysterious circumstances?'

'Mysterious circumstances . . .'

'It will come out at the inquest. No one can say till then. I wonder if Grace will stay. She can't very well without Lizzie's being there.'

'What does that matter?' I asked. 'Lizzie is dead. I can't believe it.'

I lived in a daze. There was one thought which kept coming into my mind. It was what Ben had said: 'Don't give up hope. Something will be done.'

Something had been done.

No. I would not believe *that* of Ben. He was vigorous in his pursuit of what he wanted. He had married for it. Would he murder for it?

There! I had said the word to myself. And now it haunted me and I could not get it out of my mind.

There was great anxiety in the family. We met and talked over the matter. They all said that Lizzie had been taking the drug to help her sleep. Some drugs were dangerous. It was easy to take too much.

Uncle Peter was staying at Manorleigh for the inquest.

We were all waiting for the outcome. That would either still our fears or make them realities.

We did not want to read the papers but we could not stop ourselves. They were full of the case. Everyone was talking of the sudden death of Mrs Elizabeth Lansdon . . . wife of one of the candidates in the constituency of Manorleigh. She had been found in her bed by the close friend of herself and her husband . . . Mrs Grace Hume, widow of the Crimean hero, grandson

411

of Peter Lansdon the philanthropist. Why did they have to go into those details every time they mentioned them?

There were hints as to what might have happened. Mrs Elizabeth was shy and retiring; she had given the impression that the life of a successful politician's wife had little charm for her. It was her friend, Mrs Grace, who had shone at the meetings; she it was who mingled with the people, kissed the babies and expressed general concern for the welfare of the voters . . . taking on the work and duties of the candidate's wife.

Hints . . . all the time. I was amazed how the press enjoyed the hunt for sensation. They reminded me of a pack of hounds chasing a fox. Ben had angered them. He had been too clever, too successful; and they hated that. And now was their opportunity to destroy all that success.

We heard the result of the inquest before Uncle Peter came back to tell us about it.

We were all gathered together in the house in the square. Justin and Morwenna were with us. They said they felt like members of the family and wished to share our grief at such a time.

We heard the paper boys crying out in the street. 'Inquest Result . . . Mrs Lizzie Inquest. Read all about it.'

The papers were brought to us. In thick headlines it read: CORONER'S VERDICT: ACCIDENTAL DEATH.

We all breathed with relief. I was sure the others had feared what I had that it might have been 'Murder against some person or persons unknown'.

Uncle Peter returned. Lizzie's body was to be brought to London and she would be buried in the family vault. He told us all about it.

'What an ordeal! It seems that Lizzie had been in the habit of taking the stuff. It's a dangerous habit. She should have been stopped. Ben didn't know about it. That didn't do him much good. It gave the impression that he was a neglectful husband.

'Grace was put through a lot of questioning. She was the great friend. Yes, she had known about the laudanum. No, she

412

had not thought it necessary to inform Lizzie's husband. She knew that Lizzie had difficulty in sleeping and was amazed how well and happy she was when she had a good night's sleep. Grace had thought it was helpful . . . taken in moderation. She had had no notion that Lizzie might be exceeding the dose. In fact she had thought she took it only rarely. Then she told him how she had gone to see Lizzie that morning. They had already ascertained that Ben and Lizzie did not share a room. They didn't like that very much. As a matter of fact, at this time I was getting a little worried.

'Grace was good. An excellent witness. She said Ben was a kind husband and that Lizzie was very fond of him. The only thing Grace knew of that worried her was having to face people and do what was expected of her . . . not by her husband. He was always very gentle with her . . . but by others. Grace had always done her best to help her.

'They asked if Grace was aware of certain remarks which had been made in the press. Grace said she was. And how did they affect her? She ignored them, because they were nonsense and she knew that they were made by people who feared their candidate was not going to win the election. Mr Lansdon had never behaved in any way which was not in keeping with the conduct of a gentleman and a good and faithful husband.

'Did she think that Lizzie would take an overdose deliberately, knowing the effect it would have? Grace said she was sure she would not. She could have been careless. She could have taken a dose and forgotten she had taken it and then . . . perhaps sleepily have taken more. She was forgetful. But, they said, she was aware of her inadequacies and worried about them to the extent that they gave her sleepless nights. Grace admitted this was true.

'"In view of this," she was asked, "having made yourself her protector, did you think it wise for her to have the bottle close to her bed?"

'I must say Grace was magnificent. She was so cool. In my opinion it is she who is really responsible for the verdict. She replied that the idea had not occurred to her until this moment when it had been put into her mind. "It would never have occurred to me that Lizzie would think of taking her own life.

413

In my opinion, knowing her well, it could only be that she took the overdose by mistake.''

'And so the verdict. Accidental death.'

The next ordeal was her funeral. She was to be buried in St Michael's churchyard, where other members of the London branch of the family were laid to rest. It was a short carriage drive from the house, but because of the publicity which had been given to the case, there were many people besides the family to witness the burial.

Poor Lizzie. She was more famous in death than she would have believed possible.

Ben was there, looking unlike himself, serious and very sad. I wondered if he was reproaching himself for marrying her in the first place and then neglecting her and planning divorce.

Grace was elegant in black, attempting, it seemed, to keep herself aloof. The crowd wanted to see her. I think some of them had made up their minds that she was 'the other woman' in the case and for her Ben had murdered his wife. They wanted drama and if it was not there they determined to create it.

As the coffin was lowered into the grave someone threw a stone at Ben. It hit him in the back. There was a scuffle, someone was hurried away, and the burial continued.

I watched sadly as I listened to the clods falling on the coffin and I threw down a bunch of asters which I had brought.

We walked away from the grave – Uncle Peter on one side of Ben, Aunt Amaryllis on the other. We went back to Ben's grand house. It seemed like an empty shell now. We drank sherry and ate ham sandwiches in sorrowful silence.

Grace came and talked to me. She seemed calm.

'I blame myself,' she said. 'I should have taken more care of her.'

'Blame yourself! Why, Grace, you were wonderful to her. She relied on you.'

'And I did not see what she was doing.'

Justin came to see us.

'It is a relief that this is over,' he said, looking at Grace.

414

She nodded.

'You did well,' he added.

I thought there was a faint hostility between them and for a fleeting moment it occurred to me that Justin might have believed the story that Grace was too friendly with Ben. Then it passed. It was nonsense. I was imagining things.

'I hope so,' said Grace. 'It was rather alarming.'

'It must have been,' replied Justin. 'Are you going back to Manorleigh?'

'Of course,' said Grace. 'How could I not?'

'If you do, it might look as though . . .'

'Oh, all that nonsense!' said Grace. 'Nobody believes that. It's all party politics.'

'Of course,' said Justin.

Morwenna came over. 'Oh dear,' she said. 'I do hope Ben is not too depressed by all this.'

'Here he is,' said Grace. 'He'll tell you.'

Ben stood before us and for a few seconds his gaze held mine . . . at least I suppose it was only for a few seconds. It seemed more and I felt that everyone in that room must be aware of his feelings for me. Then he said: 'What am I to tell?'

'I was just saying,' Morwenna explained, 'that I hoped you were recovering from this terrible shock.'

'Yes, thank you,' he replied. 'I am.'

'Shall you be going back to Manorleigh?' asked Justin.

'Yes . . . this afternoon. Very shortly, in fact.'

'I suppose it is the best thing . . . to get on with work.'

'It's the only thing.'

Again I intercepted his gaze. It was full of pleading. I felt quite unnerved and in that moment I did not know what to believe. I said: 'I think Aunt Amaryllis is trying to catch my eye. I had better go and see what she wants.'

It was escape. I felt I might have been acting rather strangely and that Justin, in particular, was aware of it.

I found Aunt Amaryllis. She said to me: 'Oh, there you are, dear. You'll stay, won't you? Uncle Peter is hoping you will. They will all be gone shortly.'

Uncle Peter came up and pressed my arm.

415

'I wish Ben could stay a little while,' said Aunt Amaryllis. 'It will be awful going back to that place and electioneering after this. Someone was saying it won't do any good. It will need a miracle for him to get in now.'

'We are good at working miracles in this family,' said Uncle Peter.

'I do hope it works out for him.'

I was glad when it was over. I had a quiet meal with Uncle Peter and Aunt Amaryllis and then Uncle Peter walked me home.

I said to him: 'What do you really think about all this, Uncle Peter?'

'I wish to God it hadn't happened. It's just the worst time for Ben.'

'Do you think people believe . . .'

'People like to believe the worst. It is more exciting than the best.'

'What'll happen?'

'Ben won't get in this time.'

'It will be a terrible disappointment to him. He has worked so hard.'

'He'll survive. The luckiest thing is that the verdict was what it was. It might have been very unpleasant. We have to be thankful for that.'

He kissed me goodnight.

I went into the house but not to sleep.

Uncle Peter was right. There was no miracle. Ben did not win the seat.

Uncle Peter said: 'It was hardly likely that he could.'

So there he was . . . defeated.

I said to myself: At least he is innocent of Lizzie's death. If he had planned to kill her he would not have done so at such an important time.

I felt relieved at the thought.

Ben came back to London. Grace had now returned to her own home; but she was constantly at one of our houses. She

416

said she would sort out Lizzie's clothes and send some of them to the Mission. She took them there and had a long talk with Frances. She was becoming very interested in the Mission.

I saw Ben now and then.

Uncle Peter said he was disillusioned and was talking of giving up politics. 'It will take him some time to live this down,' said Uncle Peter. 'People don't like this sort of thing to be attached to their Member. They think he should be beyond reproach, not committing the sins of ordinary people.'

I said: 'Ben has committed no sin.'

'No, but his wife died in mysterious circumstances. They'll reckon that, even if he didn't murder her, she took her own life. They'll say: Why was she so bemused as to take an overdose? It must be because she had an unsatisfactory home life. Constituents do not like their Members to have unsatisfactory home lives.'

Uncle Peter thought Ben should face it and not show himself to be in the least put out by failure. Perhaps next election they would give him a constituency up North where the people might be less aware of what happened.

Aunt Amaryllis did not give dinner parties for a while. The family was in mourning. But she did gather us all together, though; and when she did Grace, Morwenna and Justin were often of the party.

'I look upon you, my dears, as members of the family,' she told Morwenna and Justin. 'I really don't want strangers at such a time.'

So I saw Ben often. We talked a little, in snatches and quietly, because usually there were others in the room. These conversations normally took place after dinner or just before while we were waiting to go to the table.

I asked him if he felt badly about the election and he said he had expected it would go that way.

'After all your work, Ben!'

'In politics, or in life for that matter, everything can change in a week. I knew as soon as it happened that I was sunk.'

'You will fight again?'

'I expect so. But it takes a long time for them to forget.'

'By the next election perhaps?'

'Then there will be someone to bring it up . . . refurbish it
. . . dress it up as new, I dare say. It will cling, Angelet. I wish
I could have done something. It was my fault. I just ignored
her. I should have explained. It is too late now.'

'Time will pass and it will be better.'

'I keep thinking that all the time. Then we can start again
. . . you and I.'

'I couldn't talk about that now, Ben.'

'Perhaps not . . . but later.'

Grace came over to us.

'I hope I am not interrupting,' she said brightly.

'Oh no,' I told her.

'You seemed in deep conversation.'

'No, we were just talking . . . idly . . .'

I looked up and saw Justin. He was looking at us very intently.
I smiled and he came over; and the conversation turned to
generalities.

The next morning to my surprise Justin called. He was carrying
a small parcel.

I wondered why he had come so early in the morning. We
were in the sitting-room – just the two of us.

He said: 'I wanted to see you rather specially, Angelet.'

'Yes, Justin, is something wrong?'

'No . . . not just now.'

'You mean something might be? Morwenna?'

'No, not Morwenna. She doesn't know I've come.'

'You are being very mysterious, Justin.'

'I don't know how to say this or where to begin. It's just a
hunch I have. It's just something I feel you ought to know. I
never thought to tell you . . . or anyone . . . but since Gervaise
did what he did for me . . . at such a time when we were not
even friends . . . I have felt I owed you something. I've wanted
to look after you for his sake. I'm not a very admirable character,
as you know, but I really think that changed me. It's because
of that . . .'

'Justin, this is getting more and more mysterious. Why don't
you say it outright?'

418

'I will. But first I want you to read this. Then . . . when you've read it, I'll talk to you.'

He put the package into my hands. 'What is it?' I asked.

'It's a diary. I've had it for some time. Read it . . . and when you have read it, we must meet again and I will tell you what I am afraid of. You wouldn't believe me . . . until you read that and then I think you would understand a good deal.'

'A diary? Whose?'

'Angelet, I must ask you not to show it to anyone. Will you promise?'

'Of course, but . . .'

'Take it to your room. Wait till tonight. Read it when you are quite alone. That is very important.'

'I am very puzzled, Justin.'

'I know. But just do as I say. Take it straight to your room. Lock it away and when you retire tonight and can be sure of being quite alone, read it . . . and when you have read it I will come and see you and tell you why I am behaving in such an extraordinary way.'

'Why can't I look at it now?'

'Someone might come in. You would be interrupted. Please, do as I say. Promise me, Angelet.'

'All right. I'll promise.'

'Thank you. I'll go now. I'll come tomorrow and we'll talk.'

Then he left.

I looked at the parcel and was greatly tempted to open it, but having given my promise I took it to my room and locked it in a drawer.

Really Justin was behaving in a very odd manner.

I retired early that night and as soon as I was alone I unlocked the drawer and took out the package. Stripping off the paper, I found a diary. I glanced at the dates at the top of each entry and the small neat handwriting.

I undressed, got into bed, and began to read.

On the fly leaf was an inscription: 'For Mina with love from Mother.'

Mina presumably was the owner of the diary.

January 1st: I found this diary when I was getting ready to leave, and I remembered that last Christmas Mother had given it to me. She had said: 'Write in it, Mina. Then you can look back on your life at this time in years to come and it will seem as though it is happening to you now.' I thought I would, but I didn't. And now she is dead and I have to leave here and start a new life. I think it might be interesting. What to write about is difficult to know. So much will be just not worth recording. I shall see how it goes. This is my first entry and it seems I am telling myself things I already know. I don't suppose I shall continue, I am just starting because it is all new and I am leaving here and have to earn my own living. Mother never wanted that, but the little she was able to leave is not really enough to live on. I don't want to scrimp and scrape all my life. Besides, what would happen to me here? I had to take this job with the Bonners, for the only thing a woman can do when she has to earn a living and she is in my position, is to be a governess. I shall look upon it as an adventure and if it is intolerable I shall not be completely penniless. I can look for something else. So this is a start.

The next entry was a week later.

January 8th: Something worth writing. Here I am installed in Crompton Hall, Crompton, near Bodmin, Cornwall . . . a rather eerie sort of place and the Bonners are rather impossible. But they amuse us, Mervyn and me. I suppose I ought to record our meeting. I thought it was a coincidence at first that we should meet on the way to the Bonners but as we were travelling on the same day it was quite natural that we should meet, because the little branch railway line is not used by many people. It is more like a toy railway than a real one – though it is the pride of the local inhabitants' lives. It was snowing when I boarded the little train. There were only three other passengers. It was late because the main line train had been delayed. The little train was waiting for its arrival, I was told. Two of the passengers were a middle-aged couple; Mervyn was the other. I liked him from the moment I saw him. He helped me with my bags and soon we were facing each other in the carriage. I remember the conversation.

'What a day for a journey!'

'It *is* winter.'

'Still, it could have been better than this. Are you going to Crompton?'

'Yes, are you?'

'Yes. I was wondering if I should be met.'

'You are staying there, are you?'

'I'm going as governess . . . to Crompton Hall.'

He started to laugh. He had beautiful white teeth.

'I'm going to Crompton Hall . . . as tutor.'

We stared at each other in disbelief.

I thought: Now this is something to put into the diary.

That journey was quite exciting. It was long because there were so many delays on the line. I didn't mind in the least. I wanted it to go on and on. He told me about himself. He was alone in the world – no parents. They had spent all they had on educating him and now here he was forced to earn a living and fully equipped to take the post of tutor to 'a young gentleman in the country' – 'as he was described to me,' he said.

I told him I had nursed my widowed mother for years – I being the only child. She had had an annuity which had made living comfortable enough, but when she had died there was little else. Like him, I had received a good education so I was equipped to be a governess to 'a young lady in the country'.

By the time we had arrived at Crompton we were good friends and much of the apprehension I had been feeling was gone as we mounted the dogcart sent by our obliging employers; and we were conducted to Crompton Hall.

The next entry was:

February 3rd: Mother would scold me if she knew I had neglected my diary. She herself had been a great diarist, but when I looked over it after her death all it contained were things like: 'Not so well today', or 'Poured with rain all morning'. I thought that such details were not really worth recording. In

421

this book I shall write only what I feel to be significant in my life. And I feel it is beginning to be fraught with significance.

It is all due to Mervyn. How lucky I am that we should be here together. Even during our meeting on the train I felt this and so did he, I believe. We could laugh together over our employers. The Bonners were not Cornish. They had settled here only about five years before, and they were regarded as foreigners in the community, although they did not seem to be aware of it.

They think they are the lords of the manor. They don't seem to understand that to be regarded as such they would have had to live here for at least a hundred years. The servants despise them; so do the villagers. The Bonners are not gentry and there are no snobs like their kind. They are accepted by the doctor and the solicitor, the neighbouring squires and of course the vicar: 'dear bumbling old Rev,' as Mervyn calls him. 'He is the good shepherd and we are all his sheep, old and young, poor and *nouveau riche*.' We have a lot of fun laughing at them all. The children are nonentities. They have to remember that they are a lady and a gentleman now with a tutor for Master Paul and a governess for Miss Jennifer. 'How many families run to that!' as my employer would say. 'Most of them would have only one for the two, but brass is meant to be spent to get the best for the family.' That is Squire Bonner's policy; and it suits me very well, for it brings Mervyn and me close together.

Mervyn has convinced the Bonners that the children should ride. It is part of their education. He is wonderful on a horse. I never rode much. I didn't have the opportunity. He is determined to teach me. He takes me out with the children, of course, and as Master Paul and Miss Jennifer enjoy that, Bonner *mère* and *père* think it is a good thing. They are fast climbing up the social ladder and the saddle is yet another step.

The reason I am writing today is because silly little Gwennie Talbot said to me: 'I think the tutor be sweet on 'ee, Miss.'

I blushed, which made her titter, and I pretended to be annoyed. I said: 'Don't be impertinent, Gwennie.' But I was pleased. People are noticing. So that seemed worthy of an entry in my diary.

March 1st: I really am no diarist. It is only rarely that the urge comes over me to write. I suppose life has been going on in the same way all these weeks. But I have never been so happy and it is wonderful and all due to Mervyn. Each day I get up with a feeling of exhilaration. It is love, I suppose, and what is so exciting is that we are both under the same roof.

We are sometimes invited to dine at the Bonner table – the reason being that they are short of guests and we are educated – far better than our employers, I am glad to say – and we are of use to make up the numbers. This amuses us. Mervyn always has a great deal to say about the people who visit us. He is observant of human nature and can be so amusing in a wicked sort of way. I tell him he is very cruel.

A few evenings ago the vicar came and brought with him some connection of his family, not a nephew – farther away than that – a sort of second cousin, I imagine. The young man, it seemed, was a ne'er-do-well. He was rather good-looking . . . quite handsome, in fact. His name is Justin Cartwright.

When I read that I started. It was like a physical blow.

Justin! Then something else struck me. What was the name of the man we had thrown into the pool? Mervyn Duncarry. Mervyn was not a very common name. I had been wondering why Justin had thought it necessary for me to read the diary of a strange young woman named Mina. This was now taking on some significance.

I returned to the book.

He is staying with the vicar. I think he may have been in some sort of trouble. I quite like him. So does Mervyn.

March 6th: The greatest day of my life. Mervyn told me he loved me. We shall get married one day. But it is not easy for a tutor and a governess. But still, all that is to be considered later. We shall have to make plans. I am quite blissful and can think of nothing else.

March 30th: Today we rode into Bodmin. We made the excuse that we had to get some books for the children's lessons and

423

they were left in the charge of servants, so we had the day to ourselves.

I have never been so happy before. I laughed when I remembered how apprehensive I had been about coming to this place and when I think of the happiness it has brought me, from the moment I stepped into that little branch line train, I cannot believe my good fortune.

'We are going to buy a ring,' said Mervyn. 'It's a pledge.'

'I want to buy a ring for you,' I replied. 'There shall be one each.'

'Have you got the money?'

'Not much.'

'Nor I.'

We rode into Bodmin and left the horses at an inn where we had a glass of cider and a sandwich. Even the most ordinary food tastes like ambrosia when one is in the state I am in. We went to look in a jeweller's shop. It had to be gold. The prices were beyond us. Then I had this idea. Why didn't we buy one ring. He should wear it one week and I another. We hugged each other. So we went in and bought a gold signet ring which we could just manage with our combined money and we had our initials engraved inside: M.D. for him and W.B. for me.

I felt sick. I saw it again. The pool from which I could never escape. The ring I had found. I had given it to Grace and she had flung it into the sea.

'Wilhelmina,' he said, for he always calls me by my full name. He said it sounds important. Wilhelmina is grand. Mina is just ordinary. 'Wilhelmina, with this ring I make you mine for as long as we both shall live.' I was so happy. I had never dreamed there could be such happiness. How we laughed over the ring. It was big for me. I could only wear it on my forefinger; and it went on to his little finger. We would later carry out our first intention. There should be two rings, one for him and one for me – and we would always wear them because of what they meant to us.

April 5th: I suppose one cannot exist for ever on the top pinnacle of happiness. I understand how Mervyn feels. Perhaps I shall give way . . . in time. But I can't just ﹐ . . . lightly forget my upbringing, I suppose.

My mother and I were very close to each other, and although when she was so ill I sometimes lost patience with her, that did not mean that I did not love her very much. I always thought of her as so wise. And she used to say, 'A bride should go to her husband a virgin. I did, Mina; and I know it will be the same with you. It must be. I could never rest happy if it were not so. It is a sin, Mina.' I had said Yes, it was, and I promised her that I would be pure and virginal until my wedding day. It must have been in both our minds that living as I did it was hardly likely that there would be a wedding day, so it had been easy for me to give that promise. But now Mervyn was urging me. He seemed to have changed. He was fierce . . . even angry. He wanted to come to my room at night. My room was next to Jennifer's. I wondered what would have happened if she had awakened in the night and come to me for something, which she might well do. I imagined being dismissed with ignominy . . . both of us. I was sure the Bonners would take a very virtuous stance in such matters.

So I said: 'No. We must wait until we are married.'

'When will that be,' demanded Mervyn, 'in the position we are in?'

I thought we should wait. Make plans. Even tell the Bonners. They might allow us to continue working after we were married.

He said he did not think they would. Nor did we want to be here all our lives.

'What else could we do?' I asked.

'We could get away from here . . . to a little place of our own.'

'And do what? We couldn't live on my income.'

'We'll do something. In the meantime . . . I want you, Wilhelmina. This is torment for me . . . being under the same roof.'

I should have been delighted that he cared so much, but there was the ghost of my mother and my puritanical upbringing holding me back. I wanted to give way, yet I was afraid and I

425

felt I should never be quite happy if I did. Mervyn was so angry. I had never seen him so angry before. He was like a different man.

April 15th: There is a rift between us. Sometimes Mervyn will take me so tightly in his arms that I could cry out with the pain of it. I am a little afraid. He looks so fierce and angry and different. I almost give way . . . and then I see my mother and I am afraid. She had talked to me about deserted women and unwanted babies. She said, 'You see, they believe in these protestations of eternal love. And then they find they have been tricked.'

I can't believe that Mervyn would trick me. We truly love each other. I was wearing the ring all last week. He has it now. He was quite violent this evening. I was so upset. It was after dinner. He was with me when I was going up the stairs. He began urging me . . . even more insistently than usual.

I said: 'Don't talk so loudly. Someone will hear.'

He threw me from him. I almost fell. Then I ran up to my room. I think if he had come after me I might have given way. But he did not come. Later, I heard him leave the room. I am realizing that I am a little frightened of him. I did not know that he could be so vehement. He is like a different man.

I could not sleep. So I am writing in my diary.

April 16th: This is terrible. Everything I have dreamed of is gone like a soap bubble which the children blow with their clay pipes. I did not hear him come in last night, though I sat for a long time at my window. I cannot believe I dozed. I was so upset. I kept going over that scene. I kept saying to myself: It is because he loves me so much. This morning he was very subdued. His eyes were shadowed.

He said to me: 'I'm sorry, Wilhelmina.'

I said: 'It's all right. I understand. Let's get married . . . no matter what we have to arrange afterwards.'

'Let's do that,' he said. 'Oh God, Wilhelmina, if only we can get away from all this to a life of our own. We'll do anything. We'll make plans right away.'

I was happy again. He understood. Everything would be perfect.

April 16th, afternoon: Two of the village children playing in the woods found the body. It was a girl aged about ten years – one of the children from the village. She had been sexually assaulted and strangled. I was very shocked, of course. I didn't realize then that it was anything to do with us, until they came to the house asking questions.

Mervyn knocked on the door of my room. He said, 'I want to get away. I can't stay.'

I was astonished. 'Why not?' I said.

'It is necessary,' he said. 'I can't stay.' His eyes were wild. He had that mad look again.

Gwennie was at the door. She said: 'They want you to go down to the drawing-room, Mr Duncarry.'

April 16th, evening: I cannot believe it. They have taken him away. Someone saw him coming from the woods last night and they have found a bloodstained jacket in his room. So . . . they have taken him away.

April 20th: I have not been able to write since. There is a black pall over everything. They are holding him on suspicion. Mrs Bonner goes round bleating about the dangers. They had had him in their house! We might all have been murdered in our beds . . . and when she thought of her daughter she was overcome with fear and relief that they had him under lock and key.

I was bitter. I have tried not to believe it. But I do. I know it is true. I have dreamed a wild, impossible dream. Life could never be as good to me as I had for a brief while thought it might. When had I ever had good luck? I was bitter and angry with life. I had lost my lover. Suppose I had given way . . . he would never have come upon that child . . . he would never have felt that overwhelming lust which made him forget everything but that he must satisfy it. But there would have been other times perhaps . . . How could Mervyn do that? But what do we know of people . . . ordinary people who can suddenly turn into monsters of depravity driven by some incomprehensible sexual urge?

427

April 30th: I love him and I have discovered that, whatever he has done, I love him. I will take care of him in future . . . if he comes out of this. But how can he come out of it? They will find him guilty. They will hang him. I shall have lost my lover for ever. I believe I can help him. I believe I can save him. I could reason with him. I could make him explain to me. What I want more than anything is a chance to do this, to bring him back to a normal life, to do the things we planned to do before this happened. How could such a man as Mervyn . . . so amusing, so charming . . . behave like that? How could he suddenly change? It must have been a brainstorm . . . a momentary attack . . . like an illness. And I had refused him . . . and because of that . . . Oh, I could cure him, I know I could.

May 1st: The papers are full of it. They all write of him with hatred. I cannot stay here. I told Mrs Bonner that I was too shocked. I had regarded him as a friend. For once she understood. I said I had to get away. I gave her my notice. I would leave in a month. She would find someone else. It had been a terrible blow. She would never have another tutor. She would have a governess for both the children. If I cared to take that on . . . I said, 'No, I must get away.' I do not know what I shall do.

May 13th: He is going on trial for murder. It is a foregone conclusion. They have already proved his guilt. The papers have raked over his past and found that he was involved in another inquiry concerning the death of a girl in similar circumstances. Nothing was proved against him and he had gone free. If he had not, suggested the paper, would little Carrie Carson be alive today? He will die and that is more than I can bear. They are going to allow me to see him.

May 20th: I have been to Bodmin Jail. It was not easy to talk to him. There were people watching all the time. He talked in a low voice.

He said: 'Help me. I'll get away before the trial . . . We'll be together ever after . . . We'll get out of the country. Bring me something . . . a knife . . . bring me a knife . . . I'll fight my

428

way out. We'll go away. Think about it. I love you, Wilhelmina, I'll always love you.'

I said: 'I'll always love you, Mervyn.'

May 29th: Tomorrow I am leaving. I have made my plans. I shall get down to the coast. I think it would be a good idea to get a post not far from the prison. I shall be able to see him and tell him where. I am quite excited. I am making all sorts of plans. I am glad I kept this diary. I shall always know now how I felt . . . at the beginning . . . during those wonderful, wonderful days. It is something I shall want to live through again and again. I have seen clearly that I love Mervyn no matter what he has done. I suppose that is true love. I cannot lose him. I shall do everything I can to help him escape from prison and when he does he will know how much I love him. It will show him more than anything else ever could. I will cure him. I will. I know I can. I know he is not evil . . . deep down. People in the past were possessed by devils. That is what has happened to Mervyn. I am going to look after him. I am going to make him the man he was intended to be and we shall live happily ever after somewhere right away . . . perhaps out of England and in time we shall forget all this.

There the diary ended.

I was very thoughtful. I slept little that night. I could scarcely wait for Justin to call next morning.

He came as he had said he would.

'Why did you give me this to read?' I asked.

'Because I thought you might be in danger.'

'This diary . . .'

'I must explain. I was passing the house when she was leaving. I went to say goodbye to her. She shook hands with me and said she wanted to get away after all that had happened. She looked ill and shocked. I had guessed there was something between her and that man. She was getting her bags into the dogcart. No one was helping her, so I gave a hand. When she

429

had gone, I found the diary lying at my feet. It had evidently fallen from one of her bags. I picked it up and looked at it. I saw what it contained and decided I would keep it. You've guessed who she is?'

I nodded. 'Grace,' I said.

'Exactly.'

'I remember how you spoke to us in the park when you called her Wilhelmina Burns.'

He looked at me very seriously for a few seconds. 'It has cost me a great deal to tell you this,' he said. 'I am afraid I don't come out in a very good light. I wouldn't like Morwenna to know. I do trust you. You never told about my cheating at cards.'

'What good would that do? It would only hurt her.'

'Thanks, Angelet. I'll make a clean confession. I was living by the cards.'

'Cheating at them, you mean?'

'Winning eighty per cent of the time. One lost a little to win confidence.'

'I see. It was a profession with you.'

'I was the ne'er-do-well relation of the Vicar of Crompton. I used to go round visiting houses like that once, but there comes an end to that sort of thing. So I came to London. Then I saw Wilhelmina in the park. I recognized her at once. Of course, she was living under a different name. Miss Grace Gilmore. I think her own name had been mentioned once or twice in the papers when there were a few details about the house where Mervyn Duncarry was working. She obviously did not want to be connected with that. Well, I met her in the park. I told her I had the diary. She was very upset. I asked her about you and Morwenna. The truth is I blackmailed her. I knew her connection with the murderer. He'd got away . . . and she had helped him. She was very frightened and I was getting tired of the life I was living. One slip and you are finished for ever . . . black-balled from all the London clubs. It hadn't happened but it was always a possibility. I wanted a more secure living. Marriage with an heiress seemed a good plan. She told me about Morwenna's parents and her unsuccessful season. I liked

430

Morwenna from the start, I really did. It was easy to see she was innocent . . . gullible.'

'Oh, how could you!' I cried.

'I'll make no excuses. I was like that. But let me tell you this, Angelet, I'm changing. I want to be different . . . respectable . . . I want to be what Morwenna thinks I am. And then there is the boy.'

'So that little incident . . . the boy with the purse . . . that was arranged?'

He nodded.

'And then your courtship? The elopement?'

He nodded again.

'I suppose you thought an elopement was the best way. Once you were actually married they would have to accept you. You didn't want long preliminaries which might result in enquiries.'

'I know I'm unworthy but I swear to you that I love Morwenna and the boy. I'm trying, Angelet. I haven't touched the cards . . . well, only once or twice . . . since that showdown with Gervaise. But I am changing. I'm different. I like my work. I like my parents-in-law. I want to be a good husband and father. Morwenna thinks I am that already . . . so perhaps I'm almost there.'

'I think you are, Justin. You must forget the card-sharping. It won't do any good for anyone to know about it.'

'That's what I think. I want to forget my past. I'm trying and I want to be what Morwenna thinks I always have been.'

'And what of Grace . . . Wilhelmina . . .'

'She's a strong woman.'

'Why did you show me the diary?' I asked. 'Why didn't you give it back to her? What has she done? I've read it. All she did was love this man.'

'Why did she change her name?'

'Because she wanted to get away from all that.'

'She settled in, I gathered, and beguiled you all. She went to the Crimea.'

'She was a nurse. I have the utmost admiration for those women.'

'She went out to marry rich Jonnie and she came back comfortably off.'

431

'It was a legal marriage. Uncle Peter checked on that. There is no reason why she should not forget her past . . . as you will.'

'They discovered the body of that man in the pool, remember?'

'I do remember,' I said vehemently.

'How did he get there? How did he die? It was so near the place where she was staying.'

I did not answer.

He went on: 'Enough of him. He's out of the picture. She's a clever woman . . . a scheming woman. She has some money now . . . not as much as she would like. She is looking for a rich husband. She wants to be a social hostess. I can see it clearly . . . I was interested in her the moment I saw her. You know whom she has her eyes on now, don't you?'

'Whom?' I asked faintly.

'Ben Lansdon.' He looked at me ironically. 'I've observed a lot. One has to in the card business. You have to know how people react and you play accordingly. I'll tell you what I know about Ben Lansdon.'

'What?'

'That he is interested in someone else.'

'Who?'

'I think you know. Hasn't he told you? He's obsessed by you . . . and his wife takes an overdose . . .'

'What are you suggesting?'

'That I don't think she took it herself.'

'Oh . . . no!'

'Simply that it was given to her. She was inconvenient.'

'I don't want to hear any more of this, Justin. It's pure supposition. It's unfair. You don't know anything.'

'I think she was murdered.'

'No . . . no. It was accidental. The verdict . . .'

'Verdicts are not always the truth.'

'Justin, what are you leading to?'

'That two people might have killed her. One, her husband who is in love with another woman and who must have found her a great encumbrance. Two, the other woman who had plans to marry her husband.'

432

'I think this is nonsense.'

'It might not be. I don't think Ben Lansdon would commit murder. He's too clever for that. He wouldn't hate her. He wouldn't hate anyone to that extent. He is one of those men whose conduct is not always exemplary – like my own – but they can be a little more kindly than the wholly virtuous sometimes are. He didn't want Lizzie as a wife, but he had an affection for her. That was clear to me. But what of Wilhelmina/Grace? Now that is another matter. She has been ingratiating herself with the family, hasn't she? I can tell you how desperately she wants to be Mrs Benedict Lansdon.'

'What you are saying is horrible. Grace . . . a murderess! I won't believe it.'

'Of course, I might be wrong. But I just wanted to warn you. You see, you are next in line of fire. You can be sure Wilhelmina knows of Ben's feelings for you. And if you were not there . . . in a little while . . . well, she was wonderful to Lizzie, wasn't she? He would appreciate all the help she gave him at the election. She's clever. If she hadn't such a rival, she could have a good chance of success.'

'It's nonsense, Justin.'

'Maybe, but it is a possibility. That was why I wanted you to see the diary . . . because you should realize you are dealing with a woman of some purpose. She is strong. She manipulates. And Lizzie died so conveniently.'

'But why would she have killed her then? It spoilt his chances at the election.'

'People like Wilhelmina take the long view. If the moment was ripe . . . she would seize it. This is conjecture, true. But I tell you because I think you ought to know.'

'I suppose I must say Thank you, Justin. But I don't believe it. I just don't believe it.'

He bowed his head and lifted his shoulders.

'I've done my best,' he said.

Enlightenment

I was tormented by fears and doubts. What I had discovered through Justin unnerved me. I could not get Lizzie out of my mind; and I felt I should never know peace again.

Someone had killed her. My greatest fear was that it might have been Ben. I told myself again and again that if he had intended to kill her he would not have done so at such a time. If he were really so cynical as to marry her for a gold mine and then discard her when she was in the way, he would not have chosen to do it at such a time when he would know it would put an end to his ambitions for a parliamentary career. That was a thought I clung to. Then another idea came to me. Ben was clever. Perhaps he had deliberately chosen such a time because he knew that thought would occur to others.

I could not believe it. He was ambitious, ruthless perhaps . . . but he had always been kind and courteous to Lizzie. He could never have planned cold-bloodedly to murder her.

Then there was Grace. I could not think of her as Wilhelmina. What did I know of Grace? I thought of her as she had been when she had arrived at Cador . . . 'looking for work,' she said . . . arousing compassion in my mother and me, and all the time she was involved with a murderer, in love with a murderer. What was she doing in the neighbourhood of Cador . . . and why did he come there? There was so much mystery surrounding her, and although I had heard a great deal from Justin, there was much that was not clear to me.

And if neither Ben nor Grace was guilty . . . then was it Lizzie herself? Did Lizzie find her life so intolerable that she took it?

Whichever way I looked there was no peace.

Timothy came to see me. He took my hands and kissed me gently on the forehead.

'My dear Angelet,' he said. 'I have thought of you constantly. This is a terrible tragedy.'

'Thank you, Tim,' I said.

'There is nothing I can say except that you have my heartfelt sympathy. We miss you very much.'

'You mean at the Mission?'

'There and elsewhere. Fanny talks of you constantly, and she is always asking when you are coming down.'

'How is she getting on?'

'Splendidly. She is learning to read and write. She could not bear that Fiona should be able to do it and she but a child. So Fiona started to teach her. They are very good friends already, those two. Now Fanny is there with the governess in the mornings. She is making rapid progress. She is a very bright girl.'

'Does she know that her stepfather is dead?'

'No. We didn't tell her. It isn't necessary . . . just yet. If she asks we shall tell her. I don't think she will shed any tears for him.'

'Does she still talk of her mother?'

'No. But she is sad at times and I am sure she is thinking of her. We must expect that. She can't get over it all at once. But things are working out well. She is really very fond of the children. I think she is fond of us all. But you know Fanny. She is not one to betray her emotions. They are there, all the same.'

'You have done a wonderful job with her, Tim.'

'You helped. When I think of the Mission and what so many people owe to it I feel I want to dedicate my life to it.'

'Yes, I understand.'

'By the way, your friend Grace Hume has been down.'

'Down to the Mission?'

'Yes. She told Frances she would like to come. She seems very interested. Frances immediately pressed her into service. She found that she was good with accounts and that sort of thing. And that's the one field where things are in a bit of a mess down there. Grace said she quite enjoyed doing it. I stayed one evening for one of those impromptu sort of meals and we

435

talked. I told her about Fanny. I must say she did seem very interested.'

'I can't quite see Grace there. She is so much the social hostess.'

'People have many sides to them, Angelet.'

'Yes, I have learned that.'

'The important thing is, when are *you* coming back?'

I hesitated.

'Angelet,' he said. 'Let me help. This will pass. It was a great tragedy, and I know how you felt for her.'

'I think,' I said on impulse, 'I shall go down to Cornwall. It is a long time since I have been and my parents are urging me to go. I want to go down there and think . . . away from all this.'

'I understand.'

It occurred to me then that Timothy would always understand.

The thought of going to Cornwall had come to me on the spur of the moment, but as soon as I had said it, it seemed a good idea. I should get away from everything, be able to think more clearly. I had to come to terms with my emotions. I knew now without a doubt that I loved Ben; but Lizzie was between us, as much now as she had been when she was alive. I wanted to protect him; I wanted to help him. At the same time I could not get out of my mind the terrible thought that he might have been tempted to do anything to be rid of her. I knew without doubt that he loved me; and in love, as with everything else, his emotions would be intense. If he had acted on the impulse of a moment could he ever forget? Could I? I knew that in time he would want us to be married.

What would happen? I could not understand my own feelings. In the peace of the country, in the comfortable ambience of my old home, should I be able to assess . . . to think clear . . . to plan reasonably? Could I look at my feelings for Timothy, whom I did love in a quiet way? I knew he was a good man, a stable man. I could have a peaceful life with him. Rebecca would be happy. I could settle into a cosy cocoon of contentment. But would it be complete? Would I ever forget the man who could

436

arouse passionate emotions in me such as I could feel for no one else?

I longed to be at Cador with the familiar things of my childhood around me, with my ever-loving parents. Perhaps I could confide in them. Perhaps I could discover which way I must go.

It was inevitable that Ben should come to the house.

He looked pale and haggard.

'Oh Ben,' I said, 'it has been such a terrible time.'

He looked at me steadily. 'It is good to see you, Angel,' he said.

I smiled wanly.

'I had to talk to you,' he went on. 'I had to make you understand.'

'It has been such a shock.'

His next words sent a shiver through me. 'I killed her, Angel.'

'Ben!'

'As sure as if I put that stuff in her glass, I killed her. She did it because life wasn't worth living for her. That was my fault. She was so helpless . . . so vulnerable. She always hankered for Golden Creek. That was where she was happy. I married her for what she could bring me. Yes, I admit it. You were married and there seemed no hope. And there was the gold . . . waiting to be brought forth. I married her and then I neglected her. I made life so wretched for her that she decided to go.'

'You mustn't blame yourself too much. It won't do any good.'

'If I had been different . . .'

'If we had all been different our lives would not have been as they are.'

'If only I had tried to understand her. I was so immersed in my own life. She hated it all . . . the fuss . . . everything. And I had thrust her into that life.'

'She wanted to do all she could for you.'

'Yes, and it was too much for her.'

'But you have to grow away from it. You will in time.'

'No. It will always be there with me. She's dead . . . and I could have stopped it.'

I felt a sudden gladness in my heart. It was not he who had given her that extra dose. At least I was sure of that, and that made all the difference to me.

'It's too late for reproaches, Ben,' I said. 'That won't bring her back.'

'I know. You comfort me, Angel.'

Ben, in need of comfort! Ben, vulnerable and weak! I had never seen him like that before and I loved him the more for his weakness.

'I'm going away for a while, Ben,' I told him. 'I'm going to my family in Cornwall.'

'Not for long?'

'I don't know. I want to do a lot of thinking.'

'Yes,' he said, 'I understand.'

'Don't fret, Ben. It's done with. It's no use going over it. That can do no good.'

'You're right,' he said.

'You'll start again. You'll be your old self. You know you never liked anything to defeat you.'

'That's true,' he admitted. 'But I see I have taken matters too much in my own hands. I have tried to manipulate life.'

'Strong men do that . . . do they not? It is just that sometimes Fate is stronger than they are.'

'What shall you do in Cornwall?'

'Walk . . . ride . . . play with Rebecca . . . be with my family. I feel that I shall be able to see which way I have to go.'

He nodded. 'Think of me,' he said. 'And come back soon. I shall be waiting for you.'

Rebecca was delighted to go to Cornwall and see the grandparents; and with equal delight my family greeted me.

Jack was waiting for us at the station. 'They are killing the fatted calf,' he said.

And there was my old room, full of childhood memories . . . happy memories, apart from that dark one which would not go away and seemed to be at the centre of everything that had happened to me since.

I had been home only two days when my mother announced at breakfast that she had had a letter from Grace.

'She wants to come down and stay for a week or so. She says we have often told her that she will be welcome. I am writing

438

at once to say we shall be delighted to have her. I expect it is very sad for her. She was such a friend of Lizzie's.'

I felt a shiver run through me.

Grace coming to Cornwall? Why?

I kept thinking of Justin and how earnestly he had warned me. It had all seemed so melodramatic . . . Grace wanting to murder me . . . in the hope that one day Ben would marry her!

It was too far-fetched.

I thought I had dismissed the matter from my mind, but here it was back again.

If Ben had been guilty he could not have come to me and talked so earnestly. He was ruthless, I knew; but he was not a murderer. He had been sincere when he had talked to me; his strength had been broken down by a sense of terrible guilt . . . but it was not the guilt of a murderer.

But what of Grace . . . who was really Wilhelmina? She had once loved a murderer. I think she had helped him to escape. I tried to remember reports which had come out during the hunt for Mervyn Duncarry. He had made his escape by stabbing a warder with a knife. It was not understood how a prisoner could have a knife. Someone must have smuggled it in to him. That had been suggested at the time.

Who could have done that? Grace?

Was Justin's theory so wild? And now she was following me to Cornwall.

Grace arrived in due course. She looked changed in some subtle way. There was an air of purpose about her.

My mother welcomed her warmly. She had always been fond of Grace and regarded her as a member of the family.

At dinner, Grace talked about the Mission. She had been there once or twice and was greatly impressed by the work which was being done.

'Well, you know what I'm talking about, Angelet,' she said. 'There is that wonderful story of Fanny. I asked Timothy Ransome if I could go and see her.'

'And did you?' I asked.

'Yes, I did. What a lovely family! Fanny is settling in. She was quite sociable, which I gather is something she has learned there. She asked after you. She told me how you and Timothy came and took her away. She seems fond of you . . . and Timothy . . . and the children, of course. Don't you think that is a wonderful thing to have done?' she added turning to my parents. 'And that is just one case.'

My mother said it was indeed wonderful.

'I gather you are doing the books,' I said.

She laughed. 'What a mess they were in! Frances is magnificent . . . but accounts are not her line, and with all the donations coming in and the bills that have to be paid . . . Well, it does seem to be a line of work which nobody wants to undertake.'

'It's the less glamorous side of the business, I suppose,' said my father.

'But very necessary,' put in my mother. 'So what is happening, Grace? Are you giving them temporary assistance?'

'I've found it useful to have something to do. It won't be figures all the time . . . once I've straightened out the books. I should like to do a little bit of social work, too. I think I shall be there quite frequently.'

'Frances wants all the helpers she can get,' I said.

She smiled at me. There was a certain glitter in her eyes. Or did I imagine that? I could not get the picture of her out of my mind . . . going to Lizzie's bedroom . . . I saw Lizzie drowsy from a laudanum-induced sleep. I seemed to hear Grace's voice. 'Can't you sleep, Lizzie? You must. You need to be fresh for tomorrow . . . There is a great deal to do . . . Here, another few drops won't do any harm.'

Could Justin have been right?

And Lizzie had been in the way. And now . . . so was I.

I wanted to think of everything that had happened.

I rode out alone. Memories of the past crowded into my mind and when I remembered the past there was one incident which must always be there. The encounter by the pool . . . a child murdered . . . and Ben, younger than he was now . . . a little uncertain . . . acting in such a way as was to affect the rest of our lives. I could not help it. I found myself making my way to

440

the pool. There was the cottage where crazy Jenny Stubbs had held Rebecca captive not so long ago. I was thinking of the dragging of the pool, the discovery of the watch and the remains of the man whom Ben and I had thrown in all those years ago.

Violence had come into our quiet lives and it had had an effect on me which was never forgotten.

I slipped off my horse and tied him to the bush just as I had on that other occasion. It was quiet . . . no sound at all but a sudden sighing of a gentle breeze in the weeping willows trailing into the water.

Thus it had been on that fateful day. There was the spot where he had come upon me – the piece of wall exposed now as it had not been on that day before Gervaise and Jonnie had done their excavating; and Jonnie and Gervaise now both dead.

There was so much to remind me.

The eeriness seemed to surround me. I should not have been surprised if I heard the bells – not Jenny Stubbs's bells but the real ones – or the fantasy ones perhaps I should say – and perhaps the sound of monks' singing as they went into their ghostly underground chapel to pray.

I stood by the pool. It looked swollen. There had been a good deal of rain recently, and as the ground about it was flat it had advanced at least a foot.

No sound at all. Nothing but memories and the feeling that here anything might happen.

Someone was coming towards me. I saw that it was Grace. She walked purposefully.

'Hello, Angelet. I guessed you'd be here. Two minds with one thought. I want to talk to you alone. It's why I have come to Cornwall, really.'

She came and stood very close to me. The ground was slippery. I was aware of her . . . very near to me.

'This pool fascinates you,' she said. 'It's because of what happened.'

'Yes,' I agreed.

'You've never forgotten. How could you, after what you did with Ben's help?'

I said: 'I believe you know a great deal about that man.'

441

'Yes,' she answered. 'I want to talk to you about it.'

'Why to me?'

'Because it concerns you. I knew Mervyn Duncarry. He was a tutor in a house where I was a governess.'

'Perhaps I should tell you that I know that.'

'Through Justin? I thought he would tell you. He is the reformed character now. Who would have believed it? And he wants to protect you. I know Justin. I know how his mind works. I know how yours works, too, Angelet.'

'I should like to know how yours does,' I retorted.

'I believe you are afraid of me. There is no need to be.'

'What should I be afraid of?'

'That is what you have to tell me. I've just come here to talk to you. I told you that is why I have come to Cornwall. I don't know what is going on in your mind, but I am sure that whatever you are thinking is wrong.'

'Why do you think that?'

'Because there is something you have to know and I am going to tell you. I'm fond of you, Angelet. I'm fond of your family. I remember what they did for me. I don't know what would have happened to me but for them. Let me tell you all about it. Imagine a rather frightened young woman who suddenly has to go out and earn her living. I had looked after my mother for many years. My father had died and from then on I had cared for her. My parents had educated me well and I was said to be clever, so when she died and there was only a small income left to me I had to become a governess. I went to a house where there were two children – a girl and a boy. There was a tutor for the boy and a girl for me.'

'I know that,' I told her.

'I fell in love with the tutor. He was charming but there was this flaw in his character. It was like two personalities. There are people like that. They can be cured . . . with the right treatment, I believe. One night he went out and killed a girl.'

'He was the murderer,' I said.

'I loved him. I wanted to help him. You can understand that, I know. I visited him in prison. We planned to escape together. He chose a place near the sea where I would stay until he was ready to go. That's why I came to this neighbourhood. I stayed at that inn for a few nights, but I wanted to save as much money as I could, for we should need it . . . so I decided to find a sort of post . . . where I need not spend money and that's why I came to you. I went to see him in jail. I smuggled in the knife he asked for . . .'

'But you knew he could kill again.'

'I was desperately in love with this man. In spite of everything I wanted our future to be together. I believed I could take him away . . . right out of this country. I believed I could cure him. You see, it was because I refused him that he went out and did that dreadful thing. I had left clothes for him in a broken-down old hut on the moor. I put the watch there with the clothes. It had belonged to my father and I had scratched our initials on it. It was meant to be a sign that I was with him whatever happened. Then he met you.'

'And he tried to murder me.'

'I could have cured him. I was sure of it. I cannot tell you what I suffered. I thought he had deserted me. If I had known that he was lying at the bottom of the pool I could have borne it more easily. You lied. You said you found the ring near the boathouse. The boat was missing.'

'I remember. We gave it to one of the fisher boys.'

'I thought he had escaped without me and that I had helped him to do that. That was the most unhappy time of my life. I was so bitter . . . so angry.'

'You threw the ring into the sea.'

She nodded. 'And when they dragged the pool they found the watch . . . they found his remains . . . and I knew that he had not deceived me. I hated you then . . . you and Ben . . . for all the years that I had suffered when I thought he had deserted me. He had not. He would have been faithful to me. I told myself that we could have got away together. We could have found a new life overseas. And you killed him . . . you and Ben.'

'We did not kill him. He killed himself. He fell and struck his head.'

'But you hid him. You gave me all those years of anguish. I

443

hated him for what I believed he had done to me, and all the time he was lying there in that pool. He was faithful to me and I had believed him faithless.'

'So you hated us for that.'

'It was difficult to hate you, because I had grown fond of you. You and your family had been so good to me.'

'You married Jonnie. Had you forgotten your murderer then?'

'I'll never forget him. I loved once. Some people are like that.'

'After all he did! After all he was!'

'Love such as I had for him does not take count of things like that.' She seized my arm and pressed it, and for the moment I thought she was going to attempt to throw me into the pool.

I jerked myself free. I said: 'You married Jonnie for his money, I suppose.'

'I liked Jonnie. Jonnie was a good man. I worked hard in Scutari. You simplify things too much, Angelet, and people are the least simple of all things on earth. I was a good nurse. I liked Jonnie . . . I liked him very much. We were happy for the little time we were together. But there was one I cared for more than anyone else . . . and would go on caring for.'

'And Ben? You wanted Ben, didn't you?'

'I thought I would be a very suitable wife for a politician.'

'I am sure you would. And Ben?'

'Ben was looking in another direction, wasn't he? He was always besotted about you. I think that adventure you had together did something to you both. You wanted Ben and he wanted you and he was married to Lizzie.'

'And what of you? You wanted Ben, too.'

'Yes. I thought I might make it, too. Ben is a powerful man . . . the sort who was a challenge to me. He was rich . . . thanks to Lizzie's gold mine. I wanted to be rich.'

'Tell me what happened on the night Lizzie died.'

'I only know what happened on the morning after. I went in and found her dead.'

'Who killed her?'

She looked at me and her lips curled faintly at the corners.

444

'You think I might have done it, don't you? Or was it Ben? We both had our reasons, didn't we? It would have been rather silly of Ben to kill her just then because it would inevitably lose him that seat he so much wanted. On the other hand, it would be a masterstroke. People would say: If he was going to kill her why do it at such a time? On the other hand, you suspect that I may have done it. Why? Because I wanted Ben for myself. But he is in love with you. I've always known that – so what chance have I? You wouldn't expect me to kill a woman to make way for you, would you?'

'Grace, why are you saying all this?'

'Because I want you to see it clearly and I want to see it that way myself.'

Then I said: 'Why should you kill her?'

'Because . . . you would not marry Ben if you suspected him of murder, would you? I was ready to help and look after Mervyn, but perhaps your feelings do not go as deep as mine. I wasn't sure. And then, you see, there was the nice kind Timothy Ransome . . . the pleasant life in the country, the waif living there to remind you of your virtue. You had a choice. I might have thought that if you suspected Ben of murdering his wife you would have turned to Timothy. Then the field would be clear for me, wouldn't it?'

'Grace . . . I don't understand.'

'Do you believe in reformed characters?'

'What do you mean?'

'Well, look at Justin . . . card-sharper, blackmailer, adventurer . . . and now good businessman, the perfect husband and father. What a transformation!'

'I really believe that Justin has changed.'

'So do I. He was lucky. I wonder what would have happened to him if he hadn't found Morwenna and his accommodating father-in-law. Justin is one of the lucky ones.'

'And he's turned his good fortune to advantage.'

'Nobody is entirely virtuous, you know. Not you . . . nor Ben . . . nor any of us – and some are worse than others . . . Mervyn, for instance, who had that terrible affliction . . . if affliction it was. Justin the adventurer . . . and I suppose you would call

445

me an adventuress. Even Gervaise was a gambler and died owing money, didn't he? People have to be accepted for what they are. We should not judge them too harshly.'

'Once again, Grace, why are you telling me all this?'

'I am pleading for myself.'

'Why do you have to plead with me?'

'Because I have lied and cheated. I came to your family under false pretences. I have watched Justin and I have been to the Mission. I have been down to see that child Fanny and I feel that whatever one has done in the past, one could find a certain salvation in a place like that. Do you believe that?'

'Are you serious, Grace?'

She took my arm again. 'I am deadly serious,' she said. 'I am going to work in the Mission. When I have set the accounts to rights I am going to do active work. I have talked to Frances and Peterkin. They are willing to have me there. I think I can forget my bitterness, my ambition, everything . . . there. I think I have learned that there is more contentment to be found in trying to comfort others than to seek it for oneself.'

I looked at her suspiciously.

'I have been wicked,' she said. 'When I thought Mervyn had deserted me, I said to myself: I will never love anyone again. I will work for myself. I will take all I can get. I might have loved Jonnie if he hadn't died. He was very good to me. He made me independent but not content. I wanted power. And there was Ben. I did a terrible thing, Angelet.'

She put her hand in her pocket and drew out a letter.

She said: 'I held this back. I wanted Lizzie to stand between you and Ben. The letter was there by her bedside that morning. I read it . . . and I held it back. I am giving it to you now. I think it will make all the difference to you . . . and Ben.'

I unfolded the sheet of paper and read:

My dearest Ben,

I hope you will understand and forgive me for what I am going to do. There is nothing for me but pain. I knew it . . . some months ago. It gets worse. I saw it with my mother. The pain is unendurable. It is exactly what happened to her

446

and there is no stopping it. I have kept it from you all. Laudanum helps. It was good at first but it is no longer enough. I nursed my mother and this is exactly the same as what killed her. But the pain while I am waiting for death is too much. If I could have helped her out I would have.

I want to thank you for making me happy. I have always known that I was not suitable for you. You needed someone who could help you in your life. I was never good at that, but you were always so kind and never said how I disappointed you. I want you to know that I love you very much. I wish I could stay. But I know I could not hide my illness much longer and that would distress you . . . and everybody. I know I could not bear to suffer as my mother did. So this seems the best way. I wished there had been an easier way for my mother.

Don't grieve for me. Try to forget me and be happy.
Lizzie.

There were tears in my eyes and I saw that there were in Grace's also.

'She was a very good woman,' said Grace. 'An example to us all. Forgive me for withholding it. It was wicked of me. But you have it now. You have the truth. Ben must know. It is his letter. You must both forgive me, Angelet. Can you?'

I nodded. I was too moved to speak.

Grace and I returned to London that day.

I went straight to Ben.

I said, 'I have something to show you, Ben. Grace gave it to me.'

He took the letter and read it.

It was as though a burden of guilt dropped from him. He turned to me and took my hands.

There was hope in his eyes; and I shared it.

447